THE ATLANTIS IDOL

THE SIGMA FILES: BOOK 2

JOE TOPLIFFE

THE ATLANTIS IDOL

Copyright © 2024 by Joe Topliffe

The following is a work of fiction. The story, characters, setting, and events are either products of the author's imagination or are used fictitiously.

ASIN: B0D3ZZMVTV

ISBN: 9798325498794

No part of this book may be photocopied, reproduced, or distributed (electronically or otherwise) without the prior written permission of the author.

PROLOGUE

Sitting low on the horizon, the warm golden glow of the sun spread its way across the tranquil waters of the Mediterranean. A gentle breeze carried the salty scent of the ocean, as the São Vicente glided gracefully over the waves. The sails of the impressive ship rippled, as Jean de Gurrigue, the seasoned Papal treasurer, stood with a stern expression, his eyes fixed intently in the distance. The weight of responsibility sat heavily on his shoulders, for he was entrusted with a task of utmost importance.

Beside him, the ship's captain barked orders, guiding the skilled crew as they sailed with a sense of purpose toward their destination. The São Vicente was on a mission, not just of commerce, but of divine significance. It was imperative that he made it back to Avignon. The journey had been smooth thus far, but Jean was on his guard.

The French and English had been at each other's throats over Aquitaine and the French crown for the best part of twenty years, and Jean had been alerted to a feud between King Peter of Castile and King Peter IV of Aragon. While this didn't concern the Papacy or his mission, his ship was sailing through water that had become a hotspot for heavily armed galleons from both sides. The last thing he wanted was to catch the attention of either of the warring parties. His vessel wouldn't be the first to be mistaken for an enemy warship and attacked and sunk without warning.

Jean's fingers absently traced the outline of the parchment in his hand—a letter of authorisation signed by Pope Innocent VI himself. The letter granted Jean and his associates free passage beyond any inquisitive sentries; the Pope's seal was usually enough to scare off any nefarious ideas.

With the horizon looking clear, Jean headed inside the captain's quarters. He stopped at the doorway and reached out a hand to catch himself as the great ship swayed. He was no stranger to seafaring, but in his old age, he found himself losing his balance more often. The sooner he was back on solid ground, the better. The inside of the cabin was dark, save for the dim flickering light from a candle on the table in the centre. As he shut the door, the creaking of the ship's wooden frame seemed to be amplified tenfold. Rolling up the parchment with the Pope's seal and placing it on the table, he turned his attention to the thick ledger that sat in the middle of the candle's orange glow.

The ledger was still open on the last page he had scrawled on earlier that day. The quill sitting idly to the side had seen heavy use the past days as Jean logged details of every item recovered from the late Bishop Thibaud de Castillon. The bishop had amassed a vast fortune over the years, and it was no secret that this wealth was accumulated through less than moral means. But crucially, it had been kept in the name of the Church, and as the Papal treasurer, it was Jean's solemn duty to ensure that the Church's interests were safeguarded.

The Atlantis Idol

Weeks of meticulous planning had led Jean and his crew to this moment. The São Vicente was laden with supplies, its hold carefully arranged to accommodate the anticipated haul. Golden chalices, intricately adorned relics, and chests of coins awaited their transport to Avignon, where they would be secured within the Church's hallowed vaults.

A low thudding sound echoed through the air, causing Jean to look up suddenly from the table. He watched the window of the cabin, but the sun had disappeared beyond the horizon, and he couldn't see what had caused the noise.

Another low thud sounded; this time followed by the fizz of water as a large wave splashed over the starboard side of the ship. Voices began calling to each other as Jean made his way to the doorway. As he opened the door, a loud boom erupted and a large object catapulted itself through the sail, leaving a gaping hole as it splashed into the sea not far from the stern. Jean's heartbeat quickened as he placed the object in context with the sound. The cannonball had missed the mast by a matter of feet. Voices were shouting all around him as they reacted to the sudden attack. Looking to the east, his eyes widened as he spotted two ships emerging from the shadows. A surge of dread coiled in his stomach.

The captain bellowed to the crew as another cannonball splintered the side of the hull. The São Vicente wasn't well armed, and the opportunists in the oncoming ships knew that. If it was gold they were after, it was in their best interest not to sink the ship. The oncoming galleys were close enough now for Jean to see the flags adorned proudly at the top of their masts. He stared incredulously as he recognised one as Castilian, and the other as Genoan. These were no pirates, but representatives of Peter of Castile's navy. Did they not know who they were? Their own flag was clearly marked atop the

São Vicente's mast. No, Jean decided, they did know who they were. And they attacked anyway.

Their safe passage through these waters was dependent on the navies of both sides of this poxy war respecting civilians or other parties outside of the conflict. He cursed his ignorance.

It was clear from their approach that the sailors approaching the São Vicente intended to board and loot the ship. The cannonballs grazing the hull were just warning shots, part of the scare tactic. They were more than close enough to have sunk them already if they wanted to. Jean knew that the crew of the São Vicente wouldn't go down without a fight, but it was abundantly clear that they were outnumbered and outgunned. He admired their courage; it was an inspiring testament to human resilience. But to resist would be senseless. His heart sank as he realised the dire situation they were in. He clung to the railing, his knuckles white from the intensity of his grip. In that moment he knew his mission had failed.

The boarding and seizing of the ship were inevitable and had taken just minutes. The air, thick with smoke, mingled with the acrid scent of gunpowder and the briny essence of the sea. Jean and his crew were lined up on their knees, their hands bound behind their backs. The commander of the first invading vessel strode across the deck towards the São Vicente's captain. Jean looked up at the approaching man, taking note of the Castilian badge on his lapel.

"We're on Church business," the captain declared. "Order of Pope Innocent VI."

The man ignored him. Instead, he snapped his fingers and pointed to the captain's quarters. Two of his men went inside the cabin. Moments later one returned with the ledger and a small chest full of gold and silver coins. The commander took a quick look at the chest, and then opened and studied a page of the ledger. As he read the contents a crooked smile began to creep across his face.

Jean piped up. "Have you no shame? You are stealing from the Church!"

The man snapped his head around at the treasurer. "The Church's greed is of no concern to me," he replied.

Footsteps clunked on the deck as another group of people approached from the port side.

"Botafoc," came the voice of the man in the centre. From his garb, he looked like the one in charge. Captain of the Genoan ship, Jean assumed.

The Castilian commander grunted. "Yanes." He acknowledged their arrival without turning his attention away from Jean.

"What now?" Yanes asked.

There was a moment of trepidation about Botafoc before he replied. He ran a hand through his straggly beard, considering his options.

Jean took note of the strange dynamic between the two. They knew each other, at least by name. But there was distance between them. Two crews from different origins, with nothing in common except the enemy. They had spent a long time sharing this stretch of sea with nothing to do but await orders that never came. These were bored sailors itching for action. Unsatisfied by the stalemate of the war, was this their opportunity for a slice of adventure?

Botafoc looked back at the ledger, turning the page. He glanced at Jean again, and then at Yanes. Finally, he snapped the ledger shut and handed it to one of his men.

"Take everything. We divide it when we reach the shore."

**

Antonio Botafoc had spent many days and nights in his damp, dimly lit cell in the Maguio Royal Garrison. Night had fallen once more, the pale light of the moon casting shadows on the wall, partially illuminating the etchings of countless prisoners who had occupied the same space before him. Iron bars separated him from the outside world, and the occasional drip of water echoed through the dank chamber.

He sat on the lumpy straw mattress, running a hand through his tangled beard, his skin starting to bear the pallor of confinement. Memories of the Papal treasure ship, the São Vicente, danced before his eyes. Its grand sails billowing in the wind, the rush of the sea spray against his face, the camaraderie of his crew. It all seemed like a distant dream.

After commandeering the vessel and realising his luck at the treasures stowed on board, he and Martin Yanes had brought the ship to shore to divide up the spoils and head their separate ways. To hell with the war, he would start anew with his newfound riches.

It had all come crashing down on the rocky shores of Maguio, France, where the ship had been inadvertently blown aground. He remembered standing defiantly at the helm, fighting against the wind with everything he had to keep it away from the rocks.

The crew had been equally resolute, their shouts and curses lost in the howling wind. The ship had been tossed about like a mere plaything, and the tumultuous sea had exacted a heavy toll. Masts had splintered, sails had torn, and his ship's fate was sealed, cast helplessly upon the rocky shore.

The storm had come out of nowhere, with the ferocity of a vengeful god. Botafoc was not a superstitious man, but for a fleeting moment, he wondered if this was the result of divine intervention—karmic punishment from some omnipotent force.

Botafoc shook his head. His freedom had been taken from him in an instant as the local royal garrison descended on the wreck. Most of his crew were dead; killed by the storm or hanged by the authorities for their part in the crime. But here he stayed, in this purgatory of iron and stone. He gritted his teeth as he cast his mind to Martin Yanes. The Genoan captain had wasted no time in setting sail after taking their share of the treasure. He had watched the ship fade away to the east before it disappeared beyond the horizon. His counterpart had avoided the storm; of that he was certain. Botafoc spat on the ground, cursing Yanes' good fortune. The man was surely home free, living the life Botafoc had dreamed of the moment they decided to attack that pathetic ship.

The clinking of keys drew his attention. Footsteps echoed off the stone floor, and a pair of shadows approached his cell. The heavy iron door clunked as the lock engaged, and the rusted bars creaked as the door swung open. Two figures entered, silhouetted by the pale moonlight. They were heavily armoured, both resting one hand cautiously on the hilt of their swords. They stood on either side of the door inside the cell. Shortly after, a cloaked figure entered between them.

Botafoc stood up as the cloaked figure stepped into the stream of moonlight that partially lit the space. He could see part of the man's face, wizened from age. The old man lifted the hood from his robe and addressed Botafoc. "You are the one who attacked my ship?" The man spoke softly, but there was a directness to his tone.

Botafoc looked to the man's entourage. They stood motionless. His eyes fell once again on the hilt of their swords.

"They are here for my protection," said the robed man plainly. "You are safe, so long as you talk."

Botafoc cleared his throat. "I am Antonio Botafoc," he replied. "I am a captain of the Castilian navy."

The robed man stepped forward. His face became fully illuminated in the pale light that streamed through the cracks in the stone. "And you attacked my ship."

"Yes," Botafoc answered.

The ornate white robes of the old man were juxtaposed with the damp and dingy surroundings. The light reflected off the large cross hanging around the man's neck.

"You knew it was my ship."

Botafoc knew who he was looking at. In front of him was none other than Pope Innocent VI. He quickly pieced things together as his mind flashed back to the man who had pleaded with him on the ship. "Yes," he admitted.

"A pity," the Pope replied. "You have caused me a great inconvenience, Antonio Botafoc." He paused as he looked around the small cell, his expression a mixture of curiosity and solemnity. "How long have you been imprisoned here?"

Botafoc was taken aback by the question. "I, uh, a few weeks, I suppose. Have you come here to hang me?"

The Pope's face contorted into a scowl, as though disappointed by the suggestion. "I have come with a proposition," he replied.

"A proposition?"

"Martin Yanes," Pope Innocent VI said, his voice now carrying the weight of authority. "Your counterpart from the Genoan navy. Your…" He considered his next words carefully. "Accomplice."

"I do not know the man well," Botafoc interjected. The guards on either side of the doorway shuffled. Their armour clinked with the sudden movement. Botafoc knew instantly that the interruption had irked them. The Pope raised a hand, and they relaxed once more, their hands releasing their grip from the hilts of their swords. The weapons hadn't made it out of their sheaths, but Botafoc now knew how quickly this encounter could turn against him.

"How well you know him is of no concern to me," said the Pope. "He has taken something from me. The late Bishop Thibaud de Castillon's fortune belongs to the Church. That thief has taken half of it, as did you. It must be returned to its rightful owner."

Botafoc remained silent, his gaze locked onto the Pope's.

"I want him found," The Pope continued. "I want that which belongs to me." He eyed Botafoc carefully. "What say you, Antonio?"

"What's in it for me?" Botafoc finally asked, his voice gruff.

"Your freedom." The Pope leaned in closer, his voice barely above a whisper. "Or do you wish to rot in this prison?"

Botafoc's mind raced. The Pope was offering him a chance at freedom, a chance to reclaim his life. But it would not come without a price. Perhaps he would be put to death anyway after the job was done. He had questions, doubts, but one thing was clear: he couldn't remain in this cell forever.

The Pope's expression remained unflinching. "You will receive a full pardon for your crime. You will be granted a ship and a crew. You will be accompanied by my men, to ensure you uphold your end of the bargain. Once you have retrieved the treasure, you will return it to Avignon. Then you will be absolved of your sins and free to live your life as you see fit."

Antonio Botafoc considered the offer carefully.

"Agreed," he said finally, extending his hand.

The Pope nodded, a faint smile playing at the corners of his lips. "Very well. You shall have your chance at redemption."

Pope Innocent VI turned to leave. The guards gave Botafoc one last intimidating look before following him out. The sound of their footsteps echoed softly away as the jangling of keys engaged the lock to his cell once more.

The next morning, Botafoc was released from his cell and provided with fresh clothing. He was led to a chamber where he met with representatives of the Church, and they discussed the details of the mission ahead. The two guards that had escorted Pope Innocent VI the previous night were there, eyeing Botafoc cautiously. The whole time he was in the chamber discussing the plan with his new associates, he didn't feel their gaze leave him for a second. On exiting the chamber, the salty sea air entered his nostrils. He inhaled deeply, cherishing the smell. The Maguio Royal Garrison was close to the docks, and on stepping outside into the bright sunlight he caught a glimpse of his ship. It had seen better days, but it had been patched up well since the storm. The Castilian flag was fluttering proudly at the top of the mast. He felt a pang of guilt on seeing it.

Standing on the deck of his ship, his new coat ruffling in the breeze and his new crew busily preparing to set sail, Botafoc couldn't help but reflect on the path that had led him to this moment. Abandoning his post as a respected member of the Castilian navy to become a pawn in a high-stakes game orchestrated by the Church. Had it been worth it?

He thought of Yanes; the man who had escaped with half the treasure with no consequence. It gnawed at him. It was an injustice that ate him up inside, the stark contrast in their fates for the same crime. Perhaps, in a strange twist of fate, he would be the harbinger of retribution upon Yanes and his crew. For his sake, he had to hope he would be.

The sails ruffled in the wind as the ship picked up speed on its way out of the dock. Botafoc's gaze fixed upon the horizon. The promise of freedom and redemption beckoned like a distant siren's call. Determination burned within him, driving him forward. One thing was certain: he would seize this opportunity, no matter the cost.

ONE

The day was muggy and overcast as Sophie and Antoine stood before the rusty shutter door of storage unit 37B. Nestled amidst rows of similar units in the nondescript storage facility on the outskirts of Montpellier, France, it seemed like just another forgotten corner of the world. Sophie pulled out her phone, checking a message she had received that had alerted them to the opportunity presented by this particular unit.

Storage hunting was something of a hobby for the two of them. Plenty of units would be left to auction when a customer defaulted on their payments. The pair would frequent auctions, in hopes of unearthing something valuable they could make a tidy profit on.

"It's quiet today," Antoine noted, cupping his hands around the end of the cigarette that protruded delicately from his mouth. The lighter clicked on, and he sucked in a deep breath, tilting his head back as he blew the smoke out.

Sophie looked around. He was right, it was quiet today—unusually so. When an auction was on for a lapsed unit, it was usually contested by at least a few others. She scrolled through messages on her phone. Had they got the date wrong?

"Found it!" a voice called from behind them. Pierre, the balding middle-aged owner of the storage facility, held up a set of bolt cutters victoriously. "Sorry to keep you waiting." Having misplaced his copy of the key for the unit's lock, he had resorted to breaking it open.

"You're doing it now?" Sophie asked, confused. "When does the auction start?"

Pierre gave a wry smile. "No auction today. I have something special just for you two."

Antoine snapped his head round. "What do you mean?"

"This is a serious one," Pierre replied. "I've known you both long enough to know you have contacts. If I put this on auction it'll go for way less than it's worth."

Antoine looked at the sturdy padlock securing the shutter door. "How can you possibly know that?" There was no way he could know the contents of the unit. For starters, it was against the terms of the agreement. Secondly, and more curiously, Pierre was about to break it open with bolt cutters. Perhaps there was a chance he could have seen what was inside in passing as the customer loaded it or paid a visit.

"I knew the man who was using it," Pierre said solemnly. "He passed away a couple of years back. Nice guy. Bit of a strange one though."

Sophie raised an eyebrow. "Strange how?"

"I guess you could say he was a collector." He shook his head. "No, hoarder is more accurate."

Antoine tutted loudly. "Come on, Pierre. Don't play with us. Everyone who comes here is a hoarder. That's literally the reason they come here, to hoard the useless shit they don't have room for."

"Or can't bear to get rid of," Sophie added.

"So, the unit's been sat here unpaid for a couple of years?"

"No, his granddaughter was covering it," replied Pierre. "But, well, you know." He gestured to the bolt cutters. "I tried contacting her, but I've had no luck."

"So, here we are," said Antoine.

"Here we are." Pierre angled the bolt cutters towards the lock and began to clamp around the rusted metal.

"So, what are we talking?" enquired Antoine. "Antiques, retro video games, rare Pokémon cards?"

Sophie snorted.

"Hey, you laugh, but some famous rapper paid $2 million for one of those wizard cards."

"Magic: The Gathering," Pierre corrected, his voice sounding strained as he struggled against the hefty padlock. The padlock eventually snapped and clunked onto the floor. He let out an audible sigh. "This is what I'm talking about. One man's trash is another man's treasure." He bent down to pick up the now useless lock. "Damn shame. These things aren't cheap, you know."

Antoine let out another long puff of smoke, before dropping the cigarette on the ground and stubbing it out with the heel of his shoe, twisting it into the concrete. "Let's open her up." He reached for the handle to open the shutter, but Pierre caught his arm, stopping him suddenly.

"Look, we need to agree on something first." His tone had suddenly shifted to something more serious. His hand remained on Antoine's arm.

Antoine rolled his eyes. "How much?" He had expected Pierre would want his palms greased, but he was hoping he would be able to see the item in question first.

"50% of the sale price to your contact."

He hadn't given Pierre enough credit; he knew Antoine would underplay the value of the piece, whatever it was, and shaft him with a lowball fee.

"10%," Antoine countered.

"30."

"20."

Pierre exhaled deeply. "Done." He took his hand off Antoine's arm and extended it towards him for a handshake. Antoine shook it, squinting a little as the man's clammy palm gripped him a little too tightly.

"So, what is it?" Sophie asked, anxious to get inside.

"See for yourself," Pierre replied, stepping back to give the pair space.

Sophie smiled. Pierre was no stranger to people like them. He knew the thrill of this was in the unknown: the feeling of anticipation as the shutter went up and they caught that first glimpse of the treasures that lay inside.

Antoine lifted the shutter, the roller mechanism screeching as the metal sheets folded into each other. Sophie's heart began to beat faster. She loved this part.

The sight that greeted them was familiar, yet foreign. A jumble of cardboard boxes, old furniture draped in white sheets, and a musty odour that was the hallmark of disuse.

The pair entered the storage unit and began perusing the contents. Well-practised, they were methodological in their sweep of the area. The way they were carefully trying not to disturb items was akin to that of a forensic team working through a crime scene. As was often the case with such storage units, this one contained the remnants of a person's life. Sophie and Antoine respected the belongings of others and knew that it was difficult at first glance to distinguish junk from sentimental objects.

Removing a white sheet from an old piano, Sophie tapped a note with her index finger. The white key depressed without making a sound, getting stuck down after she released it.

"So, I'm guessing this didn't once belong to Claude Debussy?" she joked.

Sophie enjoyed the mystery of being alerted to something of significance in a room and having to figure it out without hints. It was a fun game Pierre had created for them, reminiscent of the many themed escape rooms that had popped up around major cities over recent years.

Antoine snapped a few photos of the contents of a cardboard box on his phone.

Sophie moved over to the far side of the space, approaching a large piece of furniture. "Am I getting warmer?"

Pierre shrugged his shoulders playfully.

Antoine lifted the cardboard box he had been carefully examining and set it down to one side, revealing a larger box beneath. He paused momentarily to gauge Pierre's reaction. The man's face gave nothing away.

"For God's sake, if you know what it is, just tell us what to look for." Antoine's patience had already worn thin.

Pierre held his hands up apologetically. "I don't know where it is. It must be in one of the boxes." He sighed. "Try that one there." He pointed to a box near where Sophie was standing.

Sophie opened the box and her eyes widened. "Woah," she said under her breath, before reaching in with both hands and carefully retrieving the item she had spotted. Antoine hurried over to get a closer look.

Sophie lifted it carefully from the confines of the cardboard box, revealing an ornate brass spyglass. She studied the pattern that had been delicately etched onto the side. The pattern started about two-thirds of the way down its length, wrapping around the spyglass until it reached the thicker end by the lens.

"That was lucky," Pierre muttered to himself.

"It's beautiful," she gasped. She carefully twisted the brass, testing how it reacted in her hands. The components responded to her touch, the layers of the brass folding into each other seamlessly. She handed the spyglass to Antoine, who held it flat in both palms to study it more closely. He then extended it once more and peered through it, one eye squinted shut. The lens was intact, and he couldn't make out so much as a scratch.

"Nice ornament," he said casually. "Did you get it from Etsy?"

"If I was trying to con you, I'd have asked for a fee upfront, not a share of the profits. Check the lettering on the bottom," said Pierre eagerly.

Antoine moved closer to the entrance of the storage unit to get more natural light onto the object. Sure enough, engraved into the brass near the bottom were two intricately written letters. Antoine admired the handiwork of the tool's creator. How such a cursive effect could be achieved in such a small surface area was beyond him. The two letters were engraved with such a flourish, that it took him a while to realise what they represented.

"You weren't kidding," he said, at last, surprise in his voice.

Pierre smiled. "So, I was right? It's worth something, isn't it?"

Antoine turned to Sophie. "Look at the lettering."

She hurried over, knocking into the side of a large bookcase that was draped in sheets. Something clattered onto the floor, but she didn't stop to pick it up. The discovery was too exciting to delay. She followed Antoine's gaze to the base of the spyglass.

"G.F." she read. She thought for a moment, then her eyes widened, and her hand covered her mouth as she came to the same realisation Antoine had.

"Tell me!" Pierre cried. "What does G.F. mean?"

"They're initials," Antoine said with a smile. "Giovanna Florelli. She was a famous maker of spyglasses like this in the late 1600s."

"That old dog," said Pierre. "How the hell did he get to have this in his possession? Stole it from a museum?"

Antoine ignored him. "Nobody has seen one in such good condition. I should really be wearing gloves for this." He looked around for something to place the antique into. "Pierre, do you have something for this?"

The man scratched his head. "Hmm, yes, I might just do." He started to head back towards his office but stopped suddenly and turned on his heel. "Am I about to become rich?"

Antoine nodded. "We'll have a buyer for it within a week."

Pierre squealed with joy and hurried over to his office to look for something soft to house it.

Sophie let out a low whistle. "I wasn't expecting anything this impressive today."

Antoine was still looking at the spyglass nestled in his hands. "I never thought I'd see a Florelli. Especially in this condition."

"I can't believe you kept a straight face when you negotiated the price."

Antoine looked at Sophie and the two shared a wry smile.

"I don't know what you're talking about," Antoine protested sarcastically.

Sophie chuckled to herself. "You're evil."

"We're evil," Antoine corrected.

When establishing contact with Pierre, the two had given him the number to their burner phone. They both knew they had no intention of following through on the deal they had made with him. The poor fool. They were about to rob him blind. They would disappear from this place, and he would never hear from them again.

Sophie made her way back through the storage unit to pick up the object that had fallen from the bookcase moments earlier. As she bent down to pick it up, her fingers brushed the spine of an old book. It was tattered and brittle with age. She picked it up with one hand, lifting the dust sheet covering the bookcase with the other. As she found the space from which the book had fallen, something caught her eye. Leaving the book on its edge alongside another like it, she reached out and wiped a thick layer of dust from the shape that had piqued her interest.

Feeling the surface of the object, it felt alien alongside the dusty old books surrounding it. Reaching out and grabbing it, she revealed an old wooden box. A brass clasp secured it shut.

Little did she know that the contents of that box would be a more significant find than they had ever discovered.

"What's that?" asked Antoine.

Sophie studied the box. "Wanna guess?"

"Closest guess wins," said Antoine.

"€20?" Sophie cocked her head at her brother.

Antoine looked at the spyglass in his hands. "Make it €100. And the loser buys dinner."

"You're on," she replied excitedly. Placing the old wooden box on the ground, she lifted the clasp and then the lid. The hinge gave a little resistance but eventually relented.

Inside lay a thin leather-bound book, its pages frayed and yellowed with age.

Intrigued, Sophie carefully opened to the first page. The script was elegant, written with a meticulous hand that seemed to belong to another era. She perused the pages, noting the way the writing didn't form prose, but seemed to be a list of sorts.

"Antoine," she said, her heart beginning to beat faster.

"What is it?" he asked, his own anticipation bubbling up.

"Italian," she muttered under her breath, recognising the language the book was written in. She turned to face Antoine, setting the book down between them. "This is old. I mean *really* old."

"I can see that," replied Antoine candidly. "What is it?"

"I'm not sure," she replied. "I think it might be some kind of ledger." Neither of them could speak Italian, and the handwriting was difficult to make out even if it had been written in a language they were fluent in.

Something else caught Sophie's attention. As she flicked to the next page, she caught a glimpse of a drawing resembling a symbol that seemed strangely familiar. She was sure she had seen it before. But where?

Antoine had cottoned on. He tilted his head to get a better look at the symbol. "Is that—"

"Here we are!" Pierre's voice suddenly interrupted the pair, followed by the sound of his office door shutting behind him. Sophie slammed the leather-bound book closed and put it back into the wooden box. She had just got the lid down and the clasp secured when Pierre came into view. He had a smile on his face and a box full of packing peanuts under his arm.

"This should keep it safe until you find something more substantial." He dropped the box onto the floor and gestured to Antoine, inviting him to nestle the spyglass inside. He did so, taking a moment to cover it from all sides with the packing materials.

"It'll do," he said, giving a quick glance in the direction of Sophie, who had stealthily nudged the wooden box out of view with her foot.

"Now, back to business," Pierre said eagerly, a twinkle in his eye. "When will you have a confirmed price from your contact?"

"Within the week," said Sophie. "You have our number, and we have yours. We'll be in touch."

Pierre looked cautiously at her, and then at Antoine. Both did their best to avoid acting suspiciously.

"Lovely," he said at last. "Are we done here?"

The man was far too trusting. She felt a fleeting pang of guilt ripple through her.

"Pierre."

"Yes?"

Antoine gave her an intense glare. She knew that look. He thought she was about to blow it.

"I've taken a fancy to something else here," she said, walking to the bookshelf. Antoine's heart pounded in his chest.

She lifted the dust sheet and retrieved an old, tattered book. "Not a first edition, but I know someone who loves this book. It's their birthday soon and this would make me the best friend ever. How much?"

Pierre didn't so much as hesitate. "Take it."

Sophie smiled widely. "You're too kind."

Pierre waved it away. "If that's all, I need to close up." Sophie noted the new padlock in his hand. "This thing is going to auction for real tomorrow."

Antoine wasted no time, clutching the padded box with both hands. "That's our cue then." He nodded at Pierre. "Talk soon."

Pierre rubbed his hands together excitedly. Sophie took one last look at the wooden box she had slid behind a pile of cardboard boxes, the clasp closed, and the contents secured.

As they climbed back inside their car, Sophie let out a long exhale.

Antoine's keys jangled as he started the engine.

"So?" he asked expectantly.

Sophie moved her arm to reveal the leather-bound ledger resting in her lap. She thought of the old, tattered book she had switched it with, that now sat in the wooden box for the eventual winner of the auction to find.

She opened the cover and carefully turned the pages until she landed on the strange symbol they had recognised.

"Shall I make the call to Sigma?"

Antoine nodded as he released the handbrake, put the car into first gear and pulled away.

TWO

The crisp mountain air nipping at her cheeks, Quinn Miyata glided effortlessly down the snow-covered slopes. Her breath came out in short puffs, creating a temporary fog around her face before dissipating into the clear, azure sky. She focused on the path she was carving as she took a brief detour off-piste from the familiar run she had traversed many times before. The freshly fallen snow crunched under the board as she switched from regular to her preferred goofy stance, shifting her weight onto her right leg as she took a winding path between a cluster of trees.

The slopes were quiet this early in the morning. A seasoned snowboarder, Quinn didn't need to think too much about each move, her body in tune with the board. The experience was cathartic, requiring just enough attention to keep her thoughts clear. She was completely engrossed in the moment.

The rush of adrenaline as she navigated the winding trails was a stark contrast to the meticulous world of archaeology that had consumed her life for the past few years. Ever since she was little, she had been fascinated by the subject, engaging with the past in such a tangible way. She had always been a bit of a history buff, and her studies had taken it to a new level.

Quinn had realistic expectations of what to expect from her career since graduating two years prior. But she couldn't help but feel unfulfilled by her work. She had never expected to be plunged headfirst into the field, excavating long-forgotten tombs in far-flung corners of the world and poring over dusty relics. The Hollywood depiction of archaeology was not something most in the profession would experience. The reality for Quinn was a stuttering economy, and open roles that were even remotely close to her area of expertise coming few and far between. She ended up taking a job working with a small team of geologists, assessing the makeup of plots of land that had grand ambitions to become housing developments or shopping centres. Testing mineral samples and handing out permits to building contractors was not exactly the exciting life she had dreamed of.

The snowboarding vacation was her yearly pilgrimage to the peaks of Aspen, Colorado. The mountain offered solace in its quiet majesty, and Quinn had found comfort in the rhythm of carving through the snow. With each downhill run, she felt a sense of liberation, escaping the boredom of the nine-to-five.

The slope began to level out as the run was coming to an end, joining onto a much gentler route that was busier with tourists. The chatter of voices came suddenly as a group of skiers passed by overhead on a chairlift. Coming close to the main hub of the resort, she weaved this way and that, eventually sliding to a stop outside the café that sat at the bottom. It was time for coffee.

She unstrapped her snowboard and took a moment to catch her breath. She gazed out at the panoramic view of the snow-covered mountains, their peaks bathed in the soft morning light. It was a sight that never failed to inspire her, a reminder of the vastness of the world and the mysteries it held.

Leaning her snowboard against the collection of others outside, she then made her way inside. The cosy interior offered respite from the cold, and Quinn settled into a chair.

Minutes later, the waitress brought a steaming cup of coffee over to her, leaving a receipt underneath the mug.

"Thanks," said Quinn.

"My pleasure," the lady replied enthusiastically. "Let me know if you need anything else."

Quinn smiled, then took a tentative first sip of the hot drink. She stretched her legs out in front of her, turning her ankles in circles as part of her cool-down routine from the ride. Her snow boots were comfortable, but after a couple of hours riding her feet began to feel it. She unzipped the pocket on the inside of her bright red jacket and retrieved her phone, setting it on the table next to her goggles and helmet. Catching a glimpse of herself in the reflection of the screen, she noticed how tightly the goggles had clung to her face. She had distinct red marks from the pressure in a perfect outline around her eyes. She chuckled to herself and unlocked the device.

Two notifications greeted her on her home screen.

The first was from Paige, her friend from college who had joined her on the trip to Aspen. While not much of a snow sports fan, Paige enjoyed everything else that came with a trip to the mountains; most notably the hot springs spa and the après ski drinking culture. She had dabbled in skiing and given introductory lessons a go but decided that it was not for her. Quinn had a suspicion that the attractive frat guys who had taken the class with her had now progressed to solo ventures on the slopes.

Quinn read the message.

Let me know when you're back. Bored as hell!

She began to type back.

I'm at the café. I'll order you a mocha.

Quinn knew Paige well enough to know that she needed more than a little push to get out of bed. Shortly after, the three dots flashed up on Quinn's screen indicating that Paige was crafting her reply.

Better make it a Bloody Mary.

Quinn let out a snort of laughter. Typical Paige. She had to hand it to her though, she handled her liquor better than Quinn did. A hangover would usually leave Quinn bedridden most of the day. For Paige, it was nothing a Bloody Mary couldn't fix. And she never lost her sense of humour, no matter how ill she felt. Quinn shook her head as she typed back.

I'll ask if they serve that.

She turned her attention to the other notification. Her heart skipped a beat when she saw Ted's name on the screen.

Hey, Quinn. How have you been?

The message had caught her completely off guard. It had been a while since they had last spoken, and Quinn had assumed their connection had faded with time.

The sight of his name evoked a mixture of feelings within her. The two had undeniable chemistry, and after spending a bit of time together it was clear it had the potential to develop into something more than friendship. But the nature of how the two had crossed paths was tinged with bad memories. They shared a trauma bond that was born from the horrendous circumstances they found themselves in less than three years prior.

A field trip to Mexico City, funded by the university during her time studying, looked like a good opportunity to get some hands-on experience learning from real archaeologists, who had recently made a discovery of great significance in Aztec history. The university had set her up with a professor from a partner university from London, who led the trip. It was there that she had met Ted Mendez, the journalism student the professor had brought with him. Just a day after they had made their introductions, they had been kidnapped by armed thugs and wrapped up in the heist of an ancient artefact. The trip ultimately ended up with Quinn and Ted being forced on a dangerous treasure hunt to uncover a priceless ancient jewel that seemed to possess unexplained power.

Having warmed up from the hot coffee, she removed her bright red jacket. As her mind recounted the events in Mexico, she subconsciously moved her hand to her shoulder, her fingers feeling the scar that had been left from the bullet that had grazed her. One detail of the traumatic experience she would rather forget, the scar was a permanent reminder of the emotional wound that bore into her, bringing the memory to the surface every time she looked in the mirror.

Quinn's fingers hovered over the keypad, torn between responding to Ted's message and letting it fade into the digital abyss.

As she sat there, she couldn't help but wonder if the unresolved tension between her and Ted was a sign of something more. Was it a chapter of her life that deserved closure, or was it the beginning of a new adventure? What was his reason for getting back in touch?

The summer after graduating had been a blast, and she had spent a chunk of it with Ted in London. Quinn recalled one evening in particular. They took a stroll through Greenwich and sat and drank in a quaint old pub tucked away in a cobblestone alley. The conversation had flowed effortlessly, laughter had filled the air, and sparks had ignited between them.

Their connection was undeniable, but there was a catch. Quinn was based in the United States, while Ted's life was rooted in London. Despite their undeniable chemistry, they had hesitated to let things develop, both aware of the challenges a long-distance relationship would bring. At least that is what Quinn had told herself. In reality, the distance was not the key issue. The truth was that connecting with Ted over video call brought up memories of the harrowing experience in Mexico. She withdrew and tried to close herself off from it.

By the time Paige arrived, the drink Quinn had ordered for her had been sitting on the table for a while. Quinn wondered how anyone could drink anything containing tomato juice, but Paige guzzled it down thirstily. When she finished the last drop, she slammed the glass down on the table victoriously. She wiped the remnants of the Bloody Mary from her lips and let out an exaggerated exhale.

"What a night," she said.

Quinn responded with a cheeky smile.

"Don't look at me like that," Paige reached across the table and playfully punched Quinn's arm.

Quinn threw her hands up in mock protest. "I'm not looking at you like anything."

Paige narrowed her eyes and pursed her lips. "I'm taking it easy tonight. No drinking."

"That's what you said yesterday."

"Yeah? Well, how about this…" Paige looked for inspiration for her retort. "You look like a sunburnt panda."

Quinn felt her face, remembering the way the goggles had marked her face, redding the areas around her eyes. She stuck her tongue out childishly. Paige reciprocated, pulling a silly face.

"You're an idiot."

"You too."

Paige looked at the helmet and goggles on the table. "How do you do it?"

"What?" Quinn asked.

"Get up at the crack of dawn and... exercise." She shuddered at the thought.

"I like it."

The door to the café opened and the sound of loud chatting and laughing came suddenly. A group of people entered and passed by their table. Quinn recognised the men of the group as the frat guys that had been in the ski school for the first couple of days they were there. Paige barely acknowledged them as they sat down at the far end of the room.

"Any updates to share there?" Quinn enquired.

"Nah," Paige replied plainly. "Can't remember everything, but I think I blew my chance with Paul."

Quinn looked at the group, spotting Paul among them. Tall, dark and handsome, he wore a permanently smug look on his face. He had his arm around a woman from their group, who was nestling into him as the group continued their loud laughing and joking.

"Pff, just as well," said Quinn. "Your couple name would be Pauge."

"Or Pail," Paige added. The pair shared a hearty laugh.

The door swung open again and a woman entered. She looked immediately lost, scanning the room as though getting her bearings. One of the women from the noisy group at the far side called out to her and waved her over.

As the woman passed by their table, she caught Paige's eye.

"Hey," the woman smiled.

"Hey," Paige smiled back.

The woman rejoined her group, pulling up a chair from the adjoining table as they started to spill out of their area.

Quinn widened her eyes, her expression asking the question Paige knew would follow.

"So, Paul is a no-go. But there might be something with Harper." She winked.

Quinn mouthed "nice" and nonchalantly reached a fist across the table. Paige met it halfway and the two shared a quiet fist bump, blowing it up after contact.

Quinn's phone lit up on the table. She glanced at the screen and then sighed.

"What's up?" asked Paige.

"Ted messaged me."

Paige slammed her fist on the table. "Shut up!" she shouted excitedly, drawing attention from the noisy group. "What does he want? Are you getting back together?"

"Stop it," Quinn replied quietly, trying to get rid of the unwanted attention from the rest of the café. "And we weren't really together."

"Like hell you weren't," Paige rolled her eyes. "You gonna text him back?"

Quinn said nothing.

"You gotta message him. Let yourself be happy."

Quinn considered the words carefully. Something got stuck in her mind, like a switch had been flicked in her brain. "I am happy."

Paige shook her head. "Don't bullshit me, Quinn. You haven't been happy since you started working at that crappy job. And you sure as hell haven't been happy since you stopped talking to Ted."

Quinn looked at her phone. She then pocketed it, stood up quickly and grabbed the goggles and helmet from the table.

"Come on," she said. "Today's the day you get your snow legs."

THREE

Ted Mendez sat across from his interviewee, a restless middle-aged man who had a lot to say about working as a train driver. The man spoke loudly opposite him, compensating for the grinding and screeching sound of the coffee machine in the small café they were sitting in. A blender started up and the man increased his volume.

The man's words flowed like a river, each sentence cascading into the next. But for Ted, they were more like distant ripples in the background. He nodded at the appropriate intervals and maintained a façade of attentiveness. In truth, Ted's mind was elsewhere. The man's voice faded into the background, drowned out by the echoes of his thoughts.

Another patron nudged Ted as they left their table. The sudden unexpected motion snapped Ted back to the present.

"It's beyond a joke now," the interviewee stated, gesticulating wildly. "How many times do we need to strike before they get the message?"

Ted could feel the man's expectant gaze on him, keeping him in a constant state of anxiety as the interview progressed.

He nodded once more, not taking his eyes off his laptop as he scribbled notes on the document he was working on. Then, something strange happened. He realised there was a distinct silence. For the first time since his opening question, asked more than fifteen minutes ago, the interviewee had stopped talking. Ted looked up from his screen to see the man waiting impatiently.

Ted blinked, realising he hadn't been paying attention at all. He cleared his throat, mentally scrambling to piece together the last few minutes of conversation.

He smiled politely, hoping that whatever the man sat across from him had asked was rhetorical.

The man continued to expound on the topic, detailing the reasons he believed he and his colleagues were underpaid. Ted made an effort to listen carefully to this point, fearing another question he wasn't prepared for. He jumped in at the first opportunity.

"It's interesting hearing it from this perspective," he said. "It's easy for the public to get annoyed at the inconvenience the rail strikes cause to their lives, but perhaps they don't see how important they are in highlighting this issue."

"I don't like it any more than the poor souls that can't get to work," the man held his hands out apologetically. "But some of those people can find another way to get there, or work from home. This is my livelihood."

Ted's phone lit up on the table next to his laptop. Excitement and trepidation bubbled within him as he glanced at it, hoping to see Quinn's name flash up. He had messaged her a couple of hours ago, hoping to rekindle a friendship that had begun to fade. He could feel her pulling away, but he wanted desperately to keep her in his life.

The message on the phone was from Carl, his friend and flatmate. He pushed the button on the side of the phone to lock it.

The feeling of disappointment enveloped him, and his mind wandered to the summer he and Quinn had spent together after their whirlwind meeting in Mexico.

In the aftermath of those traumatic events, they had found friendship and a spark that promised more. It had been a short, but wonderful time as they explored London together, shared their likes and dislikes and connected on a level Ted had never done with anyone before. A vibrant tapestry of moments with her played out in his mind, overshadowing the drab interview unfolding before him. He recalled the laughter as they ran to catch the last bus home and made it just in time, and the jokes they made as they watched a terrible movie on a whim. His mind flashed back to the first time they kissed, days before Quinn had to return home.

Video calls had made up the bulk of their relationship since, with Ted unclear throughout on how to label it. Despite their obvious connection, their lives were so separate, not only in geography but time. Many couples Ted knew had tried and failed to maintain a long-distance relationship. But Ted knew there was another reason Quinn had begun to pull away these last few months. He felt it too. Seeing Quinn's face pop up on his screen evoked a mixture of feelings: the warmth of her smile, the beauty in her eyes, and that indescribable quality she radiated that Ted couldn't fathom. But, in seeing her, Ted was transported back to those moments in Mexico when they were both fighting for their lives. Every now and then there would be a look that would transport him back to that fateful trip. It was a trauma bond they shared; one which Ted knew weighed heavy on them both equally. Being in each other's company was a constant reminder of the experience. He couldn't blame her for wanting to rid herself of the memory.

He felt the man's eyes on him once more, getting the sense that they had never left him. Then he noticed the silence that was growing in discomfort.

"Ted? Are you still with me?"

Ted snapped back to reality once more, his cheeks flushing with embarrassment. The man opposite him was visibly annoyed.

"Sorry," he replied. "Please continue."

The man looked at him with a perplexed expression. "I don't really have any more to say."

"Really?" Ted found the words leaving his mouth before he had a chance to catch them. His tone failed to hide his surprise that the man who had been practically monologuing for the best part of twenty minutes suddenly had nothing left in the tank.

Glancing at his laptop screen, both to check on the notes he had taken and to avoid further eye contact with his interviewee, Ted decided he should wrap things up. He hastily shut the lid of the laptop, pocketed his phone, and shuffled around getting his things ready to make a quick exit. The man sat incredulous as Ted extended a hand.

"Thank you so much for your time today. I think I have everything I need."

The man shook his hand. "Sure."

Ted stood up and made his way to the door. He had handled the whole interview poorly, and it was not the first time this had happened recently. He hoped his supervisor would not find out about this one. He was on thin ice already.

Keen to put as much distance as possible between himself and the situation he was leaving, he went straight for the tube station.

The cold winter air nipped at his extremities. Ted stuck his hands in the pockets of his coat and walked briskly, weaving in and out of the pedestrians ambling in the busy streets of central London.

He placed his phone face down on the reader at the barriers to Hammersmith tube station, the machine taking a second to scan the debit card details in his virtual wallet. The reader beeped and he instinctively took one step towards the barrier, before realising they had failed to open. He saw the light next to it had turned from orange to red. Suddenly a great force pushed into his back, causing him to lurch forward into the barrier. A call came from behind him as a man apologised, before moving to the next barrier along.

Ted cursed under his breath and tried his phone on the reader again. It beeped once more, this time the light turning green and the doors opening.

A Hammersmith & City line train was waiting for him on the platform. He hopped into the closest carriage and found an empty seat. It would be a long journey back to East London, but one benefit of getting on at the start of the line was nearly always guaranteeing a seat. He pulled his phone from his pocket and checked the message from Carl.

You gonna be here for dinner tonight? I'm making tacos.

Carl and his damned tacos. His friend went through phases of cooking the same dish over and over again. This time he was trying to recreate a visit to a restaurant where he had eaten what he had called the 'best tacos in the world'. No offence to the London dining experience, but Ted was sure there was better Mexican food out there.

A thought crossed his mind, taking him momentarily back to the restaurant he and Quinn had eaten at in Mexico City when they first met. They had got to the place early while they waited for Professor Thornton to join them. Ted remembered making a worse impression on Quinn that night than the burrito had made on the professor's digestive system.

Ted tapped a reply to Carl's message.

I'll be there by 7.

The train rattled through a tunnel, the screeching of the wheels on the track echoing around the carriage. Ted's phone momentarily lost signal. The moment it returned, a new message from Carl flashed up.

Can you grab salsa?

Ted rolled his eyes, before reacting to the message with a thumbs-up emoji. There was a Tesco Express just around the corner from the station. It would only be a quick detour.

Ted unlocked the door to the flat and was greeted with the smell of Carl's cooking. The scent of coriander and citrus filled the place, and he could hear the sizzling of the frying pan. In Carl's defence, the food at least smelled good. Loud music played from a speaker on the kitchen counter. Next to it was a chopping board where far too much coriander had been chopped finely. As he walked into the kitchen, Ted placed the jar of salsa next to a lime that had been cut in two.

"Legend!" Carl shouted over the music, without looking away from the hob. He was wearing a black apron that had the words 'If you're reading this, bring me a beer' written on it.

Ted peered over his shoulder, getting a glimpse of the chicken thighs that had been dusted in paprika.

"This looks good," said Ted.

"You sound surprised."

"I am." Ted patted Carl on his back in jest. He then noticed the quantity of chicken that he was cooking. He wondered if Carl had moved onto a new phase of batch cooking. This was far too much food for the two of them.

"Carl?" Ted asked curiously. "What's going on?"

"Nothing," Carl replied suspiciously.

Ted looked again at the mass of coriander Carl had chopped. It was then he noticed something was out of place in the kitchen. He had rushed in and not realised the table was missing. He walked to the doorway, peering into the living room to see the table laid out with four chairs around it. Four placemats sat neatly on top, with a jug of water in the middle.

"What the hell is this?"

"We're having company," Carl replied plainly.

"I can see that," said Ted. "What company?"

"Eliza's bringing a friend over for dinner."

Ted raised an eyebrow. "Eliza?"

The two rarely saw their third flatmate. For some reason, they had never really clicked as a trio. She worked nights a lot of the time, so they rarely had a chance to eat together or socialise. But even so, Eliza tended to keep herself to herself, with Ted and Carl rarely seeing her venture out of her room.

"We were talking, and I thought it would be fun," said Carl.

Ted was dumbfounded. "Eliza. As in, our flatmate, Eliza?"

"Yeah, man," Carl turned from the hob for the first time, eyeing Ted curiously. "She's pretty cool, actually."

Ted snickered. "She's weird."

"Ted."

"You said it yourself," Ted protested. "What, you two best friends now?"

Carl chuckled. "Jealous?"

"Devastated," Ted replied sarcastically. He turned his attention back to the food preparation. "Need some help?"

"My man," Carl smiled. "I'm almost done, but you could take over the pico de gallo." He motioned to the chopping board full of coriander and the lime that had been halved.

"Where's the tomato and onion?" asked Ted, noticing the crucial ingredients were missing as he dug into a cupboard for a bowl.

"I hadn't got that far yet."

"So, when you said, 'take over', you meant 'do the whole thing'."

"Pretty much," Carl shrugged.

The sound of voices coming from the front door could just about be heard over the loud music. Carl turned the volume down and called out to the newcomers.

"Hey!" Came Eliza's voice, followed by the sound of keys jangling. "Smells good."

"You're just in time," said Carl. "We're about to serve up."

"We?" Ted asked quietly.

Carl winked. "You can take the credit for the pico de gallo, even though I did chop the lime and coriander."

"How gracious of you," Ted retorted, getting to work on chopping the tomatoes.

A second female voice came from the other room. Carl craned his head around, as though trying to catch the conversation. It was subtle, but Ted twigged at what was going on. Of course, that was why he was making such an effort.

"Unbelievable," he said.

"What?" Carl played dumb.

"Does Eliza know you're using her to get to her friend?"

Carl made a face that told Ted to lower his voice. "Vanessa," he clarified. "Anyway, she suggested it. Just play it cool, please."

Ted rolled his eyes.

"Come on, mate," Carl put an arm around his shoulder. "I need my wingman. You know, big me up a bit."

"I think Eliza's doing a good enough job of that already," said Ted.

"Come off it," Carl dismissed. "You're still my number one." He fired a wink at Ted, before carrying the food into the other room.

Carl's extra effort in dinner preparation paid off, resulting in Ted declaring it his friend's best-tasting meal yet. The drinks were flowing, and Ted was surprised at how easy the conversation was with Eliza and Vanessa. Meeting new people was a distinct flavour of uncomfortable for Ted, but perhaps the alcohol was helping a little for all parties. He saw a side to his elusive third flatmate that he hadn't seen before. Carl was right, she was pretty cool. Ted even found one or two opportunities to crack a joke at Carl's expense. Carl of course returned the favour. All in all, the evening was surprisingly enjoyable. It was a welcome distraction.

Just as he had forgotten all about the message he had sent to Quinn that had gone unanswered all day, his phone it up on the table. Eliza was in the middle of telling him about the exhibition at an art gallery she was looking forward to seeing. Feeling a sense of déjà vu, as he weakly attempted to remain engaged in the conversation while subtly checking his phone, his heart skipped a beat as he saw Quinn's name attached to the notification.

Eliza stopped mid-sentence and caught a glimpse of the screen from across the table.

"I'm sorry," said Ted. "I need to excuse myself for a moment."

"Sure," Eliza replied, a knowing smile etched on her face.

Ted disappeared into his bedroom, his phone in hand. He sat at his desk and opened the message from Quinn. He couldn't help but smile as he read the words. It had been a while since they last spoke, but there was something in the way she wrote that made it feel like they were picking up where they had left off. There was no trepidation in her response.

His message had been simple, a tentative bridge across the miles that separated them. In the tone of her reply, Ted had a feeling that she was glad to hear from him and was not simply replying out of politeness.

He began to type out a follow-up message, eager to keep the conversation going. He was mid-way through drafting it when suddenly Quinn's face popped up on his screen, interrupting his flow. She was video calling him.

Ted was hit with a powerful mixture of excitement and anxiety. He was not expecting this, and he was certainly not ready for it. Before he had time to think, his thumb pressed the green answer button and the call connected.

Quinn consumed his screen, her bright red jacket and red marks around her eyes giving Ted an immediate sense of where she was. Behind her was a blanket of white snow. He saw his own dumb expression in the small window in the bottom corner and quickly attempted to correct it into something resembling a normal face. Whatever that looked like.

"Hey," she said, the hint of a smile creeping across her face.

"Hey," Ted replied. "What's up with your face?"

Quinn laughed. "My goggles. They're too tight."

A moment went by as Ted searched for what to say. Quinn beat him to it.

"So, I saw you were typing, and I figured this would be easier. Listen, Ted, I—" she paused as she thought hard on her next words. Ted's heart began to beat faster. Perhaps he had misjudged this entirely. Was this the part where she formally cut ties with him?

"I just want to say sorry for being so distant," she finished. "I was going through some stuff. I don't know, I guess I thought by avoiding you I was avoiding having to think about—"

"It's okay," Ted interjected. "I understand completely. You don't need to apologise." He felt a huge weight lift from him. Quinn looked relieved too.

"Okay," she smiled. "So, how have you been?"

"Oh, you know, chasing stories, uncovering the gritty truth. Journalist stuff."

Quinn laughed. "Sounds hard-hitting."

"Not really," he admitted. "I interviewed a train driver today."

Quinn pulled a face that showed her intrigue. "How was that?"

"I honestly don't remember."

Quinn chuckled again, letting out an involuntary snort.

"And you?" Ted asked. "Any interesting rocks in the mountains? Must be hard to find them under all that snow."

Ted knew Quinn was dissatisfied with her job. He had considered avoiding the topic, but from past experience, he knew she was up for joking about it with him.

"Actually, that's why they sent me here. The rocks in Colorado are all the rage at the moment. Apparently, there is a research team digging up the abominable snowman's house as we speak."

"Hey!" Ted objected. "Yetis are real. I'm telling you."

"Don't get me started on your Big Foot theories," Quinn stuck out a tongue playfully.

"Yeti," Ted corrected. "Totally different."

The pair laughed again. In that laughter, they found a glimmer of hope; a hope that perhaps, despite the miles and the complications, their story was far from over.

FOUR

The bustling streets of London stretched out before Ted as he weaved his way through the morning crowd. The city was alive with a frenetic energy, a symphony of car horns, hurried footsteps, and the distant hum of conversations in myriad accents.

The workday had flown by in a whirlwind of interviews, phone calls, and frantic typing. By the time Ted emerged from the newsroom, the city was bathed in the soft hues of twilight.

It had been a better day than yesterday, workwise at least. Luckily, his boss hadn't asked about his interview with the disgruntled train driver. She had seemed busy the few times Ted saw her gliding up and down the office, moving from one meeting to another with a takeaway cup of coffee in her hand. Despite not finding the right moment to check in with her about the progress (or lack thereof) he was making with his article, he had tried hard to keep a low profile all day.

After being ambushed with an unexpected dinner party, Ted's evening was looking tiresome. But everything had changed with that video call with Quinn. Reconnecting with her lifted his spirits, and when he joined his flatmates in the living room once more, Ted found himself engrossed in the banter between his flatmates with renewed vigor. The quirks and eccentricities that once baffled him had become a source of amusement and camaraderie. In their unique ways, Carl and Eliza had become his adopted family in this bustling metropolis.

The next evening would be another unusual one for Ted. He had promised Eliza to accompany her to visit a new art exhibition. Eliza, a free-spirited artist with a penchant for illustrating, had transformed their flat into a kaleidoscope of colours and shapes. She drew all sorts, taking inspiration from a variety of artists to create her own unique style. She had started to find success in selling prints of some of her best work. Those that she deemed not good enough to advertise online, she kept in a binder. It had been Carl's choice to display them around the flat, and Ted was fully on board. Her work was wonderful. Even the 'bad' ones.

As he approached the warehouse that was being used as a makeshift gallery, Ted wondered if he had ever done something like this before. Art galleries were not his usual scene, but he recalled visiting the Tate Modern once or twice.

Upon arrival, he was greeted by the pulsating rhythm of music, its beats reverberating through the air like a heartbeat. A DJ was standing at their decks in the far corner of the space, headphones over one ear as they concentrated on the mix. The warehouse was bathed in a surreal, multicoloured glow, courtesy of the various art pieces and projections that adorned the walls. It felt like stepping into another world entirely.

The exhibition was a sensory explosion. Ted marvelled at the creativity on display as he entered, his senses immediately overwhelmed.

Ted navigated the labyrinth of artistic expressions, each corner of the warehouse offering something new and captivating. There were sculptures that seemed to defy gravity, their forms twisting and spiralling into improbable shapes. One particularly striking piece was a massive canvas covered in intricate geometric patterns that seemed to shift and dance when observed closely.

The attendees were as diverse as the art itself. Artists, art enthusiasts, and curious souls who had stumbled upon the event mingled in an atmosphere of shared awe. Conversations buzzed around Ted, snippets of discussions about the meaning of art and the boundaries of creativity.

He caught sight of Eliza, who was chatting with a small group. She peeled away when she saw him approach.

"You made it!" she shouted excitedly over the loud music, throwing her arms around him and embracing him in a warm hug.

"This is pretty cool," said Ted. The booming bass from the speakers reverberated through him.

"What?" Eliza asked.

"I said this is pretty cool," Ted repeated, leaning in to get closer to her ear.

Eliza smiled. "I know it's not really your thing."

"No, really," Ted insisted. "This is cool. Thanks for inviting me."

He could see the joy in her face as she said it. She brought him over to the group of friends she had been chatting with before.

"Everyone, this is Ted, my flatmate," she announced. "Ted, this is everyone."

The five other people in the circle gave a polite smile or nod. Ted gave a little wave in response. "Nice to meet you," he said loudly. He wasn't sure if anyone had heard him over the music, or if they were already disinterested in him because they went straight back to their conversations.

"Hi again," came a voice from Ted's left. He turned to see Vanessa.

"Hey," said Ted. "Good to see you again."

"Likewise," she replied. She was holding a bottle of beer in each hand. She stretched one out towards Ted.

"For me?" Ted asked.

She nodded.

"Thank you," Ted gratefully accepted, clinking the neck of the bottle against hers.

"Good day?" she asked.

Ted shrugged. "Okay, I guess. You?"

She reciprocated. "Not bad."

Ted gestured to a nearby sculpture, hesitating a moment as he tried to figure out what it represented. "You into all this stuff too?"

"Erm," Vanessa pondered the question. "Not really. I mean, don't get me wrong, this is all very impressive. But it's more Eliza's thing."

"I know what you mean," said Ted.

A few moments went by as Ted tried hard to find an avenue into a new topic of conversation. He took a sip of beer, hoping to buy enough time for a wave of inspiration to wash over him. Nothing came. Usually, this was around the time the person he was talking with made their excuses and moved on to a more engaging conversation. But Vanessa stayed, the pair standing awkwardly together. He saw the way she was turned away from the rest of the group. Eliza was laughing with two of them. He realised that, like him, Vanessa was an outsider in this crowd.

"Do you know Eliza's friends well?" he asked.

"Not really. We've met once or twice at events like this. They're really into the art."

"Right." Ted was getting a sense of the dynamic.

There was another long pause as the pair took another sip of beer and glanced around the room for inspiration.

"You know, Carl's meant to be coming tonight too," Ted said.

"Oh, great," Vanessa smiled. "He seems nice."

"Yeah, he's okay. Turns out he makes decent tacos too."

"They were tasty," she agreed.

"He usually makes terrible food, so you caught him on a good day," said Ted.

"Are you trash-talking my tacos?" Carl's voice suddenly came from behind him. Ted watched as a look of concern formed on Vanessa's face, before turning to see his friend soaking wet. His jeans were a darker shade of blue than they should be, and his hair was flattened from the rain.

"Actually, I was singing their praises," said Ted. "What happened to you?"

"Bloody shower right as I got off the tube," he said. "I need a drink."

"I'll join you," Vanessa said hastily. Ted was surprised to see she had polished off the bottle of beer already. Looking at his own bottle he realised he had nearly done the same. A few too many awkward pauses in conversation, he surmised. Either Vanessa was extremely glad to see Carl, or eager to get away from Ted. He tried not to linger on the answer.

He took a last sip of beer before looking wistfully at the pair at the bar. He figured he would give them some time alone, and set off on a lap around the warehouse, wondering how long he was expected to stay for.

The Atlantis Idol

As he meandered through the event, his phone buzzed with a message from Quinn. The timing couldn't have been better.

Hey Ted, just wanted to check in. How's the art event?

Ted smiled at her message, appreciating the genuine concern in her words. He quickly replied.

It's pretty cool. Bit bored though. About to third-wheel Carl and Vanessa.

His phone buzzed again shortly after.

Eliza's friend from last night? They hitting it off?

Ted looked over at the bar and caught Vanessa laughing at something Carl said.

She's laughing at his jokes.

This time he barely had time to look away before the reply came.

That's a big fat yes. Carl's not that funny.

Ted chuckled to himself. Another message flashed up on the screen.

Hope you don't get too bored. Take some photos for me. I want to see the art!

Ted tapped out a quick reply.

Thanks, will do. Have a good day on the slopes!

Their exchange brought a sense of warmth and connection, even across the physical distance that separated them.

As Ted continued to explore the event, his thoughts occasionally drifted back to Quinn. He wondered if the renewed contact between them might lead to something more. But he was also aware of the complexities of their lives, the distance, and the pain that had kept them apart.

He was busy trying to make sense of a sculpture made from recycled materials when a distinctive voice cut through the artistic din. "Ted?"

He turned, his head reeling as he recognised the voice instantly. Julia. It had been years since he had seen her. They had been close friends during their time at university. Back then, Ted had been infatuated with her and had spent a long time holding onto the hope of romance. The last time he had seen her was in a dark pub, where over a pint of ale Julia had announced her relationship with someone else, casually placing Ted firmly in the friend zone and extinguishing any possibility that the two of them would be an item. The moment had hit Ted like a freight train. He had even missed seeing Star Wars at the cinema for the privilege. Of course, Ted didn't blame her for not reciprocating the same feelings he had. But he had been too embarrassed to continue seeing her, and their paths had diverged.

"Julia," Ted stammered, the memories flooding back.

She smiled, her eyes gleaming with nostalgia. "It's been a while, hasn't it?" Her well-spoken accent was as strong as he remembered. A sweet floral scent enveloped him, and he was suddenly transported back to the time when he was pining after her. She still wore the same fragrance.

"How have you been?" Ted asked.

Julia brushed her hair behind her ear and looked to the floor. "Oh, you know, good."

There was an uncertainty and nervousness that Ted couldn't help but sense. It felt so out of place for Julia; she had always been so self-assured and confident.

"How was that trip after graduation?" he followed up. He remembered she had told him she was planning to travel with Richard. It had been the catalyst to the realisation that the two of them were an item.

She looked sheepish as she replied. "Oh, it was lovely. We backpacked around Bolivia; saw some beautiful places, met some wonderful people."

"And how's Richard?" Ted followed up quickly.

She shifted her weight onto her other foot. "It didn't work out. Turns out we didn't have all that much in common, and in the end, I realised he wasn't what I wanted." Her gleaming eyes fixed on Ted. He felt his heart begin to beat faster.

"I'm sorry to hear that," he lied.

"Well," she started but seemed not to know what else to say. "How about you?" she flipped the question. "Editor of The Guardian yet?"

The question left Ted with a feeling of unease. She had made a comment similar to that on the night he had last seen her. The interaction had brought up a lot of uncomfortable memories.

"Not quite," he replied with a polite smile. "I *am* working in journalism though."

"Oh, really?"

"Yeah. It's okay, I guess. I interviewed a train driver yesterday."

"Fascinating," she said.

A moment went by as an awkward silence built between them.

"So, what brings you here?" Ted asked, genuinely curious.

Julia hesitated for a moment, her gaze flickering. "Actually, I'm here for business. Family business, you could say."

"Oh," Ted replied, looking around at the artwork surrounding them. Did her family produce any of these pieces? No, buying one of these pieces made more sense. Julia came from an extremely wealthy family. Her family owned an estate somewhere in the countryside. He had never seen her childhood home, but he imagined it to be an old mansion akin to those now protected by the National Trust, surrounded by acres of land.

A man walked by, touched Julia on the shoulder and whispered something discreetly into her ear. Her face dropped and her tone changed, as though she had just received troubling news.

"It was really nice to see you, Ted," she said, suddenly seeming rushed.

Ted nodded, bemused at how hastily the conversation was being wrapped up. Julia flashed another warm smile at him and reached out to squeeze his hand, before following the man towards the far side of the large space. Ted saw the man open a door and escort her inside. Just as she began to walk through, she stopped long enough to glance back at Ted. The two locked eyes for a brief moment. It was just long enough for Ted to see the tear rolling down her cheek.

The man walked through behind her and shut the door.

Ted stood still, completely perplexed at how the last few minutes had transpired. A moment later he felt something brush his hand and fall to the floor. He looked down to see a tiny slip of paper. Picking it up, he unravelled it to reveal a small handwritten message.

I'm sorry for everything. I hope you can forgive me one day.

Ted read the note again, not able to understand why it had been written. Forgive her? For what? For not liking him the way he had liked her? That was nothing to be sorry for. It made no sense. But the way she had looked at him, that tear rolling down her cheek, the man escorting her away. What the hell was going on?

Determined to get answers, Ted marched over to the other side of the warehouse, behind the DJ booth and to the doorway Julia had disappeared through moments earlier. Knowing how much he would overthink the cryptic message

The Atlantis Idol

over the course of the next few days, he decided he would catch up to her and talk it out there and then. He had come so far in getting her out of his head once. He needed closure.

He pushed open the door and found himself in a stairwell. The signage gave away that he had stepped into an emergency exit.

Hearing footsteps above him, he headed up the first flight of stairs. A loud squeak of a door opening echoed around the stairwell and the footsteps quietened. He climbed the next flight of steps, eventually finding the door Julia had presumably just entered. The door hadn't fully closed behind her, revealing a dim yellow hue of light inside.

Ted opened the door, the hinge squeaking loudly. He entered the dimly lit area to see a group of figures huddled around a table. He caught sight of Julia. There were more individuals crowded around the table, all talking in hushed tones and looking at something. Ted couldn't see what it was.

"Julia?" he said curiously.

Julia spun around, surprised to see him. "Ted? What are you—"

Ted didn't hear the end of her sentence, as he recoiled as a hand suddenly grabbed his arm. Another hand caught his other arm, and both tightened around his biceps like a vice.

"Wait, no!" Julia called out. "Don't hurt him!" Her eyes were wild.

Ted looked up at the men holding him in place. He recognised one as the man who had escorted Julia away.

"Julia, what's going on?" Ted asked nervously.

She glanced back at him, her expression conflicted. Another voice came, this time from one of the individuals who was leaning over the table.

"That's him," a woman said, stepping away from the table.

Ted caught sight of an open book laid out in the middle of the table. It looked old. Around it was an assortment of papers.

"Are you sure?" one of the men clutching his arm asked.

The woman nodded. "That's the guy. He's the reason my mother is in jail."

FIVE

The woman looked at Ted with a raging fire in her eyes. The words were swimming around his mind, as though trying to find a memory that might connect what she had just said. He had never seen her before, but this woman seemed to despise him.

He thought hard, struggling to pull his concentration away from the pressure on his arms. The two men on either side of him had maintained their grip, their fingers digging into his skin. Who was this woman? Why did she believe he was somehow linked with her mother's incarceration?

It was then that something lit up in his brain. A single image was pulled from the recess of his mind. It was of an older woman, roughly in her sixties, sitting in the back of a police car. Jasper, the professor who had invited him on the trip to Mexico, was standing at the rolled-down window of the vehicle. They were talking. She was the woman who had been behind his kidnapping. He recalled seeing her once before at the National Museum of Anthropology. She knew Jasper, but Ted couldn't remember how exactly. Something to do with academia? Another memory quickly followed; a news story with details of the museum heist, and the eventual arrest of the three Mexican mercenaries and a certain antiquities thief. Ted couldn't recall her name. But there was one name that did come roaring back: Sigma.

"Julia, what's going on?" he asked, nervously looking around the room at the group of people staring at him.

"You shouldn't be here," she replied, her voice tinged with worry.

"Who is this?" A man with a thick French accent stepped forward. He looked alarmed at the way Ted was being restrained.

"It's okay, Antoine," the blonde woman assured. "There is another matter I want to settle. It does not concern our deal."

She walked slowly over to Ted, appraising him. "You and that buffoon of a professor have caused me a great deal of pain," she sneered. "My mother is locked up in some godforsaken prison, and do you want to know why?"

Ted said nothing.

"Because people like you cannot keep your nose out of other people's business!" she raised her voice suddenly, causing Ted to flinch. "If you and that teacher's pet of a girlfriend had just done what you were told, you would have flown back home and been none the wiser. You ruined everything."

Ted was raging inside. Despite the precarious and potentially dangerous position he found himself in, he was shocked at the way this woman was gaslighting him. He and Quinn had been dragged through hell on that trip, and this woman was blaming them for it.

"What can I say?" he replied. "Journalistic curiosity." He narrowed his eyes at her.

"My mother is locked up because of you!" she yelled.

The Atlantis Idol

"Karma's a bitch," Ted muttered.

The woman paused as she tried to compose herself. Eventually, she let out a chuckle, undeterred by his comment. "You're in quite the pickle, Mr Mendez. I don't think you're in any position to taunt me." She gestured to the men holding him still.

"Natalia," said Julia. "Stop it. Please."

The woman looked at Ted long and hard. She then rolled her eyes and waved a hand to the men. They immediately loosened their grip on him. Ted stretched out his arms, feeling a strange sensation as the blood returned to his biceps.

Julia rushed over to him. "Are you okay?"

"No, I'm not okay," Ted replied plainly. "What the hell is going on here? How do you know these people?"

Julia shuffled uncomfortably. "I wasn't lying when I said I was on family business."

"What do you mean? And what was this message about?" he showed her the tiny slip of paper.

She said nothing. Her face showed signs of indecisiveness, as though she were weighing up the risk of coming clean.

Ted was growing impatient with the cryptic comments. He decided he wanted nothing more to do with this. "Screw this." He headed towards the door, but the door was now blocked by one of the men.

"Don't go anywhere," Natalia said. "I still have use of you."

"Not interested," Ted dismissed, looking defiantly at the man blocking his way. Unmoved, the man folded his arms and stared back at him. Ted attempted to push past, but the man placed a hand on his chest and thrust him back.

"I'm afraid you don't have a choice in the matter," said Natalia. She turned to Julia. "Thank you, dear, for bringing him to us."

Ted's felt a chill run down his spine. Julia had lied to him.

"Teddy," Julia pleaded. "I swear, I didn't think this would happen. I just wanted to see you and apologise for everything that happened before."

"Don't call me that," Ted replied. Julia's eyes widened. She knew she deserved that, but she couldn't hide the hurt.

"You knew about Mexico?" Ted asked.

She nodded. "My family are part of Sigma."

He looked at her incredulous. "That doesn't make sense. Sigma is a person." It was then that something came back to him from the recesses of his mind. He pointed to Natalia. "Her mum is Sigma."

"We're all Sigma," Julia said matter of fact. "It's, uh, an organisation of sorts."

He scratched his head, trying to process the last few minutes. He wished he could go back in time and stop himself from following her. Hell, he would stop himself from going to the art exhibit altogether. He thought about his friends downstairs. How long it would be before they started to worry about his whereabouts? Would they come looking for him? More likely they would assume he got bored and took off.

The clandestine nature of the meeting Ted had stumbled upon made him feel uneasy enough. Now he had learnt that these people were linked to the living nightmare of two years ago, he began to panic. He had to get out.

Without thinking, Ted launched a swift kick to the man at the door's shin. Having not expected the sudden attack, the man stumbled and let out a groan as he winced with pain. Ted wasted no time and pushed past him, shoving open the door and racing into the stairwell.

His heart pounding, his feet pitter-patting on the steps as quickly as he could, he placed a hand on the handrail and swung himself around the corner part-way down the first flight. He could hear shouting coming from behind him, and the echo of footsteps.

As he reached the bottom of the stairs, he saw the door to the main floor of the warehouse. It was closed, the booming bass from the DJ booth thumping through. If he could just make it out to the exhibition, he would be able to find safety in numbers. Surely his pursuers would not risk making a scene in such a public space. He was just a few feet away from it. As he reached the door and began to pull it open, the music from the nearby speakers launched a barrage on his eardrums. He could see the DJ, their headphones on and their back turned to him. Beyond that, the artwork in part of the exhibit and a few people milling around. He caught sight of Carl, still standing at the bar talking with Vanessa. He wanted to yell out to get their attention, but a hand suddenly wrapped around his mouth, muffling any sound that escaped. He felt his weight shift as he became quickly overpowered by the two men who dragged him back into the stairwell.

"Let's try this again, shall we?" Natalia said, a hint of amusement on her face. Ted was slumped on an uncomfortable wooden chair in the middle of the room. Having spent the last few minutes shouting for help, he came to the realisation that nobody could hear his cries. The thumping bass from the music downstairs was a cruel reminder that he was alone in this.

"I see you've had a nice little reunion with Julia," she pouted her bottom lip, producing a mocked expression that she found their friendship in some way cute. "You must have so much to catch up on."

Julia was standing with her arms folded on the other side of the room, her body language showing signs of intense remorse and discomfort in this situation.

"See, Julia belongs to a very prestigious family. Well, I'm sure that part you already knew. She doesn't exactly try and hide it, do you darling?" She flashed a look at Julia, who was now scowling at her. "Beautiful necklace you're wearing today. Bought with Daddy's money, no doubt."

"Oh, like you can talk," Julia retorted. "You're just the same."

Natalia laughed. "No. See, that is where you are wrong. My mother is wealthy, yes. But her wealth comes from hard work. We don't come from an upper-class bloodline. There are no Lords and Ladies in my family tree. We started from nothing. My mother has dedicated years to building our fortune." There was a sense of pride in the way she talked about her family.

"A fortune from stolen artefacts," said Julia.

"A fortune from years of hard work," Natalia insisted. "Those artefacts don't find themselves. We are archaeologists, historians. We're not petty thieves."

Ted knew next to nothing about archaeology or relic hunting, but as he sat there and listened, he knew what she was saying was wrong. Did she really believe that?

"What do you want from me?" he asked at last.

Natalia gave a wry smile. "I'm so glad you asked. As I was saying, Julia did a lovely job of bringing you here—"

"I swear, I didn't know she wanted you," Julia interrupted. "I just wanted to say sorry for what happened to you in Mexico. You have to believe me."

"Enough, Julia!" Natalia snapped. "Do not interrupt me again. Your father's position in this organisation, and yours, is not untouchable. You would do well to remember that." She grimaced at Julia.

The Atlantis Idol

Ted was getting a real sense of the power dynamic at play between them. What the hell was Julia and her family really involved in here?

"Your meddling in our business had a profound impact on our organisation. My mother was the driving force of our operation. Her knowledge and connections are invaluable to uncovering the hidden secrets of the ancient world."

"You need her," said Ted. "I get the picture. Can't you just pay someone with knowledge of whatever it is you're looking for next to replace her?"

She leaned closer to Ted. "Mark my words, Mr Mendez. My mother is irreplaceable." She then moved to the table and put a delicate hand on the old book that lay open in the middle. "Besides. Why pay someone for that service when I can get it for free?" She smiled slyly.

Ted was confused. It sounded like she was insinuating that he was going to help them. Then it hit him. It was not him. It was Quinn.

"No, absolutely not," he said flatly. "Leave her out of this."

"I'm afraid I cannot," Natalia said. "I am prepared to swallow my pride and admit that I need her. And the way I see things, she owes me. Just as you do."

Antoine was standing by the table, remaining close to the old book the group had been looking at. He glanced at his phone, then whispered something in French to another woman. She nodded.

"The payment has come through," the French woman declared. "I think we'll be on our way now." She eyed Ted cautiously. She looked wholly uncomfortable with the situation.

"Thank you, Antoine, Sophie," Natalia said amicably as the pair made their way to the door. "Always a pleasure."

"We'll let you know if anything else interesting comes up," Sophie said as they disappeared through the doorway. The echoing sounds of their footsteps receded until they disappeared altogether into the hubbub of the exhibition downstairs. The look Sophie had given Ted suggested she didn't approve of how Natalia was treating him. But in any case, the pair were not prepared to stick around and do anything about it. Maybe they had learned to stay out of Sigma's business.

"Interesting pair, those two," Natalia said. "Brother and sister. They make a living in antiques. I've bought a few relics from them over the years. They found this one in a lapsed storage unit in France. Actually, most of the items I get from them are from around there."

One of the men who had manhandled Ted moments ago was at the table studying the old book. "Maybe you should ask if they have friends that are storage hunting in other places."

"Oh, I have connections, dear," Natalia replied. "Oh, and Stefan," she cast an eye on her colleague. "Can you make sure their flight back to Montpellier is upgraded to first class?" She winked at Ted. "It's important to show gratitude to repeat customers."

Ted exaggerated a sarcastic smile, reiterating his displeasure at being kept here against his will.

"Now, Ted," she said. "It's only fair we let you in on our discovery here. After all, you're part of the team now."

"This is bullshit!" Ted snapped. "I'm not part of this. Neither is Quinn."

Natalia rolled her eyes. "Mr Mendez, we have been over this. The sooner you accept your situation, the sooner we can all move on. Let me be honest with you." She looked him deep in his eyes. "Your girlfriend has proven to be a very capable artefact hunter. Perhaps you as well. I need fresh minds on this job. While you are in my care, and cooperating," she lowered her tone to emphasise that point. "No harm will come to you. I guarantee it. You do this for me, and your debt with Sigma is cleared."

Ted grunted. He didn't believe that for a second. But he didn't really have much choice.

"She's not my girlfriend," he said. "I think. Not that it matters."

Natalia smiled. "Young love. So complex." She beckoned him over to the table where Stefan and Julia were looking at the old book. "Come and look at this, Ted. This is what a £100,000 book looks like."

Ted reeled. They had just paid that French pair a hundred grand for this? He looked at the tattered book. Weathered by time, the leather was cracked and worn like the lines of an aged face. It had faded to a muted sepia, the parchment yellowed, revealing the age of the pages. The ink, once bold and black, had dulled with time, creating a subtle, sepulchral elegance. The page that the book was open to bore the scars of history, with smudges and blots where the quill had hesitated, or where it had sustained water damage.

The presentation of the penmanship was a marvel of meticulous design. Columns and rows neatly ruled in ink delineated the ledger's purpose. Intricate hand-drawn borders adorned the pages, framing the entries like intricate artwork. Faded flourishes and embellishments hinted at the pride with which the ledger's scribe had recorded each item.

"It's a ledger," said Ted.

"Clever boy," said Natalia patronisingly. "It dates back to the 14th century. A certain Bishop from Lisbon, Thibaud de Castillon, had amassed quite the fortune by the time he died. This ledger details everything he had in his possession, which was claimed by the Pope in the name of the Church. Spolia, they called it."

"Okay," said Ted. "So, what's special about it?"

"This," she said, carefully turning a few pages. The layout of the book had changed from the carefully ruled lines and columns, the parchment now adorned with various drawings. "The Pope's emissary provided sketches of some of the more obscure items. Take a look at this one." She turned the page again.

Ted peered closer to get a better view of the shape. The ink was blotchy, but he could still make out what the sketch was. It was a bull, standing proudly with its head down, as though showing off its impressive horns.

"Why did they draw these?" Ted asked. "Doesn't the ledger mention everything in writing?"

"It was a long journey from Lisbon to Avignon. A few spare pages: maybe he liked to doodle."

"Avignon? I thought you said he was taking them to the Pope?"

"Keen observation," Stefan remarked. "Pope Innocent VI was part of the Avignon Papacy. One of his predecessors, Clement V, refused to move to Rome and chose instead to move his court to the papal enclave at Avignon. It was there for sixty-seven years."

"Us historians call it the Babylonian captivity of the Papacy."

"Huh," was all Ted managed. He then noticed the sketch next to it. A bearded man holding a trident. It reminded him of a character from a video game he had played. The game was centred around Greek mythology. He recognised the figure. "Poseidon," he thought out loud.

"Correct," said Natalia. "Here's where things get *really* interesting."

"I'm not following," said Ted.

"Hmm, perhaps Quinn is the better treasure hunter," she said.

"I have no doubt."

"I'll enlighten you," she continued. "The bull is a prominent symbol of the Minoan civilisation. The Minoans are intrinsically linked with Ancient Greek culture, so it makes sense that you would find Minoan artefacts alongside Greek ones." She pointed at the drawing of Poseidon. "Now," she said. "What do you make of this?" She turned the page once more, revealing a third sketch. Ted could feel a palpable energy build in Stefan as she did so. He seemed excited at what she was showing him. Ted looked at the drawing carefully. It didn't seem like much, and like Natalia's previous suggestion, seemed more like a doodle than anything else. It was nothing more than a group of circles, each surrounding the other as they grew outward.

"Concentric circles," Stefan couldn't help himself. "Any guesses?"

"No idea," Ted admitted.

"Are you familiar with Plato?" the man hinted.

"Uh, sure, I guess," said Ted. "But what does this have to do with—" He saw the gleam in the man's eye as he looked up, and the grin he was struggling to hide.

"Plato wrote of an ancient city that was built in the design of concentric circles, that through some natural disaster was lost to the sea."

The penny dropped for Ted. He looked at Stefan in disbelief. Stefan nodded knowingly. "We think this is evidence of the existence of this city. And we're going to find it."

Ted's mouth was agape. He knew what they were referring to. He looked at Natalia, who was smiling just as widely as Stefan.

"Figured it out, yet?" she asked.
"Yes," said Ted. "You're talking about Atlantis."

SIX

A moment went by as Ted realised the absurdity of what they were saying. "You can't be serious," he managed.

"Deadly serious," Natalia replied.

Ted was unconvinced. "You think this is proof of the lost city of Atlantis? This?" he gestured to the sketches on the old, yellowed parchment. "This could be anything."

"You're right to be sceptical," Stefan said. "But trust me on this. I have studied the Minoans for a very long time. The links to Atlantis are numerous. This is my life's work." He shared a smile with Natalia. "I've worked with Natalia and her mother on a few other artefact recovery missions."

"Robberies," Julia corrected.

Stefan cleared his throat. "The point being, we have found things with much less to go on in the past."

"And to clarify, there is more," Natalia added. She pulled out her phone and showed Ted an article. The headline read 'Vatican Releases Documents from Archives'.

"What am I looking at?"

"In the last few years, the Vatican has made public information from their archives that was previously sealed off. There are some very interesting things in those documents. One such thing was a mention of an agreement between Pope Innocent VI and a certain Antonio Botafoc. Botafoc was the captain of a ship in the Castilian navy, and along with another vessel, captained by a fellow called Martin Yanes, they robbed the poor soul who was transporting the late Bishops' fortune to the Pope."

"The one who wrote this ledger," Ted said.

Natalia nodded.

"So, if they stole from the Pope, how did they come to an agreement?"

"That was our question too," said Stefan. "It is well documented that after taking the belongings, the fortune was divided up between the two ships. Yanes sailed off into the sunset, while Botafoc's ship ran aground. He and his crew were captured and imprisoned. We have reason to believe that the Pope struck a deal with Botafoc to pursue Yanes and recover the Spolia. He could have his freedom; on the condition he fulfilled the task and righted the wrong."

"Sounds awfully familiar, doesn't it, Mr Mendez?" Natalia joked. "Almost poetic, really."

Ted scowled. He hated how much she was enjoying this. "This is not the same." He turned his attention to Stefan. "You said you've found things with less to go on before. This doesn't sound like much to go on."

"You're right, it's not. Good thing we have more." He excitedly took out his phone and tapped onto his photos app. He moved closer to Ted and scrolled through the photos with his thumb until he found what he was looking for. "Here," he said, landing on an image. As Ted peered closer, Stefan pinched a finger and thumb to zoom in on a specific detail.

The photo was of another old-looking document. Like with the ledger, the paper showed its age, the ink from the eloquent flicks of the quill having faded through time. Ted couldn't make sense of what he was looking at.

"This is a text from the Vatican archives," said Stefan. "It was written years after the event, but it mentions a conversation between Pope Innocent VI and a prisoner in Maguio, France. It doesn't mention them by name, but we're sure this is Botafoc."

"And?"

"And nobody else in the public eye has seen this text. We acquired it shortly after the Vatican released it. All public record of it was wiped."

"What? How?" Ted looked puzzled. Just how much power and influence did this Sigma organisation have?

"That's not important," Natalia cut in. "Having this knowledge gives us a crucial advantage."

"Why is that?"

"Because it mentions where Botafoc went next."

**

Amid the breathtaking peaks of Aspen, Colorado, Quinn revelled in the crisp mountain air as she prepared to hit the slopes once more. The snow was pristine, a vast canvas of glistening white, and the azure sky stretched above, promising a perfect day of snowboarding.

Paige, her face etched with determination and a hint of trepidation, stood by the ski lift, her snowboard wobbling under her feet. Adjusting her goggles, she glanced nervously at the sloping white expanse before her.

"Okay, Paige," Quinn said with an encouraging smile, "You got this. Remember what I told you. Keep your balance and take it slow. You'll get the hang of it in no time."

Paige took a deep breath, her gloved hands gripping the edges of the board. "Right, slow and steady," she replied, trying to sound more confident than she felt.

With a gentle push from Quinn, Paige began her journey down the slope, but her progress was marred by an almost immediate fall. She tumbled, the snowboard sliding out from under her.

"Whoa, whoa, it's okay!" Quinn called out, rushing to her side. "Just take it easy."

Paige struggled to regain her footing, her frustration growing with each tumble. The pristine snow that once seemed inviting now felt like an adversary, tripping her at every turn. She continued her descent, but it was a series of brief and unsteady moments on her feet, followed by frustrating falls.

"Shift your weight... oh no, not like that," Quinn urged, her voice laced with concern. "Try to balance... keep your knees slightly bent..."

But Paige's efforts were in vain. She couldn't seem to find the rhythm that snowboarding demanded. Her face grew despondent, her cheeks flushed with both exertion and embarrassment.

As they inched down the slope, Quinn stayed close, helping Paige up after each fall. Her friend's struggle was disheartening, but Quinn was determined to be there every step of the way.

"You're doing great, Paige," Quinn encouraged, though her words seemed to carry less and less conviction. "It's just a matter of practise."

But Paige's heart sank further as she watched other snowboarders glide effortlessly past her. The idyllic winter wonderland of Aspen now felt like a hostile place, and the allure of the slopes had turned into a taunt.

With each fall, Paige's confidence eroded. The day had become a harsh and gruelling struggle. She longed to be in the spa.

As they neared the end of the slope, Paige's enthusiasm was replaced by a heavy sigh of frustration. She leaned on her snowboard, her face weary and her spirit defeated.

"Quinn," Paige said, her voice tinged with a sense of defeat. "I'm sorry. I don't think I can do this."

Quinn, despite her concern, offered an understanding smile. "It's okay, Paige. We all have to start somewhere. Do you want to swap to skis?"

Paige shook her head weakly, her snowboarding adventure ending on a sombre note. "I don't think I'm cut out for the mountain life. Let's get drunk instead."

Quinn laughed. "It's not even lunch."

Paige raised an eyebrow. "And?"

Quinn's coffee arrived, along with a second cup that was placed in front of her friend. Paige was still brushing snow off her jacket as they settled into their booth in the café. Steam rose from Paige's cup, and she blew gently on the hot liquid as she started to take tentative sips.

"I thought you wanted a beer?" said Quinn inquisitively.

"Change of heart," she replied. "Gonna need my wits about me for the afternoon session."

"I thought you were done."

"I'm not a quitter," she said defiantly. "I may be trash at snowboarding, but I'm stubborn too. That mountain better get used to my ass sliding down it."

Quinn snorted as she laughed, spitting out a mouthful of coffee onto the table. "Could you have waited until I'd finished my mouthful?"

Paige chuckled. "That's disgusting. I'll get some napkins." She took off towards the serving area.

Quinn wiped off the coffee that had spilt down the front of her jacket. This was turning into a fun day. She hoped Paige was serious about persevering. It would be nice to have a partner on the slopes. Besides, if she even wanted a solo run, she could just go early in the morning. Paige only ever saw one seven o'clock in a day.

She took out her phone as she waited for Paige to return with the napkins. The screen was slightly damp from the small amount of snow that had seeped through her ski jacket. She wiped it with her hand, before unlocking it with her passcode. The Face ID had been playing up for some time, and instead of staring dumbly at her phone waiting for it to recognise her, she had taken to skipping right to the passcode option now. As her home screen appeared, so too did several missed video calls from Ted.

Paige returned to find Quinn with a concerned look on her face. "What's up?"

"I dunno," she replied. "It's Ted. He's tried calling me like five times."

Paige grinned widely. "Woah! Didn't you just talk to each other? The guy's obsessed with you."

Quinn pulled a sarcastic face. "Shut up. Actually, I had better go see what's up." She stood up and made for the exit to take the call in private.

"Say hi for me," Paige blew a kiss at her playfully.

The door to the café shut behind her and the crisp mountain air filled her lungs. She hit the green dial button and waited for the call to connect. After a few moments Ted's phone picked up, but it was not Ted that filled her screen. A woman with blonde hair tied back into a neat bun answered. Quinn was taken aback. Had her call been connected with a stranger accidentally?

"Hello, Ms Miyata," the woman said. Quinn's heart began to beat faster.

"Erm, hello?" Quinn replied hesitantly.

"So nice of you to answer your phone," the woman said. Something immediately felt off about her.

"What's going on?" Quinn asked. "Is Ted there?"

"Oh, yes, dear. He's here. Say hi, Ted." She turned the phone to catch Ted in the background, sitting on a wooden chair. He had his hands bound behind his back. A burly bald man stood menacingly next to him. Hands by his side, something metallic protruded from the grasp of his meaty fingers. A gun.

Quinn's stomach dropped, and with it, she almost lost her grip on the phone. The woman continued talking as Quinn watched speechless.

"I'm sure you're very confused right now, so I'll make this quick and clear. My name is Natalia. You don't know me, but you might remember my mother, Lillian Pembroke."

The synapses in her brain began firing as Quinn immediately placed the name. Sigma.

"You and your boyfriend here… Or was it just friend?" She turned to Ted momentarily and then back to the phone. "You see, he's not really sure, Ms Miyata. You caused me a great deal of pain with your escapades in Mexico. My mother is trapped in some godforsaken prison…" Her voice started to break with a flicker of anger before she caught herself. "Our organisation has a lot of work to do, and without our chief historian that has become a great deal more difficult. And that's where you come in."

Quinn's eyes shifted from side to side as she struggled to pre-empt what was being asked of her.

Natalia paused a moment. "You know what, why don't you hear it from him? He's been briefed on the situation, and so far, has been very cooperative. Isn't that right, Mr Mendez?" She pointed the phone so that Ted was fully in frame.

"Hi Quinn," Ted said, his voice steady but laden with the weight of their circumstances. Quinn was breathing heavily, her mind running a million miles an hour as she saw the fear in Ted's eyes. He looked utterly helpless.

"Ted—" was all she managed to say.

"Quinn, I'm so sorry about all of this. I didn't want you to get dragged into it too."

Natalia cleared her throat loudly, prompting Ted to get on with what he had been asked.

"Listen," he said. "These people, Sigma. They're not playing around. They told me they need you to help them find something. They have some old artefacts here that apparently prove the existence of Atlantis. Look, they said they need you, Quinn. They're pretty adamant on that."

"Okay, that's quite enough, thank you, Mr Mendez," Natalia turned the phone, so she was back on screen. "The next part is simple, Ms Miyata. You tell us where you are, and we'll send someone to come and collect you. And then you will help us on this mission. It's quite an exciting one, I assure you."

Quinn was speechless. What was she supposed to do in this situation?

"If you fail to cooperate, go to the police, or tell a single soul about this..." Natalia had a serious look on her face. "And we have ways of knowing, Ms Miyata. You will never see Ted again. Do I make myself clear?"

The Atlantis Idol

The words hung in the air, a heavy silence engulfing the space on both ends of the call. Quinn's eyes widened as the magnitude of their predicament sank in, and she tried to process all of the information she had just learned.

"I, uh," she struggled. She looked at Ted, his hands bound behind the chair, the fear in his eyes. "I'm at Aspen Mountain, Colorado."

Natalia smiled gratefully, her face the picture of smug victory. "Thank you, dear. Don't go anywhere. Someone will be there to pick you up shortly. See you soon."

The call disconnected. Quinn fell to the ground, her phone toppling out of her hands and into the snow. Tears filled her eyes, and she began to hyperventilate. What the hell was she supposed to do? How could she help Ted and get them both out of this impossible situation? What if she did help Sigma and they found what they were looking for? Atlantis? Had she heard that right? It seemed like fiction. But then, so had the last one.

Eventually, she managed to regulate her breathing and picked up her phone with a shaky hand.

Sitting back in the booth, Paige was scrolling on her phone. She immediately looked concerned when she saw Quinn's face.

"Are you okay? What happened?"

She considered what the woman on the phone had said. If she told a soul, she would never see Ted again. She felt the tear streaming down her cheek and wiped it away.

"Oh, nothing," she said. "Just this damn cold mountain wind. It makes my eyes water." She smiled reassuringly.

Paige went back to scrolling on her phone. Quinn stared into her cup of coffee, the conversation she had just finished doing cartwheels in her mind. She couldn't believe this was happening. The nightmare she had tried so hard to leave behind had come around and eaten its way back into her life.

**

"Well," said Natalia, handing Ted's phone back to him. "Your friend is very pretty. You're a lucky fellow."

Ted said nothing, unsure of what to take from the comment. Stefan was carefully packing away the old ledger as the second man freed Ted from his bindings. The man had said nothing the whole time Ted had been there. A bald muscular man who looked to be in his forties, he had the look of a cockney gangster who would not have looked out of place in a Guy Ritchie movie. Ted wondered if the man was a mercenary like the group that had kidnapped him in Mexico. Perhaps ex-military?

"Thank you, Hiram," said Natalia. "Sorry for the theatrics, Mr Mendez. We just had to make sure she knew how serious we were. I would hate for her to mess up our operation again."

The group had cleared their belongings away in a matter of seconds and were getting ready to leave.

"Shall we?" Natalia looked expectantly at Ted.

"Where are we going?"

"We got what we came for. I don't want to stay in this grubby warehouse another minute," she replied. "We're going back to the manor."

"The manor?"

"My house. It's an hour's drive, so let's get moving."

Ted stood up from the chair but hesitated a moment. A moment too long for Hiram, as Ted quickly felt the steel of a gun barrel dig into his back. He jolted at the unexpected

The Atlantis Idol

sensation. He hadn't seen the firearm until now. Had the bald man been brandishing it the whole time?

He wasted no more time in following the others out of the doorway. Instead of heading downstairs towards the main floor of the exhibition, Ted was surprised to see them moving upstairs. He gave Hiram an inquiring look and was met only with a stern face.

They climbed the stairs until finally, they ended up on the rooftop. The London rain fell steadily, puddles forming on the flat roof of the warehouse. Julia and Stefan were across the other side of the rooftop already, making their way down an emergency escape ladder. Ted figured this was how they had planned to make a discreet exit all along. Knowing they would have a hostage to boot must have been a factor. They were one scream away from drawing unwanted attention.

The drizzle irritated Ted's eyes, causing him to put a hand up to protect his face as he followed the others to the ladder.

Peering over the edge of the warehouse, he saw Julia reach the bottom, with Stefan descending quickly after her. A sharp wave of vertigo kicked in and he had to step back. He bent over and grabbed his knees, sucking in a big breath as he tried to mentally prepare himself for the climb down the ladder.

"After you, Mr Mendez," Natalia said, having no time for his hesitancy. She was no fool. Placing him conveniently in the middle of the group was the smart choice to mitigate against him making a run for it. She was not prepared to give up that position. "Now, please." Her tone shifted to one of annoyance.

Ted exhaled deeply and tentatively turned around, lowered himself down and placed his hands on the first wet metal rung of the ladder. His legs were shaking as he descended one rung at a time, making sure to have one hand tightly gripped onto the metal at all times for safety. He took considerably longer to descend the ladder than Julia and Stefan, who were waiting at the bottom next to a black Range Rover.

When he reached the halfway point, Ted heard the clanging of feet hitting the rungs above him. He looked up to see Hiram on his way down. The movement disrupted his rhythm, and his foot slipped on the wet metal. He lost his grip on the rung above him and fell suddenly. His stomach dropped as the panic of the moment set in. Flailing his arms, his hand slapped against another rung further down and he gripped on for dear life. His shoulder pulled sharply and painfully as it caught his weight and abruptly stopped his fall.

He must have fallen only a foot or so, but it was enough to send his heart racing and for his legs to turn to jelly. Finding his footing once more, he slowly continued his journey down the ladder, eventually hitting solid ground safely.

Hiram and Natalia reached the bottom as he nursed his sore arm,

"Be careful, Mr Mendez," Natalia said patronisingly. "You're no good to us dead."

Ted grimaced with pain. He thought the comment was a strange one, seeing as they had threatened Quinn with his murder just minutes ago.

Natalia marched to the driver-side door of the black Range Rover, unlocked it with her key fob and climbed into the driver's seat. The engine turned over as she twisted the key in the ignition, the lights illuminating the dingy alleyway as the vehicle came to life.

Ted was ordered to sit in the back seat, squashed in between Stefan and Hiram. Julia remained outside the car as Natalia wound down her window.

"You did well, Julia," Natalia said. "Get home safe."

Julia gave a last mournful look at Ted before the electric window began to close and Natalia put the car into first gear. Ted got the feeling he would never learn whether she had been telling the truth about not knowing Natalia wanted to involve him in this. One thing was clear: Julia's intention would have had no bearing on the situation. Ted knew enough about Sigma now to know they always got what they wanted, one way or another.

SEVEN

As the rain showed no sign of relenting, the blurred lights of the city on the windshield faded into darkness. Leaving behind the urban hustle, the well-lit motorways were replaced by poorly lit country roads. With each passing mile, the rain showed no sign of relenting, and the darkness of the night seemed to intensify. There was nothing but the car's headlights and the white-striped line of the road to show the way. Natalia never seemed to take her foot off the gas, driving the Range Rover almost into the centre of the road at sixty miles an hour as the road twisted this way and that. The country lanes were full of blind corners, but Natalia refused to slow down, despite the poor conditions.

Ted was not sure exactly where they were, but from the road signs he had caught sight of before they had diverged from the motorway, he assumed they were somewhere in Surrey. There seemed to be no other sign of life in these parts, the eerie stillness of their surroundings broken only by the patter of raindrops on the windshield.

The Atlantis Idol

At last, they arrived at their destination, a historic manor house nestled deep within the countryside. The old stone walls and ivy-covered façade exuded an aura of mystery. It was as if the manor house had been untouched by time, a relic from a bygone era.

The Range Rover's tyres crunched on the gravel driveway, Natalia bringing it to a slow stop as she parked the car. The engine sputtered to silence, and they sat in the darkness, the rain pinging against the roof like a thousand tiny drumbeats.

As they approached the old house, the building seemed to loom imposingly over them. It fit the description Ted had in his mind of what he imagined Julia's childhood home to look like. Given that her family ran in the same circles as Natalia, perhaps that was not far from the truth.

As Natalia unlocked the heavy oak door, Ted noticed a CCTV camera pointing right at him from the corner of the exterior wall. The group stepped inside, and an alarm immediately began beeping. Natalia swiftly moved to a panel on the wall and punched in a code, each entry on the keypad responding with a high-pitched blip. The alarm ceased the moment she entered the last digit. In the middle of the countryside, so far from civilisation, Ted pondered the value of such an alarm system as a deterrent for burglars. Once triggered, any criminal would surely have plenty of time to get what they came for before help arrived.

Stepping inside, Ted was hit by a distinct musty smell that was common with old buildings such as this. It was a grand place, but it felt cold and stale. It certainly didn't give off the vibe that it was lived in.

Natalia flicked a light switch, and the grand foyer was illuminated in a soft yellow hue. An impressive staircase with a red patterned stair runner was the centrepiece of the entryway, with various rooms peeling off in different directions. Natalia led the group into a large sitting room.

"Please," she gestured to the sofas that formed a semicircle facing a fireplace. There was a taxidermy deer head mounted on the wall above the fireplace.

Inside the room, Ted felt like he had been transported to another time. Tall bookshelves groaned under the weight of leather-bound tomes and dusty manuscripts. He knew Sigma had amassed a treasure trove of ancient artefacts over the years, but he was under the impression those had been seized in a raid of Lillian Pembroke's home following her arrest two years ago.

"Sorry for the state of the place," said Natalia. "I don't spend a lot of time here. This house is used mostly as storage."

Fetching logs from a rack to the side of the old fireplace, she carefully stacked them and lit a fire. It wasn't long before the room was toasty and warm.

"Don't worry, the central heating works just fine," she said. "Your rooms will be warm enough."

"Rooms?" Ted asked.

"Yes," Natalia raised an eyebrow. "You didn't think we would all sleep in here, now, did you?"

Ted was confused. He was being kept here against his will. Surely, she would want to keep a close eye on him through the night. He looked at Hiram. The burly man was sitting upright on the other sofa, his posture and general disposition giving Ted the impression that this man never relaxed. Perhaps he would be assigned to watch Ted through the night. The bald man locked eyes with him, and he quickly looked away.

"Don't worry," said Natalia. "You'll have your own room tonight. I wouldn't subject anyone to Hiram's snoring. I suspect you'll hear it through the walls anyhow."

Hiram showed no reaction to Natalia's comment. Not even so much as a grunt or a twitch. He continued to sit there silently, watching.

Feeling growing unease at the man's relentless gaze, Ted distracted himself by looking around the room. The old manor was a place where time seemed to have lost its way. The warmth of the crackling fireplace cast flickering shadows on the walls of the dimly lit sitting room. The rain outside had softened to a gentle drizzle, creating a soothing background murmur.

The air seemed to carry whispers of ages past. Ted noticed more intriguing artefacts, each a silent sentinel of history. An ornate, antique globe stood in one corner; its surface etched with cartographic secrets of long-forgotten voyages. A curiously ornate chest, its wood darkened with age, peeked out from a dust sheet. Ted couldn't help but wonder what stories it held within.

"Your family's collection," Ted started. "I thought it was all seized by police after Mexico."

The question seemed to sit uncomfortably with Natalia. She grimaced as the pain of what her family had lost bubbled back up to the surface.

"Yes," she replied. "We lost many precious items. My mother's home was picked clean. But we are not so foolish as to put all our eggs in one basket. That was but a drop in the ocean of our collection."

Ted recalled the number of artefacts that were cited in the press. If that was only scratching the surface, he struggled to comprehend just how large this collection was. Sigma had certainly been busy over the years. It was a wonder they had kept themselves hidden for this long. Each acquisition came with risks. He wondered if he and Quinn were the first to put a spanner in the works of their operations. He hoped they were. He dreaded to think what happened to any others that came before them.

"You said you use this place for storage. I guess most of your collection is here," Ted assumed aloud. Natalia eyed him with suspicion, and he instantly regretted asking the question.

"What I meant to ask…" Ted backpedalled. "You don't live here?"

"God no," Natalia answered. "Who in their right mind would want to live in a place like this? An old house such as this, in the middle of nowhere. It's the perfect place to lose your mind altogether."

"They say this place is haunted," Stefan piped up. "That is why you got it so cheap, correct?"

"Old ghost stories don't scare me," she said dismissively.

"What was the story?" Stefan asked, intrigued.

"It was nonsensical," Natalia said with a sigh that showed her disinterest in the subject. "An old lady of the manor who died and never left."

"Hmm," Stefan mused. He pulled out his phone. "I wonder if I can find the full story somewhere. What's the name of this place?"

Natalia ignored him.

A chill ran down Ted's spine. He didn't share Stefan's intrigue for ghost stories, and the very mention of such a story in this house put him on edge. He was not sure if he believed in all that stuff, but the old manor was creepy enough without the suggestion of some unexplained entity haunting it. And to bring it up right before they went to sleep? He knew the thought would eat away at him right through the night.

"You believe in any of that, Hiram?" Stefan asked.

The Atlantis Idol

Hiram took his eyes off Ted and turned his steely gaze at Stefan. Ted could see the subtle change in Stefan's expression as the discomfort of the man's stare was transferred to him.

"I don't poke around in the dead's business," he said gruffly, his thick East London accent coming through.

Stefan's eyes widened. After a moment the hint of a smile began to grow from the corners of his mouth.

"So, you do believe," Stefan said, seemingly satisfied. He sat back in his seat and went back to his phone.

"Well, I think that does it for me," Natalia said at last. "Ted, let me show you to your room."

She got up and gestured for Ted to join her. As Ted stood up, Hiram did too.

Ted followed Natalia out of the room and up the impressive staircase that loomed over the entryway. The old manor was like a maze, with dimly lit hallways that creaked underfoot. Finally, Natalia led him into a room with heavy velvet curtains and a four-poster bed covered in faded burgundy sheets. The room was cold, and the chill seeped through the old stone walls.

"Let me remind you, Mr Mendez, that you are here for a reason. I need you to cooperate. The house will be locked down tonight. Any escape attempt will be futile: there is nowhere for you to go for miles in any direction. Hiram is a trained hunter. He will find you."

Ted looked at Hiram over Natalia's shoulder. The man was looking intently at him once more.

"The harder you make this for us, the harder we will make it for you and your friend. Do I make myself clear?" Natalia asked.

"Yes," Ted replied.

She nodded, satisfied. She then held out her hand expectantly. Ted looked at it for a short time, not understanding what she was waiting for. She cleared her throat.

"Your phone, Mr Mendez."

Of course. He should have known better than to expect to keep hold of it through the night. They had kept a close enough eye on him thus far to guarantee he would not have called for help.

He handed it over reluctantly.

"Good night," she said, gripping it tightly, before leaving the way she had come. Hiram followed her back down the stairs.

Ted shut the door and breathed out a long breath he didn't realise he had been holding. He slumped onto the lumpy mattress and stared at the ceiling, trying not to linger on the thought of an old ghost haunting the house while he slept. His body was tired, but his mind was running a million miles an hour. He thought again of the artefacts he had seen earlier. Relics from history, each with their own story to tell. It was both fascinating and eerie, a reminder of the power Sigma held; power they once again held over him.

As he lay in the darkness, Ted couldn't help but replay the evening's events over and over. His chance encounter with Julia had spiralled into a nightmare he couldn't wake up from. The events of the past few hours had shattered his sense of reality. He was a journalist, not a spy or a thief. Quinn was incredibly intelligent, yes. But a key piece in a game to uncover an ancient city? Neither of them had signed up for anything like this. Yet, they were both trapped in the heart of Sigma's operation now.

Images of the ledger, the supposed link to Atlantis. Were Natalia and Stefan really onto something here, or were they grasping at straws in a desperate attempt to carry on Lillian's work while she was in prison? Natalia seemed eager to prove her value and authority in Sigma.

Ted knew he had to be cautious, to watch and listen. Every move he made was being scrutinized. But the exhaustion of the day's events weighed him down, and he couldn't help but drift off to sleep.

In the dead of night, Ted found himself waking up in a panic. He thought he heard a noise—a distant scratching sound, and the creaking of floorboards. Perhaps it was just his imagination: Stefan's fascination with the rumoured ghost story playing on his mind. Or perhaps it was the unfamiliar surroundings and the weight of the situation sitting heavily on him. Either way, he woke to the uncomfortable feeling of a full bladder. This couldn't wait until morning.

The manor was eerily silent. He felt his way around the room to the door, opening it slowly with a creak. He navigated the darkened hallways tentatively, searching for the bathroom.

Lucky for him, he didn't have to search long, with a bathroom just down the hall. After relieving himself, he made his way back towards his room. He got as far as the stairs before hearing something strange. He heard a voice, soft but distinct, echoing from an adjacent room. Intrigued and perhaps a little anxious, he followed the voice to its source and saw a faint light coming from a partially open door.

As he peered inside, Ted was surprised to find Stefan seated at an antique writing desk. The room was dimly lit, with the glow of a single lamp illuminating a book spread open before him. He couldn't make out what the man was reading, but he seemed to be reading aloud. Stefan's voice was a hushed murmur, his words indecipherable. His eyes, however, were wide and intense, fixed on the pages before him. He seemed to be speaking to the book, as if in conversation with it.

Caught between curiosity and the desire not to intrude, Ted hesitated. He watched for a moment, mystified by what he was seeing.

As if a sudden awareness had washed over him, Stefan's voice trailed off, and he closed the book quickly. He glanced around, and his eyes met Ted's, widening in surprise.

"Ted," he said, a note of unease in his voice. "What are you doing up?"

Ted stammered, unsure of what he had stumbled upon. "I... I was just coming back from the toilet. What are you doing?"

Stefan hesitated, his gaze shifting between Ted and the closed book. "Just a bit of research. I talk to myself sometimes when I'm working." He eyed Ted carefully. "It's hard to sleep in this house."

"Yeah," Ted agreed. "It's got a really creepy vibe."

Stefan chuckled. "Well, I looked up the ghost. Turns out it was a different house." He stashed the book away into a bag.

Perhaps it was the way he was looking at Ted or the tone of his voice, but he wondered if he had lied to put Ted's mind at ease about the haunting.

"Sorry to disturb you," Ted said. "See you in the morning."

As he returned to his room, Ted was left with a sense of intrigue and a flurry of questions. He could see Stefan had been caught off guard and looked uncomfortable with the situation.

The night seemed to stretch on endlessly as Ted lay in bed, unable to shake the mysterious encounter. What was Stefan researching, and why the secrecy?

EIGHT

The morning sun spilt its golden warmth through the dust-covered windows of the old manor. It had been a restless night for Ted, filled with uncertainties and the haunting ambience of the place. After finally succumbing to tiredness, he forgot all about the eerie tales of ghosts. Upon waking, he had even momentarily forgotten the predicament he was in. It was only when he realised he was still fully clothed, and his eyes adjusted to the strange surroundings of the unfamiliar bedroom, that reality came crashing down on him. This *really* was happening. It hadn't just been a bad dream.

Natalia's house was no ordinary mansion in the countryside. It was more like a treasure trove of ancient relics and secrets. Leaving his room, he spotted a bust of a bearded man carved from stone in the hallway. He hadn't noticed it in the dark of the night. There was no label or plaque to indicate what he was looking at. This was a collection after all, not a museum. Ted concluded nothing from it, other than it was probably very old and expensive.

He could hear the chatter of voices downstairs. Nobody had come to collect him yet, so he figured he had time to do a little more exploring.

As he wandered down the dimly lit hallways, more artefacts revealed themselves to him. He couldn't help but marvel at the sheer volume he had missed when wandering the same hallways during the night. Each item had its own story to tell, but with no context to each one, he could only guess at their origin and significance. The manor itself was like a time capsule, preserving history in its very walls.

Along one wall was a collection of African tribal masks, their bold, striking designs reflecting the rich diversity of African culture and spirituality. Next to this was an imposing suit of armour. Ted was no expert, but he assumed it to be a samurai piece from feudal Japan. Adorned on a headless mannequin that stood a few inches taller than Ted, it loomed intimidatingly over him. The item was in pristine condition and a testament to the craftsmanship of those who constructed it.

Next to this was a small cabinet, within which sat a meticulously detailed model of a Viking longship. The intricate carvings beautifully showcased the seafaring prowess of the Norse people during this period.

Ted moved on to the next item, a handcrafted dream catcher. He recalled seeing these in a museum once before but couldn't remember the origin of them.

"From the Ojibwa culture," a voice came suddenly from behind him, as if on cue. Startled, Ted flinched and spun around to see Natalia. "Native Americans believed that at night the air was filled with dreams, both good and bad. These were said to protect them, particularly infants, from bad dreams." She looked carefully at Ted. "How did you sleep?"

Ted hesitated a moment before replying. "I've had better nights."

Natalia's eyes narrowed. "Well, I think the sleeping conditions provided by your host are more than ample, considering."

"Considering what?" he questioned.

"Considering the pain you have caused my family. My mother sleeps in a dirty prison cell, while you sleep in clean sheets in her own house. I would say I have been more than gracious as a host."

Ted stared at her incredulous. He was being kept here against his will yet was being made to feel like he was being done a favour, as though she had been going out of her way for his comfort. She was delirious.

"Now," she said, impatience creeping through in her voice. "Care to join us downstairs?" The question was rhetorical. Ted knew he had no choice in the matter.

He followed her around the corner and down the stairs. The sound of chatter from the sitting room grew louder. He heard Stefan talking enthusiastically, but the other voice was one Ted didn't recognise. He walked into the room to see a petite woman conversing with Stefan. She turned to him as they entered the room, adjusting her big round glasses on her face as she appraised Ted.

"Ah, you must be Ted," she said heartily. "Welcome aboard."

"This is Magda," Stefan chimed in. "We work together. She'll be joining us on the expedition."

"Er, hi," Ted replied. Although they hadn't explicitly mentioned it before, he had assumed there would be some travelling to come as they followed signs to Botafoc and Yanes. But the mention of an expedition had thrown Ted momentarily.

Another thought stuck in his mind. Stefan said he and Magda worked together, but he had no context as to what work that was. Were they both permanent employees of Sigma? Was this what they did for a living? He remembered something Stefan had said the night before: this was his life's work. He had been talking about this particular discovery. He had said that he had worked with Sigma on artefact discoveries before, but the way he had said it suggested they were not permanent partners of Sigma, but contractors who had been brought in for this project alone.

"So, you're an expert in Minoan history, too?" Ted asked.

Magda's eyes lit up. "Yes. Stefan and I have studied their culture for years."

Ted looked at Natalia. "Seems like you have all the knowledge you could ever need to find Atlantis. Tell me again why you need Quinn and I." Something felt off about this.

Natalia looked around the room at the expectant faces staring back at her. She then grabbed Ted by the arm and pulled him out of the room. "Excuse us," she said politely as they exited into the hallway.

"Listen to me," she hissed, her voice barely above a whisper. Her grip was still firm on his forearm. "I'm going to level with you. Magda and Stefan are the experts in this field. They know more about the history than anyone. But I have to have contingencies. Insurance, if you will. For whatever reason, you and your friend have a knack for treasure hunting." She tensed her grip on his arm as she saw him roll his eyes. "Whether you like it or not, you do. My mother hired an expert for the Mexico expedition, and that buffoon of a professor turned out to be less useful than two students in locating what we wanted." Her eyes widened. "I think there is more to this job than history. I don't want to insult our colleagues in the other room, but if I'm being honest with

The Atlantis Idol

you, I don't think they will be enough to get us across the line. It's a puzzle, Ted. I need you and Quinn to help me solve it." She looked down as if suddenly realising how tightly she was squeezing his arm. She relaxed her grip before letting go altogether.

Ted looked at her questioningly. "Why us?"

"You have a proven track record, Ted, albeit from a small sample size. You are treasure hunters. Plus, do you think I would pass up the opportunity to acquire your services for free?"

Ted scoffed. What a disgusting way to put it. Natalia was either more delirious than he realised, or she was desperate. Both scenarios were dangerous.

"Ted, this is something huge. If Stefan is right, we could be on the verge of discovering Atlantis. At the very least we can track down two renegade sailors from hundreds of years ago and locate a fortune that went missing from history. It's exciting. And rewarding."

"I'm not interested," Ted insisted.

"Ted, I don't want to play hardball with you," she said. "Just play along. At the end of it all, we go our separate ways and you and your friend will be rich enough to never have to pay rent again."

Once again, Ted knew he didn't have any choice in the matter. This conversation was pointless.

"Your friend will be here this afternoon," Natalia said finally. She left suddenly and re-joined the others in the sitting room. Ted could hear her resume conversation with them.

Before he followed, Ted noticed Hiram standing in the doorframe. The silent bodyguard. He had been watching them, listening to their conversation. The man didn't take his eyes off Ted, waiting expectantly for him to follow Natalia into the sitting room. He felt the man's stare burrowing deep into the back of his head as he passed him and found his way to a vacant armchair.

**

Anticipation hung in the air as the old manor awaited Quinn's arrival. A black Mercedes-Benz with tinted windows sped through the countryside, approaching the old building's secluded location. Quinn was sat in the back seat admiring the view of the rolling hills, a thick layer of mist cloaking it with an air of mystery. The landscape looked both tranquil and haunting as if time itself had woven a tapestry of history into every blade of grass and gnarled tree.

The driver, who had been quiet the whole journey from the airport, occasionally threw steely glances at her in the rear-view mirror, as though checking she was still there. Quinn avoided eye contact for the most part.

Shortly after finishing her drink with Paige, she received an anonymous phone call. The number had been withheld, which ordinarily would result in no answer from Quinn. But after the upsetting call with Natalia, she knew it would be related to that. Sure enough, a young woman of about her age met her at the ski resort later in the day and drove her swiftly to the airport. There, she had been ushered onto a private jet and flown directly to London. The driver of the Mercedes-Benz had met her on the runway of Heathrow Airport and said but a few words to her. Now, here she was, hurtling through the narrow roads of the English countryside with nothing more than a go bag and the clothes on her back. She had been replaying the conversation with Natalia over and over in her head: the look on Ted's face as he sat bound to a chair, the smug look on Natalia's. Quinn was full of rage and fear in equal measure. As she wrestled with her thoughts, one thing was crystal clear to her; no matter what, she had to play along. She and Ted had crossed paths with this organisation before, and they always found a way to get what they wanted. She felt her shoulder, her fingers running over the scar that had been left from the bullet of one of Sigma's henchmen. They were already in over their heads. Whatever Sigma needed her for, she would have to swallow her pride and comply.

The car finally arrived at the imposing gates of the old manor; the wrought iron structure rusted with age. The wheels crunched on the gravel of the long path, before settling to a stop. The engine stopped and the driver stepped out, walking solemnly around to the side Quinn was sitting on and opening the door for her. The crisp air filled her lungs as she stepped out onto the gravel leading to the front entrance. The eery silence of being this far from civilisation was jarring, especially after such a long journey that had been filled with the background hum of the engines carrying her to her destination. The manor loomed before her, an ancient sentinel of history and secrets.

A crow cawed and swooped down from a tree, breaking the silence. It began pecking at something hidden in the gravel pathway.

"Ms Miyata," the voice of the woman she had spoken with on Ted's phone came from the front door.

Quinn turned to see Natalia approaching. The woman had the same smug grin on her face as she feigned delight at her arrival. The woman extended a hand to her. "I trust the journey was smooth." It felt like an expectation, not a question.

"Yes," Quinn eyed her sternly, shaking her hand.

The two locked eyes a moment, as though each were waiting for the other to blink first.

"So," Natalia said, turning towards the front door. "Please do come in. And excuse the state of the place. My family have used this as storage for some of our collection."

This woman was something else. Less than a minute in and she was lauding her wealth over her.

Quinn nodded, feigning interest. "I'm excited to see some of it."

Natalia reminded Quinn of one of Ted's friends, Julia. Or rather how she imagined Julia to be. Quinn had never met her but had pieced together a character profile from snippets and passing remarks from Carl. Ted hadn't spoken about her much, and as far as she knew the two had lost touch.

The sound of an engine turning over came suddenly, and Quinn turned to see the black Mercedes-Benz slowly reverse back the way it had come, the tyres crunching on the gravel path. Looking back at the old manor, she followed Natalia inside.

It was there she saw him. Standing in the foyer with a relieved smile on his face was Ted. His hands were no longer bound, and he appeared unharmed. Her heart skipped a beat as they locked eyes for a moment. It had been so long since she had seen him in the flesh. Without another thought, she raced forward and embraced him tightly. Their reunion was a moment of warmth and tenderness, overshadowed only by the complexities of the situation that had brought them together.

"Are you okay?" she asked. "What happened?"

"I'd like to say it's a long story, but it's actually pretty short," Ted replied, a hint of humour in his voice. "Sigma isn't done with us. They ambushed me at the exhibition, and that's when they called you."

"What do they want with us?" Quinn asked. The front door slammed shut, making her jump. She turned to see

Hiram leering at the pair. Where had he come from? She hadn't noticed him before.

"Please, this way," Natalia called from the sitting room. The stocky bald man remained in the way of the front door, his imposing presence enough to deter any fleeting thoughts of escape. Quinn and Ted entered the sitting room, where Quinn was immediately greeted by Magda and Stefan.

"Lovely to meet you, Ms Miyata. I'm Magda," Magda said enthusiastically. Before Quinn could react, the woman had pulled her into a hug.

"Hi," was all she managed.

When Magda freed her from the unexpected embrace, Stefan approached with a more formal handshake. "Stefan," he said.

"Quinn," she replied.

"Excellent," Natalia said. "We're all finally together. I'm sure you must be tired from your travels, Ms Miyata, but we have lots to discuss."

Both Quinn and Ted could sense an urgency in her voice. Or was it impatience?

"This is the reason you are here," Natalia continued, leading them to the ledger that sat in the middle of a coffee table in the centre of the room.

Quinn eyed the aged book carefully. It was open on a page that contained sketches of various kinds. She peered closer, examining the shapes. The bull with its head lowered, showing off its impressive horns. The bearded man wielding a trident.

"These are Ancient Greek," Quinn said. "Or Minoan."

"Yes!" Magda couldn't mask her excitement at Quinn's recognition of the symbols.

"I was right," Natalia smiled. "She knows her stuff."

Quinn's hand hovered over the corner of the page. "May I?" she asked, looking up at the others. Stefan and Magda nodded in unison. She carefully lifted the page and turned it over. It was there she realised instantly why she had heard the word 'Atlantis' on the phone the previous day. She recognised the concentric circles, and the fact they had been drawn alongside Poseidon was telling. The Temple of Poseidon was widely believed to be a focal point of the ancient city. The Greek god was thought to be an idol of great significance to the Atlanteans. The temple in the heart of the city was a tribute to this idol.

"What is this book?" she asked.

"It's a ledger, written by the Pope's emissary in the 14th century," said Magda. "It details the belongings of the late Bishop Thibaud de Castillon, which was claimed by the Pope in the name of the Church."

"Spolia," Quinn breathed.

"That's right," the historian's eyes widened in delight behind her large round spectacles.

"I told you. She has remarkable knowledge for someone so young," Natalia remarked.

Quinn winced at the patronisation in the comment. She tried to shake it off. A thought then hit her and she looked up from the ledger.

"14th century. Is that the period when the Papacy resided in France?"

"Spot on," replied Stefan encouragingly.

"I feel like there is a lot to this I'm missing," she said.

"Let us start from the beginning," Stefan offered. "Bishop Thibaud de Castillon lived in Lisbon, Portugal, where he had amassed a substantial fortune during his life. The means by which he did so have been scrutinised by some historians. Although it is cited as 'commercial activities', it is widely assumed his wealth was created, shall we say, not in keeping with the moral values of the Church."

"Shocker," Ted scoffed.

Natalia threw a disapproving glance at him as Stefan continued.

"When he died in 1357, Pope Innocent VI laid claim to the man's fortune in the name of the Church and sent an emissary to Lisbon to recover the treasure and bring it back to Avignon. This ledger was used to detail each item in the bishop's collection."

"This is where it gets interesting," Magda chimed in. "On the way back to Avignon, the emissary's ship was attacked by two other ships; one of the Castilian navy, and one of the Genoan, commanded by Martin Yanes and Antonio Botafoc. They had been loitering in the Mediterranean, somewhere off the coast of Cartagena, while the War of the Two Peters stretched on."

"Botafoc's name loosely translates to Fire Blast, or Fire Fart," Stefan added.

Ted let out a snort as an unexpected bout of laughter erupted from within him. "Are you serious? Fire fart?" He looked around at the others for a reaction. Magda gave him a cheeky wink.

Magda picked up the story again. "They divided up the spoils between them and went their separate ways. Yanes was never seen again, but Botafoc was eventually captured and imprisoned." She paused. "Have you heard about the Vatican archives that were released not so long ago?"

Quinn nodded. "It rings a bell."

"Good. We are in possession of some of the documents that were made available. I should add that there are no copies of this. Well, outside of the ones I have made." She flashed an innocent smile in the direction of Natalia, who looked less than impressed. Quinn sensed a lack of trust in this dynamic. If Natalia was the powerhouse behind this operation, Magda was smart to protect herself like this. Knowledge was power, and keeping a personal archive gave her a little bit more power, just in case.

"The document talks of a visit from Pope Innocent VI to an unnamed prisoner in Maguio, France. The very place where Botafoc was captured and imprisoned. It talks of a deal that was struck between the two. It is our understanding that Pope Innocent VI granted Botafoc's freedom in exchange for Yanes' location. He sent the man after him to recover the other half of the bishop's treasure."

"Did it say where he went?" asked Quinn, who was now sucked into the story.

"No."

Alarm bells rang in Ted's head. "That's not right. You told me the documents did say where he went."

"Yes, and they do," Stefan said defensively. "But not so black and white." He gestured to Magda, who retrieved a binder from under the coffee table. Inside were old worn sheets of parchment individually protected in plastic sleeves.

"Here is the account," she said, sliding the binder in front of Quinn. The old text looked to be written in Italian.

"I don't speak Italian," she said plainly.

"Then take our word for that part," said Magda. "Look here." She placed her finger on top of the plastic sleeve towards the bottom of the page. Quinn leaned forward to inspect the text more closely.

"Is that Latin?"

"Yes," Magda confirmed. "That's the part that we've been trying to figure out. It is unclear who the documents from the Vatican archives were written by. Some of these documents were written second-hand much later than the event. We have examples that bear the seal of the Pope, and even some signed by name, so we can date those somewhat. But not this one, unfortunately."

Quinn read the text slowly. She was no expert in Latin, but she had dabbled here and there. She read it again, aloud this time.

Insula, ultra columnas Herculis, prope domum ancestralem thesauri.

"What does it mean?" asked Ted.

"An island, after Hercules' column," said Magda. "Then something about treasure and the ancestral home."

Quinn looked at Magda and Stefan. "Are they referring to the Pillars of Hercules?"

"Exactly," Stefan nodded.

"What's that?" Ted asked.

"The mouth of the Mediterranean, where it meets the Atlantic," said Quinn. "In the Strait of Gibraltar. There are landmarks there known as the Pillars of Hercules."

"So, an island after this? In which direction?"

"Beyond the pillars, towards the treasure's ancestral home," said Magda. "We think they mean where the treasure came from: Lisbon."

Stefan pulled out a tablet and opened up the maps app. He pinched his finger and thumb on the screen to zoom in on one part, revealing the coastline of Portugal. "So, the home of the treasure is here," he pointed to the landmass consuming the right-hand side of the screen. "Which means we're looking for an island close to here." He scanned the area, shifting the view to zoom in and out. With each pass of the coastline, he found himself searching further and further into the Atlantic Ocean.

"See, this is where we're stuck," he admitted. "There is nothing that resembles the island the text is referring to. Beyond the Pillars of Hercules and near Lisbon. There's just nothing there. You'd have to go as far as the Azores or Madeira to find an island."

The group were quiet while they stewed on the issue Stefan had presented.

Quinn read the Latin text again. They were definitely missing something.

"Why are you heading east from the pillars?" Ted asked curiously. "Why does beyond the Pillars of Hercules have to lead out into the Atlantic?"

"Because that is the way to the Portuguese coast, towards the ancestral home," replied Stefan matter of fact.

"Well, maybe that isn't the ancestral home," Ted suggested.

Stefan pursed his lip, pondering the thought.

"Do you mind?" Quinn asked, reaching her hand out towards the tablet. Stefan nodded, taking his hands away and giving her a respectful amount of space to use the device. Quinn set about pinching and swiping on the screen, adjusting the view until it was hovering above the Strait of Gibraltar.

"Ted's right, we're making a huge assumption here. What if beyond the Pillars of Hercules is not in an easterly direction, but west?"

"Towards the Mediterranean?" Magda asked.

"Yes." Quinn traced a path along the coastline of the southern end of Spain, across France and towards Italy. As her finger ran along the eastern coast of Italy, she stopped partway down. "The Vatican," she said. "That's the ancestral home."

Stefan raised an eyebrow sceptically.

"You said it yourself. It's unclear who wrote some of these texts, and when. What if this account was written here by a member of the Church long after the papacy had returned to Rome?"

"So, we're looking in the wrong place?" Natalia interjected.

"It's possible, but again it's just another assumption based on a different interpretation of the text."

"So, this island that Yanes would have been heading for, where Botafoc followed. You think it's off the coast of Italy? Somewhere like Sardinia or Corsica?" said Natalia.

"Those islands are pretty big," Ted chipped in.

"I have no idea where we to start," Quinn admitted.

"That's okay. Because I do," Magda had her phone out and was smiling to herself.

Stefan looked over her shoulder. "What am I looking at?"

"This is off the shores of Ponza, Pontine Islands. Do you think this could be our guy?" She was looking at an article detailing the many shipwrecks recorded in the area. Scrolling through the list, she settled on the one that had been described as a galley, estimated to be about five hundred years old.

"Zoom out," Stefan instructed. Magda pinched her finger and thumb together until the small archipelago was barely visible. Instead, what he could see was the shoreline of the outskirts of Rome.

"Looks promising," he smiled. "Well done," he turned his attention to Quinn, and then Ted. "Natalia was right about you two."

NINE

Giovanni Rossi strode through the narrow, cobbled streets of Trastevere. The echoes of his footsteps faded against the centuries-old buildings as the amber glow of streetlights cast long shadows on the worn facades. Born and raised in Rome, the forty-five-year-old private investigator knew these streets better than anyone.

The subject of his current case, an elusive art thief, had led him on a chase through the city's winding alleys. He had lost sight of them some time ago, but Giovanni hadn't given up hope just yet.

Weeks of preparation had led to this moment. Giovanni was no stranger to cases like this: wealthy individuals who had valuables stolen from them. Valuables that, when recovered, may raise questions with the authorities as to how they ended up in their possession in the first place. He was efficient and guaranteed discretion with his services and had a proven track record that had earned him many high-profile cases. It certainly made a change from the cases he had started his career as a PI with, after his early retirement from the police force: insurance investigations, background checks, or stalking cheating partners to gather evidence of the unfaithful party during a divorce.

It had taken longer than usual to track them down, but he had finally done it.

This thief, however, was no fool. They had sensed they were being followed and quickly found a way to elude him. For now, at least.

He passed a quaint restaurant with wrought-iron chairs spilling out onto the cobbled street. A particularly noisy party of diners shouted and clinked glasses in celebration, adding a splash of life to the otherwise weathered surroundings of this part of the city. Giovanni smiled politely as he passed by, keeping his pace swift but casual to blend in. His target could be anywhere, and he knew better than to rush things. Let them reveal themselves to him.

As he rounded a corner, he found himself with a decision to make. The tight alleyway forked into two paths. He took stock of his options, his hand moving to his face as he rested his thumb on his chin while rubbing the left side of his nose with his index finger. After a moment's thought, he pressed on to the right. The Wooden shutters of a window crashed closed above him. He looked up to see a balcony, adorned with potted plants that leaned precariously outward.

A couple stumbled into view, approaching from the far side of the alleyway. One let out an excited giggle as her companion pinched her backside. The two stopped to share a passionate kiss as Giovanni squeezed past. He pulled out his phone and checked the time. It was getting late, and he was missing his window of opportunity. Perhaps he needed to try again another night. That would involve more planning. If the target got spooked and switched up their routine it would set him back. Detail, intuition, patience. These were the reasons he was as good as he was at his job. He was not going to wait for another stolen painting before he made his move.

Passing by a bakery that had closed much earlier in the day, loud noise from a television streamed out of an open window on the floor above. Giovanni rounded the corner of the alleyway, stepping out into Piazza di Santa Maria.

He stopped suddenly. There they were. The elusive thief who had given him the slip just minutes ago was making their way across the square. Their pace was hurried. Whether it was Giovanni's doing or not, something had them spooked.

The square was busy enough; Giovanni would not need to worry about pursuing from a distance. He would blend in without trying. He headed after his target, closing the distance as much as he could without breaking into a jog.

He passed the fountain that posed as the centrepiece of the square, keeping his eyes firmly on the figure. They were wearing a coat with a hood up to conceal their appearance. It would not help them now; Giovanni had identified them and would not let them out of his sight again.

They were headed north, towards the river. He could sense they were getting close to their destination. Giovanni couldn't shake the sense of satisfaction that came with unravelling a mystery. It had been one of the things he had loved most about being on the force.

As the years went by, the bureaucracy of the role seemed to weigh down on him more and more. What was once an exciting investigative position had turned more into pushing papers and waiting for permission to do his job. Now, he was his own boss, and he could do things on his terms. As far as he was concerned, he was not straying too far from the direction his moral compass pointed in, despite operating in a greyer area than the law allowed. He knew life to be much more complex than the black-and-white moral code the law abided by.

The hooded figure turned into Piazza de' Renzi and then into another side street. Giovanni tailed them from a safe distance. He felt in control of the situation once more as he watched from the shadows while they stopped in front of an apartment complex. He waited patiently while they pulled a set of keys from their pocket, the metal jingling as they searched for the right one, before using it to unlock the front door. They disappeared inside, and the front door banged shut behind them.

All the while, Giovanni waited. He had got what he came for. Now he knew their base of operations, temporary or otherwise, he could figure out the rest. But he would have to do it quickly before they moved on to a new place and took the focus of his investigation with them. Now began the most tedious part of his case: the stakeout.

There was nowhere inconspicuous to wait while he watched for the thief to leave their apartment. But it made no difference to Giovanni. Before leaving the scene, he had placed a remote camera on the underside of the alcove above the doorway of the building. It monitored activity in and out of the building like a remote webcam doorbell. While he waited at home, his phone buzzed each time the camera picked up activity going in and out of the building. A short recording of the person captured in the footage taken by the camera was sent to an app on his phone. It was a small complex with few inhabitants, and as a result, there were few comings and goings.

While he waited for his target to leave their apartment, he had wasted no time in performing the crucial research that would lead them right to their door. Exercising his sleuthing skills, he had tapped into the rental history of each apartment within the complex. It didn't take long to determine the apartment that belonged to the thief he had been investigating. All that was needed now was the signal that the place was empty, so he could enter the apartment unseen.

It was a little after eight in the morning when his phone lit up on the arm of his sofa, the soft hum of the vibrate function alerting him to movement. He opened the app and watched the short recording. His thumb rested against his wiry beard as he rubbed the side of his nose with his finger. The figure entered the frame, and he got a glimpse of their face. It was them.

His window of opportunity had opened, and he would need to make the most of it before it slammed back shut. He was up and out the door before the recording had finished playing.

It was just a short fifteen-minute walk from Giovanni's place to the apartment complex. That had been a key factor in his decision to go home and wait it out from there. Arriving at the scene, he had one last check of his phone for fresh notifications of movement from the building's front door. Nothing. He walked up to the entrance and looked up into the alcove at his discretely placed camera. Before he retrieved it, a thought struck him. He decided to leave the camera where it was. His next challenge was the front door. With no key, he would have to get creative. It would not be the first time he had blagged his way in as a postal worker, or as a visitor of a friend who had a busted intercom, who had advised them to ring a different door buzzer to let them in.

Just as he was deciding which angle he would explore this time, the door lock clicked and the door opened. An elderly man slowly walked out, using a walking stick to steady themselves. Giovanni stood to one side, making way for them

The Atlantis Idol

to pass. The old man nodded in appreciation and continued slowly on. Giovanni caught the door just as it swung back, preventing it from closing. He nonchalantly stepped inside into the lobby. He took stock of his surroundings, taking note of the doors of the ground-floor apartments to each side, and the stairs straight ahead. To his immediate left was a series of numbered pigeonholes. Some had letters sticking out of them. He found the number of the apartment he was looking for: nine. The space was empty.

Turning his attention to the stairwell, he recalled the layout of the building from schematics he had found online. He needed to head up two floors to reach apartment nine. As he reached the bottom of the stairs, he noticed the old lift tucked away on the ground floor. The iron shutters gave it a vintage look and immediately validated his assumption that the stairs would be the quickest route.

He took them quickly, rounding the staircase to the next floor and following it again to the floor after. Each floor had four apartments, neatly ordered with two at the front of the building and two at the rear. Based on the layout of the ground and first floor, apartment nine would be the first on his left as he reached the top of the stairs.

Sure enough, there it was. Unlike the apartment opposite, which had a tattered welcome mat lying in front of the door, apartment nine was devoid of any character. The number itself was crooked, epitomising the distinct lack of homeliness of the place. A quick background check of the current tenants, who had been renting the place for just four months, revealed that they were subletting the place on short-term leases.

There was nobody around, so Giovanni took advantage of the quiet, pulling his lock-picking set from his back pocket and quickly getting to work. He inserted the thin paper clip-type pins into the low-quality lock that separated him from his goal. It was child's play. An old apartment complex such as this was easy pickings—quite literally. The springs glided into place as he worked his magic, and before long the satisfying click of the door unlocking sounded. He turned the handle and the door creaked open.

The space that greeted him spoke volumes of the transient nature of the thief's occupancy here. The living area was adorned with an assortment of mismatched furniture, and the artwork on the walls would have been right at home in an inexpensive hotel room. The absence of personality bore the hallmark of a living space that was not well-liven. The small kitchen area and bathroom were nothing to write home about, and as he walked into the centre of the living room, Giovanni noticed just one doorway leading off to a bedroom. He wondered how much the tenant was charging for occupants to stay here. In a location this central, it would likely still be a premium rate. Location was everything, after all.

It didn't take long for Giovanni to find the items his target had developed quite the reputation for. Framed paintings that had been covered in dust sheets were arranged in a haphazard manner throughout the apartment. Giovanni lifted the corner of the nearest sheet, revealing a painting that looked vaguely familiar. In fact, he recognised it as a painting that was housed in the Galleria Spada. He was not aware that this painting had been stolen. He moved to the next dust sheet, the shape being of a similar size to the first. He lifted it off just enough to see the artwork beneath.

He did a double-take. It was the same painting as the previous one. Then the thought hit him. His experience with this type of scam came to the fore as he recalled a case when he was still on the force. The paintings were a remarkable replication of the original, and the heavy ornate frames were a nice touch. But this was a forgery. The original was, for now at least, likely still safe and sound in the gallery. Art thieves would have convincing fakes made of a specific painting, and when the time was right, they would steal the original. The intention was never to keep the original away from its rightful place for too long. They needed just long enough for their black-market trades to be wrapped up, and for their fakes to be in the hands of wealthy, yet naive, buyers, who believed to be in possession of the stolen original. By the time the original was restored to its rightful place and the buyers realised what had happened, the con artists would be long gone. It didn't fool the most critical eye, as the forgeries could be easily detected by someone who knew what they were doing. But there were enough who fell for the scam to make it worthwhile.

His phone buzzed in his pocket. His heart rate began to increase as the realisation quickly sunk in. He dropped the dust sheet and reached into his pocket, seeing the notification of new footage from his remote camera. He hastily reviewed the footage and breathed a sigh of relief to see someone he didn't recognise on the video. He had more time.

Placing his phone back in his pocket, Giovanni made his way around the room to search for the painting that had been stolen from his client. It didn't take long for him to find what he was looking for. The landscape painting was much smaller than he had anticipated, and couldn't have been much larger than A3 size, plus the thick frame surrounding it.

His client was no fool; they knew the difference between a fake and the real thing. They had given Giovanni some key signs to look for when assessing the painting on scene. Giovanni threw the sheet off the frame and studied the work: the intricate brush strokes, the earthy colours the artist had used in what was, in Giovanni's opinion, a drab landscape.

Despite the piece not being to his taste, this was clearly the real deal.

Now came the final phase of the job. He could make the call now to his client to confirm the location of the piece, and they would send a team to recover it with force. He was being paid for surveillance and information, not for retrieval. Besides, he was not expecting to be able to transport the item himself.

He dug into his pocket once more, retrieving his phone. Unlocking it with his Face ID, he began to type in the number his client had given him to call when the job was done. But just as he was about to tap in the final digits, another notification popped up from the remote camera.

He immediately stopped what he was doing and switched his attention to the camera app. The video played and revealed something that made his stomach drop. His target had made their way back into the building. Giovanni knew he needed to move, and fast. He looked at the front door, and then back at the painting. It was much smaller than he had anticipated. There was a risk the thief would empty the place by the time his client came to collect. He could wrap this up here and now.

He grabbed the dust sheet and threw it back over the painting. He then lifted it and made his way to the front door. Leaving the apartment, he let the front door close behind him, the latch locking with a loud click. He could hear the target's footsteps on the stairs. His escape was cut off. Then he saw the open lift. Without a second thought, Giovanni entered with the painting in hand. He pushed the button for ground floor with his elbow and set down the painting, leaning it carefully against the wall as he grabbed the shutter door and pulled it closed with a screech. The lift shuddered to life and started moving, slowly. The footsteps grew louder as the target was already on the first floor. After what felt like a lifetime, the lift finally descended below the second floor. Giovanni tucked into the side of the dark cabin, but as the lift descended past the first floor, the target was nowhere to be seen. The footsteps were still audible, but they were coming from above him now. They had crossed paths at just the right moment to avoid contact.

Tucking the painting under his arm, he pulled open the iron shutters with his free hand the moment the lift came to a stop on the ground floor. He was out like a shot, and before long was outside and on his way to safety.

**

Hours later, Giovanni's evening had settled into the familiar rhythm of solitude, the soft glow of his desk lamp casting shadows around his sparse, book-lined study. His apartment exuded an aura of refined simplicity and lived-in comfort. Nestled in an old, ochre-hued building with weathered facades, his home was a sanctuary from the bustling city outside.

Lost in the quiet contemplation of the documents spread across his desk, the abrupt buzz of his phone distracted him. Face down on the desk, the soft light of the screen crept out from under the device. Upon picking up the phone and flipping it over, Giovanni saw a familiar name: Bianca; an old colleague from his days on the force. He hit the green button and put the phone to his ear.

"Pronto."

"Gio," his old friend's voice came through the receiver. "How are you?" Her voice was a welcome sound in his ears. Giovanni leaned back in his creaky chair as he relaxed into conversation.

"It's been a while," he replied, not answering her question.

"It has," Bianca's voice sounded hesitant, as though there was a topic she didn't know how to broach. Giovanni had clocked it straight away.

"So," he said expectantly.

"I asked you how you are," she said.

"I know. But that's not important. Tell me what's up."

"Gio," Bianca sighed loudly. "Always so straight to the point."

"I'm just messing with you," he smiled to himself, his chair squeaking as he twisted in it a little. "How's Andrea?"

"She's good," she replied, a noticeable change in her voice. "Are you keeping well, Gio?"

"You know, same old."

A long pause filled the dead air before Giovanni spoke again. "So, tell me. What do you need?"

"This one's big," she said. "I'm knee-deep in a tangled mess here. I need your keen eye."

Giovanni's brows furrowed at the mention of a case. Bianca was already a good detective, but what made her better than the others on the force was her lack of ego and ability to ask for help when she needed it. A good detective utilised the tools at their disposal, instead of trying to solve everything themselves. Like Giovanni, Bianca knew the best way to get things done was to make use of the skills of those around them. Whatever this case was, it must have been bigger than anything her department had handled since his retirement. The force hadn't come so earnestly for his expertise since he went solo.

"Did Marco sanction this?"

"He doesn't know I'm contacting you."

The Atlantis Idol

Figured, he thought. Marco would never allow his pride to be dented by enlisting the help of a PI. Besides, he knew the chief had held a grudge against him since the day he left the police.

He had long left that part of his life behind, content with his private detective work. But there was an undeniable spark of interest in Bianca's plea for assistance.

"Tell me about the case," he said.

"Antiquities," she replied. "Which is why I need your expertise."

"Black market trade?"

"Collector, we think. But there's something else about this. It goes deeper than we realised. We're talking about a shadow organisation."

"What's in it for me?" he inquired.

Bianca knew from the question that it didn't matter. He was already in. "Give me a couple of days to figure a few things out. Meet at our usual place, say Thursday at nine? I'll fill you in on the details. Breakfast is on me."

"Okay."

"I'll send you some bedtime reading," she added. "See if you can make sense of it."

The phone disconnected, and Giovanni looked out the window at the sunset casting an orange glow over this historic part of the city.

A moment later, his phone buzzed with an email from Bianca. He opened it to find an attachment. The PDF seemed to be a transcript of an interview with an associate of the shadow organisation Bianca had referred to.

Giovanni scanned the document, looking for anything that immediately stood out to him. He scrolled down the page with his thumb, before landing on a word that stuck out to him. He considered it a moment, as though trying to recall why it rang a bell in his mind. As he scrolled down further, the word was repeated. He had found the focus of this new investigation.

Sigma.

TEN

A sense of anticipation crackled in the air as the boat Natalia had chartered chugged steadily through the Tyrrhenian Sea. The group had left the mainland behind, venturing toward the distant shores of Ponza Island. The boat's gentle sway matched the rhythmic waves that lapped against its hull, creating a melodic cadence that seemed to whisper tales of the approaching land.

With one hand on the rail fixed to the side of the vessel, Quinn watched as the island grew bigger as they drew nearer. Sat next to her, Ted was dealing with a sudden onset of seasickness. He had managed to keep down his breakfast thus far, but the nausea remained as long as the boat continued to bob up and down over the gentle waves.

A thin layer of mist had settled in the area, masking the island. As they grew closer, the mist lifted, revealing a picturesque vista of sheer cliffs carved by the relentless sea over centuries.

"There it is," Magda thought aloud. "It's beautiful."

"Take us into the southern end," Natalia instructed. "You'll see the opening for the harbour."

Stefan, who had been at the helm, responded with a firm nod and proceeded to guide the boat with delicate movements. He had surprised Quinn and Ted with his seafaring skills. As they launched from the small port outside Rome, he had regaled the pair with tales of fishing trips with his buddies. Nothing particularly interesting seemed to happen on those trips, but Stefan had a certain charm in the way he told the stories that held their attention.

The boat skirted the east coast of the island, and the harbour came into view. Beyond that, Quinn could see quaint pastel-coloured houses emerging like vibrant brushstrokes against the backdrop of a rugged hillside. The chime of buoy bells mingled with the gentle hum of the boat's engine, while seagulls swooped and called overhead. As they entered the mouth of the harbour, the activity of the port surrounding it grew busier. The rhythmic chatter of locals and tourists alike, punctuated by laughter and snippets of animated conversation, filled the air as Stefan manoeuvred the boat so it faced parallel to the dock, just a couple of feet away. He then jumped to the wooden walkway of the dock with confidence, tying a thick rope around the vacant piling. The boat gently bobbed closer to the dock until it was nestled in close. He then signalled to the others to follow.

Stepping off the side and onto the wooden walkway, Quinn looked around at the other vessels of similar sizes. Three white boats sat idly side-by-side with the same logo of a tour company adorned on the side of the hull. What Quinn would have given to be there as a tourist for the day, and not in the circumstances she found herself in now.

Ted breathed a huge sigh of relief as he disembarked and found himself on much sturdier ground. Unfortunately, his churning stomach received no respite as the smell of fish overpowered the group from a nearby fishing boat that had recently returned from sea.

"You feeling okay?" Quinn put a hand on his shoulder.

Ted said nothing, putting a hand up to indicate he would be fine, even if he was still struggling.

"This way," Natalia said impatiently. She was waiting with Magda and Hiram further up the walkway. Quinn turned to see Stefan busy tying knots and securing the boat.

"You should hurry," he winked at her. "That woman scares me. I'm almost done, I'll catch up to you."

The pair tentatively followed the rest of the group, the wooden walkway of the docks leading onto the stone-paved street of the port. Ponza welcomed its visitors with open arms, a heady blend of briny sea salt intermingled with the sweet fragrance of blooming bougainvillaea and jasmine. From the docks, the streets meandered, revealing a treasure trove of charming shops, open-air cafés and gelaterias that invited exploration. The radiant sun cast its golden rays upon the harbour, bestowing a glistening sheen upon the azure waters that lapped at the shoreline. A large group of tourists squeezed by in single file, following their tour guide as they came up from the other direction in a narrow street. The guide held up an orange paddle as they walked, talking in Italian and then English as they gave some information to their group.

Quinn marvelled at the beauty of the place, the island rich in history and adorned with natural beauty. Its allure lay not only in its captivating scenery but in the promise of endless discoveries awaiting those willing to wander its labyrinthine alleys. Onwards they walked, led by Natalia, until they reached a café that was tucked away from the busier parts of the area. They found a quiet corner to settle into.

Quinn was taking her first sip of the espresso she had ordered when Stefan entered the café. He smiled as he sat down in the vacant seat next to her.

"I'll never get over how beautiful the Mediterranean is," he announced. "I honestly could live here. Italy, Greece, Malta, take your pick. Put me on any island around them and I'll be happy."

Magda chuckled. "He says this every time he comes back from holiday. Yet you still live in that dingy flat in Ealing, don't you, Stefan?"

Stefan rolled his eyes. "You have to spoil everything, don't you?"

"I'm just saying, you're full of it," she stuck out her tongue playfully. "I know you. You'll be bored after two weeks. Here," she finished, carefully sliding a small cup of espresso across the table. Stefan's eyes lit up as he gratefully accepted the hot drink.

"Grazie."

"Prego," she replied warmly.

Quinn and Ted sat next to each other, sharing a feeling of unease as they sat casually at the table with their captors. To the staff working in the café or the other patrons enjoying their cup of coffee, they seemed like another group of tourists. Little would they know of the predicament the two were in, and the desperation they were feeling. Quinn had half a mind to make a break for the door or call out for help and explain the situation to someone, anyone. But they had been down that road before with Sigma. There was no stopping them.

Magda took out her phone and opened the file she had saved of the article that detailed the shipwrecks in the area. She scrolled down to the one that had been described as a galley, the age of which roughly matched the vessels they had believed Botafoc and Yanes to have been at the helm of. Since

The Atlantis Idol

the discovery back at the old manor, Magda and Stefan had been researching furiously to find any more details on the shipwreck. Unfortunately, their efforts had been fruitless. Aside from the vague description that had been given in the article Magda had found, they had no new information to add any credibility to the wreck's supposed identity. They had found more sources that cited the existence of the shipwreck, however, which added fuel to their excitement. Something was lurking in the depths of the Tyrrhenian, and whatever it was, they were about to discover it.

Natalia had finished her drink and was busy tapping away on her phone. The whoosh sound of an email being sent came from the device and she put it face down on the table.

"The diving gear will be loaded onto the boat for when we get back," she said.

Quinn was sceptical about the way Natalia had casually dropped in the diving gear. Who was dropping it off into the boat? Why was it such a shady transaction? She caught herself mid-thought. This was Sigma; of course they could forge contacts on the island who had access to diving gear. The covert nature of the transaction actually made sense; if the authorities got wind of a planned dive near a known wreck site, they would be on them like moths to a flame. Whatever antiquities that lay beneath the surface of the sea were protected.

"Are you worried about forensic markings?" asked Quinn.

Natalia looked quizzically at her.

"I read something recently about artefacts from protected wreck sites being made traceable."

"That new technology?" Stefan interjected. "No. That hasn't made its way over here yet, luckily for us."

"What technology?" Ted asked curiously.

"It's been used in the UK to deter thieves," said Quinn. "The stuff they cover the wrecks in transfer to diving gloves and pretty much anything that touches it."

"Like anti-vandal paint?" Ted offered.

"Yes, I suppose. A bunch of wreck sites around the British Isles have been protected by it now. The 17th-century Dutch warship, the Klein Hollandia, the German submarine, the UC-70. This area has known wrecks too. What's to say they haven't put something like this in place yet?"

"Trust me, they haven't," insisted Stefan. He locked eyes with Quinn.

Magda let out a dejected sigh. "I'm getting nothing."

"So, what now?" asked Ted. "If we can't figure out where the wreck is…" there was a tinge of hopefulness in his voice as if he had a shred of belief that this might be the end of the line. "I mean, say we get a rough location. How were you planning to find the ship? I've seen documentaries. You'd have to be right above it to see it from a dive."

"We have the technology to locate it, even in deep waters," said Natalia. "But we need a firm location."

"We can't just go sailing around hoping we stumble on it," added Stefan. "Is there nothing online that hints at where it is? Which part of the island at least?" He turned to Magda.

"No, it's so strange. The wreck itself is well documented, but all hints as to its exact location are absent. It's as if someone removed them."

"The government?" suggested Stefan. "It's strange. The tourist board usually encourage excursions."

"Maybe they knew something about this one," said Ted. "Maybe you're not the only one after this ship, and whoever removed all traces of its exact location either wanted to protect it. Or keep it a secret for themselves."

The Atlantis Idol

A moment of silence went by as Ted's words lingered in the thoughts of each other person sitting around the table. He tried to gauge their expressions, as though wondering if they had really believed they were the only ones who had gotten wind of the significance of this particular shipwreck. And if not, did that add credibility to what they believed it would lead to?

The café door opened and three men with thick straggly beards walked in. They immediately began speaking loudly with the barista operating the coffee machine as if they knew each other. Ted flashed a look at the sudden activity, making the quick assumption that they must be regulars. The trio eventually sat down at a nearby table. One propped up a vacant chair opposite their own so they could put one foot up on it as a footstool. A waft of the smell of fish that they had experienced by the docks suddenly hit them. The trio must have brought it with them. Ted then guessed that they must be fishermen taking a break from work.

"So, what now?" Quinn said at last.

"Somebody on this island knows about this shipwreck," Natalia was staring at the new arrivals to the café. "If we probe hard enough, we'll find it."

The weather had turned as the day wore on. More boats were coming into port as the sea became choppy and conditions were worsening. Dark clouds amassed overhead, shrouding the once-blue skies, and the gentle sea breeze intensified into a tempestuous wind. The tranquillity of the scene rapidly dissipated as gusts of wind rattled the café's windows, and the distant waves turned tumultuous. According to the weather forecast Magda picked up on her phone, a thunderstorm was on the way. Stefan decided that whether or not they learned anything new about the wreck's location, it would be too dangerous to go out and look for it until the weather improved. For now, they had set up camp in the heart of Ponza. Natalia had checked the group into a hotel, and they were currently sitting in the large suite waiting for Magda to return from the assignment she had given her.

With her proficiency in Italian, having studied in the country for some time, Magda was the best person to mingle with the locals and try and find a way to get info about the wreck sites off the island. Natalia's theory was that two groups of people would be bound to have some knowledge of the wrecks in the area: those in the local fishing trade, and the tour company that owned the boats they had seen docked in the harbour. Magda was posing as a filmmaker who was researching the area for a documentary for a lucrative streaming service. Her hope was that the promise of TV money and a feature in the documentary itself would be incentive enough for some information to be offered up. It seemed to have hooked in at least one person, as later that day there was a knock at the door to the suite.

Magda entered with a tall pale man, who had a big smile on his face. By the look of him, he was no older than twenty. He also seemed a little taken aback when faced with five new faces when entering the room.

"Everyone, this is Matteo. He works on a fishing boat with his father. He has lived on the island his whole life. I think he would be perfect for our documentary."

"Hi," Natalia said heartily, flashing a big smile and moving swiftly across the room to shake his hand. "I'm the producer, Natalia."

"Nice to meet you," Matteo beamed. "Your colleague tells me you are making a documentary about our beautiful island?" His accent shone through as he spoke. With the capital city the closest part of the mainland, it was common for the Romanesco dialect to be used here. Even when speaking English, Magda could pick up on the nuance with which he spoke. She had a friend from Rome who spoke in the same way.

"Your island is fascinating," said Natalia. "It must have been an interesting upbringing."

"Compared to the big city, of course," Matteo smiled. "My cousins live in Rome, so I would visit them a lot as a child. But my father and I have lived in Ponza since I can remember. It is home. Magda told me you have a special interest in the, er…" he paused and said something briefly in Italian to Magda.

"Maritime history," Magda translated aloud.

Natalia nodded. Matteo was getting straight to the point. Probably eager to learn what his role in the production would be.

"We are historians," she said. "The waters surrounding the island are steeped in rich history. The studio read about a 17th-century galley that was sunk off the coast. I'm sure it must be very well known to you."

"But of course," said Matteo. "The ghost ship."

"Ghost ship?" Ted couldn't help but pipe up from the back of the room.

Matteo chuckled. "Don't look so alarmed. That one," he paused again, looking for the right words. "Not much is known about it. The fishermen like to make up stories. Somehow that one became known as the ghost ship. I do not know why. It is probably not haunted."

"Probably," muttered Ted under his breath. "What a relief."

"Fascinating," said Natalia. "I'd love to learn more about it. Would it be possible to film it for the documentary?"

Matteo looked cautiously at her. Natalia wondered if she had played her hand too early; so eager she was to get things moving and locate the ship. She didn't want to force the poor man into cooperating. But if this didn't pan out the way she had hoped, she might be left with no other option.

Matteo looked at Magda, and then back at Natalia. "I know where you can find it."

Natalia's heart raced. It was working.

"But," Matteo added. "I won't tell you where it is. I will show you. And you must promise not to reveal the location in your documentary. It is protected."

"We understand," Magda put a reassuring hand on his shoulder. "We want to be respectful of the island and its history."

"Quite," affirmed Natalia. "We will only document the shipwreck. There will be no footage above water while we are in the area, to ensure there are no landmarks in the shot that might give anything away."

"Okay," Matteo smiled. "And my payment?" He was direct with his question.

"I will inform the studio. We'll settle that before the storm passes."

ELEVEN

Stefan readied the boat as the sun peeked over the horizon. His practised hands swiftly untied the mooring lines, freeing the vessel from the wooden embrace of the dock. The storm had raged through the night, finally subsiding at dawn. The group had been eager to get out on the boat as soon as they were able and had asked Matteo to meet them at the harbour. The young man had got to work right away when joining them, helping Stefan to ready the boat for launch. Quinn and Ted sat in the boat, sandwiched between Magda and Hiram as they awaited the start of their journey out to sea in search of the shipwreck.

The engine roared to life at the twist of a key, its rumble harmonising with the lapping of waves. With a nod to Matteo, who had jumped back into the boat after some final preparations, he skilfully steered the boat away, easing the throttle for a slow, steady departure. As they left the harbour behind, he guided the vessel confidently toward the open sea.

The morning sun cast a warm, golden hue upon the landscape, the boat chugging away over the azure waters surrounding Ponza. As the boat picked up speed and the waves grew larger, Quinn put a hand on Ted's knee, giving it a gentle squeeze. He grimaced, the relentless bobbing of the boat only serving to increase his discomfort. He appreciated the gesture, which made him feel less alone with the feeling.

Seabirds soared gracefully overhead, their calls echoing across the tranquil expanse as Ponza's coastline receded into the distance. Turning to the bridge, Ted saw Matteo had taken control, with Stefan standing to the side, watching the horizon. Matteo navigated them through the open sea with the familiarity of someone born amidst these tides. The boat cut through the water, leaving a fleeting trail of ripples behind it.

A sense of anticipation filled the air as they sailed further from the safety of the island's embrace. The sea, once calm and welcoming, now carried an air of mystery and adventure. Ponza's rugged cliffs gradually faded from view, a thin layer of mist masking them as the view was replaced by an expansive seascape that stretched infinitely in every direction.

The journey progressed, the boat gently bobbing atop the undulating waves. The salt-laden breeze tousled Quinn's hair.

"How can he know where we're going?" asked Ted. "It's just water and mist everywhere."

"There." Matteo's voice came perfectly on cue to answer the question. A cluster of jagged rocks emerged from where he was pointing, jutting out from the water like ancient sentinels. Matteo guided the boat closer and steered them around to the right of the rocks, using the structure almost as a road sign to change course. They headed in the new direction a minute longer before Matteo eased off the throttle and the chugging of the boat quietened. He returned control to Stefan and made his way to the rest of the group.

"We are here," he announced.

The Atlantis Idol

Natalia sprang to her feet, an excitement pulsing within her. She signalled for Hiram to fetch some equipment from one of the bags on board.

"How are we going to find the ship?" Quinn asked, looking out around the boat at the open water. "There's no sign of it above the surface. How can you be sure we're in the right spot?"

Hiram returned with a device Quinn didn't recognise.

"Oh, I see," said Ted. "I saw this in a documentary. "That's LiDAR, right?"

"No," Magda chimed in. "Sonar. You can use LiDAR to detect things underwater, but the water must be calm and clear for it to work. Sonar is more accurate in these conditions."

"Oh," replied Ted. "How does that work?"

"I thought you said you were filmmakers," Matteo said, casting a suspicious look at them.

"He's new," Magda replied, pivoting quickly in the lie. "Intern."

Ted played along with an apologetic smile.

"I'll show you how it works," Magda continued. "You too, if you're interested." She gestured for Matteo to sit with them.

Moments later, Magda had a laptop open, the device resting on her thighs as she tilted the screen towards the others. The sonar equipment had been set up by Natalia and Stefan and the data had started to be recorded.

"It uses sound waves that bounce off the sea floor. These sound waves return a signal to the ship. I'm recording these signals to produce an image here. If we find other structures between here and the floor, we'll know we've found something of interest."

"Like our shipwreck," said Ted.

"Precisely."

Stefan killed the engine and the boat bobbed gently on the sea's surface. The crew prepared the sonar equipment for their underwater search. As Stefan rigged the sonar device at the boat's stern, the crew peered at the laptop screen as it came to life, displaying data from beneath the waves.

The machine emitted sound waves, a sonar pulse, which travelled through the water and bounced off objects submerged below. The screen displayed the echoes—varying shapes and densities on the sonar display—as signals bounced back from different depths and textures.

Stefan nodded to Matteo, who started the engine once more and nudged the boat gently forward. He manoeuvred the boat in a methodical grid pattern, ensuring complete coverage of the immediate vicinity.

The rest of the group watched Magda's screen intently. Nothing was happening.

Ted broke the silence. "How do we know when we've hit—"

Before he could finish his sentence, the sonar waves emitted a high-pitched ping, the signal reflecting as a series of dots and lines on the screen. Each distinct echo indicated a potential obstacle, either natural formations or man-made structures.

Another ping emitted as the sonar picked up more objects. The crew watched intently as the sonar data slowly built a three-dimensional map of the underwater terrain, revealing anomalies that hinted at unnatural formations below the surface.

"We got it!" Magda shouted to the bridge. Stefan raised a hand in acknowledgement and signalled to Matteo to slow the speed of the boat to a stop once more.

Suddenly, the boat lurched as though it had been bumped into. A knocking sound came from the bottom of the vessel.

"What the hell was that?" Ted asked worriedly.

"The mast," Matteo called back. "The top of it is just below the surface."

"We're right on top of it," Quinn breathed. She couldn't help a sudden feeling of exhilaration take hold of her as they were within touching distance of history.

Magda adjusted the sonar settings, fine-tuning the frequency and angle to refine the readings. Scanning the depths, she analysed the data on her laptop screen, catching glimpses of intriguing shapes and shadows as more of the wreck revealed itself.

"Is it our ship?" Natalia asked. "I don't want to waste time exploring the wrong wreck."

"No, this is definitely it." Magda didn't take her eyes away from the screen as she replied. "Unless there is another galley we didn't know about."

"Okay, let's take a look," Natalia decided.

Stefan killed the engine as anticipation surged among the group. Hiram was busy helping Magda ready their diving gear. The time had finally come to uncover the mysteries concealed beneath the waves.

Ted peered over the edge of the boat, seeing the shadowy outline of the shipwreck's mast just visible beneath the water. The grand scale of the shipwreck was almost impossible to comprehend as it stretched down into the depths of the sea. It was an overwhelming sensation, one of dread that bubbled to the surface of Ted's mind. The sea had that kind of power, to strike fear and wonder of the unknown in equal measure to those who dared to stare into its abyss.

It didn't take long for Hiram to change into the diving gear while receiving a briefing from Natalia. After checking the equipment, he was poised on the boat's edge, zipping up his diving suit. Magda was helping to secure the scuba tank on his back. The sun blazed overhead, casting shimmering rays onto the crystal-clear waters. His breath hitched with anticipation as he adjusted his mask and tested his oxygen regulator. An experienced diver, something Ted had attributed to a possible special forces background, the burly man had an air of confidence about him as he readied himself for the venture.

"Good to go?" Magda asked.

"Yes," he replied matter of fact.

"Aren't you forgetting something?" Matteo was looking around at the group with a quizzical look. "Where are the cameras? You don't want to document the dive?"

Natalia and Magda shared a look before Natalia cleared her throat. "This is just research. We'll get some footage on the boat another time. But we don't want to bring out the big cameras until we're sure we have something worth shooting."

"I have my underwater camera," Stefan said, holding up a small cube-shaped device. He strapped it to Hiram's wrist. "The fancy cameras can't handle the pressure at these depths." He pushed a button on the small camera, and it beeped as it switched on, a small red light blinking to indicate it had started recording. "See you on the other side, big guy," Stefan said.

Hiram gave one final adjustment to his mask and fixed his regulator, giving a quick breath through it before throwing himself backwards off the side of the boat. With a splash, he entered the sea, the water enveloping him in a cool embrace. The sensation of weightlessness surrounded him as he descended beneath the surface, the outside world dimming

The Atlantis Idol

into a tranquil aquatic realm. His movements were deliberate and controlled as he made his way into the submerged world.

As he got his bearings, the ancient ship's mast came into view. He had already passed the fragments of the crow's nest that remained, the rest long eroded. The underwater landscape unfolded before him—a mosaic of shifting light and shadows. Guided by the sliver of sunlight piercing the surface, he delved deeper into a world where time stood still.

The ghostly silhouette of the galley loomed below, shrouded in an ethereal haze. The ship appeared like a colossal shadow against the luminous undersea landscape, its timeworn frame telling tales of countless voyages and the tumultuous seas it once navigated. It was as though the vessel's weathered remains had been sat frozen in time.

Hiram kicked his legs, feeling resistance from the water against his flippers. There was a cadence to his movements, a rhythm learned from hours spent training, each motion deliberate and efficient. The diving gear acted as both a facilitator and a limiter in his journey into deeper waters.

He descended, following the line of the mast down to the deck. He switched on a torch, the light cutting through the murkier depths, illuminating the ship's haunting architecture. He traced the remnants of the hull, running his gloved hand along the once-mighty timbers now surrendered to the relentless embrace of the ocean. The whole wreck was now encrusted with barnacles and draped in undulating ribbons of seaweed.

The hum of bubbles escaping from the regulator accompanied Hiram's controlled breathing. The deck of the ship was close now. Directing the beam of the torch into the shadows ahead, the light revealed more of the eerie galley.

While he was not sure exactly what he was expecting to salvage from the site, the instructions from Natalia had been clear. He would explore as much of the wreck as his oxygen tank would allow and report back with the footage from the underwater camera. He found an entry point into the interior of the ship via a gaping hole in the side of the hull. Given the way the vessel had sunk and rested on the seabed, Hiram surmised that the damage had been caused prior to its sinking. He felt a palpable sense of reverence, the maritime relic telling him its story. There had been a battle in these waters. The hole was likely the result of a cannonball or even some kind of larger explosion.

As he entered the heart of the ship, a school of fish darted playfully around the sunken timbers. Enclosed within the wreck, he glimpsed the remnants of ancient cargo. He placed a hand on the ship's hull and propelled himself inside, passing a rusted anchor and decaying barrels. He was careful to keep a decent amount of clearance above him to give space for the air tank on his back. The tank itself was a source of both reassurance and apprehension; a finite supply of air that dictated the length of his exploration. Hiram didn't much enjoy diving, but he was well-practised at it, nevertheless. The limited oxygen supply strapped to him limited the exploration, as well as his comfort. But it also added a ticking clock in an environment that he would much rather take his time to work carefully and methodically through.

Navigating through the dark, eerie corridors of the sunken galley, the remnants of the ship stood as a solemn testament to a bygone era. Venturing deeper into the vessel, visibility worsened, Hiram relying almost completely on the torch as his eyes had to adjust to the subdued light that filtered through broken planks and openings in the hull.

Passing through fragmented doorways and overgrown openings, he followed the remnants of the galley's structure, the muted colour of decaying wood creating an otherworldly atmosphere.

He came across the space where he assumed the cabins would have been—now encrusted with marine life—where the crew once rested between arduous journeys. Not much remained of the interior, betraying the life that once thrived within these walls. It was there he discovered the first of many skeletons, lying at awkward angles on the floor of the cabin. He angled his wrist to ensure the camera that was strapped to it fully captured the scene. When the ship went down, it had taken the crew with it. He wondered about the gaping hole that had been blasted out of the hull. Surely there had been time for these sailors to swim out to safety. He surmised that these poor souls must have been killed before that point. It was plausible that the vessel had been sunk after the battle, or at the very least after fighting had taken place below deck. He passed over a skeleton, its hand resting next to a rusted cutlass. The weapon looked largely intact, its hilt simple in design yet iconic for its time. He would make sure the team recovered this. While she was a collector of all kinds of antiquities, he knew Natalia was particularly fond of old weapons like this.

Passing through another cabin, he glided through the shipwreck, the mesmerising remnants of a bygone era surrounding him. A sudden presence interrupted the quietude—a thresher shark gracefully manoeuvring through the heart of the ship. Startled by its unexpected appearance, Hiram's pulse quickened. At around ten feet long, this shark looked to be fully grown. It had likely entered the wreck on the hunt for fish. Given the schools of small fish Hiram had seen throughout his journey through the old ship, he wondered if the shark was a regular in these waters.

Noticing that he was taking in more hurried breaths, he tried to steady his breathing. He knew this type of shark. The long tail fin was a giveaway. Despite being a deadly predator to a large pool of marine life, the thresher shark was no threat to humans. So long as he kept his cool and let the shark get on with its business, he would be okay. Thresher sharks are not inherently aggressive, and if undisturbed, tend to keep their distance from divers.

Remaining calm, Hiram admired the majestic creature's sleek form and long, whip-like tail. The shark, sensing no threat, continued its exploration of the wreck, its movements fluid and unhurried. Its large, dark eyes appeared curious yet composed, a silent acknowledgement of Hiram's presence.

He observed it as it passed through a hole in the hull and out of sight. Checking the levels of his oxygen tank, he took stock of how much time he had left to explore. He still had plenty of time to delve further.

Continuing his journey into the heart of the wreck, Hiram entered a spacious chamber. He knew instantly that this was the area he had come to find. The remains of the ancient vessel's captain lay atop a small collection of trinkets. As with the rest of the crew, time had rendered the remains a mere skeleton. While not feeling particularly connected to this expedition, save for his fee, Hiram felt a sense of reverence for the figure that lay before him.

He gazed upon the remains, trying to discern the stories etched in their silent bones, imagining their struggles as fate decided that the submerged wreck would become their tomb. He retrieved a zip lock bag from a small pouch that had been fixed to his wetsuit and began to pick up items off the floor around the skeletal captain. He started with a small round object, bringing it closer to his mask to inspect it. Rubbing it between his fingers to clear a layer of dirt off, he saw that it was an old coin. He placed it into the bag and reached for the next one. Just as his hand brushed it, something caught his eye. His hand halted before he had picked up another small coin as he took in the sight. He placed the torch on the floor of the boat, angling it so that it shone onto the object his eyes had settled on.

It was a small wooden box. A rusted brass clasp was keeping the lid closed. It took some effort, but he was eventually able to lift the clasp and pry the box open.

Inside lay an object that looked strangely familiar. Hiram had seen it very recently, in one of Stefan's books. He dusted away at the silt covering it, creating a small cloud in the water. He then reached for it with his other hand, the zip lock bag tightly closed between his middle and ring finger as he pinched with his index finger and thumb. He brought his other hand around and adjusted his grip, inspecting the object more closely. It was miraculously intact for an object that had such shapely, delicate features. It seemed to be a bronze figurine of some sort, no bigger than a small action figure a child might play with. While tarnished, the features carved into it had survived the erosion of the sea all this time. Enough at least to make out the lines at the bottom of the figure's face representing a long and wizened beard. The most prominent feature that proved to be a dead giveaway of what the figure represented was the arm that wielded a long staff with a fork-like shape at its tip. A trident.

TWELVE

Stefan was grinning widely as he held the small figurine in his hands. The tarnished bronze gleamed in the sunlight as the group huddled around, their expressions a mix of awe and contemplation.

"Poseidon," he breathed "I can't believe it." He studied the statuette with an air of reverence. As Quinn and Ted watched on, they could see what this discovery meant to him. Just how significant this was in unravelling one of history's most fabled mysteries—the lost city of Atlantis—they were not sure. But, despite the dire circumstances that had led them to this point, it was difficult not to get swept up in the pure joy radiating from Stefan.

"You lied!" Matteo's voice cut through. "You said you wouldn't disturb the site." His voice carried the weight of a solemn promise, his eyes burning with white-hot rage.

Natalia swept her hair back and let out a frustrated sigh. "I'm sorry we lied to you, Matteo. You are right to be angry, we have used you. And I'm sorry, but we will not be returning this."

"This is wrong."

The Atlantis Idol

"What's done is done, you cannot change it. And I strongly suggest you cease your protestations now." She gave him a piercing look that allowed him to read between the lines.

"You..." Matteo stopped as he looked at the concerned look on Quinn's face. "You are not filmmakers."

Natalia didn't reply.

Matteo cursed under his breath in his mother tongue. He sat quietly across from the group, ashamed of his naïveté. He should have known better than to trust them. Something had felt off when he reached the hotel room with Magda, but he had chosen to ignore it, blinded by the money that came with the information he provided. That, and the prospect of being part of the documentary.

"May I?" Natalia reached out and clasped a hand around the figurine before Stefan had a chance to respond. She took the artefact, turning it in her hands as if unlocking secrets held within the ancient bronze.

"It's exquisite," Magda murmured, eyes fixed on the intricate details of the sea deity. "This is an incredible discovery."

"All this time, just waiting for us to find," added Stefan. "A piece of history untouched for centuries. Well done, Hiram."

"So, it was the Pope's ship?" asked Ted.

Stefan shook his head. "Not the Pope's ship. It's difficult to say exactly which, but it is either Botafoc's or Yanes'. This small statue all but confirms it; one just like it was detailed in the ledger."

"So, how do we know which it is?" Ted followed up inquisitively.

Stefan paused a moment, before turning to Hiram. "You said you found remains of the crew?"

The grizzled man nodded.
"Can we review the footage?"

Moments later, the underwater camera was hooked up to Magda's laptop. The group watched as she navigated to the camera's storage drive, located the video file and initiated playback.

For a moment the image was stuck on a still of Stefan's face, the background of the sea just visible behind. The fisheye lens homed in on his facial features before the footage began to play. Stefan's face moved away from the camera, and moments later Hiram fell backwards into the sea. The sound became muffled as bubbles filled the screen and the waters of the Tyrrhenian Sea consumed the feed.

They watched intently as the video focused on the depths below their boat, with Hiram swimming deeper. The tall wooden mast was visible at first before the angle changed and the camera tilted downward. The old ship loomed slowly into view, and a palpable energy was felt among those watching the laptop screen. This was their first view of the ancient vessel. Stefan leaned in eagerly, his fingers drumming the side of the laptop in anticipation. Natalia, her brow furrowed with concentration, watched as Hiram swam further into the depths.

As the murky blue hues continued to dominate the screen, the deck of the ship grew bigger with every second. The smaller details of the wreck became clearer through the fisheye lens of the underwater camera, the swaying tendrils of underwater plant life surrounding the wreck becoming more visible. The camera jostled along with Hiram's movements, capturing glimpses of the sunken ship's remains.

The Atlantis Idol

They watched as Hiram entered through the hole in the hull and made his way through the cabins. Stefan leaned in and watched intently to take in as much detail as he could.

He jolted and let out a guttural sound as the thresher shark suddenly filled the screen.

"Holy—" Ted exclaimed, too shocked to find the right expletive to finish his sentence. "There's a shark down there?"

"A thresher," Hiram grunted. Ted looked at the man agape, wondering how he was so nonchalant about it.

The shark's large eyes were searching yet seemed to ignore Hiram's presence. Its long tail fin moved gracefully from side to side as it passed by slowly and out of view.

Eventually, the recording reached the point in the dive where Hiram had located the box containing the bronze figurine of Poseidon. The skeleton of the ship's captain came into view. Stefan waited for the right moment before pausing the recording. The group looked at the skull that had filled the laptop screen.

"Any ideas?" Stefan asked.

"Hard to tell," said Magda. "Little is known about either of them to identify them easily."

"What about the ship?" Quinn chimed in. "Does it have any distinguishing features that tell us it was Genoan or Castilian?"

"Excellent point," Magda smiled, clicking her fingers as though having the light bulb moment herself. She leaned forward to take control of the trackpad on the laptop, rewinding to the point where Hiram was approaching the deck, approximately fifty yards out.

"Quinn's right," she said. "There is something unique about this ship that can help us identify it. Well, at least distinguish Botafoc's from Yanes'. It's a pretty big one, actually." She chuckled. "I can't believe we didn't see it already."

Natalia was leaning over her. "Care to share, dear? I'm afraid I'm not following you."

It was not Magda who answered, but Quinn. "Botafoc and Yanes were part of the navy, and the documents from the Vatican archives say that they were heavily armed, right?"

"Yes," Natalia agreed. "But they both were."

"Right," Quinn continued. "They had ballistae, which would have been spread across the deck."

"Ballistae?" asked Ted.

"Like large crossbows," Quinn clarified.

"Cool," Ted said to himself.

"They would have had at least eight on a ship this size," Magda chimed in. "Do you see any remains of them on this ship?" She tilted the laptop screen so Natalia could see it more clearly.

"No," she admitted.

"Exactly. Because this wasn't Botafoc's ship, or Yanes' for that matter."

"I don't understand."

"Botafoc's ship ran aground after making off with his share of the treasure. Chances are, that ship was in no fit state to sail. I think the Pope gave him another vessel to captain to seek out Yanes and the rest of the fortune."

"It's not a warship," Stefan agreed.

"It had seen battle," Natalia countered. "Just look at the holes in the hull."

Magda nodded. "We don't know what happened. Maybe Botafoc tracked down Yanes and was attacked by him. Maybe it was something else."

"So, that means the skeleton Hiram found is Antonio Botafoc," Natalia surmised.

The Atlantis Idol

"It seems so."

A few moments of silence followed. Quinn pondered the situation and wondered what thoughts were running through the rest of the group's heads. They had found Botafoc, but they hadn't found what they really came for. The bronze statuette of Poseidon was the only evidence they had found that there was any link between the late bishop's treasure and Atlantis. In fact, they couldn't even attribute it to Atlantis at this point. Poseidon was a prominent figure in Greek and Minoan history, and it was entirely likely that the statue was a relic taken from either of those cultures.

Stefan chewed his lip, as though deep in thought. He stood up and went to the other side of the boat, leaving the laptop with Magda. Quinn watched as he paced the deck, his face exhibiting conflict. No doubt the exhilaration he had felt just moments ago at discovering the statuette had been replaced by the frustrated feeling of reaching a dead end.

Quinn turned to Ted. He gave her a warm smile. Their reunion had been stranger than either of them had imagined. What should have been a joyful reconnection had become the very thing that had kept them apart in the first place. Quinn couldn't help but feel that by letting herself feel the giddy excitement that came with a rekindled relationship, even briefly, she had opened herself up to the pain that always seemed to come around the corner. Fate had decided that happiness was not something she should have so easily. Her spirit dampened with the harsh reality of their situation, she wondered if there was a world in which they could be together without the imposing shadow of Sigma looming over them. Perhaps this was the universe's way of telling her it was not meant to be, and that she had been right to cut herself off from it the first time.

Almost as though sensing a change in her, Ted placed his hand in hers, their fingers interlocking. Quinn cast aside the negative thoughts, returning the smile he had given her a moment ago. To hell with fate. They survived this once before, and they did it together.

"Woah," Magda breathed. Stefan, who had been leaning over the side of the boat, staring into the deep blue of the sea, suddenly perked up and looked at his colleague with a glimmer of hope.

"Stefan," Magda said, an urgency in her voice. She didn't have to say anything else, as Stefan hurried over to perch alongside her.

Magda pointed at the laptop screen. The display was filled with a still image from Hiram's video recording. She had been reviewing the footage and had spotted something.

"Can you enhance this? Right here," she said, pointing to a small, blurred section of the video.

"This?" he asked, placing his finger on the screen, leaving behind a fingerprint smudge. Magda nodded.

Stefan took the laptop and began furiously swiping at the trackpad and tapping on the keyboard. Eventually, the section of the screen Magda had been pointing out was blown up, the image gradually becoming less pixilated as it was enhanced.

"What are you looking at?" Natalia asked curiously.

The image slowly came into focus, and the question was answered for her. Around the neck of Botafoc's skeleton was a necklace. A ring was hanging from it, having been threaded onto the chain of the necklace. Protruding from the ring itself was a small shape.

"That ring," Magda said. "It looks strangely familiar."

"What is that coming off it, an X?" Quinn had joined and was leaning in over Magda's shoulder.

"A cross," Magda corrected.

"A crucifix? Doesn't the Christian cross have one longer end?" Ted asked.

"Not this one," Stefan clarified. "It has the same symbolism. But this shape, with arms of equal length, is known as the Greek cross."

"The Greek Orthodox Church," Magda added.

"What's Antonio Botafoc doing wearing a Greek Orthodox ring?" Stefan asked, his voice quiet as though he were asking himself. He had the look of a detective poring over his notes and fragments of evidence, trying to connect the dots.

"You said it looked familiar," said Natalia. "Why?"

"Stefan," Magda said, ignoring Natalia's question. "Is there any mention of a ring like this in the ledger?"

"No," he replied assuredly.

"I've seen it recently," she insisted, scratching her head. "I'm sure it was—" she trailed off before the memory she was looking for came to the front of her mind. "The archives! There was another document that referenced it. But it was from a much more recent entry. I think it was Benedict XV. I remember finding it odd to read about the Vatican keeping Greek Orthodox trinkets in their collection." She turned to Hiram. "How much oxygen is left in that tank?"

With a splash, Hiram disappeared beneath the surface of the water once again. This time he had a clear objective and better knowledge of the shipwreck layout. It would not take him long to retrieve the ring and the other items he had been sent back for.

On the deck, Natalia was becoming impatient. "This is a waste of time."

The faint hum of an engine could be heard in the distance. Quinn looked up and saw a speedboat with flashing red and blue lights coming towards them. The rest of the group had taken note of the approaching boat too. Natalia stood up suddenly, a concerned expression etched on her face.

"What the hell?" Stefan muttered, surprised at its sudden appearance.

Natalia looked at the approaching speedboat for a moment, her mind racing. She knew exactly what this was. The police were coming to shut them down. How did they know they were here? Had someone tipped them off to their activity? If they knew exactly what was going on here, it was over. They would be arrested and locked away in an Italian jail while they awaited trial. She turned around and looked at Matteo.

"You!" she hissed. "What did you do?"

He said nothing, looking at her defiantly.

"We took his phone," Natalia said, turning her attention to Stefan and Magda. "How did he alert them?"

"Maybe he had suspicions and told the police to check the area just in case?"

Natalia sighed. She hadn't given Matteo enough credit. It didn't change the white-hot rage that was building inside her, however.

"You are an accomplice," she threatened the young fisherman. "Do you understand? You assisted us willingly for your personal gain. If we go to jail, you'll be coming with us."

A siren sounded as the police boat came within fifty yards of them. As the boat got closer, the siren stopped and a voice came through the tannoy, speaking first in Italian, then English.

"You are disturbing a protected historical site. Stand up and put your hands clearly where we can see them. We will now board and perform a search of your boat."

The voice pierced the air, the odd word masked through the muffled nature of the tannoy system. The message got through loud and clear, though; it was game over.

The police boat slowed down and pulled up alongside theirs. There were two officers aboard. The man who had been driving shut off the engine, while the other, who had been speaking to them through the tannoy system, tethered their boats together with rope. Shortly after, both officers were on board and standing imposingly in front of the group. They said something in Italian to Matteo, who responded, passionately gesticulating towards the others as he made his point. This was not looking good. Matteo had thrown them firmly under the bus.

The two officers carried firearms attached to their belts. Quinn couldn't help but stare at them, their presence alone enough to create a sense of unease. That was largely the point, she supposed; the implication of threat, in the hope that the guns would never need to come out of their holsters.

The officer from the tannoy spoke loudly and clearly. "If you are filming in this area, I need to see some permits."

Matteo shouted something before the others had a chance to reply, gesticulating wildly again. While Quinn and Ted didn't speak Italian, they could guess that Matteo was helpfully alerting the officer to the fact that they were not actually filmmakers.

The group were stood in a line with their hands behind their heads while the second officer searched them one by one.

"I need you to present any and all items you have taken from the site," the first officer said. The second had finished their search of Quinn and Ted and was currently patting down Stefan.

Matteo got up and retrieved the bronze figurine, bringing it to the officer.

He took the statuette, inspecting it with intrigue. He muttered to Matteo, before addressing the group.

"I've seen enough." He placed the statuette aside. "You are all under arrest. My colleague—"

The officer's eyes suddenly widened, and his face contorted into a grimace of pain. Quinn watched in horror as blood seeped from his mouth. Ted grasped her hand, his face as white as a ghost. They looked from the officer's terrified expression to the blade that had been plunged into his back.

Standing behind the officer was Hiram. Having resurfaced from his dive, he had snuck on board the adjoining boat, waiting for the right moment to attack the first officer with the only weapon at his disposal: the cutlass he had recovered from the shipwreck.

The second police officer reacted a split second too late. As he turned to see the bloody scene that was playing out behind him, Hiram had plucked the handgun from his colleague's holster and fired off two shots into the man's chest. The crack of the gunshots was deafening. The officer went down, instantly becoming limp. Another two shots rang out and Quinn watched in horror as Hiram had finished the brutal assassinations with bullets to the heads of both police officers. The shocking assault had taken just seconds.

The tension was thick on the deck of the small boat. For a few moments the lapping of the waves of the Tyrrhenian Sea was all that could be heard, the group stunned into silence.

Matteo was quivering in fear in the opposite corner of the boat, petrified by the unexpected violence that had just occurred. Calculated and emotionless, Hiram approached the young fisherman, his feet clunking heavily with each step. He took a look at the man who had betrayed them, then raised the gun once more.

THIRTEEN

Amidst the urban cacophony of Italy's capital, the sunlit rooftop terrace stood as a serene escape from the bustling streets below. Perched atop an ancient building, the rooftop bar offered an unparalleled view that stretched across the river Tiber, reaching the grandeur of Vatican City in the distance.

Sunset hues painted the sky, casting a golden glow over the Eternal City, as the dwindling light kissed the domes and spires of the Vatican. From this vantage point, the contours of St. Peter's Basilica emerged; an architectural marvel that commanded reverence even from afar.

Quinn leaned against the wrought iron railing that ran around the edge of the rooftop. A gentle breeze swirled, rustling through the leaves of potted plants that dotted the terrace. It was difficult for her to enjoy the spectacular view while her mind was still reeling from the savage murders she had witnessed at the hands of Hiram hours earlier. A pang of guilt weighed heavy in her stomach. Those poor souls. She had to keep reminding herself that she was a prisoner in this situation and that there was nothing she could have done to stop it. Yet, she felt as though she were complicit in their deaths. She couldn't get the image of the police officer's petrified face out of her head. The way the blood had seeped from his mouth as the sword was plunged through him, the deafening gunshots, the way Hiram had approached Matteo with the look of a cold-blooded killer. The scene was replaying over and over in an infinite loop.

"Quinn," a hand touched her tenderly on the arm. She snapped back to the present and saw Ted standing alongside her. His face reflected the exhaustion they both felt, the torment of the day's harrowing events mirrored in his eyes. She knew he was suffering just as she was.

He handed her a glass of water. She took it gratefully, sipping from it as she looked back out at the panoramic view.

"They're saying they've got an apartment nearby. We're going to stay the night there," said Ted.

"Of course they do," Quinn kept her gaze firmly on somewhere in the distance. She loathed how easy it was for Sigma to go from place to place, breaking laws, hurting people, and getting exactly what they wanted every time. One such example was the rooftop bar itself, which was eerily empty for an establishment in the heart of the city that boasted such a beautiful vantage point. Natalia had made some arrangements to book the space under the pretence of a private function. After having some cash flashed at them, the manager had promptly kicked out the tourists who were already enjoying their drinks on the terrace. Money talks, Quinn decided.

The sun's final rays cast long shadows that stretched across the Roman rooftops. It would be dark soon. A drop of rain landed on her hand as she clutched the glass of water. Then another on her head. Soon the pitter-patter of droplets falling increased in volume and frequency. Before long the sudden rain shower had intensified, and the terrace was becoming soaked. Ted took Quinn by the hand and led her inside, where the others had taken shelter.

Magda was wiping the screen of her tablet, which had been open on a series of scanned photos from the documents they had acquired from the Vatican archives.

"I suppose we'll need to continue this at the apartment," she said, eying the bartender waiting patiently at their post, ready to serve while they wiped a glass clean. They felt as though they had the privacy to discuss what they had found and plan their next move from the terrace, but the space inside was more cramped. While not giving off any eavesdropping signals, the bartender's proximity was enough to put Magda off.

"I'll text the address to Hiram," said Natalia. "We'll get him to meet us there."

After the unexpected encounter with the local authorities, and the quickly escalating violence that had followed, they had left Hiram to clean up the situation while the rest of the group headed back to shore. What exactly that involved for Hiram, Quinn and Ted were not sure, but it was implied the bodies had been disposed of at sea, along with the police boat. Another vessel lost to the sea under nefarious circumstances.

With them was the item Hiram had been sent back to the wreck to retrieve: the necklace Botafoc had been wearing, with a ring hanging from it. Magda had been certain that this ring, or one exactly like it, had been described in one of the documents from the Vatican archives. While she had perused them in their entirety once, the documents they had acquired were numerous. She couldn't pinpoint exactly where she had seen reference to the ring with the Greek cross on. The ring itself had a distinctive feature that had reignited Stefan and Magda's excitement, after momentarily reaching a dead end.

Engraved on the outside was a small series of concentric circles. It was yet another link to Atlantis that they couldn't ignore. Magda was certain that whatever that link was would be made known to them once they located the passage in the documents that mentioned the object.

Gathering their belongings, they headed to the exit. Natalia took a roll of Euros out of her pocket and looked for the bartender to settle their bill. While they had been stood behind the bar a moment ago, they were now nowhere to be seen. A faint clinking of glasses could be heard just over the hammering rain outside. The bartender had gone to clean up the terrace. Natalia let out an audible tutting noise, before leaving the cash on the bar and leaving.

Ted pressed the button to the lift that would take them down to the ground floor. A moment later, the doors opened with a high-pitched pinging sound. Ted recoiled as an unexpected figure appeared from inside the lift.

"Hiram," Natalia called, surprised to see him.

Hiram stood quietly in the lift. Ted felt his pulse quicken and a sudden knot form in his stomach at the sight of the imposing figure. There was something about the man's presence that had changed since the boat. Both Ted and Quinn felt it. His sudden appearance in the lift instantly brought a feeling of dread, as though they were in the presence of death itself. Knowing first-hand what he was capable of had been the difference maker. They had known he was the muscle of the operation, but until then there was a small part of them that wondered if it was all for show. It certainly wasn't.

One thing they were acutely aware of was how little Natalia seemed to be phased by Hiram. How many events like the one on the boat had she been involved in for it to be desensitised so much for her?

"All settled?" Natalia asked.

"Yes," came the gruff reply.

Quinn winced at the way Natalia had asked. It was so blasé. She wondered if Natalia would treat it with more sincerity if she had to do the dirty work herself. There was a distinct lack of empathy in the woman, a cold heart that demonstrated a failure to value life.

As they reached street level, Natalia was on her phone arranging for a taxi to take them to their home for the night. They stood under the awning of the building to keep dry, while the rain splashed in large puddles on the road. The tooting of a car horn came suddenly, followed by the shouts of a driver, as a Vespa weaved dangerously in and out of traffic.

Across the street was a convenience store. It was getting late, but the inside was lit up and it looked like it was still open.

"Magda," Quinn said sheepishly. "Sorry to ask, but do you have a, erm…"

Magda squinted as she tried to follow Quinn's train of thought.

"I need to use the restroom. I think I'm early."

"Oh," Magda suddenly twigged. "Of course! Here." She reached into her bag and retrieved a sanitary pad, handing it discreetly to Quinn.

"Thanks," Quinn smiled. "I'm going to ask if I can use their restroom," she announced loudly to the rest of the group. Before waiting for a response, she marched across the road into the pouring rain.

Natalia looked up from her phone. "What is she… Hiram! Go after her!"

The tall bald man followed her at a jog.

"She's just going to the toilet," Ted defended.

The Atlantis Idol

"Hiram will keep an eye on her," said Natalia firmly.

Quinn entered the shop, a jingling noise sounding as she pushed open the door. She watched as Hiram caught up. The man hesitated a moment, before pulling the door closed and standing guard outside. She was relieved he had at least given her some privacy. There was not much chance of her escaping, but that was not her intention.

As she walked through the convenience store, passing aisles of various food and drink items, Quinn saw a sign at the far end that signposted the way to the toilet. There was a notice next to it, that from her best guess said something about it being only for paying customers.

Quinn decided to make a beeline for the counter. A bored-looking woman was sitting on a stool, her head buried in her phone. The young woman's eyes flicked up towards Quinn as she approached, but then went swiftly back to her phone.

"Buonasera," the woman said softly.

"Buonasera," Quinn repeated. She paused for a moment, taking in the wall of electronic items behind the counter. Plug adapters and phone chargers of various sizes and colours adorned the wall. Quinn glanced to the doorway. She could see the back of Hiram's head through the glass pane in the door. She then turned back to the shop clerk.

"Posso…" She tried hard to remember the phrase she had once learned. "Er, il bagno?"

"Uno, due, tre, quattro," the woman replied.

Quinn recognised the numbers. The combination for the lock on the restroom door. She smiled as she appreciated the simplicity. 1, 2, 3, 4.

"Grazie," she said warmly. She looked back at the wall of electronics, finding what she had been looking for. She pointed at a basic-looking mobile phone hanging from one of the racks in vacuum-formed plastic. It was one of those cheap prepaid phones she had associated with burner phones from TV; something a criminal might use to communicate incognito.

"Quanto?" she pointed at the phone.

The clerk looked up from her own phone for more than a second, following Quinn's eyes to the wall.

"Venticinque," the woman replied.

Quinn took one last look at the doorway, before dipping into her pocket and pulling out the cash she had swiped from the bar after the rest of the group had headed to the lift. She placed two ten and one five euro notes on the counter.

"Prego," she said.

The woman eyed the cash and gave a heavy sigh. She took down the phone from the wall and placed it on the counter. With a push of a button the old till drawer pinged open with a loud ringing sound. The clerk placed the notes inside and shut the drawer again.

"Grazie," they each said to each other as Quinn made off toward the restroom. Punching in the combination, she turned the handle and hurried inside, locking the door behind her. Placing the lid of the toilet down, she sat on the seat and pried open the plastic to get at the phone.

She had been patiently waiting for an opportunity to call for help without Natalia and her associates noticing. With her own phone being confiscated, she hadn't had a chance to do so until now. Switching on the handset, she waited for it to start up. The screen lit up and a few moments later she was greeted with a sight she hadn't seen since she had her first phone years ago. She thought for a moment about the right number to call. Emergency services? As she was about to punch in the numbers, she noticed that the icon in the top corner of the screen depicting the strength of the signal had

The Atlantis Idol

no bars. It seemed like the toilet stall was a dead spot. Quinn swore under her breath, her hands starting to shake.

A knock on the door came suddenly. Quinn jolted.

"Ms Miyata," Natalia's voice came from the other side. "Everything okay? The taxi is waiting for us."

Quinn fumbled with the phone, switching it off and wondering where to stash it. Her pockets were tight; it would bulge out and be instantly noticeable. She bent down and lifted the leg of her jeans, tucked the phone into her sock and rolled the jeans back down. She assessed her foot. It seemed a bit less conspicuous. She wiggled her foot around to test if the phone stayed put.

Natalia rapped on the door again. Quinn flushed the toilet and turned on the sink tap. A moment later she opened the door to an agitated Natalia.

"Everything okay?" she asked, feigning concern.

"Yes," Quinn lied. "Just got caught short. Aunt Flo came early, and Magda helped me out."

"Happens to us all, dear," Natalia smiled. "Now, we really must be going. The taxi is just out front."

FOURTEEN

A short drive away, the luxury penthouse Natalia had taken them to stood as a testament to opulence and sophistication, perched atop a grandiose high-rise building. The air was alive with the distant echoes of Rome—the murmurs of traffic, the joyous laughter of families enjoying an evening stroll, and the distant chime of church bells.

After speaking briefly with the smiling security staff on duty in the lobby, Natalia had taken them up to the penthouse. The button in the lift that took them to the penthouse level was operable only to those who had a valid security card. The lift doors slid open, and they were greeted by a large open-plan space, adorned with sleek minimalist furnishings and grand floor-to-ceiling windows offering panoramic views of the cityscape.

Entering the main living space, the opulent interior unfolded before their eyes. The tastefully decorated open-concept area housed a fusion of modern and classic Italian design elements. Chic leather sofas and velvet armchairs surrounded a sleek glass coffee table, accentuated by intricate handwoven rugs that added warmth to the polished hardwood floors.

Natalia let out a sigh and set down her belongings. "Make yourselves at home," she said, heading straight into the kitchen to make a coffee from the professional-grade machine that sat proudly on a granite countertop. Stefan joined her, taking a seat at the breakfast bar that sat on an island in the centre of the kitchen.

"This is stunning," said Magda. "Do you own it?"

"Not this one," said Natalia. "My mother wanted to sample different areas of Rome before settling on one. It's just a rental, I'm afraid."

Just a rental. Ted tried hard not to scoff audibly at the privilege that dribbled out as she spoke.

Magda couldn't wait to get the tablet back out and pick up from where she had left off at the rooftop bar. She sat at the breakfast bar alongside Stefan and continued perusing the scanned pages of the documents they had saved on the cloud.

"Let me help," said Stefan, taking out the laptop they had used to log the sonar readings on the boat. Magda was switching between the scanned pages and a spreadsheet that had a list of numbers mapped to a few lines of text.

"What's that for?" asked Ted curiously.

"It's how I organise things," Magda replied. "There are so many documents, it's hard to keep track of everything. I numbered the pages that were taken from the same document, so I could logically group them. And for each group, I have a description of what it talks about."

"I'm guessing you didn't describe one as 'Greek cross ring Atlantis clue'?" he joked.

Magda chuckled. "Unfortunately not. But I'm narrowing my search to documents that were written in the last century. I'm sure it was from a more recent entry."

"Recent?" Ted scoffed. "Are we classing anything up to a hundred years ago recent?"

"Considering the Vatican Apostolic Archive was formed in 1612, yes," said Stefan plainly.

"Okay… So, how many entries are we talking?"

"Only a fraction of the total archives has been digitised, and of that fraction, over seven million scanned images have been taken."

Natalia filled up the coffee machine with fresh beans and water. "It's going to be a long night. Let's get to work."

Hours passed, and the night drew on. Empty coffee cups lay on the island in the middle of the kitchen. A yawning Stefan returned from another room, stretching his arms as though limbering up as he prepared to sit alongside Magda for another stint scouring through the ancient documents. All the while, Quinn and Ted sat idly with the group. There was a part of Quinn that was so intrigued by the mystery that she wanted to help. Magda let her watch as she worked, but despite the potential time saving benefit of having Quinn take on some of the reading herself, she hadn't been allowed to review the texts alone.

"I'm going to take a quick break, stretch my legs," said Ted, climbing down from a stool and heading off.

Natalia fired him a glance that conveyed suspicion.

"I need to pee," Ted clarified.

Natalia looked at Hiram, who dutifully stood up and began to slowly shadow Ted out of the kitchen.

"Come on," Ted protested. "I promise I won't try and escape. We've been more than cooperative so far, just as you asked."

Natalia eyed him carefully.

Ted continued. "If you want to stand by the front door, just to make sure, fine."

Natalia nodded and Hiram made his way to the lift doorway, which served as the front door to the penthouse.

Ted passed a large luxurious bedroom as he headed toward the bathroom. Tucked just inside the room were the group's bags. So eager to get on with their work for the night, they had thrown them there and used the room as temporary storage. Ted noticed a tan canvas satchel propped up against the wall, its clasps unfastened and the flap open. It was Stefan's. He remembered back to the night at the manor when he had interrupted Stefan while he was reading a book. He had been muttering to himself, as though reading aloud. But there was a quickness to his whispering. Ted remembered it vividly. It reminded him of the hushed tones someone used to pray, or how a Catholic would recite their well-practised Hail Mary.

He checked back towards the kitchen. He was out of view, and Hiram was standing sentinel by the front door. He would need to be quick, but he was hidden, for now. Reaching into the satchel, he felt the leather of the book he was looking for. He lifted it carefully out with one hand. The old leather-bound book had no writing or inscription on the front. Turning it over, he noticed the same was true for the back, as well as the spine. It was unusual for a book to be completely unlabelled this way. He saw that the book had several yellow sticky notes acting as bookmarks. He opened the book carefully to a random one. The page to the left-hand side had a large drawing on it. Ted knew instantly what it represented: the large temple in the centre, with buildings and farmland surrounding it, the depiction of water weaving in between each circle of land cascading out from the centre, with bridges connecting them all. This was Atlantis. But there was something off about the way it was drawn. The temple was crumbling. The lowest levels of the land were being consumed by the water. This was a scene of destruction.

He looked at the text written on the right-hand page. One line was underlined in blue ink.

And so it was, the island lost to sea. As was the will of Poseidon - to destroy his own land to make way for something new.

What was this book? An interpretation of Plato's story of the ancient city? He turned to another page that had been bookmarked with a yellow sticky note. Another passage was underlined in blue ink.

To the idol, the offering will set forth rebirth and renewal. A new beginning.

"What the hell are you doing?"

Ted jumped, swivelling around to see Stefan standing in the doorway.

"I, er," Ted fumbled, closing the book, and trying hastily to put it back inside the satchel.

"Leave it," Stefan said, his voice stern. Ted could see a look in the man's eyes he hadn't seen before. He knew immediately that he had stepped on turbulent ground.

"I'm sorry," Ted attempted to apologise. "I shouldn't have pried."

"No," Stefan said. "That book is very personal to me."

"I'm sorry," Ted said again. "What is it, if you don't mind me asking?"

"I do mind," replied Stefan coldly. A moment of awkward silence followed. Eventually, Stefan took in a deep breath in and exhaled exaggeratedly, as though he were trying to centre himself. Or calm himself. "Would you ask a believer of God to share their personal copy of The Bible with you? Or pry into the journal of a person's private thoughts?"

"Of course not," Ted admitted.

"Then please respect my privacy. My work is very important to me, and I like to keep it to myself. If you were to ask Magda, I'm sure she would be the same."

"Right, of course. I'm so sorry, my curiosity got the better of me. I promise I won't make this mistake again." Ted was eager to get out of this uncomfortable situation.

"Apology accepted," said Stefan, his demeanour changing instantly. He looked again like the perfectly pleasant man he had known these last few days. Ted took the opportunity to leave the room and head for the bathroom.

"Oh, and Ted," Stefan called after him. Ted stopped in his tracks, a sudden pit forming in his stomach.

"Yeah?"

"I'm happy to let this little indiscretion stay between us if you are?" Stefan offered a smile.

"Yeah, sure," Ted replied. "Sorry."

"It's already forgotten," Stefan whispered, winking playfully at him, before turning to return to the kitchen.

Ted entered the bathroom, flicked on the light switch, shut the door, and locked it. He let out a huge breath, and with it the tension that had built up inside him from the interaction. Looking into the mirror, he took his glasses off and wiped them on his sleeve.

"What the hell have you gotten yourself wrapped up in, Ted?" he muttered to his reflection.

After relieving himself, flushing the toilet and washing his hands, he slid across the bolt for the door to unlock it. As he exited, he was surprised to see Quinn. She smiled warmly at him.

"Hey," she said.

"Hey," he replied. "The craziest thing just happened to me."

"Oh?"

"Yeah." Ted suddenly noticed Hiram had left his post by the front door and was hovering nearby. "I guess I'll tell you later."

"Okay," Quinn stepped into the bathroom, her hand subtly giving his a quick squeeze as she passed him.

As Ted went back to the kitchen, Quinn closed the door, locking it with a slide of the bolt. Wasting no time, she reached down and lifted the leg of her jeans, revealing the mobile phone she had stashed into her sock. The screen was just visible as it stuck out the top of the sock. She retrieved it and switched the device on.

"Okay," she breathed, her heart rate elevating as she punched in the number for the emergency services. Before she pressed the green call button, the bathroom door handle began to move. The handle went up and down over and over, as though someone were desperately trying to get in.

"Quinn," Natalia's voice came from the other side. "Open the door, please."

"Shit." She pressed the red button on the phone and desperately tried to stuff the mobile back into her sock. The door handle was wobbling frantically now, with much more force. Without warning, the screws locking the bolt in place bent and the door was wrenched clean off its hinges. Quinn yelped in surprise as the door swung back open. Hiram pushed the door aside and reached out for her, grabbing her forcefully on the arm.

"What are you—" Quinn started to say before a twinge of pain cut her off.

Hiram pulled her out of the bathroom and dragged her back towards the kitchen. Natalia was walking just in front of them. When they reached the kitchen, the others looked shocked at the sudden commotion.

"Quinn!" Ted exclaimed. "Let go of her!"

Hiram let go of Quinn's arm but remained standing right behind her to block any attempts to exit. Natalia was standing with her arms folded.

"I'm disappointed, Ms Miyata."

"What's going on?" Magda and Stefan had stopped working and looked on with concern and confusion.

"Do you wish to tell them, or shall I?" Natalia said, drawing out the moment.

"I don't know what you—"

"Oh, cut the bullshit, Quinn!" Natalia shouted. Quinn noticed that this was the first time Natalia had used her first name to address her. All pretence of respect through formality had gone out the window.

"Fine," Natalia sighed. "Hiram, if you would."

Hiram patted Quinn down, searching her pockets. Moving around to face her, he methodically made his way down her trouser legs, before settling on the lump sticking out from her ankle. Lifting the bottom of her jeans, he grasped the mobile phone from her sock and handed it to Natalia.

"What the—" Stefan murmured, seeing the burner phone in her hand.

"I would say you have a lot of explaining to do," Natalia said. "But I think it's pretty clear what this is. Let me warn you again about the dangers of crossing Sigma. If you call for help, from the authorities or anybody outside of these four walls, you can be assured it will not end well for you."

Quinn caught Ted's eyes. She recognised the look he was giving her. It was not one of concern but of pride. Despite the threat before them, she had almost found them a way out of this mess.

Natalia dropped the phone on the ground and stamped on it, cracking the screen. "I will say this for the last time, to both of you." She looked from Quinn to Ted, a finger pointed right at them. "Cooperate, and you live. That's it. That's all I'm asking." She picked up the broken phone and handed it to Hiram. "Dispose of this," she commanded.

It was another hour before Magda looked up from her tablet screen, nudging Stefan on the arm.

"Hey, take a look at this. I think I found it."

Stefan leaned in closer as she showed him what was on her screen. "I was right, it *was* a more recent entry."

Stefan looked at the number marked on the bottom of the scanned image. Fifteen. He referred to the table on the spreadsheet Magda had previously prepared.

"Benedict XV," he said.

"Yes," she smiled. "It's as if there was no mention of this ring at all until 1920."

"That we know of. There are still countless documents that haven't yet been digitised."

"True," she admitted. "But look at this extract. Tell me that's not describing this perfectly." She gestured to the ring that lay on the counter between them.

Stefan looked at the text she had zoomed in on. He read silently for a minute.

"Well?" Natalia asked impatiently.

"Hang on," Stefan waved her away. "Just a moment." His lips moved as he continued reading silently. He turned to Magda, who was smiling widely. "You're right."

The two shared a chuckle and a warm embrace. The breakthrough had finally come.

"If your keen eye hadn't spotted this ring on the end of that necklace, we would never have made it this far," enthused Stefan.

"Care to share with the rest of us?" Natalia chimed in again.

Stefan and Magda composed themselves and set the tablet down. Magda began to explain. "I knew I had recognised this ring before," she started. "Pope Benedict XV had mentioned it, or another ring just like it, in this document." She gestured to the tablet on the kitchen island. "The passage is of course written in Italian, but the translation is accurate enough to convey the description and the context. With the documents we have acquired from the Vatican Apostolic Archive, we are learning a lot about the Vatican. This here is one of the few times we have seen reference to collaboration between denominations, particularly concerning the Catholic Church. Pope Benedict XV writes about an agreement between the Catholic and Greek Orthodox Churches. Somehow, the Vatican had a number of Greek Orthodox artefacts in their possession. Perhaps as a result of cases like Bishop Thibaud de Castillon, who had acquired them at some point in their lives, only for the Vatican to lay claim to them after their death. The point is, Pope Benedict XV writes here that one such artefact was a pair of rings: one with an engraving of concentric circles, just like this one, and another with an engraving of a trident. Both have the sign of the Greek cross hanging from the ring like a small charm. Again, just like this one."

"They were kept on chains that were thought to be worn around the necks of priests," Stefan added.

"Greek Orthodox priests?" asked Natalia.

"Yes, presumably. Later in the text, it talks about the agreement. The Vatican found ways to keep items like this locked away in their vaults, without returning them to their original owners."

"Sounds like a few museums I know," said Ted.

"Pope Benedict XV wrote here that they agreed to keep them safe, as is the holy compass of the Church."

"The holy compass?"

"Like I said, it's not a perfect translation. I think they're referring to the moral compass of the Church. The promise they have agreed to keep."

"That's it? Seems vague," Natalia looked disappointed.

"Well, the translation isn't perfect, and there is some Latin mixed in."

"Of course. Just to make it difficult for us," said Natalia. "You know, a minute ago you two were acting like you'd found the missing piece to this whole thing. Sound to me like there's a lot of guesswork and unanswered questions."

Magda was smiling knowingly. "Then, I think you'll like this part." She showed a specific part of the text to Natalia. "I've translated it loosely as this." She transitioned to another window where she had taken the snippets of text and written in her translation below. Quinn and Ted leaned over Natalia's shoulder to see what it said.

With these rings, maintaining the compass of the Church, the kingdom taken by sea will be protected.

"The kingdom taken by sea," Quinn said. "Atlantis."

Magda beamed. "It has to be, doesn't it?"

FIFTEEN

Nestled along the serene banks of the Tiber River, Giovanni entered the small square that he had once frequented with his old colleague. The green space emanated an air of tranquillity amidst the bustle of the capital. A verdant haven embraced by nature; the park boasted lush greenery that swayed gently in the soft whispers of the river breeze. The feeling of walking back into this space transported Giovanni through time, bringing back memories of his long chats with Bianca. The two would often escape the sterile atmosphere of the precinct to catch up or hash out details of a tricky case together. The park was usually quiet, providing the perfect backdrop for a leisurely lunch without feeling like your conversation was privy to half a dozen strangers.

He spotted Bianca across the square, sitting on the same bench they had sat on so many times before. She was even sat on the same side she always had. He wondered if it was an unconscious choice, or if she was playing into the nostalgia of the moment.

She caught his eye as he approached, giving a wave as Giovanni made his way along the cobblestone path that ran around the perimeter of the square. The path was flanked by an array of tall trees, their outstretched branches providing a natural canopy shielding visitors from the sun.

"It's good to see you, Gio," Bianca said warmly. She stood up and welcomed him in with a hug. Giovanni was not the most comfortable with physical affection, but he accepted the hug. Bianca had been a good friend to him over the years. Giovanni didn't have a lot of friends, but Bianca was definitely one; perhaps even his closest.

"It's good to see you, too," he replied. Bianca sat down on the bench. "Please," she said, patting the space next to her. Giovanni sat alongside her, the view from the seat causing a host of memories to come flooding back.

"It feels strange being back here."

"Me too, actually," said Bianca. "I haven't been back for a while. It lost its charm a little." She smiled at him, a tinge of sadness showing in the corners of her mouth.

"I have missed this, you know," he said. "Not the job. But this."

Bianca reached into a bag she had propped up against the side of the bench. She pulled out a brown paper bag with two pastries inside, handing one to Giovanni. The cornetto she had handed to him was a staple of their morning meetings at this park.

"Don't get soft on me now. I need the Gio I remember. Laser focus, no emotion. You, know, the one who doesn't give a crap," she said tongue in cheek.

Giovanni paused as he bit into the cornetto. "I don't know whether to be offended or not," he said, with a mouthful of flaky pastry.

She laughed. "I meant it as a compliment." She nudged him playfully. "You're the best detective I've ever worked with. Trust me. They brought in some new guy last year—young gun; thinks he owns the place." She sighed. "I hate him."

"You don't invite him for breakfast?" Giovanni teased.

"Yuck, don't even joke about that. You know, one time he made a pass at me, on duty. Walked right past my desk and asked me out, out of nowhere. Creep. Should have seen his face when Andrea picked me up from work." She shifted and patted Giovanni's knee. "She says hi, by the way."

Giovanni nodded, finishing his mouthful. "So, tell me about Sigma. I read the files you sent."

"There he is!" Bianca exclaimed, letting out a hearty chuckle. "I knew the real Gio was still in there. I didn't even get to finish my cornetto."

"You know me, Bianca. I not one for small talk."

"I know, I know. I'm just busting your balls. And hey, I like your company. Give me a break."

"Look," Giovanni felt an unusual pang of guilt. "I'm sorry I've been a bad friend. I should make more effort."

Bianca shook her head. "You're not a bad friend. Just return my messages from time to time, okay? Maybe come over for dinner? Andrea is a really good cook."

"Okay," he said. "I promise."

"Good. I'll hold you to that," she replied with a mouthful of food. She wolfed down the rest of her pastry, dusted off her hands and got down to business. "You've got more experience in antiquities theft than anyone else on the force. That's why I need you. Interpol has been all over this case for years, and after a key arrest a couple of years ago it seemed to have cooled off."

"Lillian Pembroke," said Giovanni. "I saw the file from Mexico City."

"Exactly. Then Chief got a call from Interpol that her daughter had entered the country."

"It's not illegal for her daughter to travel."

"No, but she's on the watch list. She's a known associate of the organisation. With her mother in prison, she is thought to be heading up the operation."

"Family business," said Giovanni.

"We don't know how deep it goes. Could be her, could be others."

"Why doesn't Interpol just shut them down?"

"We don't even know if they're still operating the way they were. Maybe there's been nothing that sticks since Mexico."

Giovanni thought hard, staring out into the centre of the square where a stone statue was housed under a vine-covered pergola. His thumb moved to his chin as he began to rub the left side of his nose with his index finger. Bianca recognised his ticks and knew he was deep in thought. The silence grew as she gave him the space to work things through in his mind.

"I'm missing something," he said at last. "There's no evidence to suggest her daughter is doing anything illegal."

"I guess you haven't seen this," Bianca pulled out her phone and showed him a missing person report. "This was filed this morning."

Giovanni looked at the report. "Ponza?" He looked at Bianca quizzically. "Why did this reach your office?"

"Because Natalia Pembroke was spotted there. Along with a British former Special Forces soldier." She saw the look on Giovanni's face and followed up quickly. "Come on, you know this isn't a vacation between friends."

Giovanni looked at the report once more. "What did you have before this morning?"

"A feeling," Bianca looked sure of herself.

"A hunch?"

"Don't give me that, Gio. How many times did you have a feeling about someone, and while you're waiting for something concrete, they go and commit a crime? You know this isn't a coincidence. I don't know what's going on, but something is happening with this damn organisation. I'm right about this, and deep down you know it."

Giovanni looked at Bianca and smiled, before shaking his head as if thinking of something funny.

"What?"

"Seems like you're giving me all the answers," he said.

"So?"

"So, I'm wondering. What do you need me for, Detective?"

Bianca rolled her eyes. "Gio, come on. This is your world. You've got contacts. And I'm sure that only grew recently. I'm not going to ask how many of your clients have been antiquities collectors just like this one."

"I wouldn't tell you, anyway."

She shifted uncomfortably.

"What are you asking of me?"

"I just want you to shake some trees. Somebody knows something."

Sucking in air, Giovanni pondered it a moment. "Okay. I'll see what I can do."

"Thanks, Gio."

"I'll be in touch if I find anything."

Bianca hesitated. "Actually, that's the thing."

"What?" Giovanni raised an eyebrow.

"Chief needs to be in the loop on this one."

Giovanni scowled and bit into his bottom lip. He knew it was too good to be true. And he knew exactly what was coming next.

"I know you're not going to like this, but you need to come in and get the briefing from him, too. It's got to be above board."

Bianca was smart, and a damn good detective. But one thing that grated on Giovanni was her reluctance to go against protocol. Had the roles been switched he would have happily kept the arrangement between themselves. Not Bianca, though.

"You already told him?"

She nodded apologetically.

The precinct stood as an amalgamation of aged Roman architecture and modern facilities. Nestled amidst the hustle and bustle of the city, the building exuded an air of authority. Its exterior, weathered by time, boasted a facade of intricately carved stone, reminiscent of Renaissance design, hinting at the building's historical significance.

Giovanni stepped through the revolving door with trepidation. He had banked on never having to set foot in this building again. The spacious lobby, adorned with a balance of classical and contemporary architecture, welcomed him in and invited a walk back through memory lane. The floor was polished to a glistening sheen, the squeaking of shoes echoing through the impressive space.

The walls, adorned with commendations and accolades from successful cases of yesteryear, bore witness to the precinct's storied past. Giovanni passed the mahogany reception desk, manned by an officer he didn't recognise. The ambient buzz of radio communications blended with the clacking of keyboards and occasional phone rings. That particular dynamic symphony was a sound Giovanni had almost forgotten.

He walked into the bullpen, spotting his old desk. An officer he didn't recognise was sitting at it, their head buried in the monitor of the computer. Seeing the pair approach, they waved at Bianca, who reciprocated. They then cast a curious gaze at Giovanni, obviously wondering who he was.

"Caio, Tommaso," said Bianca.

"Caio," he replied, his eyes still firmly locked on Giovanni.

Giovanni glanced down at his old desk as he passed by. The transformation from his tenure was evident. What was once a neat and tidy workspace, with his belongings organised at just the right angles, was now a chaotic mess. Papers were strewn about haphazardly, partially covering the keyboard the officer was busy tapping on. A small photo frame stood upright to the side of the computer. In the photo was the officer in plain clothes, with a woman and child standing with him as they smiled at the camera.

Bianca moved to her desk, a comparatively tidy workspace to Tommaso's. She reached down to a set of drawers to the side of her desk, unlocking the top one with a small key. She pulled out the drawer and rifled through. Eventually, she plucked a file out, before locking it again.

"Chief's expecting us," she said. She led Giovanni to the Chief of Police's office. Giovanni felt a sense of trepidation as he reached the door. He had walked through that door many times before, and the conversation had always been a little frosty. He and the Chief, Marco, had never seen eye to eye, and even before he left the force they hadn't been on the best of terms.

He could see the silhouette of the old man sitting beyond the frosted glass of the door. Before he had time to steel himself, Bianca had pushed the door open. The grey-haired stalwart of the force looked up as the pair entered the room. He stopped what he was doing and smiled as he saw Giovanni.

"Giovanni," he greeted his former colleague. "It's been a long time." He reached out with a hand. Giovanni shook it firmly, the two maintaining eye contact throughout.

"Marco," Giovanni replied. "Must be getting close to retirement now?"

"Take a seat," Marco said, purposefully ignoring the question and sitting back behind his desk. "I understand Bianca has filled you in on the details."

Giovanni should have expected no less. In many ways, they were actually very similar; perhaps too similar. That had likely been part of the problem while they worked together. They both liked to get right down to brass tacks, but they were also extremely stubborn.

"I told him everything we know, plus the missing person report that was filed this morning." Bianca handed over the file she had brought into the room with them. Marco moved a plain white coffee mug from the corner of some papers on his desk to make way for it.

Checking the contents, he cleared his throat. "Ah, yes. Matteo Cattaneo. Twenty-one years old, local fisherman, no criminal record. No known affiliation with Sigma." He slid the file back across the desk to Giovanni. He took a look at the face of the young man who had gone missing.

"Are we sure this is linked to Sigma at all?" asked Giovanni.

"What, you think the guy just disappeared on a fishing trip?"

"Ponza is a small place," Bianca interjected. "According to police records, nothing like this has happened in a long time. Interpol told us Natalia Pembroke was spotted in Ponza the day before this individual's disappearance."

"It's an assumption," said Giovanni.

"It's a lead," insisted Bianca.

Marco slid two more files across the desk to Giovanni.

"What's this?"

"Two more missing person reports," the old chief said.

Giovanni scanned them, picking up the connection quickly. "They're both cops."

"Coast guard, stationed in Ponza," Bianca added. "Both went missing around the same time as the fisherman. They never returned from their shift."

"Are they all presumed dead?" Giovanni knew the answer to that question already.

"While you're out shaking trees with your contacts, I'm heading straight for Ponza to see what I can learn," said Bianca.

"You seem pretty fixed on this Ponza connection. But you contacted me before these reports were filed. What's the bigger story here?"

"Interpol," said Marco bluntly. "If this Sigma group are up to something, they want them put away for good. I'm putting my trust in you, Giovanni. Bianca was insistent on your involvement in this case, due to your experience in antiquities. If she's right, and it is Sigma we're dealing with here, I'm going to need you on the top of your game. Can I count on you?"

Giovanni looked at his former boss with a bitter taste in his mouth. This had been a pointless meeting. He hadn't learned anything new from the Chief's briefing, save for the information about the two officers who had also gone missing. And that was something Bianca could have looped him in on at the park. He knew the reason he was there. It was a power play. Marco just wanted another chance to remind him who he worked for. Screw it, he thought. May as well give the sad old man this one last moment of enjoyment.

"Yes, sir," he replied at last. "You can count on me."

SIXTEEN

The Belvedere Courtyard was renowned for its beauty, history, and stunning Renaissance design. As Quinn stepped into the expansive open space, she felt the grandeur of it wash over her. This part of Vatican City, much like the wider city of Rome, felt like a time capsule of art and culture.

Taking in the magnificent buildings surrounding the courtyard, she admired their splendid frescoes and decorative motifs. The elaborate balustrades, arches, and columns, each adorned with an intricate design, added to the wonder of the place.

"Quite a sight, isn't it," said Magda, catching the look of wonder on Quinn's face.

"I've always wanted to come here," she replied. "Just, well…"

"Under different circumstances," Magda finished for her. "I get it."

Truth be told, the courtyard was one of the lesser sights Quinn had witnessed in the last hour. On entering Vatican City, she had found the looming presence of Saint Peter's

Basilica stunning. That spectacle was topped only by the walk through the Sistine Chapel, where even Ted had looked awestruck at the masterful work of Michelangelo.

Those had been the heavy hitters, but there was something about this courtyard that really took Quinn by surprise. It was not the surrounding buildings, the marble sculpture that sat as the focal point, or even the sound of gently flowing water from the ornate fountains that did it. It took her a while to come to the conclusion, but it hit the moment she reached the far end and turned back to take in the view from the other side. The symmetrical layout of the courtyard was what made it so interesting. The view was spectacular from every angle.

Crucially, the Belvedere Courtyard served as the entrance to the Vatican Apostolic Library, which played host to the real purpose of their visit.

Approaching the entrance, Quinn felt a sense of reverence carried in the air, mixed with a deep-rooted anxiety that chewed her up from the inside. By the time they had stepped inside, her palms had become sweaty. The doorway itself, adorned with intricate carvings and symbols, stood tall and imposing. It was a testament to the institution's significance, and a cruel reminder of the weight of the decision each of them would make inside the archives. Morally, Quinn felt as though what Natalia had planned for them was on the tamer end of the scale—the woman's decisions to this point had resulted in the deaths of three innocent people, after all. However, for some reason, within this historic hall, the magnitude of the crime that would shortly follow seemed especially great.

She took a deep breath. Ted had reminded her not to blame herself for anything that was happening with this group. It hadn't stopped her from doing so, however.

Quinn was acutely aware that the atmosphere had changed the moment she had stepped foot inside the building. The ambient noise from outside had diminished, replaced by a subdued hush that echoed within the high-ceilinged halls. The architecture itself was awe-inspiring. Ornate vaulted ceilings adorned with intricate frescoes depicted scenes of religious and scholarly significance. The whole interior of the grand building had an ethereal quality.

Natalia led the group in the direction of a member of staff who was waiting in front of a wooden door. Quinn looked at the security guards standing imposingly on each side of the old door and knew this must have been the entrance to the archives. She remembered the plan they had spent the last few days preparing for.

After making the connection between the ring found on Botafoc in the shipwreck and the rings mentioned in Pope Benedict XV's entry, Magda and Stefan were adamant that the rings described there would be found here.

With these rings, maintaining the compass of the Church, the kingdom taken by sea will be protected.

The entry seemed clear. Somewhere in the heart of this building was the answer to the mystery they had been searching for—the location of Atlantis.

It was not as easy as just visiting the library and asking to view the rings. The archives were off-limits to tourists and visitors. Only scholars, historians, or academics were able to apply for access to the archives for their professional work. Even then, the application needed to be accepted and could take a while to process.

Stefan and Magda were eligible to apply as historians, and of course, they embellished a little in their application. The response from the Vatican was that the pair would be able to have access to the archives the following week.

This was an unsatisfactory response, at least to the ever-impatient Natalia. Of course, she was her mother's daughter, and she had ways to expedite the process and bump up the date of entry. In her words, there was only one thing the Vatican loved more than God. She was more than experienced enough in the art of persuasion and found ways to grease a few palms to get what she wanted. Quinn was not sure what the price had been in this case, but it had worked. It was probably just a drop in the ocean for Natalia and her family.

Natalia was not content with letting Stefan and Magda go in alone. It was clear she had her doubts about their loyalty, but the other thing causing a headache for her was Quinn and Ted. Maybe it was paranoia, or perhaps it was her recent history with the pair, but she didn't trust them to keep out of trouble while Stefan and Magda were inside the archives. Ted had attempted to flee at their first meeting, and Quinn had nearly succeeded in calling the police. If either of them tried anything and alerted someone to their plan, Stefan and Magda would be promptly arrested. Natalia would be back to square one.

The solution to that problem was to split Quinn and Ted up. She had told Magda to include a reference to Quinn on the application, citing her as her apprentice who was studying with them. 'Collateral' was the word Natalia had used when Quinn asked why.

"Caio," said the member of staff waiting by the door as they approached.

"Caio," Magda said, taking the lead.

"English?" the man asked.

"Please," she responded with a smile. "We're here to access the archives. Here's our letter." She presented an envelope with a slip of paper inside.

The man took the envelope and removed the paper, studying it carefully. A long and tense moment went by as the man's eyes flicked back and forth across the page. A stern look formed on his face, and he let out a heavy sigh. He then looked at Magda, then at Stefan, and finally, his eyes rested on Quinn. He looked down his nose at her, as though seeing through the group's ruse. He took another long look at the paper, inspecting the bottom of it closely.

"Okay," he said, a smile suddenly appearing. "Follow me, please." He turned to the security guards and nodded. "Please place any bags you're taking with you here for inspection."

Stefan went first, pacing his small bag on the table that stood next to the door. One security guard began rooting through it, while the other asked him to raise his arms. He obliged, and the guard began to frisk him.

The uniforms of the guards were unique, and it took Quinn a moment to remember that the Vatican was guarded by the Swiss Guard. The attire was reminiscent of the Renaissance period and reflected the origins of the Swiss Guard's service to the Papal States. The combination of blue, red, orange, yellow, and black in the striped tunic with puffed sleeves and beret-style hat was eye-catching and drew attention to the guards wherever they were posted.

Magda went next, followed by Quinn. The policy had been clear and came as no surprise; nothing would be taken in that could potentially be used to damage or tamper with any document. Pencils and paper were allowed, but the Vatican went so far as to ban the possession of cameras or mobile phones in the archives to protect the contents from the public eye.

"Thank you," the staff member said, placing a large iron key in the lock of the wooden door. The old mechanism clunked as the bolt shifted with a turn of his hand.

"We'll let you know when we're finished," said Stefan casually to Natalia.

"I hope you find what you were looking for," she replied jovially. Stefan knew the underlying sentiment; he had better find what they were looking for. "We'll wait for you where we agreed," Natalia added.

Quinn gave a half smile to Ted, but her eyes showed a mixture of apprehension and dread. "See you in a bit," she said. She followed Magda and Stefan towards the open door.

"Wait!" Ted caught her hand with his, taking her by surprise as he spun her around. Before she had a chance to react, he planted a firm kiss on her lips. His hand was still grasping hers tightly. After a moment, he took a step back. Surprised by the unexpected kiss, her eyes searched his, as though looking for a clue as to what to say. Her heart began to beat a little faster. How she had missed him.

"Good luck," whispered Ted.

Before Quinn had a chance to find the right words, Natalia exaggeratedly cleared her throat. Snapping out of the moment, Quinn hurried to the doorway and followed Stefan and Magda through.

The doorway led to a narrow stairwell that twisted down in a spiral to the sub-level of the building. The dim yellow hue of lights strung up along the outer wall illuminated their path. The member of staff went first, with one of the Swiss guards at the rear, shepherding the trio into the archives. The second guard had remained behind, standing sentry at the wooden door to keep unwanted visitors from following.

"Watch your step," their guide called from the front. "It is quite steep."

The Atlantis Idol

As they reached the bottom, the string of lights weaved around to reveal a narrow passageway. The ceiling was low, and Stefan had to bend down slightly for fear of bumping his head. A few paces in, a larger space opened in front of them. The ceiling eventually lifted as they entered the space. The staff member reached for a switch on the wall. It flicked on, bathing the first bookcase in light. A second later, a light a little further down came on, revealing the next set of bookshelves. Another light struggled to come to life, flickering as it tried to awaken with the rest of its kind that were switching on one by one down the long stretch of corridor. It was not until the final light flickered to life at the end of the long room that they could fully comprehend the scale of the ancient archives. Rows upon rows of wooden bookshelves stretched far and wide, some within reach and others locked inside cage-like structures, visible and tantalising close, but protected by a strong wire mesh. Quinn wondered if those were the collection of documents that were not yet seventy-five years old. The Vatican had a policy that any documents that hadn't yet reached this age were off-limits.

The room was dusty, and the scent of aged paper and leather bindings mingled in the air. Quinn could feel a contained excitement in Magda and Stefan. For a historian, this was a once-in-a-lifetime moment. Being here to study would have been exciting enough, given the library's rich history. But with the particular mission they were on, there was a palpable energy radiating between them. They were both clearly trying to keep their emotions in check in the presence of the Vatican staff member and his accompanying guard. Quinn was not sure how they might arouse suspicion from this alone, but they were trying to keep their feelings at being there covert all the same. Perhaps it was a mark of respect for the ancient tomes preserved in the archives, mirroring the ambience of solemnity and reverence in this venerable repository of wisdom. It was akin to the way one might enter a place of religious significance. It was a strange thought that observing silence was the default custom in such situations.

The group began to walk down the long corridor between the rows of bookshelves. Passing by the first of many, Quinn glanced at the spines of the ancient books. Each tattered volume was almost indistinguishable from the next; the faded beige of the binding was met with a nondescript and unlabelled spine. The Vatican Secret Archives was home to the largest collection of Catholic books, documents, and doctrine in the world. It was said to also boast letters from well-known figures such as Abraham Lincoln and Mary, Queen of Scots. Quinn wondered how anyone would be able to find them among this sea of books, files, and shelves. Like all libraries, they must have had a system. It was unlikely that the Dewey Decimal system was in use here. The best guess Quinn had was that the shelving units were organised by chronology.

"So, your application says you intend to study a collection of documents from Pope Benedict XV?" the man leading them through the corridor stopped suddenly, addressing Magda with a smile. He held his hands together in front of him always, even as he was walking. It was similar to the way a priest did the same, their hands concealed into the long sleeves of an alb. It looked strange to see it on a man wearing plain clothes, where his hands were in full view the whole time; he held them as if he were giving himself a handshake. Quinn found herself staring a little too long, the man's eyes moving to hers. She looked away sheepishly.

"Yes, that's right," Magda replied. Her voice betrayed the casual demeanour she had been trying to keep, a small amount of apprehension escaping with her words.

They had given that collection of documents in their application out of formality. The truth was that what they were looking for was not contained in any book in this vast library. Their destination was the vault that rested on this sub-level of the building, beyond the far end of the rows of shelves. Getting in this way was a means to an end. Of course, accessing the vault was out of the question, at least as far as those governing the Vatican were concerned. Stefan and Magda had other ideas, however. The only question now was how, and when, they would make their move.

The last few days had been one of intense planning for the pair, along with Natalia. They had dug up every photo, schematic, or account that existed on the interior of the Secret Archives. Most of that information came from the dark web. Plans for the two storage vaults under the Apostolic Library and Vatican Museum were drawn up during the papacy of Paul VI. The bunker that housed the vault was eventually inaugurated by John Paul II in 1980. It is a fire-proof, two-storey reinforced concrete structure that serves as the resting place of countless priceless artefacts. If the rings Pope Benedict XV had described were indeed kept in the Vatican, that was where they would be.

The member of staff unclasped his hands for what Quinn was sure was the first time in their short meeting. He took a pair of white gloves from his pocket and placed them on each hand carefully, stretching his fingers to reach the end of each space and ensure a tight fit. He then bent down to the bottom shelf of the bookcase they were standing next to. He muttered to himself in Italian, as though reading the spines of the books to navigate through them. Quinn bent down to see for herself, but, as before, there didn't seem to be any labels on the spines of these books.

Finally, the man stood up. He was holding a pale-coloured book with tattered edges. It looked in much better shape than a lot of the tomes resting on the shelves of the Secret Archives. It was, after all, only a hundred years old; a spring chicken of a document, by comparison.

He presented it face up to Magda, like a waiter presenting a fine bottle of wine.

"I believe this is the first book on your list," he said expectantly.

"Yes," Magda replied, looking to Stefan for his input.

"Excellent!" was all Stefan managed.

The man holding the book nodded, satisfied. "Please, right this way." He gestured to a small collection of desks poised in the centre of the long room, where a larger space between bookcases had been cleared for the seating area. "You can read the book at your leisure."

"Excellent," Stefan said again. Magda glared at him through her large round glasses, and the two shared an extended eye contact that gave Quinn the impression that they were communicating almost telepathically. She could tell from Magda's expression what that conversation was; Magda was telling him to keep it together.

They followed the man to the space and proceeded to untuck the wooden chairs that were nestled neatly underneath the desk, before taking a seat. The man gracefully placed the old book in the centre of the desk, the cover facing Magda.

"If you will," he said, presenting another two pairs of gloves to them to wear while they handled the book.

"Of course," Magda replied, putting the gloves on immediately to show her commitment to the preservation of the book.

"We will be close by if you need any further assistance," the man smiled, before leaving them to it. The Swiss guard remained close by as the man shuffled off, disappearing into the dark corridor with the low ceiling.

Moments later, the muffled thump of the old wooden door at the top of the winding staircase could be heard. Then two sets of footsteps, first quiet, and then more accentuated as the man returned with a newcomer. Walking behind the staff member was an elderly man with a scruffy grey beard. The bearded man was wearing a dark grey suit with a patterned tie and sported small round glasses. After receiving his book from the member of staff, he took a seat at the desk furthest from the trio, but not before first appraising them with a long hard look. Sat facing away from the man, Stefan didn't acknowledge him at all. Quinn gave a warm smile, and Magda a polite but hushed "Caio." Yet the man said nothing, simply sitting down and diving right into the book he had requested. Quinn noticed he was taking notes with a pencil on a notepad. The policy in the archives was strictly no pens allowed; once again, nothing that could permanently damage the books.

Stefan let out a frustrated sigh. They would have to wait a while to execute the next phase of their plan.

An hour passed, the trio making hushed idle chit-chat as Magda and Stefan took turns reading passages from the book and making notes on their laptops. The member of staff hadn't exaggerated when he said he would be close by. He and the Swiss guard had remained just within earshot, their presence felt throughout as they watched the trio while they worked. They had expected the close monitoring—after all, they were handling a rare and precious document.

There was a lamp on each of the desks, with a brass base and a short pull cord to switch it on and off. The elongated top of the lamp that housed the bulb had the iconic shade of green that was common in grand libraries. The bulb was hot now from prolonged use, the old book underneath bathed in its muted yellow glow. Magda read the pages carefully, tapping away on the laptop she had brought in with her. The tablet the pair had used extensively during the trip had been left back at the apartment; a conscious decision knowing the rules they had agreed to when entering the archives. The same was true of their mobile phones; any device that could photograph the space or any of its contents was strictly prohibited.

Eventually, the elderly man packed away his belongings and signalled for the member of staff to return the book he had been studying. The moment they had waited for had finally arrived. If they wanted to cause as little chaos as possible, they would need to take advantage of being the only visitors inside the archives, however short that moment was.

Quinn took the opportunity to stretch her legs. Part of the plan had been to spread out and make it impossible to keep eyes on each of them at the same time. She got up from the desk, her chair scraping loudly on the floor as she pushed back, drawing the attention of both the elderly gentleman and the member of staff. She smiled apologetically as she passed the man who had guided them there. She then moved towards the deepest end of the archives, on the opposite side from where they had entered.

Magda waited for the elderly man to be escorted back up the stairs before getting up herself and walking casually along the corridor between the two long rows of bookcases. The Swiss guard looked immediately uncomfortable with the sudden change in pace. Not one minute ago he had an easy task of standing nearby as four historians sat quietly at their desks. Now suddenly three out of four were up and roaming in all directions in a room full of priceless documents. He decided to follow Magda, who was closer to the exit. He stayed a respectful distance away, all the while ensuring his presence was felt.

Quinn was now at the far end of the underground room. She could see the panel on the wall where the door was that led in the direction of the secret vault. It was not obvious to the naked eye, but having seen the schematics of the place she knew what to look for and where. Knowing there was something behind that wall made the panel easy to find. Cleverly, the security panel that required a key card to access was not on the wall alongside the door but hidden on the back of one of the bookcases nearest the wall. Even then, as Quinn reached it, she had to brush away a layer of cloth from the back of the bookcase to locate it. With one hand keeping the cloth to one side, she bent down to inspect the security device. She suddenly felt some resistance in one of the front pockets of her trousers. There was something in there, protruding from the fabric as it tightened with the bend of her knee. She took her hand off the cloth, the material swaying back and settling into place, concealing the security panel once more. Quinn reached into her pocket and felt for the foreign object. Her fingers touched something metallic. It was round, and as her fingers ran across it, she recognised the feel of it. The chain links running down from the ring gave it away. She pulled the item from her pocket and inspected it. A keyring. Hanging from the end of it was a thin cuboid object. She had seen this before, or one very similar to it. Instinctively, she twisted the middle of it and a small part of the bookcase in front of her was illuminated with a feint purple light. A UV penlight. She used to have one just like it on her set of keys. But this one didn't belong to her. Where had it come from?

How had it found its way inside her pocket? It was then Quinn noticed the small tag attached to it. She brought it closer to her face, seeing that there was a handwritten note on it. Ted's handwriting.

For good luck.

She smiled to herself. How the hell had he smuggled that into her pocket without her knowing? And how had the security guard not detected it when she had been frisked? Her mind then flashed back to the moment Ted had caught her by the hand, spun her around and kissed her right before she went into the archives. That sneaky little fox. That had been after the pat down.

"Excuse me, madam," a voice came from beside Quinn, making her jump. She looked up to see the member of staff standing over her, his frame half-hidden by the corner of the bookcase. He had a look of suspicion on his face. He had startled her, and Quinn couldn't help but feel like he had returned freakishly quickly from escorting the elderly man out of the archives.

"Yes?" she replied as casually as possible, trying to ignore the fact that her heart was now beating very fast.

"Can I see that?" the man asked, looking at the UV penlight in her hand.

"Oh, it's just a light," Quinn protested, acutely aware that the man was accusing her of bringing in a prohibited item.

"Madam, I must insist," his eyes narrowed.

Quinn stood up and reluctantly handed it over. The man reached out to take it from her, but his hand twitched as he was about to grasp the item. His face contorted into a pained expression and his pupils went wide. A second later, he collapsed backwards, his limp body falling into the arms of Stefan who had been standing behind him. Quinn then saw what had caused the man to fall suddenly unconscious. There was a small syringe sticking out of his neck.

Laying the man gently down on the floor, Stefan looked back in the direction of the desks, and beyond that, the entrance to the archives. Quinn followed his gaze and saw the Swiss guard lying motionless on the floor. Magda was jogging down the corridor towards them.

Stefan then turned to Quinn, an unsettling smile on his face.

"Are you ready?"

SEVENTEEN

Quinn could hear her pounding heartbeat in her ears as the fear of the moment played havoc with her nervous system. Her breath was laboured as they raced down the corridor on the other side of the archive room. All three of them had memorised the schematics and knew exactly where they were going. With the member of staff's key card in their possession, plucked from a lanyard that hung around his neck and had been tucked into the inside of his clothing, Stefan had opened the door in the discreet wall panel and was leading the way towards the vault. He looked up at the security cameras that lined the corridor. It wouldn't be long before the security team in the Vatican would pick them up. He just had to hope they were able to move quickly enough to evade the gaze of anyone watching on the monitors. Hiram had assured there would likely only be one person stationed in the security room at any one time, and with so many cameras throughout the Vatican, it was unlikely they would be watching at the exact moment the trio passed by each of them. He also pointed out that it was far more likely that the cameras surrounding the perimeter of the buildings would be monitored more closely. Who would suspect that the Secret Archives, already manned by two Swiss guards, would require the most external monitoring that day? The only danger came when someone noticed that they couldn't get hold of the two unconscious men in the archive room and came looking for them.

It didn't take long before they had found their way to the vault. Standing before the large, imposing locked door, Quinn felt a cold tingle run down her spine. The surface of the reinforced steel door was cold to the touch, reflecting the faint flicker of dim overhead lights in the corridor. Its presence was daunting, a testament to its impenetrability. The steel face of the door was a mosaic of rivets and bolts, giving it an industrial appearance that was juxtaposed with the ornate building seeped with history that it sat within.

Magda kept putting her hand on the back of her head, as though feeling for something, or nursing an injury.

"Are you okay?" Quinn asked.

"I'm fine," she replied. "I think the tape just irritated my skin a little."

Quinn thought back to the small syringes full of tranquilliser they had administered to the two men in the archive room. The fast-acting serum had knocked them out instantly. They were non-lethal, Hiram had assured. Quinn didn't know whether the statement was more, or less trustworthy, coming from a killer. She supposed if he had intended to kill the pair, he wouldn't have been afraid to hide that fact.

To smuggle in the syringes, they had taped them to the back of Magda's neck; they had been hidden underneath her hair. Of course, the needles had been contained within thin plastic tubes to avoid any nasty accidents. Quinn hadn't seen the point at which she had removed them from the back of her neck, handing one to Stefan as they divided and conquered. The precision with which they had executed the plan both reassured and terrified her. She had come to expect this level of premeditated and clinically delivered violence from Hiram, but not these two. Just what else were they capable of? On the other hand, had they fumbled their way through it and made mistakes, the three of them could be on their way to prison. Should she have been grateful for that?

Now that part of the plan was over, Magda had tied her hair back to keep it out of her way.

"That's better." She turned her attention to the reinforced steel door of the vault; the next, and most difficult step in their plan.

Quinn was about to learn exactly just what else the pair were capable of, as they focused on the dials of the vault door. It was marked with a grid-like pattern and secured with a massive, polished brass wheel that was adorned with an intricate lock mechanism at its centre. The lock itself, a maze of tumblers and cylinders, taunted the trio, almost inviting them to try their luck.

To the side of the heavy door was a biometric scanner. To enter, they would need the fingerprint of an authorised member of staff. Luckily for them, Stefan had acquired just that. The man lying unconscious on the floor who had guided them into the archives just happened to be one such authorised member. Using a specially designed gelatinous material, disguised as a packet of gummy sweets, the fingerprint residue of oils and sweat had been carefully lifted. It was then gently pressed onto a clean film of silicone to retain the fingerprint pattern. To replicate the touch of a finger, the silicone would need to be pressed onto the surface of the scanner using a precise and controlled technique. To ensure that the print left behind a clear and accurate impression that mimicked the original fingerprint, it was crucial that Stefan didn't distort or smudge the pattern during the process.

He used utmost care in placing the copy of the fingerprint on the scanner. Then he waited with bated breath as the device read the print. A loud beep sounded shortly afterwards. A red light flashed on.

"Shit," Stefan cursed. He readjusted the silicone that contained the imprint and tried again. The scanner read the print once more, but this time it took a little longer to respond. Eventually, the device beeped loudly again, but instead of a red light, it presented a green light to confirm it had accepted the fingerprint. Stefan whistled in relief, giving a thumbs up to Magda who was poised by the dials on the steel door.

"Have you done this before?" asked Quinn.

Magda gave her a quizzical look. "If I hadn't, do you think we'd be here?"

"Right."

"Vault doors, like this, no," Magda added candidly. "But I've manipulated a few safes in my time. Sort of a hobby of mine."

"She's full of surprises, isn't she?" Stefan winked.

"I'll say." Quinn was impressed, but looking at the dials on the vault door and the tentativeness with which Magda began working on the first, she was worried about how long this was going to take. "How long does that tranquilliser work for?"

Magda shushed her as she put her ear to the door. "I'm going to need absolute silence for this next part, please."

The wait was excruciating, but after determining the contact points, figuring out the number of wheels in the mechanism and graphing the results with help from Stefan and his laptop, Magda had the first lock done. It had already been fifteen minutes since she began, and there were at least two more dials she hadn't yet touched.

The anticipation grew, and with it did Quinn's anxiety levels. Stefan assured her that they still had plenty of time before the tranquillisers would wear off on the pair in the archive room, but it did little to alleviate her stress.

Eventually, the last lock clicked into place, and a loud clunking sound echoed throughout the heavy metal frame. Magda stepped back, a wide yet surprised smile etched on her face.

"I did it," she breathed. She turned to see Stefan beaming at her. The two embraced with joy, letting out a squeal of excitement.

Stefan then approached the brass wheel and gripped it. For a moment he looked like the captain of a ship, standing proudly at the helm. He turned the wheel anti-clockwise with both hands, feeling the mechanism respond to his movement. The clicking of the steel bolts as they began to slide was a satisfying sound. Stefan continued to twist the wheel around and around, faster with each turn. The brass wheel then came to an abrupt stop, and he felt the resistance of the bolts reaching the end of the chamber. With a long exhale, he gripped the wheel and pulled. The door opened and the interior of the vault revealed itself to them.

Bright white lights flickered on, triggered by the vault door opening. The trio then took in the interior of the space.

The first thing Quinn noticed was the cool air that escaped, causing the hair on her arm to stand on end. The sudden drop in temperature was a subtle reminder of the controlled climate kept inside the vault—the secure room needed to maintain an optimal environment to effectively preserve the artefacts.

The walls were lined with built-in lockers that were constructed from a sturdy fireproof material and marked with identification numbers. A central console stood in the centre of the room, atop a long table that was presumably used as a viewing area. It reminded Quinn of a high-tech version of the parcel lockers she had used to send packages.

She then noticed the security cameras in each corner of the room, the red lights next to the lenses demonstrating the silent vigilance they maintained over the vault's contents.

Magda had wasted no time in accessing the central console. Presented before her was a computer terminal, the display showing a simplistic program that served as a database of artefacts. Various categories were shown for her to browse through, along with folders with collections of numbers that corresponded to the lockers lining the walls. She got to work navigating her way around the software. She was still wearing the gloves the Vatican employee had given her to handle the old book; a convenient way to protect her from leaving fingerprints at the scene as she tapped on the touch screen. Not finding what she was looking for right away, she found a search function. A virtual keyboard popped up, allowing her to input her key terms into the system. She typed in 'ring', which returned more entries than she had anticipated. She amended the search, adding 'cross', in reference to the Greek Orthodox cross that was connected to the rings.

One result flashed up. Magda's eyes lit up when she saw the description.

Pair of rings, adorned with Greek Orthodox cross. One bears a symbol of a trident, the other concentric circles.

There was a photo of the items attached. Magda clicked on the link and a high-resolution image slowly loaded from top to bottom.

"Bingo!" she exclaimed.

"What's the number?" asked Stefan hurriedly.

"One second." She tapped a few more times. "0178." She looked for the command to unlock the locker.

Quinn scanned the wall of lockers, tracking the numbers. She pivoted on the spot, following the numbers around one wall. "There," she said, pointing to the locker that matched the number Magda had just read out.

Moments later, the door to the locker clicked open. Magda marched over and opened it up. Inside was a small safety deposit box.

Quinn looked up at the red lights of the security cameras. They had been in and around the vault for some time now. Nobody had come for them yet, but she couldn't shake the feeling that they were seconds away from unwanted company.

Stefan cursed loudly. Quinn saw the pair standing around the safety deposit box on the table in the centre of the room, next to the console. It was still closed.

"Where the hell could it be?" Stefan's voice portrayed a mixture of frustration and desperation. Quinn looked closer, seeing what had got him so riled up. The safety deposit box containing the rings they were after was locked. It was just a simple lock that required a small key. However, the key was nowhere in sight.

"Check the terminal again," he demanded.

Magda raced back to the console and checked everywhere she could think to, but it was no use. After a few more taps she was back on the screen where the images of the rings were displayed. Quinn had a good look at them both, as though trying to see if that would help give a clue. It didn't. But there was something else that caught her eye. Something about the rings…

"What's that?" Magda asked suddenly. Something had drawn her attention across the room. It was coming from the locker they had taken the safety deposit box from. There was now a dim red glow coming from the cavity inside it. She went over to inspect it.

"What is it?" asked Stefan. His voice was notably more worried. Quinn sensed a real change in energy in the room. Not a moment ago, the other two had been full of confidence. Now, they appeared to be floundering, just as she had been.

A pit formed in her stomach as she noticed something on the monitor of the centre console. "Erm, guys."

Stefan whizzed around the table to see what she was looking at. A small message had appeared in the corner of the screen in bold red text.

Silent alarm triggered.

Stefan's face went pale. "What did you do?"

"Me? I didn't do anything!" Quinn protested.

"What's happening?" Magda called from across the room.

"She pushed the silent alarm," Stefan said, enraged. "She's trying to sabotage—"

"No, I didn't!" Quinn insisted, cutting him off. "It just appeared like that."

Magda turned back to the inside of the locker that was still glowing red.

"I don't think it was Quinn," she said. She thought for a moment longer, then dashed over to the table, picking up the safety deposit box. She hurriedly took it back to the locker and placed it back inside. The moment she took her hands away, the red glow disappeared. "How about now?"

Quinn looked at the screen once more. The bold red text that issued the silent alarm warning was gone. Instead, it was replaced by another message.

Silent alarm deactivated.

"It's been turned off," she said. "We must have triggered it when we took the box out."

"How does that even work?" Stefan was pacing the room like a caged animal.

"Maybe there's a protocol for taking the boxes out," suggested Magda. "Maybe we missed something."

"No shit we missed something!" Stefan shouted. "Where the hell is the key?"

"I think it's too late for that now," said Quinn. "Someone will have noticed that alarm. If they weren't coming for us before, they are now."

Stefan snapped, slamming his fist down on the table. "Shut up, you little bitch!" He looked her in the eye, a crazed look on his face. Quinn hadn't seen this side to him before. "You, and that little weasel of a man, Ted. I have just about had enough of the both of you."

"Stefan," Magda called from across the room.

Stefan ignored her. "Natalia was right about you. You have a knack for ruining everything you touch. Why can't you just do as you're told?"

"Screw you!" Quinn retaliated. "Ted and I didn't want anything to do with this." She felt her own rage building. "I hope they arrest us all. I'll tell them everything. It will be worth being locked up just to see them wipe that smug little look from your face."

Stefan looked like he was going to lose it. "Watch your tongue. Such an American, running your mouth off. Let's see you act tough when I wring your neck."

"Stefan!" Magda stepped between the two, facing her colleague with a stern expression. There was almost a foot in height between them, but Magda looked unfazed by him.

"Step aside, Magda. Screw the ritual. We'll find someone else. I want to get rid of this one now."

Magda put out a hand and made a shushing sound, trying desperately to shut him up. He was shaking with anger, and a long moment went by as Quinn wondered if Magda was going to have to physically restrain him. She didn't want to fight him, but she would if she had to. She wondered what Magda would do if that were the case. They could take him together, but if Magda sided with her colleague, it would be game over.

"Stefan," Magda said, lowering her voice in an attempt to dictate the tone of the rest of the conversation. "I need you to take a breath and back away two steps."

Stefan looked at her, then at Quinn. They were both looking at him expectantly. He did as Magda instructed, but not before cursing under his breath. He sucked in a deep breath, then let out a frustrated noise as he exhaled.

"We're done here," he said at last. "Magda, grab the box. We'll break into it later."

"We need to see what's in there," said Magda. "What if the rings link us to something else in this vault? We won't get another chance at getting back in here."

It was then that they heard a faint echo come from outside the vault. It sounded like a door slamming. Then, the sound of shouting. It was coming from the direction they had come from, back in the archives.

"No time," said Stefan. "We need to get out of here. Right now."

EIGHTEEN

Quinn was standing alone inside the vault. Not two seconds earlier, Stefan had heard the noise coming from beyond the corridor outside and bolted. Magda had then grabbed the safety deposit box and followed swiftly behind. The moment had been a real fight, flight or freeze moment, and Quinn found herself in a state of freeze. She cursed under her breath, chastising herself for stalling. This was unlike her. Truth be told, she was still reeling from the heated argument with Stefan. It had escalated so quickly. It was like a switch had flicked in the man's head, and a side he hadn't shown before was suddenly awakened. Had this been the real Stefan all along, wearing his friendliest face for as long as he could, before being able to take no more and snapping? There was something he had said in the heat of the moment that stuck with Quinn.

Screw the ritual.

What ritual? What the hell were Stefan and Magda involved in? And what did it have to do with her?

Something snapped Quinn out of her spiralling thoughts. Perhaps it was her subconscious willing her to get the hell out of there, or maybe it was the banging sound that came from somewhere much closer than before. She had to move.

She set off, leaving the vault behind as she darted into the corridor. Loud voices were echoing all around, bouncing off the old stone walls. She could hear the shouts of the people making their way swiftly in her direction. They were coming from the direction of the archives, following the route they had gone down to get to the vault. She looked around for an escape route and saw a door she hadn't noticed before. It was ajar, the darkness inside not giving away any clues as to where it led. Suddenly, a hand appeared, grasping the edge of the door, and pushing it open. It was Magda.

"Come on!" she called.

Quinn didn't freeze this time. Magda disappeared into the darkness beyond the door, with Quinn following closely behind. She pulled the door shut behind her. Their pursuers would surely follow once they saw that they had left the vault, but she thought it wise to buy them a little more time and not immediately give away their position.

Quinn's eyes struggled to adjust to the darkness as she tried to take in her new surroundings. She could hear the hurried footsteps of Magda racing off down what she thought to be another long corridor, based on the way the sound echoed and the footsteps growing further and further away by the second.

"Wait!" she called out. No answer came, and before she had time to think her legs had begun to carry her forward. She ran with her arms out in front of her to feel for Magda or anything else that might be ahead. She heard the muffled sound of people arriving at the vault. Quinn dared not turn back.

Up until the last few minutes, things had very much gone to plan. Plan A was to leave the way they had come in, bypassing the two unconscious members of staff in the archives. So long as they walked quickly and didn't stop to address the other Swiss guard at the entrance outside the old wooden door, they should have been able to get away before they realised they hadn't been escorted out. It would take them a while to discover their colleagues and realise what had happened. That had been the plan, but as they well knew, plans go wrong.

This eventuality had been planned for, but very loosely. Quinn knew that Magda and Stefan had identified an alternate escape route, but she hadn't known exactly where the door to it was. Much like the secret panel on the back wall of the archive room, the door she had just entered blended very well into its surroundings. Set off from the side of the vault, it had been hidden in plain sight. The vault door, with its imposing steel frame, had drawn their attention, keeping it for the duration of their time manipulating the lock to access the vault beyond.

Trying hard to remember the schematics of the building, something cold and metallic struck her knee. A loud clunk sound accompanied the searing pain that shot through her leg. She stumbled, her hand hitting the ground hard as she caught herself from falling over. Reaching out to the source of the object she had collided with she felt a series of metal pipes lining the lower part of the wall. It jogged her memory, triggering a snapshot of the diagram she had seen that presented the layout of the sub-level of this very building. Her surroundings suddenly made sense. She was in the service tunnel that ran underneath the Apostolic Library, around the edge of the Belvedere Courtyard, eventually reaching the Sistine Chapel, and beyond that, Saint Peter's Basilica.

The Atlantis Idol

"Still with us, Quinn?" Magda's voice echoed through the long drab tunnel.

Quinn let out a wince of pain, pushing her hand off the floor to get her back to her feet. She was acutely aware that Magda's voice had been distant, and there seemed to be no attempt by her to retrace her steps to check on Quinn personally. At this point, Quinn knew the score; Magda may have cared for her wellbeing, but not enough to risk her own capture. Stefan had made it clear that she was dispensable—perhaps Magda felt the same way.

She tried running again, but the pain in her knee was intense. Nothing was broken, she was sure of that, but she had caught it in such a way that running would be extremely difficult for the next few minutes. She hobbled onward, hoping with every step that she wouldn't hear the door to the tunnel being wrenched open. She had put some distance between herself and the entrance now, but in her current state, she would be a sitting duck.

She could hear Stefan's voice for the first time since leaving the vault, ushering Magda to hurry up and catch up to him.

"Come on," Quinn said to herself under her breath. "Come on." She willed herself to keep going, the pain lingering with each step. Her mind raced as she fought onward. The sound of Stefan's voice had triggered a replaying of the last moments inside the vault again in her brain.

Screw the ritual. We'll find someone else.

Quinn couldn't shake the words from her head. She began to spiral, second-guessing everything about this whole expedition. Natalia had been so insistent that she needed Quinn and Ted to assist in the hunt for Atlantis. She had doubted it at the time, but why else would the woman have insisted? Why would she have flown Quinn halfway across the world? Natalia had said that she owed her. She was bitter about the fact her mother was in prison, yes, but a woman like her, with the money she had and the power that came with that—if she needed help to find the ancient city, there would be much more capable people who were willing to do so: Magda and Stefan for one. Why did they need Quinn's help? They were the experts. But then again, she had steered them in the right direction after Stefan had misinterpreted the documents that hinted at the destination of Botafoc's ship. He had wanted to go west from the Pillars of Hercules, towards Portugal. It was she who had pointed them in the direction of the real ancestral home the documents were citing, the Vatican.

Screw the ritual. We'll find someone else.

The words floated around Quinn's head once more. A realisation hit her like a freight train; a realisation that should have come to her much sooner than it did. Stefan had been bluffing. He had known all along that the Vatican was the ancestral home. He had probably known about Ponza too. He had made a deliberate error to convince Quinn that she was an essential part of the expedition. The truth was they didn't need her at all, or Ted. They needed someone for a ritual.

She remembered what Ted had told her about the book he had found, and how guarded Stefan had been about it. The signs were all there; this was a cult.

But what was the ritual? A sacrifice? Of course, she thought. The pieces were all coming together. Stefan and Magda wanted to find the ancient city to perform whatever violent act that served their mysterious cause. Who better to fund the operation than Sigma? And the bitter leader of the organisation knew exactly who she wanted to fill the role of the unsuspecting victims of said ritual.

Suddenly, the sound Quinn had been dreading came from the end of the tunnel she had been moments earlier. The door opened and the voices of those who had been pursuing them came once more. The dim light of torches danced on the walls and ceiling.

Quinn refused to look back. Her teeth gritted in determination, she pushed on. The tunnel wound around a bend. Her eyes had adjusted fully to the dark now, and she could see the faint outline of a connecting passageway. She stopped at the opening and heard footsteps receding into the dark. Magda and Stefan were not too far ahead. Quinn's leg had recovered somewhat, and she had caught her second wind. Magda was shorter than she was, and Quinn was confident she was fitter than her too. Stefan wouldn't wait for her, but he sure as hell would wait for Magda. Quinn could feel it, she was gaining ground on the pair.

There was a distinct change in the air in this new tunnel. The walls closed in, and the stonework was different there. It felt like looking into a deep hole, dug as part of an archaeological excavation, where different layers of rock indicate changing periods. Except, in this case, Quinn had ventured no deeper than she was before. It took her a few moments to realise where she had found herself. It was not until her hand felt the grooves of the crevices dug into the wall that she confirmed it. The Vatican Necropolis. She had just walked into a catacomb. The change in air came with a drop in temperature and with it the eerie feeling of being surrounded by death.

Quinn was having a horrible feeling of déjà vu, and she started experiencing flashbacks of walking through the winding catacombs that were hidden beneath the pyramid they had ventured into at Teotihuacan. Why did being with Sigma always seem to lead to places like this?

The shouts from the people behind her were getting closer. Quinn needed to keep up the pace if she wanted to evade them. She rounded a corner, following the contour of the stonework with her hand as she tried to work her way through. Eventually, she saw a light ahead. A sharp corner was illuminated by a dim bulb that hung around the corner. Rounding the corner, she found herself in the part of the Vatican Necropolis that was open to the public. Tours frequented the area throughout the day. She saw the flicker of two shadows on the wall: Magda and Stefan. They were gone in a flash.

Quinn hurried after them, just as she heard new voices coming from up ahead. A woman was speaking loudly in English, and then in Italian. Quinn rounded the corner quickly and found herself face-to-face with a startled tour guide. The middle-aged woman was surprised to see her come bursting out from the darkness, and the group of tourists even more so. One gasped, and another shrieked. Quinn stood still a moment as the group of ten or so tourists stared at her. One began clapping, mistakenly thinking the scare was part of the experience.

"Quinn!" Magda's voice came from the other side of the room. Quinn saw her waving her over, a wide-eyed look on her face. "Hurry!"

Quinn pushed through the small crowd of people still looking at her in confused silence. Moments later, the first of the Swiss guards that had been pursuing them emerged from the darkness, shouting after them in Italian.

Quinn followed Magda and Stefan through the winding path of the tourist route through the well-lit section of the catacombs. They passed a mural on the wall and found signs for the exit. Up ahead, the sound of radio static came suddenly, and another Swiss guard appeared. He was looking away from the trio and hadn't noticed them yet. He brought the radio to his mouth and began speaking into it. The next thing he knew, Stefan had barrelled into him, sending him flying. The shoulder barge knocked the unsuspecting guard to the floor, the radio clattering out of his hands and across the stone floor. The guard shouted after the trio as they exited the catacombs and made a break for stairs leading up and outside.

As they climbed the steps, the fire alarm sounded. The shrill noise pierced Quinn's ears. She kept up her pace, tailing Magda and Stefan, who seemed to know exactly where they were going. The shouts of the Swiss guards echoed through the winding stairwell behind them. They were very close now.

Still carrying the safety deposit box in his hands like a Rugby player protecting the ball, Stefan burst through the exit at the top of the stairs and into the sunlight. Quinn was just seconds behind him, the exit door swinging back on its hinge as she reached it. She pushed it open again and winced as the blinding sunlight hit her eyes. She had been inside for so long that the sudden light was an assault on her retinas. It was akin to the feeling of leaving a cinema during the day after a long movie.

Alarms were still blaring from inside Saint Peter's Basilica. Groups of tourists stopped and looking as the three of them hurtled through Saint Peter's Square. Passing the ancient Egyptian obelisk in the centre of the iconic square, the frantic shouts of the Swiss guards could be heard behind them.

Quinn could hear the sirens of police cars now. They continued running towards the far end of the square. Up ahead, the squealing of tyres was quickly followed by the roaring of an engine. A black Range Rover with tinted windows pulled up on the side of the road, causing two or three startled pigeons to fly in all directions to avoid being hit. The car came to a sudden stop, and the back door of the vehicle flew open. Ted was there.

"Come on!" he shouted, willing the group to make it before the authorities caught up to them. Hiram was at the wheel, gripping it firmly, waiting for the moment to slam his foot back on the accelerator. Natalia sat anxiously in the passenger seat next to him, watching as Stefan grew close.

Stefan hopped into the car and immediately pushed Ted back with a strong hand. His other hand still cradled the safety deposit box. The motion had made just enough room for Magda to jump in next to him. Ted looked out the window as Quinn was still a few feet away. The flashing lights of a police car reflected off the rear-view mirror, and Ted twisted in his seat to see it approaching at speed.

"Come on," he breathed, the tension building as he saw the Swiss guards gaining ground. She was almost at the car, and Magda reached out a hand towards her, ready to grab her and haul her inside. The guards were almost on her now, there wouldn't be enough time to wait for her to climb in before Hiram hit the jets.

Out of nowhere, a police officer intercepted Quinn from the side, tackling her to the ground. Ted's heart sank as he realised it was too late.

"No!" he screamed as the Range Rover took off like a shot and left Quinn behind. Ted looked out the rear window as the police officer pinned Quinn to the ground, a knee placed firmly in her back as they began to fix handcuffs on her.

Hiram spun the steering wheel and the car turned sharply into a side street, and then she was gone.

NINETEEN

The Range Rover careened around the corner, its tyres screeching as it left behind black streaks on the road. Hiram steadied the car and shifted gears as the sound of sirens came from multiple directions. Ted was still looking out of the back window, the image of Quinn being tackled and pinned to the ground burned into his mind. She had hit the ground hard, the officer using great force to dig their knee into her back while they wrenched her arms back to place her under arrest. The lasting image he couldn't shake was her face contorted in pain as they left her behind.

The vehicle hit a bump in the road and Ted was knocked into the air, his head banging against the roof. Nursing his injury, he promptly turned around and reached for the seatbelt to strap himself in. However, the safety feature locked in place as he pulled at the belt. Ted swore loudly as he continued to yank at the seatbelt until it finally yielded. He then fumbled around for the buckle, eventually feeling the satisfying click that it had been secured in place.

And not a moment too soon.

A speeding police car came from nowhere and slammed into the back corner of the Range Rover. The tough vehicle skidded violently from the sudden force, but Hiram fought the wheel to keep them from spinning out of control. The squad car that had hit them had bounced off, leaving a large dent in its front bumper. Glass from the passenger side headlight was shattered across the road. The crunch of the impact was immediately followed by the deafening sound of metal scraping against metal and the squeal of the police car's tyres. The Range Rover had fared much better in the collision and exited relatively unscathed.

Another police car approached from up ahead, cutting off their route. Having navigated through several small alleyways, Hiram had been forced to turn back onto a main road. Now that the authorities had caught up, it would be a hell of a task evading them.

Hiram glanced in the driver-side wing mirror. The car that had hit them was some distance behind, but it was picking up speed as it doggedly pursued them. He would have to find a way to shake them off, but the car heading against traffic in their direction was his immediate concern. With the speed they were travelling, combined with the speed of the oncoming car, he had just a few seconds to make a decision. He made his choice in just one second, slamming on the brakes, shifting down gears, and pulling up the handbrake. The car twisted violently into a ninety-degree turn to their left, rubber burning against tarmac as Hiram executed a pinpoint handbrake turn into another side street. When the car had levelled against the perfect angle to hit the opening, he released the handbrake and hit the accelerator again. The engine roared as the Range Rover lurched into the small single-lane street. Luckily for them, he had entered a one-way street the correct way, but to the group's dismay, they saw a slow-moving family car blocking their path ahead. Hiram pressed the horn firmly, giving a long blast, followed by shorter, more frantic ones. The car in front didn't react, and they were quickly getting boxed in. They passed a busy restaurant with patrons dining out on the pavement a few feet from the road. Hiram waited until they had passed them, before shifting into a lower gear and pulling the big car to the side. With one wheel on the pavement, they straddled the kerb and passed the other car. Ted watched out his window as the children sitting in the back seat of the family car looked on in shock at the imposing vehicle passing them. Hiram just managed to get ahead with enough clearance to tuck back in, narrowly avoiding a post box that was fixed to the pavement. Ted looked out the back window to see the flashing lights of the police cars behind the car they had just overtaken. There was not enough room for them to pass too, so for now they were stuck, giving Hiram a chance to put some distance between them. They were not out of the woods yet, but there was a shared feeling of relief inside the car.

"We have to go back for her," said Ted urgently.

Nobody said anything, their minds firmly in the moment.

"We can't just leave her!" he insisted.

"I'm sorry, Mr Mendez. She's gone," Natalia said plainly.

Ted looked at her reflection in the rear-view mirror, seeing how unfazed she was by it. He turned to Stefan and Magda, who were both intentionally ignoring him. Feeling completely alone and helpless, he punched the back of the seat in front of him: Hiram's seat. The large bald man barely registered it, his focus firmly on the road.

"Ted, I'm really sorry, but there's nothing we can do," Magda said quietly, still not making eye contact with him. "She'll be okay."

Ted dismissed her empty sentiment. How could she possibly know that? They had just broken into the secret vaults of the Vatican, stolen priceless artefacts, and attacked people in the process. She would be far from okay. Ted was sure she would be on her way to a local police station right now to be questioned and charged.

The sound of sirens was still strong and seemed to be coming from multiple directions, even now. They flew through a junction, running a red light at speed and narrowly missing a taxi, the driver of which gesticulated while beeping their horn ferociously at them. The police cars they had temporarily evaded were back, their flashing lights just visible in the rear-view mirror.

Up ahead, Hiram spotted an opportunity. Another junction was looming, the red brake lights of a line of cars glowing as they slowed down to a stop. The light had just turned green for the traffic to their left, who took off and crossed the junction. The whining noise of a Vespa engine came, as the rider twisted the throttle all the way up to get ahead of the pack. It was then that the others in the car saw the opportunity Hiram had spotted. A large tanker rumbled up to the junction, its many giant wheels crunching on the tarmac as it followed the stream of traffic. With a final look in his rear-view mirror, Hiram shifted down gears and slammed on the accelerator to get a quick burst of speed. Ted felt his body being forced back into the seat as he watched the tanker come perilously close. Finding the gap that he was looking for, Hiram pulled the Range Rover behind one car, inches in front of the tanker. Ted closed his eyes as he braced for the impact that would surely come. It was not until the deep horn of the giant vehicle sounded that he opened them again. The sound was coming from behind them. He looked back to see the tanker stopped in the middle of the junction, blocking the

The Atlantis Idol

entire road. The two police cars were nowhere to be seen, hidden somewhere beyond the tanker. Ted could still hear their sirens blaring, but as they put distance between themselves and the junction the sound grew faint.

Twenty minutes later, Ted, Natalia, Magda, and Stefan were standing on the pavement of a street they didn't recognise. Having decided to drop them off somewhere away from their apartment, just in case, Hiram took off in the Range Rover to do exactly what he had done once before with their boat in Ponza. Natalia had suggested he just abandon the car where he had dropped them off; the car would be firmly on the radar of any police officer in the city at this point, and he could end up driving himself into more danger. However, Hiram had other ideas. As he drove off, Ted wondered what the hell that man did next. Would he drive it into the river, set it on fire, or put it in a compactor and crush it down to scrap metal? He wondered if Hiram secretly relished this part of his job.

Magda and Stefan purchased hats from a souvenir shop on the way back to the apartment, along with a tote bag to place the safety deposit box inside. It all felt very amateur to Ted, but they did manage to keep a low profile all the way back to their base of operations.

"So, you're just going to let Quinn take the fall for it?" Ted questioned as they arrived back inside. He had kept his mouth shut the whole journey back but didn't wait a second longer to tell the group exactly what he thought of them.

"The police aren't stupid," Natalia replied. "They'll try and use her to get to us. And I'm sure she'll sing like a bird."

"I would, too," Ted's eyes narrowed.

Natalia flinched but caught herself before she got sucked in. "Mr Mendez, let's just be thankful it wasn't any worse."

"Any worse? How could it be any worse?"

"We could all be going to jail, for one," she said.

Ted let out a despairing sigh. There was no use in trying to reason with someone like Natalia. She was only interested in one thing: herself.

"Pout all you like. We got what we came for." Natalia saw the forlorn look Ted was giving the front door. "Don't even think about it. Just because Hiram isn't here doesn't mean freedom is that bit closer. Even if you made it out of here, you wouldn't be free. We know how to find you." She turned to face him as she drilled the next point home. "And we know where to find your friends. Carl and Eliza, isn't it?"

Visibly defeated, Ted said nothing. These people were merciless.

Satisfied she had got her point across, Natalia allowed herself a smug half smile, before asking Stefan to bring the safety deposit box to the kitchen. She was eager to see if the trouble of the day had been worth it. Stefan placed the tote bag on the kitchen island, carefully extracting the safety deposit box and placing it in front of Natalia. She appraised the simple lock that secured the lid shut.

"Should be child's play for you, Magda," she said. "Why didn't you bust it open when you were in the vault?"

"We didn't have time," Magda replied. "We weren't expecting the keys to be missing, and..." She put a hand on Stefan's arm, noticing him tense up at the mention of it. Natalia noticed it and gave a quizzical look.

"Things escalated a little from there," Magda clarified. "We realised right before we had to leave."

"You have what you need here?" Natalia chose not to dive further into that avenue of conversation. It could have been seen as a recognition of Stefan's discomfort on the subject, but everyone in the room knew it was simply because Natalia didn't care.

"Of course," said Magda.

"Then what are you waiting for?"

Magda chewed her lip. She was excited to get to work on the lock; that went without saying. There was just something about the way Natalia made demands of her that irked her. Natalia had made it clear from the start that she held the money, so she called the shots. But Magda was getting a little tired of being pushed around to fuel the power trip that stuck-up woman was on. They had been treated much better by her mother, Lillian, on the few occasions they had worked together. She was crooked too, of course, but Lillian at least had respect for her and Stefan.

"I'll grab my tools," Magda said at last, swallowing her pride.

Sitting at the kitchen island, Magda stretched her fingers as she prepared herself. She loved history. She loved the discovery of information, of understanding more about the world and of cultures past, as well as and the parts that lived on. But there was something special about the work she did with her hands. Working out in the field, researching, and working alongside archaeologists, that was where she got her kicks. It was there she could interact with history in such a tangible way. She supposed that was why she had taken to manipulating and picking locks as a hobby. It had started as a child with the Rubik's cube she had been given on her birthday. It had taken her months of trial and error, but that first time she cracked it gave her a feeling unlike any other. Now she could solve it absentmindedly in under a minute. The cube, locks, history; all of it was a puzzle to solve. She was in her element as she picked up her tension wrench.

Inspecting the lock, she was satisfied that it had been kept in good condition. That was the first thing to check, always—rusty locks were no good for picking. Nothing a little WD-40 couldn't solve, but since she didn't have any of that to hand, she was thankful it was not required here.

Inserting the tension wrench into the keyway and turning it gently, Magda felt how the plug shifted inside the lock. A few moments later, she had got a good sense of the position where the pins were bound in the lock mechanism, freezing it and stopping the plug from turning. Inserting a pick into the keyway as she held the tension wrench steady, it didn't take long for her to identify the binding pin. Maintaining consistent pressure with the tension wrench, Magda slowly lifted the first binding pin little by little. The tension wrench began to turn the plug very slightly, and then the first pin was set in place. She carefully repeated this process calmly and methodically, setting all the pins until the lock opened with a satisfying click.

She let out a long exhale, as though she had been holding in that breath the whole time. Magda was eager to open the lid and see the contents they had gone to so much trouble to obtain. She could sense Natalia lurking, expecting to have the right to do the honours. Magda denied her, lifting the lid herself. The room grew silent as the group took a collective breath. Inside the box was a layer of cloth, with two gold rings nestled inside.

Without a second thought, Natalia reached over and plucked the first ring, before holding it up to the light. She inspected the Greek Orthodox cross hanging like a bracelet charm from the ring and saw the engraved concentric circles on the ring's surface. It was identical to the one they had retrieved from the shipwreck.

"Nicely done," Stefan said, as Magda tidied away her tools.

"Piece of cake," she replied. "You just watched me break into a vault, and this little lock impresses you?"

Stefan shrugged. "I didn't say that wasn't impressive too."

There was an obvious change in Stefan the moment they had broken open the lockbox and seen the rings. The man had been quiet since leaving the Vatican, and downright irritable when addressed directly. Ted could sense something was not quite right with him, as though this particular part of the expedition had changed him. But the moment Magda lifted that lid, and the rings came into view, he was back. The transformation was instant.

"I was half expecting them not to be there," said Magda, watching as Stefan took the other ring in his hand and inspected it in the light. The two shared a warm smile. Ted recognised that look. Relief, mixed with excitement.

"Hang on, there's something else here," said Natalia, moving the cloth inside the safety deposit box. Beneath the material was a page of weathered parchment, crumpled and stained with brown blotches. She carefully lifted it from the box and saw the elegant cursive ink of the handwritten note adorning the page. After taking a moment to study the flicks and patterns that made up the handwriting, she picked out a few words that she recognised as Italian. She promptly handed the parchment to Magda, who read the note aloud, translating it as she went.

As per the agreement, I uphold my sacred duty to keep the secrecy of the site known as Atlantis beneath the church that bears my name.

"It's signed 'Benedict XV'."

A palpable energy built up in the room. This was the first time the word Atlantis had been used in writing. While they had been pretty sure that this was where they were headed, this eliminated any shred of doubt that remained.

"The church that bears his name?" asked Ted. "Benedict?"

"No," said Stefan confidently. "His family name was Chiesa. Giacomo della Chiesa was his full name."

"So, we're looking for a church named Chiesa?"

Magda whipped out her phone and performed a quick search. After a moment she turned to Stefan. "Do you want the good news or bad news first?"

"Good news."

"Okay. The good news is I've found a church named after Chiesa."

"Okay," Stefan started to get his hopes up. "And the bad news?"

"I've found like a hundred others too."

"Shit." Stefan's face dropped. He turned his attention back to the ring he was holding.

The air was taken out of the room as the task became more difficult once more. Playing with the ring in the light, Stefan looked deep in thought. Then the man's expression changed again, something catching his attention, almost as if the ring had changed form in his hand. Ted could see the symbol of Poseidon's trident prominently on the side facing Stefan.

Magda had noticed what Stefan was looking at too. "What is it?"

"I don't know," he replied, turning the ring slowly, trying to angle it to catch the light just right. "I thought it was just scratched up pretty badly, but that's not it at all." He caught the light on the inside of the ring. "Right there," he said. "You see that?"

Magda moved in closer. She squinted as she tried to make out what he was looking at. Then her eyes widened.

"Those aren't scratches," she agreed. "They're numbers." She turned to Natalia. "Check that one too. Right here." She showed the engraving on the inside of the ring Stefan was holding.

Natalia twisted her ring to catch the inside in the light. Sure enough, she saw the same on hers.

"124843" she read aloud. "Is yours the same?"

Stefan squinted as he read the small numbers. "No. 415758."

"Weird," said Magda. "What's that about?"

"A date?" Natalia suggested.

"No, I don't think so. Why are they so different?"

"Lock combinations?"

"But for what?" Magda asked.

Ted chimed in for the first time in the conversation. "Is there a letter before each one? N or W, maybe?"

Magda looked at the trident ring. "No."

Natalia cocked her head at Ted. She knew exactly what train of thought he was on and wondered how the hell he had been the first one to suggest it.

"Try both variations," Ted said. "See where it takes us."

"Both variations of what?" Magda looked puzzled.

"Coordinates."

Magda and Stefan shared a look, before turning their attention back to the numbers. Six digits: two for degrees, two for minutes, two for seconds. They fumbled to pull up the map app on their phones.

"Don't forget to convert it from degrees, minutes and seconds to decimal degrees first," said Magda.

"I know."

They each tried one combination. Magda tried the numbers from the concentric circles ring first, adding in those from the ring with the trident to the end. Her brow furrowed. "Hmm. This is putting me in Ethiopia. You?"

Stefan had finished inputting his combination. He was looking at his phone screen with the same expression he had moments earlier when discovering the engraving on the inside of the ring.

"Holy shit," he breathed.

"What?" Magda put her phone down and hurried over to her colleague. She looked at his phone screen as he zoomed out to reveal the outskirts of Rome.

"It's right here."

TWENTY

Watching the clock on the pale grey wall tick away the minutes, Quinn sat at the bare table in the interrogation room. A single overhead light, harsh and unyielding, cast a focused beam onto the surface of the table. It left shadows under her eyes, accentuating her exhaustion. She had been kept waiting for hours, with no hint as to what fate awaited her. The overall ambience of the room was one of controlled intensity. The minimalist design and deliberate discomfort contributed to an environment meant to elicit information while maintaining a sense of authority. The chair she was sitting on felt internationally uncomfortable, lacking any passing semblance of luxury. The vacant identical chair across the table from her waited ominously.

Quinn sensed it was all an intimidation tactic, but little did the authorities know it was not needed. She was no hardened criminal; she was already terrified. Frankly, all she wanted to do was talk to someone and give them as much information as possible to help track down the others, free Ted and put an end to this nightmare.

The hands of the clock ticked on and on, the sound all Quinn could hear while she waited endlessly. In that time, she had been granted a short toilet break by a surly officer, and since returning to the room the noise from the clock had seemed to intensify. The soft ticks now sounded like loud clunks in her head.

She flexed her wrist, the cold metal of the handcuff that chained her to the table cutting into her skin. The chain was short, giving her just too little freedom of movement in her left arm. She glanced up at the CCTV camera in the corner of the room, the lens pointed in her direction and the little red light next to it reminding her she was being watched.

The worst part of being in the room was the large one-way mirror that spread along one wall. The camera was one thing, but knowing there might be any number of people on the other side of the mirror watching her throughout her wait was unnerving.

The door to the room opened suddenly, catching Quinn off guard. In stepped the police officer who had escorted her from the bathroom earlier, followed by a man Quinn hadn't seen before. A little older than the officer, perhaps early to mid-forties, the man was in plain clothes. A detective? Or was this a lawyer that had been sent to attempt to give her a semblance of defence? Not that it mattered; she was guilty, and there would be zero doubt in anyone's mind about that. He sat down across the table from her, placing a briefcase to the side and setting up a recording device. He said something in Italian to the officer, who took out a small key and unlocked Quinn's handcuffs. She nursed her hand, feeling a little stiff and sore. The officer left the room, giving a subtle nod to the man at the table on the way out.

"Sorry about the handcuffs," the man said in heavily accented English. "Can I get you a glass of water?"

The Atlantis Idol

Quinn was still trying to get a read on the man. "Erm, no, I'm fine."

The man saw her cautiously eying the recorder on the desk. "Don't worry about that. It's just a formality. Let's get that part over with, shall we?"

Quinn looked confused. "Okay."

The man had reached over to hit the record button before she had time to prepare herself. He checked the time on the wall clock, before announcing the date and time into the recorder. He then addressed Quinn, his eyes piercing. "Ms Miyata, in your own words, please state for the record why you visited the Vatican Apostolic Archives today."

Quinn felt a lump form in her throat. She had her answer; this guy was a detective, not a lawyer. It seemed like he was getting right to the point, wasting no time in getting her confession on record so they could pin the whole thing on her and be done with it.

She cleared her throat, buying herself some time before replying. The way he was expectantly looking at her was intimidating. Should she try and defend herself? Or did he already know everything? Screw it, she thought; she would just be honest.

"We were looking for an artefact that was kept inside the vault."

The man across from her took out a notepad and pen from his briefcase and began scribbling notes as she talked. He stopped momentarily.

"Two men were found unconscious inside the archive. Was that your doing?"

Quinn looked at him with a calculating look, before continuing. "Not me, but the people I was with," she clarified. "See, I didn't have a say in the matter. The people who did this, they have been holding a close friend of mine and me against our will for—"

He put a hand up to stop her. She paused mid-sentence, wondering if he was going to interject with a comment about what she had said. The two waited a moment in silence, the man's hand still raised. A few seconds later the lights in the room flickered off and on again. Lowering his hand, a wry smile crept on his face, and he moved the hand to the recorder, hitting the button to stop recording.

"What's going on?" Quinn asked, completely thrown by what was happening.

"Once again, I'm sorry, Ms Miyata. I had to wait while my colleague cleared the viewing room." He gestured to the one-way mirror running the full width of the wall to his right, and Quinn's left. "I had to put on a show for the officers who brought you in, but I think we're in the clear now." He nodded at the one-way mirror. "Thank you, Bianca."

Quinn looked at the mirror, feeling as though she also needed to address the unseen colleague behind the glass. She smiled awkwardly at it.

"Let me start things properly. My name is Giovanni Rossi. I'm currently working on a case with Interpol investigating the activity of Sigma."

Quinn's eyes widened at the mention of the organisation's name. Not only did this man know about them, but they were investigating them. "Interpol?"

Giovanni nodded. "They've been tracking their activity for some time. It's quite a secretive organisation, no?" He opened the clasps on his briefcase, pulled a file from inside and took out some papers, sliding them across the table to Quinn. "It's all quite shady if you ask me."

Quinn took one of the pieces of paper and looked at the text written on it. It detailed a case of stolen antiquities in

Dubrovnik. She took another one and proceeded to read through a report of an archaeological dig that hadn't been sanctioned by all the required parties. The report brought to light concerns about illegal excavations and the looting of artefacts. In the top corner of each page, written in red pen was the word 'Sigma'.

"There are plenty more where that came from," said Giovanni. "They've got quite the reputation."

"If that's true, why hasn't Interpol arrested them before?" Quinn lifted her head from the papers, casting a curious eye on the security camera in the corner of the room. The red light by the lens had switched off.

Giovanni twisted his head around to follow her gaze. He realised what she was looking at. "Only a select number of people in the building are aware of the case. Hence the secrecy."

"You work for the police?"

Giovanni smiled. "For now, yes." He shifted in his seat. "I'll be transparent, as a gesture of goodwill. But I will expect honesty in response, as a courtesy."

Quinn nodded. She had no reason to keep secrets.

"I specialise in the illegal trade of antiquities. And I have a lot of questions about this organisation you are a part of."

"I'm not part of it," Quinn said firmly. "And neither is Ted."

Giovanni cocked an eyebrow and wrote the name down on his notepad.

"My friend. He's still with the others."

"The others. Tell me about them."

Quinn let out a long exhale, as though wondering where to start, or even how to. "Natalia Pembroke. She's the daughter of Lillian Pembroke, the leader of Sigma."

"I know of her, yes," said Giovanni. "She's incarcerated in a Mexican penitentiary."

"That's right," said Quinn. "Ted and I were involved in that, too. Again, completely against our will."

Quinn proceeded to tell Giovanni everything. She spared no detail, filling him in on everything from their first brush with Sigma in Mexico to this expedition. She talked about the bishop's treasure, the documents that hinted at the existence of Atlantis, Ponza and the Vatican vault. When she had finished, Giovanni scratched his head.

"Your friend will be able to vouch for you saying all of this was against your will?"

"Yes," she replied. "You only need to look at the police reports from Mexico City to see this is a repeat crime."

Giovanni nodded. "Now, there's something I'm failing to understand. Why you and your friend?"

"I'm sorry?"

"The people you described; they all play a role in this organisation. The historians, the Special Forces soldier, the financier. I don't mean to sound presumptuous, but I don't see where you and your friend fit in."

Quinn was not sure whether to be offended by the statement. The truth was, she had wondered the same thing herself.

"Revenge," she said. "Natalia blames Ted and I for what happened to her mother. That's the other thing I haven't told you. There's something weird about this expedition they're on. Things got a bit heated in the vault. I had an altercation with one of the historians, Stefan. He lost his temper and said something about a ritual. Mentioned that he would kill me there and then and find somebody else for it."

Giovanni squinted, as though sensing he had misheard her. "A ritual?"

"I was thinking about it. Ted found one of Stefan's books. The man was very protective of it."

"What kind of book?"

"It talked about Atlantis. But the things it was saying, the way it was written. It was quite…" she struggled to find the right words. "It gave me the vibe of a secret society of some sort."

"A cult?"

She nodded.

"Hmm." Giovanni rested his thumb on his chin as he scratched his nose with his index finger. "It's not unusual for wealthy people to be involved in such things."

"No," Quinn corrected. "I don't think this is Sigma. Natalia is using Stefan and Magda for their knowledge. They're using her resources to find the place to conduct their ritual."

"Does she know?"

"Of course. And that answers your question. Why us."

"Revenge, you said."

"Yes, and this is how she will enact it; by handing Ted and me over to this cult they're a part of."

"That seems a stretch," said Giovanni. He saw Quinn's face drop. "But I'm inclined to believe you."

Quinn felt relief wash over her. This whole time she had felt helpless. Now there was somebody on her side. She was desperate to catch up to the others, to make sure Ted was okay. If her suspicion about Stefan and any cult he may be a part of was right, she had no time to waste.

"And that brings us nicely to my next question," said Giovanni. "What now? They took artefacts from the vault. A pair of rings, you said?"

"Yes. They didn't get the safety deposit box open while I was with them, so they hadn't seen it then. But I'm sure they have by now."

"Seen what?"

Quinn chewed her lip. "Can I have my belongings?"

"What? No," Giovanni scoffed. "Tell me first, then let's see if I'm satisfied with what you say."

"Oh, I'm sure you'll be satisfied," said Quinn.

Giovanni eyed her carefully, and Quinn could read the thought process he was going through. Eventually, he stood up and stepped outside the room. Quinn could hear him calling to someone.

Returning to the room, Giovanni sat back in his chair. "I'm placing a lot of trust in you," he said candidly.

Quinn said nothing. She was not about to say thank you for the gesture, but she got the message loud and clear; he was reminding her just how easy it would be to revoke any privileges or niceties he had granted her thus far.

A few minutes later, a police officer entered the room and returned the items that were taken from Quinn's pockets during the arrest. She quickly found the UV penlight keyring, taking it in one hand while rolling up her sleeve.

Giovanni looked perplexed.

"When I was in the vault I saw images of the rings on the computer," said Quinn. "The rings have an inscription on the inside. I managed to scribble it down while the others weren't looking. She pressed a button on the penlight and a soft purple light lit up the skin of her forearm. Giovanni leaned in closer to see the faint outline of a number. Quinn scanned the light slowly across her arm. The handwriting was far from neat, but the numbers could be made out clear enough.

415758

124843

"What am I looking at?"

"Coordinates," said Quinn. "41° 57' 58", 12° 48' 43". Degrees, minutes, seconds."

Giovanni said something in Italian under his breath. He looked dumbfounded by what he was seeing.

"These people are smart," she said. "It won't have taken them long to work this out." Quinn clicked the penlight off, looking him dead in the eyes. "You want to take down Sigma? That's where they're headed."

TWENTY-ONE

Giovanni escorted Quinn out of the police station and led her to his car. Quinn couldn't help but notice the fishy looks she received from a couple of officers on the way out of the precinct. Were they are surprised as she was that she had been released so quickly? She had just broken into the Vatican secret vault, after all.

Walking through the car park, they passed a row of squad cars, before Giovanni stopped at a white Fiat 500. The car did not scream detective; it didn't even seem to fit the archetype of a typical unmarked police car. Maybe that was the point. He unlocked the car with the key in the driver's side door. It felt odd to Quinn that people still had cars old enough to not have a key fob with remote locks these days. At least, outside of classic car collectors.

Giovanni opened his door but stood and waited for her to climb inside before he got in himself. The look he gave her as he did so told her everything at that moment: he still didn't trust her, not fully. He waited for Quinn to get in and shut the door behind her before doing the same. As he squeezed into his seat alongside her, Quinn became acutely aware of how cramped the little car was. She reached her arm back, feeling for the seatbelt. She pulled it around her and had an awkward moment of trying to buckle it in while Giovanni was blocking it slightly with his body. She nudged it past him, and the buckle clicked it into place. Giovanni didn't even bother with his seatbelt until long after he had finished reversing out of the parking space and turned into traffic.

They arrived at their destination across the city sometime later. Quinn looked out the window at the apartment building they had parked opposite. When Giovanni had told her they wouldn't be going straight for the location the coordinates on her arm pointed to and would be making a stop at his apartment first, she had protested. Eager to catch up with the others, or more specifically, with Ted, she wondered why on earth they would make a detour. Time was of the essence. Giovanni had insisted that he needed to make a stop at his place first, to prepare themselves. The sort of preparations he was talking about became immediately clear when they entered the apartment and Giovanni headed straight over to a safe, where he extracted a handgun.

"Don't officers carry firearms on their person?" Quinn asked. She didn't know much about the police force, but it did seem strange that he would have his gun stored where he lived, not in some locker in the precinct.

Giovanni eyed her carefully as he adjusted the holster inside his jacket. He could see the doubt creeping through her mind. "This isn't standard issue," he said, coming clean. "Polizia di Stato issues a Beretta 92FS. Same as your American police. They call it the M9. It's durable and reliable, 15-round magazine. I never really liked it, though." He inspected the revolver he had retrieved from the small safe, opening the barrel to check the high-calibre bullets nestled inside, before flicking his wrist to lock it shut. "I prefer something with a bit more…" he made a face and a fist gesture with his other hand. Quinn got the message.

"And they let you use what you want?" Quinn probed.

Giovanni smiled. "You wouldn't believe the paperwork involved," he said. "But eventually, yes. The force like you to have a weapon with sufficient ammo in the clip."

"That's not something you're worried about?" Quinn surprised herself at her tenacity in her line of questioning.

Giovanni smirked to himself as he placed the revolver into the holster and wrapped his bomber jacket around it to conceal it. "No," he said. "With this, it only takes one bullet. And I don't miss."

The man made his way across the apartment and started packing things into a go-bag. Quinn took a moment to take in the space. The apartment was quite characterless, the decor reminding her of a low-budget hotel room. A landscape photo of a mountain range hung from the wall above a small sofa. She craned her head back to peek into the kitchen and noticed two more small rooms leading from the living room, which served as the main hub of the apartment and focal point as you entered through the front door.

"Can I use your bathroom?" she asked.

Giovanni nodded.

"Thanks." She took a chance on one of the rooms leading off from the living space and poked her head around. She had guessed wrong, finding herself looking into Giovanni's bedroom. She doubled back and tried the other door, finding the bathroom.

As she sat on the toilet, she let out a long exhale. She found herself needing to take more and more moments like this to recentre herself and avoid spiralling out of control. She had spent so long trying to come to terms with everything that had happened the last time she had crossed paths with Sigma.

Her coping strategy had been one of avoidance, and it had almost cost her relationship with Ted. She supposed she had handled it about as well as anyone could expect from a person who had survived a kidnapping and attempted murder. There was more that had gone unprocessed, but Quinn had tried to blank that out. She had chalked up what they had witnessed inside the heart of the pyramid in Teotihuacán to nothing more than shock. As far as she was aware, even Ted had done the same. Maybe they should have talked about it more.

At that moment, her mind did something it hadn't done for a long time. It flashed back to the moment the mercenary Sigma had hired reached out for the Heart of the Jaguar—a jewel of unparalleled beauty that had once been sought by conquistador Hernán Cortés—and a strange energy seemed to pulse out of it into the man, consuming him. Quinn and Ted hadn't talked of the encounter again, but she knew that they would never forget the way the man's eyes glowed after touching the jewel, and how he had become instantly aggressive, almost rabid with rage. It was as though the jewel had passed on some kind of supernatural strength to him, one that he couldn't control. Of course, that was nonsense. It had to be. There was no explanation for it.

A knock came at the door. Quinn was suddenly pulled back into the present. She finished up and flushed the toilet. When she opened the door, Giovanni was waiting on the other side.

"Let's go," he said.

As they headed for the door, a thought flashed in Quinn's mind. She was putting a lot of faith in this man. While he was be acting in the name of the law, he was the only other person who knew the situation they were in. Quinn wanted a backup, just in case. She looked at the laptop sitting on the desk in the corner of the room.

"Hang on," she said. "Can I please use your computer for a moment?"

Giovanni narrowed his eyes, as though trying to read her mind. At last, his face relaxed. "Sure."

She fired up the laptop and opened a private window in the browser. She no longer had her phone, thanks to Natalia. The only way to get in touch with someone she knew was by logging into one of her social media profiles and messaging through that. She quickly faced a hurdle, as the platform required her to access a code sent to her email to verify it was indeed her trying to log in.

"Shit," she cursed under her breath. She opened another tab, praying she wouldn't face the same issue when accessing her email. Luckily for her, her email was not as secure. There was the email she needed, informing her that someone was trying to access her account from an unfamiliar location. "Yes, me," she muttered, entering the code to grant herself access.

Upon accessing her account, she went straight for the messages section to begin a new draft. She hesitated a moment while she considered the recipient. She decided to send it to both Eliza and Carl. But just before she did, she noticed two unread messages. One was from Carl. She opened it to see a short message from him.

Hey, have you heard from Ted? Dude took off one evening and we haven't seen him since. Heard you guys might be back on and figured he was with you. Let me know, getting worried…

Quinn was about to start typing a reply when she noticed another unread message. It was in her message requests folder; from someone she was not friends with. She opened it curiously.

Hi Quinn, it's Julia. You don't know me, but I'm friends with Ted. I went back and forth on whether I should be doing this, but I couldn't sit idly by any longer. Not when my friend's life is at stake.

Quinn's stomach dropped. The message from Julia was long, and it confirmed everything she had feared. Julia revealed that she knew about Sigma's plan to corner Ted at the exhibition and had even helped orchestrate it. She sounded remorseful, going on to talk about her family's connection to Sigma and how she had had no choice in the matter.

I've been looking into The Order of Poseidon. Quinn, it's worse than I thought. These people are delusional. I swear, I didn't know what Natalia wanted Ted for, and I would never have complied if I did. Knowing what I know now, I fear for his safety.

The Order of Poseidon? Was this what Stefan was a part of? Quinn's mind spiralled. Her deepest fears were coming true.

If you read this, call this number. I've been blocked from making contact with her, but I think she will listen to you. Screw my family, they can go to hell for this. I'm sorry, Quinn, I really am. I hope it's not too late.

Quinn's heart was beating out of her chest. She felt her fingers shaking as she read the phone number Julia had written in the message. Copy and pasting it into the search bar of a fresh tab, she hit enter. The wait, while only a few seconds, was excruciating. Her eyes widened as the search result loaded, revealing the name of a penitentiary in Mexico

City. She then instantly knew who Julia was asking her to get in touch with.

**

The sound of footsteps tapping on concrete echoed through the long corridor of the cell block. Sat alone in her dark cell, Lillian Pembroke stared at the cold, weathered concrete. A sliver of natural light filtered in through the small high window, illuminating the page of the book she had positioned in just the right place to pass the time with some light reading. The library in this place was limited, but it hadn't taken her long to find the right people and pull the right levers to have books ordered for her. Lillian had made a career from getting what she wanted. Collecting antiquities was a venture for the rich, and her wealth gave her a natural advantage in manipulating others to achieve her goals. Everyone wanted something, and it hadn't taken her long to learn the lay of the land, even from behind bars.

Sat on her narrow cot, the springs creaking underneath the uncomfortable mattress, she turned the page and shifted in place. It had been over two years since she had started to call the dingy cell home, and while some things had become normal, that mattress still felt jarring to sit on.

The footsteps echoed more loudly on the cold concrete as they tapped closer to her cell. They stopped right outside, and a prison guard appeared at her door.

"Teléfono," she said. The guard didn't wait for Lillian to respond before unlocking the cell. It had not been a question. The door squeaked open, the old hinge struggling as the bottom of the door scraped against the floor. The guard waited expectantly in the doorway.

The Atlantis Idol

Lillian took note of the page number of her book, before closing it and tucking it under her pillow. She eyed the guard cautiously. "I'm only a few chapters from finishing," she said in Spanish. The guard said nothing.

If she came back to find her book gone, it wouldn't have been the first time. Lillian's influence only extended so far. Everyone wanted something, and sometimes that was something she had. If another inmate had something better to offer than Lillian, she shouldn't be surprised to have to wait a few weeks to learn the conclusion of the novel she was reading.

The guard watched her carefully as she exited her cell, staying a couple of paces behind her as she started to make her way down the long corridor. The journey through the prison was a labyrinthine experience. The narrow hallways were lined with cells on either side. Inmates could be heard shouting from one of the common areas. Another inmate was being released from their cell to join a group in their daily exercise. The jingling of keys added to the cacophony coming from the common area. The shouts grew louder, and as Lillian passed by, she could see a group of inmates surrounding two women who were tussling on the floor. The guards watched for a moment, letting the fight play out a few seconds, before blowing on a whistle and intervening, pulling the two apart. The raucous chants from the other inmates eventually subsided as the women were subdued and marched back to their cells.

Lillian had kept herself to herself as much as possible throughout her stint, avoiding this kind of trouble. She felt too old for fighting, but one day she was confronted by a fellow inmate of a similar age and stature in the canteen. She knew the protocol, and she rose to the challenge. She hadn't won the fight, but she had left a large enough bruise around the other woman's eye to make her think twice about taking her lunch again. That was the only trouble she had gotten into.

She passed through the security checkpoint, the heavy metal gate clanging shut behind her as she was passed to the next guard. This one had an even sterner expression on her face—if that was possible. Rounding a corner, Lillian was led into the designated area for accepting phone calls. A row of landlines was secured to the wall, each separated by partitions to offer a semblance of privacy. Signs in Spanish were written next to each phone, reminding inmates of the strict time limits for calls. The hum of conversation filled the air as two other inmates were using the phones. Lillian was directed to the furthest phone from the entrance, which was hanging off the hook. She walked over to it, giving a glance back at the guard before lifting the receiver. The guard waited some distance away, yet kept her firmly in her eye-line.

Lillian turned the other way, putting the receiver to her ear.

"Yes?"

"Lillian Pembroke?" a young woman's voice came through.

"Speaking."

"This is Quinn Miyata. I err—"

Lillian reeled as Quinn's voice faded slightly. The name triggered a feeling that had been pushed down for some time.

The voice came back through the receiver. "You probably don't remember, but we met—"

"Oh, I remember you, Ms Miyata," Lillian interrupted. "Yes, you and that boy, Ted. You really did a number on my trip to Mexico City."

The Atlantis Idol

Quinn paused, as though wondering how to continue. She was acutely aware she was speaking with the woman she had a hand in putting behind bars. But she needed answers.

"Listen, I know you probably have no interest in talking to me, but I really need your help," she began. "Natalia has kidnapped Ted and is working with people who might be trying to use him for some sort of ritual."

"Slow down, dear," said Lillian calmly. "It may surprise you to learn, but I don't harbour ill feelings toward you. Not anymore." She paused as she took in a deep breath. "You and your friend should never have been involved in the matter in Mexico. It was that blasted old fool, Jasper. Had he done his job properly, neither of you would have been tangled into that fine mess of an expedition."

Quinn gave a thought to Jasper. He had been foolish, yes, but the professor had been conned into helping Sigma. He had lost his job for his troubles but could count himself lucky that it had ended there. He had fared much better than Lillian.

"What has Natalia gotten herself into?" The tone Lillian used was that of a disappointed mother.

"She's working with two historians, Stefan, and Magda. They're looking for Atlantis, and I think they're close to actually finding it. Stefan said something about a ritual."

Lillian let out an exhausted sigh. "Natalia, you silly girl," she muttered under her breath. "I'm sorry, Quinn. My daughter has always been hot-headed. I'm sure you'll understand that she hasn't handled my incarceration well. She has failed to let go of her anger and is taking it out on you both. It is misplaced anger, but I'm not sure she sees it."

"I'm worried about what will happen to Ted if they find what they're looking for," said Quinn worriedly. "What do you know about The Order of Poseidon?"

"These historians, Stefan, and Magda. I've worked with them before," said Lillian. "Lovely people, but they are quite strange when you delve below the surface. The Order of Poseidon is a small society. They're very secretive."

"A cult," Quinn added.

"If you want to be so crude," remarked Lillian. "This particular sect... I don't know a lot about them. They have an odd fascination with the mythos surrounding Atlantis. Plato alluded to a natural disaster that destroyed the kingdom. But they believe it was the work of Poseidon. According to their beliefs, Poseidon was angry with the world and made an example of the very kingdom that had been built to worship him to demonstrate his anger. In doing so, he remade the world. The followers of The Order seek the Temple of Poseidon: the highest point of Atlantis and the focal point of the ancient city. It is there they think they will be able to perform a ritual to repeat the act of Poseidon and restore the world as it should be."

Quinn listened intently, trying to take in everything she was hearing. All the while, she was trying to find any detail that could give her a lifeline in trying to stop Stefan and Magda.

"What can we do?" she asked once Lillian had finished.

"My dear, you realise where I am? I cannot do a thing."

"Tell me what I can do. Please." He voice relayed the desperation she was feeling.

Lillian paused a moment, as though trying to put together a plan on the spot. "How close are they to finding it?"

"Very."

"Then you better catch up quickly. From my conversations with Stefan, I remember he talked about a knife that was used ceremonially in the temple. These people are very particular. My advice to you is this: if that knife exists, get hold of it. They won't perform the ritual without it."

Quinn went pale as she thought of the knife and Ted in the same context.

"There's nothing more I can do for you, my dear," said Lillian. "But I am truly sorry. Neither of you deserve to be where you are." Quinn noted the slight breaking of her voice. She had meant it.

Quinn ended the call and handed the phone back to Giovanni. "Thanks," she said.

He took one hand off the steering wheel to take the phone, before placing it into his pocket. Quinn looked out the window, deep in thought as the scenery rushed past. She had wasted no more time after reading the message from Julia, insisting on taking the call on the way to the location the coordinates pointed to. Casting a glance at the sat nav, she took stock of their route and estimated time of arrival. It wouldn't be long now. She hoped they were not too late.

TWENTY-TWO

Nestled in the picturesque countryside of Tivoli, the church named Chiesa was a serene sanctuary that exuded rustic charm and timeless elegance. Leaving their newly acquired car on the road, Natalia led the group up a narrow path. As they approached, they were greeted by the sight of a quaint stone structure, its weathered façade bearing the marks of centuries gone by. The path diverged from the road and into the large grassy area that laid host to the small church. The gravel faded into the grass until it split into two smaller routes that snaked around an unkempt section growing intrusively throughout. The weathered and crumbling stone wall next to the area leading up to the church entrance added further signs of neglect. Two large olive trees thrived in the vicinity, and ivy crept along the ancient walls of the church exterior.

The church could well have been used still by locals, but there were no obvious signs of activity. The terracotta roof had a small spire in the centre where the church bell hung dormant. There was a gentle sound of chiming, but it came from the corner of the building, around to the left on the side of the entrance. A small set of wind chimes hung from the awning that stretched over the entrance, the gentle breeze blowing them about and playing a quiet song.

Natalia furrowed her brow as they approached the tiny church. "Are you sure this is the right place?" she asked.

Magda caught up to her and took in the scene. "It must be. The coordinates lead right here, and the church matches the name."

"It doesn't exactly scream 'Lost City of Atlantis', does it?" Natalia was unconvinced.

"No," agreed Magda. "But the clues were pretty clear." They walked a few steps more, then suddenly she stopped in her tracks, her eyes becoming wide as a realisation hit her. "What if it isn't the lost city?" She turned to Natalia as if waiting for her to finish her train of thought.

The woman looked at her quizzically. "What are you getting at?"

Before Magda could elaborate, Stefan's voice came from behind them. "A shrine. We've visited many of them over the years, to pay our respects. Several members of The Order have built shrines to honour Poseidon. I hadn't expected this to be one too." He looked at Magda. "Is it possible Pope Benedict XV was a member of The Order?"

"What good is a shrine to me?" Natalia interjected. "We didn't come all this way to pay our respects to an old bloody sea god."

Lagging behind, Ted caught a glimpse of Stefan's hand clenching into a fist as Natalia said it. It was subtle, but it seemed like it irked him. Ted was sure that the fact that Natalia had used the word 'me' rather than 'us' hadn't been lost on Stefan either. Some cracks were appearing in the group, growing larger with each setback. Like a fracture in a sheet of ice, the slightest disturbance could cause the whole thing to split apart.

"We don't know what it is yet," said Magda pragmatically. "Let's just go in and have a look around, shall we?"

Entering through the wooden door, the group got their first glimpse of the interior of the quaint church. Daylight streamed through the arched windows on either side, bathing the church in a soft golden hue. The walls matched that of the white stucco exterior, the darkened wooden beams even more pronounced against the pale walls. Wooden pews lined the space leading up to the altar. Seemingly serving only a small congregation even at its busiest times, there were just four rows, with a walkway on each side of the pews in the centre. The walls were adorned with religious iconography, each telling a story of faith and devotion. A statue of Jesus stood in the left-hand corner of the church by the small wooden lectern, facing the group as they walked in.

Ted took in the scene. He always felt a little uncomfortable in churches. He tried to put his finger on the exact feeling that was causing it. The closest he could get to was guilt. He remembered being taken to church in his youth, but he had never really connected with religion. He had an open mind about faith and hadn't made his mind up one way or another about what he believed. Agnostic was perhaps the best word for it. Believers seemed to just know that their way was the right way, but Ted couldn't get his head around that when so many believers of different faiths were adamant that theirs was the only true one. He had decided the whole thing was just not for him. He thought hard about the feeling of guilt that struck him every time he walked into a place of worship. God or no God, he felt like there was a presence there that was disappointed in him for not committing to the faith he had been immersed in at a young age.

Hiram entered the church last and shut the door behind him. It closed with a loud thud which echoed around the space.

"So?" asked Natalia expectantly. "Does this look like one of your shrines?"

Stefan and Magda scanned the inside of the church. From the way their eyes were searching, there were no obvious signs of this place being one of the shrines to Poseidon they had described.

"It looks like an ordinary church to me," said Magda at last.

Natalia tutted, frustrated at the prospect of another dead end.

"But that's a good thing, right?" Ted chimed in. "If it was just another shrine, it wouldn't be what we were looking for. What did the note say?"

Magda recited it from memory.

"As per the agreement, I uphold my sacred duty to keep the secrecy of the site known as Atlantis beneath the church that bears my name."

"Beneath the church," Natalia repeated. "So, it could be right below us."

"Possibly," said Magda. "But how do we find out?"

"Isn't that a question I pay you to know the answer to?" Natalia fired a questioning look at Magda. To her credit, Magda didn't take the bait, instead flashing a smile and walking further into the church.

The group spread out through the space, taking a closer look for anything that could give a clue as to where to go from there. Ted looked at the large mural on the far wall of the church. Stretched across the wall behind the altar was a depiction of the Last Supper. The scene was iconic and seemed to be a recreation of the famous scene once painted by Leonardo da Vinci. Ted took in the sight a moment, appreciating the reverence with which it sat. A focal point of the church, Ted found it strange that a recreation of such an iconic painting would be positioned there. Churches he had seen usually had ornate stained-glass windows which depicted various religious objects, figures, and stories. It was strange to see a direct replica of the Last Supper serving as the main feature of the interior. Perhaps there were others like it.

He looked at the mural on the left-hand wall that Magda was studying with great interest. He walked over to join her. The mural was set into a large chunk of stone and seemed to depict a scene involving Jesus. At least, the character in the centre looked like any other depiction of Jesus, complete with robe, beard, and long hair.

"The Parable of the Sower," said Magda knowingly. "Jesus used a metaphor of different types of soil to explain how they represent people's hearts and responses to God's word."

"Oh," was all Ted managed to say. He peered at the mural. How had she identified that particular story so quickly? It didn't seem obvious to him. It was quite faded, but he supposed it did look like the person depicted in the mural was throwing seed onto a field.

Something then caught his eye. He hadn't noticed it at first, but Magda's sleeve moved to reveal a part of the corner of the slab of stone that had been concealed before. Ted squinted as he looked closer. His glasses were dirty, and he cleaned them on his shirt before stepping in closer and inspecting the thing that had caught his eye. It was a number, protruding from the stone. The number five. It looked odd sticking out of the stone the way it was.

"Hey! Over here. I think I've found something!" Natalia's voice called suddenly. Ted swung around, startled by the sudden commotion. Natalia was crouched by the mural of the Last Supper. Stefan had caught up to her.

"What is it?" he asked.

"Here," she pointed. "There are numbers underneath the mural." She placed a hand on them and applied a slight pressure. "They move!"

"What?" Magda's voice came from beside Ted. "What do you mean?"

"Come over and look."

Magda hurried over to see the two crouched down, inspecting the set of numbers that seemed to be attached to a slider of sorts.

"They spin independently, going from zero to nine," Natalia declared. "Like a combination lock." She looked at Stefan, then at Magda. "Is this typically the kind of thing you find in your shrines?"

"No," Stefan said confidently. "This is different."

"What does it mean?" Magda asked.

Ted looked back at the number five protruding from the side of the mural he was next to. "Maybe it has something to do with this?"

Magda hurried back over and saw what he was pointing out. Her eyes went wide, and she gasped. "This was right next to me! How did I miss it?" She smiled at Ted. "Good eye."

"Fascinating," Natalia turned her attention back to the combination lock underneath the Last Supper mural.

"It's like a weird escape room," said Ted. "But I feel like we're missing an important element." He looked at the murals that were similar to the Parable of the Sower. Two more sat on the walls on the same side of the church, and three more were opposite. "Magda, do you know what those other murals represent?"

Magda studied the next one along, looking at it with a curious expression for a moment. "The Parable of the Lost Sheep," she declared at last. "There's another number sticking out from the side of this one too." She put a finger on it. "It moves around on a dial, from number one to six." She moved to the others. "The Parable of the Tenants, the Parable of the Good Samaritan, the Parable of the Prodigal Son, the Parable of the Mustard Seed. They all have numbers too."

"You got that from those murals?" Stefan asked, clearly as perplexed as Ted by how easily she identified them. "They're not very clear."

"I'm pretty sure," she replied. "So, what's the link? Why the numbers?"

Silence entered the room, everyone thinking hard about what Magda had said.

"Are there numbers mentioned in each of the parables?" offered Ted. "Maybe that corresponds to the numbers on the side?"

"Hmm, no I don't think so—" Magda trailed off as she noticed something from her crouched position. "What's that under the altar?"

Stefan darted over and stooped down to check where she was pointing. He let out a sound that was equal parts shock and joy. "Magda, you genius!" he exclaimed. "Just look at this!"

Natalia muscled her way in under the altar and looked up the underside of the old wooden table to see what they had found. Carved into the wood was a scratchy message. Stefan tried to make out the words, but once again quickly realised it was written in Italian. He called Magda over, and she read it aloud.

Learn your lessons in order

And find the right answer from the final gospel
B

"B," Natalia emphasised. "Benedict XV. He left a clue. This is definitely the right place."

"Does the message relate to the numbers we found?" asked Ted from across the room.

Stefan stood up, turned back to the mural behind the altar and then shot a glance at each of the murals that depicted the parables Magda had described.

"Learn your lessons in order," he muttered to himself. "Of course! The parables were lessons that gave a spiritual meaning. He must be referring to the murals."

"But what does he mean by 'in order'?" Natalia chimed in.

"Alphabetical?" suggested Ted. "Based on the name of the story? So, starting with the Good Samaritan and ending at the Tenants?"

"Could be," said Stefan. "Try it. I'll help you." The man excitedly hurried over to the right-hand side of the church to flick the numbered dials next to the murals to place them in alphabetical order. Ted got to work on the other side. Before long the last dial was flicked into place. A long silence ensued as they waited for something to happen.

"Nothing," said Stefan. "Should it be obvious if it worked?"

"Try something else," came Natalia's voice.

"Ideas welcome," called Stefan.

No ideas came.

Magda was deep in thought. Without saying a word, she walked over to the first row of pews and reached behind to find a copy of the Bible. She flicked to the New Testament and searched for signs of one of the parables. Eventually, she found what she was looking for.

"I think the order is how they appear in the Bible," she said. "If we can figure out the order in which they appear."

Stefan went to pick up another Bible to help. Opening the page, he realised again why he had needed Magda's help with the previous step. His Italian was not nearly as proficient as hers.

"There's an easier way to do this," said Ted. "Can't you just look it up with your phone?"

Magda stopped reading and looked at Ted. She then caught Stefan's eye, who was having the same realisation she was.

"He's got a point," she admitted. "Stefan—"

"Way ahead of you," the man replied, already with his phone in his hand. A quick search and a few taps later Stefan had found a resource that detailed all the parables in the Bible, along with the chapter and verse they appear in within the gospels. He began to make note of each, so they could order them by first appearance.

"Some are there in multiple books," he said. "Was Matthew before or after Luke?"

"Before," said Magda. "Let's take the first account of each one and see where that gets us."

Soon they had all parables ordered by their first appearance in the New Testament. Satisfied they had aligned the corresponding dials correctly, Stefan flicked the last one, the Parable of the Prodigal Son, so it showed the number six.

An audible click sounded as the number slid into place, and the feedback reassured Stefan that they had made the right choice. A moment later a low rumble sounded through the walls of the church. An echoing thud then came, followed by silence.

The group looked at each other in turn. Natalia was the first to speak. "What now?"

Magda turned her attention back to the carving in the wood underneath the altar.

Learn your lessons in order
And find the right answer from the final gospel

"The second part must be related to the numbers under the Last Supper," she said. "Find the right answer from the final gospel."

"Who was the final gospel?" asked Ted.

"John," Magda replied instantly.

"So, something to do with John in the Bible? 'The right answer', what does that mean?"

"I'm not sure," Magda stepped out from the altar and studied the room as if looking for inspiration.

"Were any of these parables mentioned in John's gospel?" Natalia offered.

"Hmm, no. John's gospel was a bit different. The other three are closely related in content," said Magda, pursing her lips as she tried to find the missing link.

"What are we missing?" Stefan wondered aloud. "Is the clue in the question?"

"Find the right answer from John," Natalia looked at the mural of the Last Supper. "Which one is John here?"

Everyone followed her gaze, looking at the iconic scene. Stefan relied on his phone again, putting in a search for the figures in the painting. He quickly found a resource that annotated the scene with the name of each person sat at the table.

"Here," he said, showing Natalia the image on his screen. He then approached the mural and shot a finger up to point out that John was the figure sitting immediately to the left of Jesus when facing the painting.

"Of course. He looks like a John," said Ted. The others fired him a perplexed look. His humour was obviously not appreciated here.

"How many digits is the code?" Magda asked. Natalia went back to the numbers hidden underneath the mural. "Six," she said. "Each of them goes from zero to nine."

"Find the right answer," Magda repeated, as though hoping that by saying it over and over the answer might reveal itself to her.

Ted eyed the Last Supper scene carefully. A thought came to him that he considered not sharing aloud, as it felt too simple. He decided to go for it anyway. "What if the answer *is* in the question," he suggested. Natalia eyed him carefully, her eyebrow raised with a hint of scepticism.

"Find the right answer from the final gospel. Maybe the answer involves the right, as a direction."

He paused, waiting for the other's reaction.

"Go on," said Natalia.

"Well, how many people are sat to the right of John, from his perspective? Five." Ted waited to see if it evoked a reaction in anyone else. They just continued to stare at him expectantly.

"The answer is five," he said.

"There are six digits," Natalia's tone seemed annoyed.

"I know," Ted persisted. "But you said they go from zero. Why don't we try five zeros and a five?"

Natalia laughed. She then saw the look on Ted's face and realised he was being serious. She gestured mockingly for him to give it a try.

Ted gingerly walked past her and approached the large mural behind the altar. He got down on his knees and inspected the dials. One by one he manipulated them so they each showed zero. Then, with bated breath, he slid the last one, so it showed five. He closed his eyes, bracing for the barrage of insults that were sure to come from Natalia when nothing happened.

But something did happen. The moment he set the last digit in place, it clicked, the subtle feedback enough to convince him the combination was correct. A loud echo then sounded as something else was triggered by the mechanism.

TWENTY-THREE

Natalia stood speechless. She couldn't believe that it had actually worked. After the last digit had clicked into place a noise came from behind Ted, causing him to spin around in surprise. The old wooden altar creaked as a part of the surface came away at the corner. The thin panel slid slowly out, revealing a shallow hidden compartment. Ted moved in for a closer look. Underneath the thin veneer was the indent of a small round shape, with a tiny cross below it.

The others had raced over and were now staring at the inside of the compartment. They saw that another panel had come away from the other corner on the same side of the altar, revealing another identical indent. Nobody said a word at first, but they were all thinking the same thing. They knew exactly what the indent was for. Natalia called Hiram over, snapping her fingers and holding out her hand expectantly.

"The rings."

The big man obliged, pulling out the two rings they had acquired from the vault. He placed them into her hand. Natalia took another look at the indent. It didn't seem to matter which of the two rings went there. She carefully placed the trident ring into the circular indent. It was a perfect fit. The small Greek cross that hung from the ring like the charm on a bracelet nestled perfectly into the cross indent just below. A clicking sound came, giving instant feedback that another part of the mechanism had been unlocked. The panel the ring now lay on seemed to sink lower, a small T-shaped handle coming out from the wood. She looked at Stefan and Magda, the faint signs of a smile spreading across her face. Instinctively, she took hold of the handle and gave it a gentle twist. The ring rotated ninety degrees until it couldn't move any further. The mechanism gave some resistance, and the moment Natalia let go it sprung back to its original position.

"Weird," said Stefan. "Try the other side?"

Natalia placed the concentric circles ring into the indent on the other side of the altar. It too fit perfectly and gave a satisfying click to reveal the T-shaped handle. Natalia tried twisting that one too but got the same outcome.

"Together," she instructed, looking at Stefan, who took up position by the first handle. "On my count."

"On three, or after three?" Stefan asked.

Natalia hesitated a moment. "On three," she decided. They each readied themselves by the handles.

"One. Two. Three."

The moment the word left Natalia's lips they both twisted the handles completely in sync. This time the rings stayed in place ninety degrees from their starting position. A loud screech and scraping sound came as the floor began to vibrate. The vibrations intensified until the floor felt like it was coming away beneath their feet. Ted felt pressure on his foot and looked down to see the altar moving across the ground, pushing him as it went.

"Out of the way!" he yelled in alarm. "It's moving."

They all shuffled away, giving space for the altar as the great wooden table scraped along the floor towards the mural of the Last Supper. Moving around to the front, Ted looked in surprise at the space that was being revealed where the altar had been. The altar remained rooted to the stone floor, but a whole section of the stonework had now lifted and was sliding over the section of the floor they had just been stood on.

The altar came to a stop just short of the mural, and Ted could see the mechanism of pulleys and chains that had allowed the floor to move in this way. In the space vacated by the altar was a dark hole. Ted could see a set of steps running down into the darkness.

"Do other shrines to Poseidon have this?" Ted broke the silence that had enveloped the room after the mechanism had come to a stop.

"I can safely say no," Magda replied, her eyes wide. Another moment went by, the group staring at the ominous dark of the hole.

"Shall we?" Natalia asked, having been promptly handed a torch by Hiram. She clicked it on and began to descend the steps.

One by one they entered the hole. Ted let Stefan and Magda go, before turning to Hiram and tentatively gesturing for him to go on ahead. Unsurprisingly, the act went unappreciated. The bald man looked at Ted, unimpressed. Of course, Ted thought. Hiram was not stupid. Ted went on down the steps, ducking to avoid knocking his head on the stone floor that quickly became a ceiling as he descended below the surface.

As he reached the bottom, Ted saw from Natalia's torchlight that they were entering a tunnel. A claustrophobic feeling set in as Hiram squeezed in behind. The ceiling was low, and the walls closed in from both sides. He could see

Stefan just ahead of him, and the occasional flicks of light from Natalia's torch just gave enough context to his surroundings and the direction they were headed. Ted shuffled through, wondering where the tunnel would lead.

He didn't have to wait long to find out. The ceiling suddenly disappeared as the group entered a much more spacious area. They had reached what looked like a bunker at the end of the tunnel. Daylight streamed in from holes in the ceiling, the natural light illuminating the space in concentrated beams. It was just enough for Natalia not to need her torch anymore. She clicked it off as they took in the scene.

Ted struggled to make sense of what they had stumbled on here. Certainly, this was not Atlantis. There were no ancient ruins, no signs of civilisation from long ago. What he saw instead was what looked like some kind of art installation. There were several giant round balls suspended in the air. Rusted metal poles protruded from them, connecting some of them at points. In the centre was a giant ball that rested on the ground. Around the ball was a series of cogs that connected to the metal poles, and Ted could see metal wheels that sat invitingly at four different points around the circumference. As he took in more of the scenery, he decided that this didn't look like an art installation. It looked more like an interactive exhibit at a museum. What was this place?

The room had a domed shape, with several mirrors spread around the place at different angles. The domed ceiling evoked a distinct memory for Ted of being at the Greenwich Observatory. He had sat in the planetarium and watched a show about the different constellations of stars visible in the night sky. It was then he started to make sense of the structures.

"Is it the solar system?" he wondered aloud.

"That's what I was thinking," Magda agreed. "This here in the middle is the sun." She pointed at the giant ball in the centre of the room. "And the smaller ones suspended on these pipes are the planets."

"Why would Benedict XV lead us here?" Stefan began to walk around the room, taking in the strange objects and trying to make sense of the mechanism that linked them together.

Ted counted the planets, remembering the mnemonic he had learned at school.

"My very easy method just speeds up naming plan—" he paused, realising he had run out of planets in the room. "Where's Pluto?"

"Hmm, odd," Magda counted them silently, pointing to each ball as she did so. "Strange."

"It's a dwarf planet," said Natalia. "Sometimes it gets removed from the line-up because of that."

"Actually," said Stefan. "I think it's the opposite in this case. If Benedict XV had a hand in making this, it wouldn't have included Pluto because it hadn't been discovered yet. Benedict XV died in 1922. Pluto wasn't discovered until 1930."

"Woah," said Ted. "Is that true? We've only known about Pluto for less than a hundred years. That seems wild."

"It's true," said Stefan.

Ted took another look at the ceiling, spotting something he hadn't seen the first time he looked. The whole underside of the dome was painted. He squinted to see what the painting was showing. He could see the outline of shapes clustered together. As he looked at it a bit longer, following the shadows of shapes in the dimly lit room, he began to make sense of it.

"A map," he thought aloud. "It's a map."

"Amazing," breathed Magda. She turned her head, viewing it from another angle. "It's the Aegean Sea. Look at the outline here," she pointed, tracing her finger up and around the underside of the dome. "This is mainland Greece. Athens should be around about there. Here's Crete. And these," she pointed to the small clusters of shapes. "These are the islands. Naxos, Paros, Santorini, Tinos, Andros."

"There's so many," said Ted.

"I recommend a visit," said Magda. "They're all different in their own way. And beautiful, of course. The sunsets from Santorini are famously stunning."

"Yes, I've seen pictures," he replied.

"Doesn't come close to the real thing," said Magda, pursing her lips as she studied the map.

Ted continued to scan the ceiling, looking at the islands pictured. He didn't realise just how many there were. It was then he noticed something strange about the gaps in the roof that was letting the daylight stream through in concentrated beams. "What do you think of these?" he asked, pointing up to the nearest one.

Magda looked at it for a moment. "Doesn't look like a natural formation." She tilted her head, squinting her eyes as she studied the hole in the roof curiously. "These gaps are inconsistent in size, but they're definitely man-made. I wonder what it's all for."

Stefan was at one of the wheels connected to the series of pipes and pulleys making up the centre of the space. "This is one way to find out," he replied, turning the wheel anticlockwise. The wheel was stiff, but eventually gave, the turning motion accompanied by the intense screeching of rusted metal. The light in the room dimmed, before eventually fading to black. Ted had been looking up and saw that the tiny holes in the ceiling had been covered over, the thin beams of light that passed through disappearing. Stefan continued to turn the wheel, feeling it had more room to move. A moment later the light returned to the room as new holes appeared in the ceiling. Ted was certain that these new holes were in different places from the first set.

"Interesting," he said, noticing that the others were also seeing what he was seeing.

Stefan turned his attention to another wheel. Gripping it firmly, he turned it. The rusted mechanism creaked as it shook off decades of dormancy. It gave an ear-piercing screech as it began to move, the metallic scraping of cogs filling the room as the mechanism came to life. Ted stood wide-eyed as he watched what happened. The three planets around the edge of the space began to move, the metal pipes holding them suspended in the air swinging them around. Ted watched as one of them swung just over his head, another turning on its axis as it came around more slowly. While operated by the same wheel, the planets seemed to behave differently in the way they moved. While one swung around in its orbit of the sun in the centre of the room, another moved more slowly, turning in small circles as the mechanism brought it around the room in an anti-clockwise motion. While they had started off huddled together, the three planets quickly became very spread out from one another.

"Huh," was all Stefan said, as he stopped turning the wheel and the planets came to a stop. He looked at the remaining five planets, and then at the two other wheels posted around the sun he had yet to try. He went to the next wheel along and turned it. More screeching, and the three planets in the middle of the solar system began to move. They behaved very similarly to the others, with the planets moving further apart, and then closer together again as they completed their orbit. Finally, Stefan turned the last wheel. The two smallest planets began to spin around, completing much tighter orbits of the sun.

As those last two spun around, Ted caught sight of a flash of light reflecting from one of the giant balls. It was gone again in an instant.

"Hey, did anyone see that?" he asked the room.

"No." Stefan stopped turning the wheel.

"I did," said Natalia. "Turn it back this way."

Stefan turned the wheel the other way, reversing the mechanism. The planets spun back in the other direction.

"Slowly, slowly," instructed Natalia. "Stop when I tell you."

Stefan slowed the pace of the turning wheel, the planets gradually making their way back to the spot where Ted and Natalia had seen the flash of light. Then, it happened again.

"Stop!" called Natalia.

Stefan let go of the wheel and came around to where Natalia was standing. He looked up at where a beam of light came through the ceiling and reflected off the top of the ball representing Venus. The light bounced off a mirror that was positioned on the ceiling, causing the flash they had seen.

"There's mirrors on top of the planets," said Magda. "It's catching the light from the holes in the ceiling and reflecting onto the other mirrors."

"It's a puzzle," said Ted. "We have to turn the planets in just the right place to reveal something."

"Another puzzle," Natalia muttered. "Reveal what, exactly?"

"The map," said Magda, seeing where Ted's train of thought was headed. "Maybe if we can angle it just right, the light will bounce to a part of the map."

The penny dropped and Natalia felt the hair on her arm stand on end. She immediately snapped into execution mode and barked instructions to Stefan. "Keep spinning those wheels. Let's solve this."

Through trial and error, they moved the planets around until the light bounced off them at just the right angle to reflect off one of the mirrors on the ceiling. But no matter how they manipulated them, they couldn't figure out a definitive solution.

"The light isn't hitting the map that strongly. Should it be more obvious?" asked Magda.

"Maybe we're missing something," said Stefan. "Hiram, come and help me. I'm doing all the work here."

Hiram trudged over to the centre of the room and took up his station at one of the wheels.

"What if we try aligning the planets?" suggested Ted. "See if that does anything."

"Worth a try," said Stefan, and he began to turn the smallest set of planets to get them aligned one behind the other. He then moved to the other wheel while Hiram turned his to do the same with the three planets he was controlling.

"A clue from our old Pope would be good about now," said Ted.

Hiram aligned his planets, but they were offset from the rest. It took a lot more coordination for him and Stefan to manipulate the cluster of balls into the right place so that they were perfectly aligned one behind the other. As the last one fell into place, a concentrated beam of light shone brightly onto the ceiling. Everyone fell silent as a collective feeling of awe hit them. The light bounced off one planet, onto one of the ceiling mirrors, then back onto a different planet, then back to a different ceiling mirror, and so on until it finally hit the ceiling in a concentrated beam of light. However, the light was not hitting the map of the Aegean Sea, instead veering off to the side of the painting.

"Woah," said Ted at last. "I think we're close."

"So, what, we just keep trying this at different angles?" Stefan wondered aloud.

Magda was looking at the way the light bounced around the room, doing some rough calculations in her head like a snooker player assessing the angles to line up their next shot. She found herself becoming distracted by Hiram, who was studying the underside of the ball that represented Neptune.

"Hiram, what is it?" Natalia had noticed it too and fired a curious glance at the ex-military man. Hiram took out a torch and shone it on the area. It was then they all saw the etching he had spotted. Three small symbols: concentric circles, a trident, and the Greek Orthodox cross.

"Of course!" Magda exclaimed, the words coming out of her mouth like she had had a revelation.

"What?" Natalia turned to her.

"Neptune. The light needs to bounce off Neptune last. Think about it. The location of Atlantis is revealed by the planet Neptune. It has to be."

"I'm not following," said Ted.

"Neptune, the Roman god of the sea. Remind you of anyone?"

"Holy shit," Ted realised the connection. "Poseidon."

Magda smiled. "It makes sense, right? Benedict XV made that connection too. Look at the symbols etched into the ball. It's the perfect meeting of Roman and ancient Greek culture, a representation of the agreement he had kept with the Greek Orthodox Church. The Temple of Poseidon is revealed by Poseidon himself: Neptune."

"Magda, I could kiss you," Stefan enthused as he wasted no time in turning the nearest wheel to swing the outer planets around until they lined up neatly in a row once more. It took almost a full orbit for it to happen, and the planets ended up around ninety degrees from their previous position. He and Hiram worked together to line the other planets up with them, which took longer. The last planet settled in place, but the light didn't shine brightly onto the ceiling this time.

"It was better before, I think," said Natalia.

Stefan let out a frustrated sigh. "What are we missing now?"

Ted looked up at the mirror they had expected the light to bounce off and onto the mirror that was attached to the top of the Neptune ball. He then turned his attention to the tiny holes in the ceiling. He moved across the room to the first wheel they had come across, remembering how they had started by closing one set of holes in the ceiling to reveal another.

"What are you doing?" asked Stefan.

"Just trying something." Ted turned the wheel anti-clockwise. The room was plunged into darkness. He continued to turn the wheel until the other set of holes opened and the light returned. He peered around the large ball representing the sun to look hopefully up to the ceiling. Nothing.

"Worth a try," said Magda.

Ted looked again at the ceiling. He could have sworn there was a hole a little smaller than the others, almost as if it had opened only halfway. He gripped the wheel again and heaved it further anti-clockwise. The wheel responded, the mechanism screeching and the light disappearing from the room once more. A second later the light returned, and the small hole Ted had seen was now fully open. His hunch was right; there was a third setting.

"Oh my God," he heard Magda say before he had a chance to check the beam of light that had become concentrated on a small part of the map. He stepped around

The Atlantis Idol

to take in the view. The planets were in perfect alignment to shine a thin beam of light onto the top of a tiny island on the map.

Stefan was looking at Ted with a look Ted thought to be relief.

"It was in the middle setting when we arrived," Ted said. "When you turned it clockwise it reached the end of its movement, but there was another setting the other way."

The group looked up at the map and to where the light was shining. The island it was pointing to was very small, nestled between a group of larger ones.

"Where is that?" Magda squinted as though trying to recall the island from memory.

Natalia already had her phone out. "Irakleia. It's on Irakleia."

TWENTY-FOUR

Rising majestically from the waters of the Aegean Sea, the shores of the island of Irakleia slowly loomed into view. Ted leaned against the side of the boat as he took in the picturesque scene of rugged coastline that was adorned with cliffs and scattered vegetation. Night had fallen, the outline of the small island just visible from their boat. Their approach to the island was very different to when they had arrived in Ponza just a few days prior. Despite the magnitude of what they were anticipating discovering there, the darkness had taken away some of the grandeur of the moment. Nonetheless, there was a nervous energy about the group, with barely a conversation from the moment they left port.

As they drew nearer, the distinctive silhouette of the Greek Orthodox Church could be seen perched atop a hill. The church, with its whitewashed walls, stood as a beacon of faith against the backdrop of the island's natural beauty. Overlooking the Aegean Sea, the waves of the water lapped against the rocky shore far below.

After solving the puzzle in the subterranean space beneath the church of Chiesa, the symbol of the Greek Orthodox cross had the group convinced that the location they were looking for on the tiny island was another church. A quick search on the maps app on their phones showed that the church they were approaching now was the only one on the island.

"This has to be it," said Natalia, a rare tinge of nerves coming through in her voice. "It has to be."

Stefan manoeuvred the small boat they had commandeered into the bay. Natalia had flexed her finances to charter a private flight from Rome to Naxos, from which they had sailed across to Irakleia. They disembarked and ascended the winding path that led to the church.

The air was filled with the soothing melody of cicadas and the scent of salt carried on the gentle breeze.

As they approached the entrance, Magda and Stefan stopped to take in the scene. Ted could imagine how they were reflecting on their journey. He remembered what they had said about this being their life's work. As he watched Stefan taking in the old church, he realised what a surreal moment this was for them. He wanted this journey to be over, so he could get back to his normal life once more. But a part of Ted wanted it to be over for Stefan and Magda to see their work finally pay off. He didn't give a damn about Natalia. She was there to exploit and profit from the work of others, nothing more.

The weathered façade of the old church bore the marks of centuries past, yet it exuded an aura of solemn reverence and spiritual sanctity.

"No lights on, by the look of it," said Natalia, breaking the silence and no doubt ruining the moment for the pair of historians. "Come on, Hiram." She walked to the entrance and tried the door. It was locked. She wiggled and pulled at the old handle, but it was no use.

"Come back tomorrow?" Ted suggested. His comment was tongue in cheek, as he knew very well that was not an option. Not for Natalia.

"Hiram," she said expectantly, stepping back from the doorway. The big man moved to the wooden door and stood to one side to face it shoulder-first. He slammed his meaty frame into the door, the handle clanging and the thud echoing around in the quiet of the night. He launched himself at the door again, another thud sounding. He readied himself for a third attempt, just as the sound of rustling came from inside. The sound of a deadbolt being slid unlocked came before the door opened with a creak. It was open just enough for two beady eyes to be seen, illuminated in the flicker of candlelight from inside the church.

The face appraised the man who had been trying to break down his door, and then at the group standing behind him. In a hushed but deep voice, the person then spoke in Greek. Seeing the perplexed looks on their faces he switched to English.

"Closed."

He was met with a steely look from Hiram. Unsure who these people were and why they were persisting, the man opened the door further and stepped out to address them properly. The man had a long and straggly beard, his black hair mixed with the odd patch of grey. He wore long black robes that draped onto the ground around him. A kalimavkion sat atop his head, the stiff cylindrical black head covering an iconic part of the Greek Orthodox priest garb.

"I'm sorry, the church is closed," he said slowly. "If you would like to come back tomorrow."

The Atlantis Idol

Suddenly, the man's eyes widened, and his face quickly turned purple as Hiram grabbed him by the throat and pushed him back inside the old church. The startled man let out a guttural shout and his hands went to Hiram's thick hand that was clenched around his windpipe. When they were both inside and out of the way of the door, Hiram let go. The man slumped to the floor and began to cough. The air returned to his lungs, and he gasped for breath. Hiram stood aside to allow the others into the church. Ted was the last to enter and locked eyes with the poor priest, who hadn't yet got back to his feet. Hiram then shut the door and slid across the deadbolt to lock it. He then stood with his arms folded in front of the door like a nightclub bouncer.

Ted took in the interior of the church. Soft candlelight flickered against the walls, casting dancing shadows across the floor. The feint scent of incense entered his nostrils, and he found himself enveloped by the hushed tranquillity of the space, which fell in complete juxtaposition to the violent act from Hiram that had got them inside. The nave stretched out before them, its lofty ceiling disappearing into the shadows above. An ornate iconostasis divided the sanctuary from the nave, its gilded icons gleaming faintly in the candlelight. Each icon bore the solemn visage of saints and martyrs, their eyes seeming to glare at Ted as he moved into this sacred space.

The priest eventually got his voice back and cried out in Greek. The man then turned his attention to Hiram, a mixture of rage and fear in his bloodshot eyes.

"Stop! Please, stop! What do you want?"

Hiram said nothing. Natalia approached the priest and bent down next to him.

"We're looking for the Temple of Poseidon."

The man looked at her with a perplexed expression. "This is not Athens," he replied plainly.

Natalia grimaced. "Don't play dumb. We followed the signs. This is the church that conceals Atlantis. Show us how to get to the temple."

"I don't know what you're talking about," the priest insisted.

Hiram grabbed the priest and pulled him from the ground. The man let out a whimper as the ex-special forces soldier's big hands gripped him.

"Please, don't hurt me," he pleaded.

Ted couldn't stand by any longer and watch this poor man be attacked. He cut in front of Natalia and placed a hand on Hiram's arm, attempting to pull him away from the priest. "Hey, that's enough. Leave him alone."

Hiram shrugged Ted off like it was nothing. Natalia, irritated by Ted's interjection, walked around him, and confronted the terrified priest. The man had his hands on Hiram's, trying in vain to free himself from the brute's clutches. Natalia had spotted the ring on his finger. She moved in close and gently placed her thumb and index finger on it, turning it around his finger to fully reveal the symbol that had been partially in view. The trident.

She smiled to herself. The priest instantly knew how knowing that smile was, as his grip on Hiram's hands seemed to slacken.

"Who are you?" he asked quietly.

"Like I said, we're looking for the Temple of Poseidon," said Natalia. "I know it's here. Take us to it."

The man looked at her with a renewed sense of determination. He had looked defeated the moment he saw her recognition of the ring, but another thought had crossed his mind.

"You are treasure hunters," he said solemnly. "You are not worthy of visiting the temple."

Hiram let go of the priest suddenly, the unexpected movement causing the bearded man to stumble backwards. Hiram reached into his pocket and drew a handgun. Without a word, he cocked it and aimed it at the priest's head.

"I'll offer you a choice," said Natalia, beginning to pace up and down like a villain from a bad action movie. "Either you tell us where the temple is and how to get there, and we spare your life. Or you can die right here and now, and we find out ourselves anyway. I prefer the first option as it will save us some time, but the choice is yours."

A moment went by, the priest staring down the barrel of Hiram's gun as the tension in the air grew thick. The flickering flames of the candles dotted around the old church danced upon the ancient stone of the walls, casting shifting patterns of light and shadow that seemed to come alive.

The priest looked desperate as he turned his attention to Natalia, then to Ted, Magda, and Stefan in turn. Nobody was coming to his aid. Left with no choice, he took in a sharp intake of breath, closed his eyes, and nodded his head.

"I'll take you."

Hiram lowered his firearm as Natalia grinned widely. She enjoyed getting what she wanted, even more so from a position of power.

The priest walked slowly through the church, passing the aisles of pews with their polished wood that had been worn smooth by centuries of use. In the dim candlelight, the church took on an otherworldly aura, its ancient stones steeped in mystery and reverence. Ted could feel that this place was special in some way, and he was sure his companions could feel it too. It was a place where time seemed to stand still, where the boundaries between past and present blurred. Ted looked up as they followed the priest through the nave and towards the iconostasis. The dome-shaped roof was cast in a dark shadow from the dim candlelight, but he could just about make out that the whole underside of the dome was coloured with religious iconography.

The priest led the group beyond the iconostasis, opening a door that led to the sanctuary. There he walked sheepishly over to the far side of the smaller room. Murals lined the wall, depicting more significant biblical events. He turned to the right, facing the corner where the curved backside of the church met the right-hand wall. There he stopped and reached out a hand, palm facing up as though expecting someone to place something in it.

"You have the rings, I presume?" he said.

Magda, who had been keeping the rings in her pocket, stepped forward and placed them in the priest's waiting hand. He appraised the rings a moment, then nodded and proceeded to feel his way down the seam where the two walls met. Eventually, he stopped and applied firm pressure to the seam. He then walked over to the wall parallel, where the curved back of the church met the left-hand wall and repeated the action. Finally, he approached the altar in the centre of the sanctuary. As with the church of Chiesa on the outskirts of Rome, the first step triggered a mechanism within the altar to come alive. Ted watched as the priest placed the rings inside two compartments that had been revealed. The only difference was that the two compartments were close together, so the priest was able to activate them both simultaneously himself. The moment he did so, part of the curved wall at the back of the sanctuary clunked open, revealing a secret door.

"Through here," he said, heading towards the newly revealed passage. The group couldn't see in, the darkness beyond so thick that it was impossible to see what was there. Natalia signalled for Hiram to keep close behind him. He did so, keeping his gun raised. Ted shuffled in behind Natalia, his vision deteriorating in a matter of milliseconds as he slipped into the dark passage beyond the wall.

TWENTY-FIVE

Before Ted had a chance to gain his bearings in the darkness, he stumbled as he found that the ground beneath his feet gave way suddenly. Seeing the bobbing heads of the others in front of him, he quickly realised he had entered a steep staircase.

"Watch your step," he called back to Stefan and Magda, who had just entered the dark space behind him. He was a little miffed that Natalia hadn't issued the same warning before him.

The stone steps began to wind around. They descended further into the hidden space beneath the church, and Ted was beginning to sense a pattern in their adventuring. He wondered why every sought-after ancient ruin had to be in such dark, damp, claustrophobic places. The thought didn't stay with him long before he decided on the answer. Of course, if they were in well-lit places above ground they wouldn't be as difficult to find. Still, he wished for better conditions as they went further underground.

But despite his aversion to his surroundings and the horrendous circumstances in which he always found himself in these places, Ted couldn't shake a surprising underlying feeling: excitement. He had never thought himself a thrill-seeker, or even the adventurous kind. Most of his pastimes involved staying at home, unwinding within his bubble. Watching TV, reading, and playing video games were on the agenda most of the time. Perhaps that was one of the things that had drawn him to Quinn. She enjoyed a lot of the same hobbies, but she also had an adventurous streak in her personality that brought Ted out of his comfort zone when they were together. Reflecting on it now, he decided that he liked it. He loved a puzzle, and one of the few things he liked doing out of the house was testing himself in escape rooms with his friends. After a weekend of watching video tutorials, he had also satisfactorily mastered solving the Rubik's cube. But the act of solving it had now become routine; a series of movements that flowed naturally from his fingertips like muscle memory. The mystery was not there anymore, it had become something to occupy his hands while he worked or thought. And now, he found himself excited by the challenge ahead of Sigma. Not the danger, the kidnapping or the murder that came with the nefarious shadow organisation. It was the mystery. Hell, Ted had even started to become fascinated by the history and mythos of it all. Perhaps Quinn had rubbed off on him more than he realised.

The steps continued to wind down into the earth beneath the church. Eventually, Ted heard the trickling of water. It sounded as if it was coming from the walls. Brushing his hand against the cold stone, it felt dry. The staircase then straightened out and the final steps led into a narrow corridor, much like that of the secret archives in the Vatican. Ted felt as though his eyes had finally adjusted to the darkness, but then he realised that the reason he was managing his surroundings so much better was because of a light coming from up ahead.

The light was accompanied by a sudden burst of heat. Exiting the narrow corridor, he found himself inside a cavernous chamber. Around the edge of the space running away from the entrance on each side was a horizontal line of fire. Flames licked from a shallow well, akin to a guttering system. The smell of oil filled the air. Ted caught sight of the priest placing a box of matches back in a pocket beneath his long black robe. Ted took in the scene, along with the others. This was something straight out of a cheesy archaeological adventure movie. Ted was pretty sure he had seen this room, or something extremely similar, in a video game.

Along the walls that were glowing a pale orange from the flickering fire were faded murals. Ted recognised the central figure of many of them: Poseidon. The murals painted a picture of various stories involving the god of the sea. In each, the bearded god, the idol of Atlantis, wielded his iconic trident. To the right of the chamber was a pool of water, which was trickling gently from an open vent in the wall. But it was the centrepiece of the area that captured the attention of the group most keenly and had caused Magda to gasp when seeing it. They were completely in awe of the sight. There, on the far side of the chamber, facing the entrance they had just come through, was a giant statue of Poseidon. In his left hand, standing upright and pointing toward the ceiling, was his trident. In the statue's right hand was the handle of a wooden bucket. The bucket was suspended over an empty basin that looked like it once contained water.

"Here you are," said the priest.

"This is the temple?" Natalia asked.

The priest shook his head. "This is the proving chamber. If you are to visit his ancient temple, it is customary to prove to Poseidon that you are worthy." He pointed to the far side

The Atlantis Idol

of the room, where a small pedestal stood by the wall. "You must find the key to unlock the door."

Hiram gritted his teeth and put his gun to the side of the priest's head.

"I thought we had skipped all that," Natalia sighed. "No more games. Take us to the temple. Now." The tone of her voice became stern.

The priest looked at the great statue of Poseidon. From where it was positioned, the face of the statue seemed to stare at the group with judgment. Ted wondered what was going through the poor man's mind at this moment. He watched as the priest closed his eyes.

"I am sorry," he said. "This is how it must be." Then, with one last bid for survival, the priest grabbed the gun and pulled it, along with Hiram's hand, up towards the ceiling. The two grappled a moment, the priest fighting for control of the firearm. Then the deafening sound of a gunshot rang out all around the chamber. Ted instinctively ducked down and put his hands over his ears. His heart pounded as the sudden explosion of sound evoked a primal fear response in his body. The gunshot had reverberated around the space, the chamber amplifying the sound. Ted's ears rang with a temporary bout of tinnitus, before gradually fading away as his body began to regulate and slowly returned to normal function. It had all happened in a matter of seconds.

Taking his hands from his ears, he realised he had been closing his eyes. He opened them to see a figure on the floor. A pool of blood surrounded them. Hiram was standing over the dead frame of the priest, the poor old man's robe sprawled out on the ground, the pool of blood beginning to soak into the fabric. In the moment the gun had gone off in the struggle, the firearm had still been pointing at the man's head. The bullet had gone right into his temple, killing him instantly.

"You idiot!" Natalia snapped, fire in her eyes as she looked at the ex-special forces soldier with disdain.

Hiram said nothing. He just holstered his gun and stood there, seemingly unfazed by his actions.

"Jesus, Hiram," Natalia continued. "What a fine mess this is. We needed him."

"Did we?" Stefan's voice came unexpectedly from across the room. He was looking at the murals on the walls above the pool of water on the right-hand side of the chamber. Ted noticed how he too seemed oddly unfazed by what had just happened. It was as if he had no regard whatsoever for this poor innocent person's life. Were they so fixated on their goal that they were blind to the devastation they were leaving in their wake? Or was their body count so high that they were desensitised to death, and one more innocent life taken had no impact at all on them?

"He said it was a proving chamber. We have all the tools we need to access the temple. We just need to prove we are worthy." Stefan maintained his focus on the murals.

"No more puzzles," said Natalia defiantly. "I'm not spending another second putting objects in order, only to be led on another wild goose chase somewhere else."

"It isn't a wild goose chase," said Magda. "This is it; I can feel it."

Natalia tutted, irritated.

From out of his backpack, Stefan had retrieved the leather-bound book he had been so protective of. He flicked through the pages, his lips moving quickly as he read from it quietly.

"It doesn't mention anything about the proving chamber here," he said at last.

"I guess we're on our own, then," said Magda. She joined him by the pool of water, looking up at the murals on the wall.

Ted looked at the body of the priest, lying still in the pool of blood, and then at the two historians. They were carrying on as if the man's death was nothing more than a small inconvenience.

"Have you no compassion at all?" Ted asked the room. "This man is dead because of your actions. Same as Matteo. Is this quest of yours more important than the lives of these innocent people?"

He was met with silence, which told him everything he needed to know. Something snapped inside Ted, and suddenly the feeling of excitement he had shared with them was extinguished. He no longer cared about the mystery of Atlantis, the Temple of Poseidon, or any of it. No discovery, no matter how great, was worth the bloodshed. He sat on the ground, a flood of emotions pouring out. He felt a wave of guilt for having been excited, even for a moment, by this quest. The temporary transition it had granted him from prisoner to partner made him feel accountable for the deaths of the priest, Matteo, and the police officers in Ponza. He thought about Quinn, and how they had thrown her to the wolves in Rome. God knows how she was, facing the consequences of Sigma's actions alone. Tears streamed down his cheeks as his resolve finally relented.

In front of the pool of water on the right-hand side of the chamber, Stefan and Magda turned their attention away from the murals of Poseidon and to a cluster of smooth round shapes that protruded from the wall. The round shapes had flat surfaces, each with a symbol carved into them. The shapes seemed to sit on a thin line that had been cut into the wall. The grooves in the wall ran around like a track in a rough figure of eight shape. The hollowed-out line then became much thinner, resembling no more than a crack in the wall that ran down from the bottom of the figure of eight towards the centre of the pool of water, stopping just a few inches above the water level. To the right of the figure of eight was another group of shapes. This time the shapes were aligned horizontally and cut to look like cogs of different sizes. From the bottom of each cog was a crack in the wall that ran down towards the pool, before meeting at a single point.

Something caught Stefan's eye and he turned his attention to the small pool of water. Where the water was trickling from a small opening in the wall lay a small black object, the water running gently over it. Moving in closer, he was just able to lean over and reach it. His hand dipped into the water, and soon after he pulled it back out with the black object in his grasp.

"What is it?" asked Magda.

"I'm not sure." Stefan held the object up as he inspected it. It was a thin piece of iron, which could have been about eight inches long and an inch thick. It had some weight to it, and as he turned it, he saw that there were tiny grooves cut into it on two sides. The very top of the object was pointed like the tip of an arrow.

"An old tool? Or weapon?" suggested Magda.

"Perhaps," Stefan looked back at the open vent the object had been sitting in. He then glanced at the murals on the wall, with the cracks leading down towards the water. Walking over to the left-hand side of the room, he peered down into the empty basin below the hand of the statue of Poseidon that held the bucket. It was then he saw the thin pipe that led up from the basin, running up against the wall, before curving over and dangling over the bucket.

The Atlantis Idol

"Check this out," he said. Magda came over and watched as he pointed to the pipe. "Looks like a—" Before he was able to finish his sentence, he saw the lever sticking out of the ground near the basin.

"A pump," Magda finished for him, spotting it too. She then followed the perimeter of the basin, realising that there was a small channel that had been dug underneath the centre of the chamber. She walked back across to the small pool of water on the other side and saw that it connected with it there. Looking at where the channel met the pool, she had a realisation.

"We need to raise the water level," she said. "The water needs to come through that channel so we can pump it into the bucket."

"Okay…" Stefan looked at the bucket held by the massive statue's hand. "And then what?"

Magda shrugged. "We see what happens."

"Good enough for me." Stefan looked back to the pool of water. The cracks in the wall running from the two sets of arranged shapes stopped at different heights above the water. He looked at the open vent that he had retrieved the black arrow-like object from.

"I think these cracks in the wall lead to more openings where the water comes through." He put his hand to the wall, feeling for a crease to prize it open. The line of fire running the length of the wall through shallow channels of oil was now just a couple of feet above him, and he felt the heat from the flames warm his face. He pressed his palm against the wall but had no luck finding anything. If there was another vent there, it was sealed tightly shut. He followed the cracks back to the collections of shapes. "More puzzles it is, then."

He addressed the first set of shapes. Three round stones with a flat surface were aligned in the centre of a figure of eight track that had been made from grooves in the wall. Each of the stones had a symbol on its flat surface. Each was very similar, and it took Stefan a second to distinguish the difference between them. The first was a trident, with the three prongs at the tip pointing upwards. The second looked like a trident too, but on closer inspection, Stefan saw that there were only two prongs.

"A bident?" he wondered aloud. He then looked at the last one, which only had one prong. He opened his other hand to inspect the black iron object. "A spear?"

Magda pursed her lips while she thought. "Is it a numbers game? Something to do with the number of prongs." She looked from the shapes to the cracks in the wall. "They're arranged largest to smallest already, so maybe we reverse the order?"

Stefan wasted no time in moving the stones around to swap the first and third. The stone circles felt heavy, but they glided smoothly along the grooves in the wall. He moved the first around the top of the figure of eight, while the third went around clockwise underneath. When they were aligned on the middle row once more, he let go and the stones sat still. Nothing happened.

"Okay, not that," Magda sighed. She took a step back from the wall and tried to use the new perspective to find something she might have missed. It worked like a charm, and a moment later a thought crossed her mind, causing the hint of a smile to appear on her face.

Stefan saw the change in her. "Go on."

"The two-pronged one, the bident. Who wields that?" She turned to Stefan with one eyebrow raised.

The penny dropped. He smiled. "Hades."

"Bingo."

"So, the spear isn't a spear at all," Stefan continued. "It's a lightning bolt."

"Zeus," said Magda, following his train of thought.

Stefan looked at the figure of eight pattern of the tracks running around the shapes. The sweeping circles running around the edge allowed for easy manoeuvrability of the stones, but the focus should have been on the top, middle and bottom sections, for which there were small grooves in the centre of the lines.

Stefan moved the single-pronged stone to the top. "Zeus, god of the skies." He then left the trident in the centre while he moved the bident to the bottom. "Poseidon, god of the sea. Hades, god of the underworld." He slid the bident stone in place, then waited. Nothing seemed to happen at first, but then he noticed a change in the sound of the trickling water. It had intensified into a gushing noise. He turned to the space below where the cracks in the wall disappeared. Sure enough, there had been another vent concealed there. It had now opened, and water was pouring in. The water level began to rise. It eventually stopped just below where the next set of cracks in the wall ended.

"Hey, look," Magda reached into the pool of water and pulled out another black iron object. "This fell out of the vent." She handed it to Stefan. He inspected it, before holding it up next to the other iron object. It was smaller than the first, again with an arrow-like tip. Unlike the first, this one was shaped at a right angle. Stefan knew what to do with it right away. Sliding the edge of the new object into the grooves on one side of the first, he combined the two and completed two prongs of a trident.

Without another word, Magda turned her attention to the next puzzle on the wall. They knew exactly what the next part would lead to.

The stones arranged here again had flat surfaces with symbols on them. However, this time the stones were shaped like cogs, and there was no track to move them on. They were instead arranged in different sizes on an invisible horizontal line. There were four: the trident, a bull, concentric circles, and a fish. To the left of the first shape in the row was a handle protruding from the wall. Magda reached over and gave it a turn. The first cog began to follow the movement. She stopped when the trident was facing up.

"Okay," she said. "I guess we try getting them all to face up?"

Stefan nodded. "Let's try it."

"Magda turned the handle again, but only the trident cog moved once more. The other three sat dormant on the wall.

"How do I—" Magda accidentally put too much pressure on the handle, and it clunked as it sunk deep into the wall.

"Is it broken?" Natalia's voice came from somewhere behind. Magda looked back at her with wide eyes. She had almost forgotten they were not alone in this chamber.

"It's like she has a sixth sense for finding opportunities to blame someone," Magda whispered to Stefan as she turned back to the wall.

"Just a bit longer," said Stefan reassuringly.

"I'm not working with her again," whispered Magda, her tone sincere. She then began to turn the handle from its new position deep into the wall. This time the last two cogs turned in unison. The concentric circles stone was smaller than the fish and also turned at a faster rate.

"Okay, it's like the planetarium puzzle," Magda smiled to herself. "We need to change modes on the handle to turn them into the right place. I can do this." The concentric circles had an opening on the outer ring that Magda took to be an indicator for the top side. She spun the handle around until the concentric circles stone was in the right place. But the fish was now pointing to the bottom left.

Pulling the handle back very gently, she felt the mechanism slip and the handle move into a different position. It felt like the chain of a bicycle slipping between gears. She moved the handle once more and was surprised to see all four stones moving together, this time all at the same speed.

"Woah," she said. "Not what I expected."

"Can you figure it out?" asked Stefan unhelpfully.

"Is that a serious question?" she replied, not taking her focus off the stones.

With a lot of trial and error, Magda finally got the hang of the relationship between the stones and the way they moved in each setting. A few minutes later she had all four lined up to face the same direction. The concentric circles stone had been the trickiest, as it turned at a faster speed than the others. The stones were not yet facing directly up, but she knew she could quickly fix that. She moved the handle back into the middle position, the mechanism clicking as it responded to her command. She then turned clockwise, all four stones moving in unison, rotating slowly until they all pointed up. When they fell into place, she took her hand off the handle, stepping back to watch as the last vent opened and the water rushed in from somewhere unseen. Out came another black iron object, carried by the current of water and splashing into the pool as the water level rose further. Magda watched as the water rose high enough to reach the channel that ran underground from the pool to the basin on the other side of the chamber. The trickling sound of the basin filling up soon followed.

She reached into the pool and plucked the last piece of the iron trident, before handing it to Stefan. He slotted it into the central piece, completing the three prongs.

"Now what?" he wondered aloud.

Magda looked at the water that had filled up the basin on the opposite side. "We haven't used the pump yet. Let's see what happens." She walked over to the lever and began to pump it up and down. The water in the basin began to bubble, gently at first but then more intensely as she continued. The first splashes of water then found its way into the pipe. Magda continued to pump until the water was carried up the pipe and over into the bucket. The bucket, the handle of which was secured to the hand of Poseidon, swayed to and fro as the water rushed in. The bucket filled up, and the group watched in awe as the statue moved. The weight of the bucket pulled the great god's arm slowly down. The left arm followed suit, the trident that was gripped in its hand tilting forward. The bucket reached a stop by the water's surface, the arm having moved about ninety degrees from its original position. The trident was now pointed out towards the far side of the room, perfectly horizontal. The arm then began to teeter, before moving back towards its starting position. Magda watched as the bucket moved in the same reversing motion. She then saw why. The bucket had a hole in the bottom, and water was slowly trickling out. As the weight of the bucket decreased, it lifted back towards its resting place at its highest point.

"Hmm," Magda pursed her lips while she thought. "Are we missing something?" She remembered the trident Stefan was still holding in his hand. She looked at the hole in the bucket. Surely the intended solution to this puzzle was not to plug the hole in the bucket with that. There had to be a bigger purpose for it. Was the bucket supposed to have a hole in it?

She then remembered how the priest had pointed to a pedestal on the far side of the chamber, explaining that they must find the key to unlock the door.

The Atlantis Idol

"Stefan. That's the key," she said.

Without a word, her colleague marched to the pedestal. He looked at it, noticing the three holes in the top. He took one last look at the iron trident, before plunging it into the holes.

Nothing.

He shrugged at Magda, then lifted the trident key back out and faced his colleague with a dejected look.

It was then that the realisation hit him, and his eyes went wide. Looking back towards Magda from the far side of the chamber, he noticed the mural on the wall that housed the entrance they had come through. He had seen the mural earlier, but it was only now he noticed the small detail that hadn't stood out to him before. The mural depicted a story of Poseidon he knew well. The god of the sea was pointing his trident at a goddess, Athena. Having competed to become the patron god of the city of Athens, Athena emerged victorious. Bitter in defeat, Poseidon was said to have sent a monstrous flood to the Attic plain to punish the Athenians for not choosing him. The way the trident was pointed maliciously at Athena in the mural was a very on-the-nose representation of his fury. He studied the angle at which the trident was being held and called to Magda.

"Try the pump again."

Sensing he was onto something, Magda obliged. The water was pumped again up the pipe system and out of the top, tumbling into the bucket. The bucket filled up and the statue's arms began to move downward. Stefan waited for it to reach the lowest point of its movement, then watched as the arms slowly began to rise while the water trickled out of the hole in the bottom of the bucket. He concentrated hard, his eyes flicking back and forth from the mural to the statue. When the arm looked to be in the right place, he took a deep breath and slammed the trident back into the holes in the pedestal.

TWENTY-SIX

The moment the trident plunged into the holes in the pedestal, two things happened. First, the statue's arms froze in place, suspended in a pose that matched that of the mural. The water continued to trickle out the bottom of the bucket until it was empty. Yet the arms stayed still. Second, the ground underneath the pedestal, and under Stefan, began to groan. The floor seemed to judder as a large round crack formed in the floor, creating a circle around the pedestal. The circle of flooring then began to turn slowly. Stefan stumbled, the sudden unexpected movement causing him to lose his balance momentarily. He regained his composure just as the floor stopped moving again.

They could see that the circle around the pedestal had descended into the ground by a foot or so, just enough to give a clue as to what it was that Stefan had now found himself standing on. From where the platform had descended, he could see the mechanism dug into the wall around the circumference of the space surrounding where he was standing.

"It's a lift!" he called back to the others. "Come on, quickly. I don't know when it'll start moving again."

Magda hurried over to join Stefan on the circular platform.

Ted stood still, refusing to take another step in this journey. "I'm done," he said. "You said you would let me go once you found it. You don't need me to go in with you."

Natalia rolled her eyes, visibly fed up with him. "You can go after we find the temple. We haven't found it yet."

"I think it's pretty clear this is it," he replied. "You can just let me go now; I'll find my own way home."

"Mr Mendez." Natalia waved her hand towards Hiram, who dutifully reacted by drawing his firearm. She didn't need to say anything else; Ted knew he had no choice in the matter.

Hiram stood behind Ted and nudged the gun into his back, ushering him onwards to the others. Ted trudged on solemnly. He stepped down onto the platform, feeling the surface vibrate as Hiram followed.

"I hope it's built for this many people," said Stefan anxiously.

The group waited as if expecting the mechanism to kick in once they had all stepped into the circle.

"I guess we need to activate it somehow," said Magda. She approached the trident key that was still stuck facing down at the top of the pedestal. She wrapped her hand around the short shaft of the trident that served as a handle. She twisted her hand, testing the mechanism. Sure enough, the trident moved. The whole section inside the top of the pedestal rotated anti-clockwise ninety degrees, before locking in place once more. The platform began to groan and judder. A second later it started to move. It continued its slow spiralling motion, working its way deeper into the earth on a corkscrew track.

The Atlantis Idol

As they moved slowly around, Ted saw them pass a part of the wall that had ladder-like grooves dug into it—presumably an emergency access option to get back up if the lift got stuck at the bottom.

The lift continued to descend. The smooth walls all around them were painted with the muted colours of faded murals, much like the ones they had seen inside the chamber. The scenes depicted in the murals told a visual story of the rise and fall of Atlantis. Ted could see a vibrant and thriving city built in concentric circles on a bed of water. Poseidon sat proudly on a throne atop a temple in the very centre. This city was his, and he looked satisfied. It was a far cry from the fury with which he had been depicted on the mural in the chamber that told of his failed attempt to become the patron god of Athens.

The murals on the walls of the inside of the lift showed the passage of time in Atlantis, with things slowly taking a turn for the worse. Eventually, Ted could see the ancient city's demise at the hands of Poseidon himself, with the sea god creating earthquakes and terrible tsunamis that led to the city being swallowed by the sea.

"The island lost to sea, as was the will of Poseidon: to destroy his own land to make way for something new," said Stefan. The man was watching the murals with a look of reverence. The words triggered something in the deep recesses of Ted's mind. It took him a moment to remember, but he eventually recalled that he had read those exact words in Stefan's book. The leather-bound tome the man had kept close to him, and the book he had been so protective of when Ted had been caught reading it.

The lift continued its course past the final mural that showed the destruction of Atlantis. As the last muted colours of imagery disappeared, the lift finished the final few feet of its journey to the bottom. It continued to spin slowly around and eventually revealed the first glimpse of the place the group had come so far to see.

They had arrived at a cave, the air cool and musty, heavy with the scent of damp earth and the tang of salt from the nearby sea. Moonlight filtered in from a narrow fissure high above, casting dappled patterns of light and shadow across the space. The cavern was vast, its walls lined with jagged stalactites that dripped with moisture, creating a symphony of faint drips and trickles. The ground was strewn with rubble and debris, the remnants of ancient stonework that once could have belonged to a structure made thousands of years ago. Broken pillars rose from the rocky floor like ancient sentinels, their weathered surfaces bearing the scars of countless centuries. Moss and lichen clung to their crumbling stones.

In the centre of the cavern stood the remains of an altar, little more than a flat slab of stone set upon a pedestal of weathered rock. Cracks spiderwebbed across its surface, emphasising the passage of time and the relentless force of nature.

The lift slowly twisted down the final inches of its descent, coming to a rest at the bottom with a deep thud that reverberated around the place. Ted saw that Magda and Stefan were holding hands, taking in the moment of the discovery together.

Natalia was the first to step off the lift. The historians quickly followed, their hands separating again as they began to explore their surroundings. Ted noticed how this time Hiram hadn't waited for him to go on ahead. He knew the big man hadn't suddenly come to trust him—Ted simply had nowhere else to go. He gave a longing glance behind him at the ladder-like indents carved into the wall of the lift. It was a long way back up. With a sigh, Ted followed the others into the cavern and towards the ruins. He took in the impressive scene. If you were to lift the ruins out from this place and set them down somewhere else, they would look like any other nondescript temple ruins. But after the journey they had been on, the clues they had followed and the evidence that pointed them to this spot, there was no doubt about it. This was the Temple of Poseidon.

There was little left of the fabled building, and it was much smaller in scale than Ted had imagined, but that didn't detract from the grandeur of the moment. Despite the decay and ruin that surrounded them, there was a palpable sense of reverence in the air. Ted knew instantly that this was a special place, and that they were standing on sacred ground. The echoes of ancient prayers seem to linger in the shadows, whispering secrets of a lost civilization.

"There isn't much left," said Natalia.

"Indeed," Stefan replied. "The temple was at the highest point of the kingdom. If anything else survived, it will be below sea level. But…" he smiled to himself as he stepped onto a stone step leading up to the centre of the temple. "This is what we came to find."

Natalia noticed the pool of water where the sea seeped into the cavern and couldn't help but wonder about what else lay below the surface.

"I don't understand," she said. "If this was the highest point, why is it now contained in a cavern at the bottom of an island?"

Stefan shrugged. "One of history's great mysteries."

"The sea level has risen over time," Magda chimed in. "And the island might have been formed by the catastrophic tectonic movement Plato described."

"The earthquakes Poseidon caused?" asked Natalia.

"If you choose to believe that."

"Oh my God." Stefan's voice echoed through the cavern. The others looked at him, seeing him kneeling in front of the altar in the centre of the small temple. He was holding something in his hands.

"What is it?" Magda moved closer.

"It's here," Stefan replied, rising carefully with the object nestled carefully in his hands. He turned to Magda to show her. She gasped when she saw it.

In his hands was an ornate dagger. The hilt was embossed with colourful stones that glinted in the stream of moonlight that cut through the fissures in the cave wall. The curved blade, though dulled from time, looked menacing as Stefan laid out his hands for the others to see.

Ted took note of the way Magda glanced back at him right after seeing the dagger. The look on her face in that tiny moment struck him as odd. It was not the one of awe and wonder that was painted on Stefan's. It looked like sadness. Ted suddenly felt uneasy.

"A ceremonial knife?" Natalia asked as she too approached the altar.

"Yes," Stefan replied. "I can't believe it's still here after all this time."

"It's beautiful," Natalia admired the hilt of the weapon. She then flashed a stern look at Stefan. "It's coming back with me, you understand. For my collection."

Stefan frowned. He understood the terms of their deal, but he couldn't help feeling aggrieved by it all the same. Natalia didn't appreciate the importance of this object one bit. She didn't know the significance this weapon had for the world as they knew it. To her, it was just another trinket to put in her old Manor House.

Another thought then crossed his mind.

The Atlantis Idol

"To the idol, the offering will set forth rebirth and renewal. A new beginning." He recited again from his book.

Natalia rolled her eyes. "Do we understand each other, Stefan?"

"Absolutely," he said with an uneasy smile. "But, you know, we ought to learn to stop getting hung up on possessions. It was part of what made the world so toxic and broken. The new world will be better."

"Spare me the lecture," she dismissed. You know I'm not into all of that." She then looked at Ted for a moment, before focusing on Stefan again. "If you don't mind, can we please move things along?"

"What's going on?" Ted asked, his heart starting to pound in his chest. Something felt very wrong here.

"We've reached the end of our journey," said Stefan proudly. "My life's work. Magda's too. It's all led to this moment. Isn't it wonderful?"

Magda was turned away from Ted. It was as though she couldn't look at him anymore.

"This is an exciting moment," Stefan continued. "A pivotal moment in the history of the world. Today marks the end of an era and the beginning of a new world. We will cleanse the world, as Poseidon did for the Atlanteans, and make way for something new. Something better."

"What?" Ted had no idea what Stefan was talking about.

"Ted, you're a smart man. And a curious one, at that." Stefan pulled the leather-bound book from his bag and held it aloft. He was now clutching the dagger by the hilt in his other hand. The curved blade pointed out to the side, the jewels in the hilt reflecting magnificently in the streak of moonlight that illuminated the altar.

"Don't play coy now," he continued. "You saw what's in here. Truth. Promise. Destiny. When the world falls to ruin, it is the will of Poseidon to set things right. As he did with Atlantis."

"What are you talking about?"

"Look at the state of the world, Ted. It's plagued with greed, corruption, inequity."

Ted looked over at Natalia, who was looking disinterested in what Stefan was saying. The man seemed to be talking nonsense, and she was acting like she had heard it all before.

"As his disciples, it is our responsibility to enact this change for him," Stefan said with a proud look on his face. "The offering will set forth rebirth and renewal. Ted, you are the chosen one. Your offering will please the idol of Atlantis and set about the change we desperately need in this world."

Ted's mind raced. He was fixated on the dagger in Stefan's hand. The ceremonial knife, as Natalia had called it. They were going to kill him, as a sacrifice to Poseidon.

"Have you lost your mind?" Ted's lips began to tremble. He started backing away towards the lift. They had left the trident key inside the top of the pedestal. If only he could get to it and activate the lift before they caught him.

"That's far enough, Mr Mendez," Natalia was wise to his thinking. Hiram pointed the gun at Ted and circled him, the gun trained on him the whole time while the big man put himself between Ted and the lift.

"This is a great honour, Ted," said Stefan, as though trying to reassure him in some sick way.

"So, this is a cult, is it?" Ted looked around desperately for options. "You're insane, you know that?"

"Cult is such a derogatory term," Stefan dismissed. "We are The Order of Poseidon. And our community has searched for decades for this very spot: the altar inside the very temple that he was once worshipped from; the place he loved the most. He sacrificed it to make way for something new. And now we must sacrifice to do the same."

"That doesn't sound like a fair trade," said Ted. "He gave up a temple, a city at most. Not his own life."

Stefan's eye twitched. "It is his will. The scripture is very clear on that." He motioned to the book. "Do you think you know this better than me?"

Ted's eyes darted from place to place, desperate for something, anything, to help his cause. He finally settled on Natalia.

"Please, do something."

Natalia looked unfazed by what was happening and made no attempt to help him. Ted realised this had been planned all along.

His mind flashed back to the exhibition when he had followed Julia to the Sigma meeting. He remembered how Natalia had said that he and Quinn owed her for putting her mother behind bars. This was not about repaying a debt; however misguided Natalia was in that claim. And despite what she said, she didn't need Ted and Quinn to follow the clues to this place. She had made the argument that they had proven themselves to be capable treasure hunters. But the more Ted thought about it, the more he was convinced that they had known all the answers they needed to know themselves. He and Quinn had been made to think they were somehow important in that aspect. But no, that was a lie. This was not about finding Atlantis, not for Natalia. This was about revenge. The Order of Poseidon needed the clout and connections of Sigma to help find the temple. And crucially, they needed a sacrificial lamb for whatever ritual they were planning to perform. Of course, Natalia had the perfect candidates in mind for that.

Ted felt a meaty hand on his shoulder, and the barrel of a gun bury itself into the small of his back. He felt numb as he was pushed forwards to the steps leading up to the centre of the temple. Stefan waited expectantly, the book in one hand and the ceremony knife in the other.

"Here," Stefan instructed, pointing to the altar. Hiram lifted Ted effortlessly onto it and pinned him down on his back. There was no way out, no means of escape. His death was coming, and he was powerless to stop it.

TWENTY-SEVEN

Ted stared at the ceiling of the cavern, watching as particles of dust floated by in the dim patch of moonlight that crept in through the fissures in the cave wall. His senses had dulled as his mind prepared him for the end. Hiram's thick arm was held around his chest and throat, pinning him to the cold, damp, cracked stone of the altar. In the corner of his vision, he could see Stefan gesticulating with the dagger, the leather-bound book open in his other hand as he read aloud from it like a preacher.

Ted thought about the lies Natalia had fed him throughout this journey. From their very first encounter at that exhibition, he had known her well enough to know she was not to be trusted. She was someone with an agenda, and the means to ensure that she moved all the pieces she needed to fulfil that agenda. But Ted still felt foolish for clinging onto the hope that after they had located Atlantis, she would make good on her promise to let him go.

His mind went to Quinn. He had been so worried about her after they left her in the dust back in Rome. Taking the fall for Sigma's crimes felt like the worst thing that could have happened to her, but in hindsight, it was the best possible outcome. Hopefully, the authorities would believe the truth, that she was being manipulated and held against her will by this nefarious organisation. Hopefully, she would escape without punishment, or at least with minimal punishment. At the very least, she would escape with her life, and with any luck, she would be rid of Sigma now, for good. In that regard, she was faring much better than he was.

He thought about the time that had passed since they drifted apart after their last encounter with Sigma. Strangely, it was Sigma that had brought them together in the first place, but the organisation had a lot to answer for as to the trauma bond they shared that had eventually become too much for them to face. The time since they reunited had been so fleeting. It was not fair. Sigma had brought the love of his life to him, and in the next act ripped her from him. And just as the pain the organisation had caused had healed long enough for them to reunite, they had been ripped apart once again. He wished they could be allowed to live a life together. Surely, they deserved that.

Stefan continued to speak from the book and gesticulate wildly with the dagger. Ted wondered if this man really believed in all this supernatural stuff. He had been suspicious of him since discovering the man's book, but he had taken it to be nothing more than a strange interest than anything as sinister as this. Sacrificing Ted to Poseidon to 'remake the world'; it seemed incredibly far-fetched, to say the least.

He was not sure if it was a result of his fear causing his mind to hallucinate, or if the ritual Stefan was conducting was actually creating some supernatural effect, but Ted started to feel strange. The dust particles floating in the light began to move more quickly, as though they were dancing in response to something Stefan had said. A cold wave rushed over Ted, and he began to feel lightheaded.

Stefan then came closer, and Ted could feel the ritual was almost at its climax. Stefan laid the book down on the ground next to the altar and spoke a few final words as he knelt next to Ted. He clutched the dagger in both hands and lifted it high above his head, readying himself for the killing blow that would complete the ritual. Ted felt Hiram's arms grip around him a little tighter, and he instinctively started to struggle with all his might. He kept his eye fixed on the dagger, the jewelled hilt glinting in the light as Stefan prepared to plunge it downward. Ted watched the last few seconds of his life play out with frantic thoughts racing through his mind.

Time seemed to stand still as the dagger hovered high above Stefan's head. Ted then heard Quinn's voice come from somewhere deep in his mind. It sounded distant, like an echo. She was calling his name, the pitch of her voice high as though she were screaming at him.

Stefan's head turned and Ted watched as the man relaxed his grip on the ceremonial knife, taking one hand away as he was distracted by something. Ted turned his head to the left to see two faint figures near the lift where they had entered the temple. His senses came rushing back and the strange feeling he had felt during the ritual subsided.

He heard Quinn's voice again and realised that she was one of the figures he was seeing. He squinted to focus his vision and confirm what he thought he was seeing. She was really there.

"Get the hell away from him!" she shouted. The man next to her had a revolver raised, pointing at Stefan.

"What is going on here?" the man had a commanding voice. "Sir," he addressed Stefan. "Put the knife down."

The group were so stunned by the newcomers' arrival that nobody said anything for a moment. Ted felt Hiram shift his body slowly as the ex-military man reacted to the danger by trying to access his gun without drawing attention. With the stone altar low to the ground, Hiram had crouched down behind it, wrapping his arms around Ted to keep him in position. The man had taken an arm away to try and reach his firearm. The man holding the revolver next to Quinn was fixed on Stefan and hadn't noticed Hiram reaching down for his gun.

"Watch out!" Ted called, alerting them to the situation. As he did so, he pulled down on the arm that was keeping him restrained, lifting his head to pull Hiram forward. He used all his core muscles to heave upwards, throwing Hiram off balance with the sudden movement. He knew he had no advantage from this position, and Hiram would quickly regain his composure, but all he needed was a moment to attract the attention of Quinn's companion.

Hiram lurched forward from the sudden movement, letting out a frustrated grunt as Ted pulled him towards the altar. The plan worked, as Hiram missed grabbing the gun, and the man next to Quinn switched his focus to them.

Hiram quickly regained his balance and used his superior arm strength to pull Ted back down onto the slab of cracked stone, giving himself more leverage to attempt to reach the gun once more.

"Hey!" The sound of the revolver's hammer clicking down sounded, the cylinder twisting around to place a bullet in line with the barrel, ready to fire. Hiram stopped and looked up to see the man next to Quinn training the gun on him. An experienced killer himself, Hiram recognised another of the same ilk. There was something about the man that separated him from the others in the cavern.

The man moved in closer to the steps leading up to the altar. "Take your hands away from him and put them in the air where I can see them."

There it was. The line sounded too well practised.

"Police?" Hiram spoke, the gruff sound of his voice alien to Ted, who couldn't remember the last time he had heard the man speak.

"Yes," the man replied. He pulled a badge from his bomber jacket pocket with one hand, the other still firmly on the grip of the nasty-looking six-shooter. "Detective Giovanni Rossi." Giovanni glanced around the space, taking a mental note of the number of people and their current state. So far, he hadn't seen any other weapons besides the gun Hiram was reaching for and the large, curved knife still in the hands of Stefan.

"We have ourselves a situation here," Giovanni continued. "I would appreciate your cooperation in ensuring everyone's safety while we figure it out. Nobody has to get hurt."

Hiram stared at the revolver being aimed in his direction, and at the look in the eye of the man wielding it. The barrel of the weapon was long for a sidearm. Hiram knew the model; those things packed a punch. He was not ready to give up just yet, but he was wary of making a move for his own pistol.

"Ted, are you okay?" Quinn called across the cavern. Her voice carried every bit of worry she felt in it. Seeing the scene of the ritual playing out as she and Giovanni descended the last rung of the ladder into the cavern, she realised how close they had cut it. One more moment and Stefan would have killed him.

Ted was lying flat on his back, Hiram's meaty arm still across him, restraining him.

"I've been better," he replied sarcastically, trying hard to mask his fear with humour. "It's good to hear your voice," he added with sincerity.

Quinn smiled. "You too." She took in the scene of the cavern, her brain trying to process the historical magnitude of what she had just walked into, while simultaneously fretting for Ted's safety. Following in Sigma's footsteps, she had put together the same pieces they had to trace their path to the location of the lost city of Atlantis. Or at least this very small part of it.

Giovanni climbed the short stone steps up to the temple ruins, passing one of the giant pillars. All the while he kept his attention on Hiram. Quinn followed close behind.

"How much?" Natalia asked.

Giovanni didn't take his eyes off Hiram. "What?"

"Money," Natalia said condescendingly. "How much do you want to leave now and let us go about our business?"

The moonlight glinted off one of the jewels in the hilt of the dagger Stefan was still holding. Giovanni maintained a safe distance from Hiram as he began to circle him. He stopped when he reached a point where everyone was in his field of view.

"I'm not interested in your money," Giovanni replied.

"Are you sure?" Natalia persisted. "I have rather a lot."

Giovanni's expression remained flat; his mind focused on the task at hand. He carefully considered his next move.

Ted was breathing hard, his mind racing. Not a moment ago Stefan had been hovering in his field of vision, preparing to end his life with a stab of the blade. Death had seemed like a certainty. To say he was relieved to hear Quinn's voice interrupting the ritual would be the understatement of the century.

The Atlantis Idol

He turned his head to see the man approaching cautiously. A detective. Quinn had worked wonders here. Instead of being locked up, she had somehow convinced this man to aid her in going after the group. They would have had to trace them to the church of Chiesa and then from there to this church in Irakleia. She really was brilliant. Maybe they actually had a fighting chance of escaping.

"Whatever was happening here is over," said Giovanni. "I've got backup on the way. They'll be here any minute. You are all under arrest for counts of kidnapping and murder. You have two choices. One, you do as I say. You accept your arrest, and everybody leaves this place safely. Or…" he narrowed his eyes as he flicked from Stefan to Hiram. "Two, you resist, and I put you down. It will be easy for me to write it off as self-defence. And please believe me," he kept the gun trained on Hiram. "I won't miss."

Stefan's eye twitched. Still holding the ceremonial knife defiantly, he was seething on the inside. He had come so far, and the ritual was almost complete. The damn fools who had interrupted him had no idea just how important this work was for humanity.

"You don't understand," Stefan said, his voice cracking as he tried to keep his composure. "We are so close. The world needs change. We can fix it right here and now."

"Drop the knife," Giovanni instructed. "And you," he addressed Hiram. "Take your arm off him and step back slowly."

Hiram didn't cooperate, keeping his arm braced around Ted's chest.

"This place is special," Stefan continued talking, seemingly indifferent to Giovanni's instructions. "There's a palpable energy here. I can feel it. Poseidon is calling to us, willing us to answer. I have spent my life studying, and learning. Everything led me to this moment. All he requires is a small sacrifice, and the reward is bigger than you can possibly imagine."

"Drop. The. Knife." Giovanni enunciated each word slowly.

Stefan cocked his head at the man holding the revolver. Ted could see Stefan's face in the moonlight. His eyes were dilated, as though he were under the influence of something. Whether it was the build-up to this moment or some unexplained mysticism of the temple itself, something had changed in the historian. He looked almost possessed in the moment.

Giovanni narrowed his eyes at Stefan, not appreciating the lack of cooperation. The way the man's pupils were dilated gave him cause to worry. He had seen that look before, and it never ended well.

Stefan turned his head to look Ted dead in the eye. "It is his will. It is too late; the ritual has already begun. We must provide this offering!" He gripped the dagger tightly in both hands and lunged at Ted.

TWENTY-EIGHT

Everything in the next moment went by in a blur. Seeing Stefan lunging at him with the dagger raised, Ted threw a leg up, his foot planting into the crazed man's chest and stopping him from getting too close. The dagger had come down and was teetering right above Ted. The old blade looked rusted and worn from age, but there was no doubt it would kill when used with enough force. Ted kept pressure on his leg, struggling to keep Stefan at bay. His hands were spread apart, having caught Stefan's on their way down. Ted could feel the hilt of the ceremonial knife on the thenar space between his thumb and index finger on both hands. He tried with everything he had to keep the blade from piercing his chest. Stefan's face contorted as he struggled against Ted's defence. The dagger vibrated as the two struggled against each other like an unconventional arm wrestle. Being above Ted with the blade pointing downward, Stefan had a clear advantage. Ted wouldn't be able to hold him off for long.

At the same time, Hiram had taken advantage of the distraction and picked up his gun from the ground next to the altar. Taking his arm away from Ted, he had spun around to take aim at Giovanni. His finger caressed the trigger. A gunshot cracked suddenly. But it was Hiram who let out a grunt of pain, dropping his firearm as the bullet from Giovanni's revolver hit his wrist. He fell to the ground behind the altar, and his fingers involuntarily spread apart as the pain seared and blood began to pour from the wound. The high-calibre revolver round had met its mark and delivered a hefty blow.

Startled by the gunshot, Stefan had given Ted just the opening he needed. With his left foot still planted on the man's torso, Ted leaned back against the cold stone altar, his hands supporting himself on the surface as he pushed off. Stefan reeled from the movement and stumbled backwards. It didn't take long for the man to regain his composure, however, and before Ted could move, he saw him lift the knife into the air again for another stab.

In a final desperate attempt, Ted kicked out with his right leg, connecting perfectly with Stefan's arm and knocking the dagger out of his hands. The blade spun in the air as it disappeared over Ted's head, landing with a clatter somewhere beyond the perimeter of the temple. Stunned, Stefan watched with concern as the dagger tumbled away and out of sight. The object was critical to his mission, and if he was to complete the ritual, he would need to retrieve it.

Stefan gritted his teeth. These petulant fools were refusing to accept their fate. He was growing tired of this.

Suddenly, something smacked the side of his face. A small rock bounced on the ground by his feet, and Stefan turned to see Quinn standing at the top of the steps to the temple. Her aim had been true, but the stone had merely cut his cheek. He clenched his fist and began to walk towards her, his mind flashing back to the moment right before he left her in the vault underneath the Vatican. He had so wanted to hurt her then, but for Magda's intervention and an urgency to make their escape. Nothing would stop him this time. His mind raced as he relished the chance to finish the job. He only needed one of them for the ritual—he could dispose of Quinn first any way he wanted.

A weight smashed into Stefan as he was suddenly tackled to the ground by Ted. Sitting up on the altar, Ted had seen Stefan set his sights on Quinn, and in a white-hot rage, he had run at him full pelt, barrelling into the man and sending him flying forward. Stefan's face smashed into the hard stone floor of the temple as Ted landed hard on the man's back. Stefan let out a muffled grunt of pain as his face took the full force of the fall.

A cry then came from somewhere behind the pair, and Magda appeared as if from nowhere.

"You bastard!" she screamed, pulling Ted up off her colleague. As she did so, Stefan threw back an elbow, catching Ted in the sternum. The wind was knocked from him, and Ted's eyes went wide as he struggled for breath. Magda threw Ted to the ground, discarding him as she tended to Stefan. He had lost a front tooth, and one eye was shut, with a deep cut in his brow. However, he was still conscious.

"Stefan. Talk to me," she pleaded.

Stefan spat blood onto the floor. He tried to speak but instead coughed violently. "Get... the knife," he managed at last, between gasps for breath.

Magda looked up in the direction the dagger had gone spinning off to moments earlier. But before she could set off looking for it, a gunshot cracked, and she froze.

Giovanni had fired his revolver upwards to the ceiling, demanding the attention of everyone within the cavern.

"Listen to me," he said with authority. "This ends now." He made his way towards the entrance to the temple, where

Magda knelt by the prone Stefan. "Stay there and don't move." He turned to Quinn. "Find that knife and bring it to me." He then addressed Natalia, who had been keeping out of the way throughout the short fight, as though either trying to get away unnoticed or bide her time to make an attacking move. "I'd like you to join your friends here." Giovanni gestured to the entrance to the temple, where Magda knelt next to Stefan.

Natalia hesitated, before begrudgingly cooperating after taking stock of her limited options.

"It took years of work to get here," Magda hissed. "You don't realise what you've done." She saw how bloodied Stefan's mouth was, feeling an anger rising that she had thus far managed to keep in check.

"And what have I done?" Giovanni questioned.

"You are standing in the way of the new world!" Stefan spat. "Poseidon will grant us a better world if only we give him a small sacrifice in return."

Giovanni raised an eyebrow, wondering why he had bothered asking. He had dealt with all manner of unstable delusions in his career and was no stranger to individuals who believed that their violent acts were justified by some sort of higher cause. But he had to admit he had experienced nothing quite like this before.

"The knife, please," he held out a hand expectantly. Quinn, who was now across the cavern searching in the dark for the dagger, felt a change in Giovanni's voice at that moment. She had only spent a few hours with this man, but that was the first time he had appeared to lose his patience.

"Why are you meddling in this?" Magda asked. "What do you stand to gain from denying the world of change?"

"Quiet," Giovanni dismissed.

Magda continued defiantly. "This planet is full of selfishness, greed, and suffering. Even Atlantis, Poseidon's own kingdom, turned in a way that required change. Poseidon destroyed that land to make way for something new. Something better. It is high time we did the same again. You value this idiot's life enough to prevent the advent of a better world?" She looked at Ted, who was still lying on the ground catching his breath.

Quinn gritted her teeth. "He's not an idiot." The glint of the jewels in the hilt of the ceremonial knife revealed the object to her, and she picked it up, studying it while she felt the ancient material in her fingers. "Ted is exactly what is right with this world. Kind, intelligent, and courageous. He is the kind of person you want in your new world."

"Which is why he is the perfect sacrifice," said Magda. "Giving up a life that is pure is a bigger sacrifice than ridding the world of a sinner. There is a reason the Church have ties to the protection of this ancient rite. They saw the parallels with the sacrifice of their own saviour. Theirs gave their pure life so others would be saved. Ted will give his so the world can be remade with the purity of his heart."

Natalia scoffed. "So pure. Such an angel," she said sarcastically. "He would never do anything to hurt anyone. Oh, except get a woman put away for a crime he was guilty of, separating her from her daughter in the process."

"You are delusional," Quinn laughed. "You know full well that Ted and I were prisoners in that whole debacle. The crime was your mother's, and she is paying the price for it. You can be bitter all you like." She looked Natalia dead in the eye. "But you are the problem."

"Hey," Ted's voice came as he tentatively picked himself up from the ground. "I am not anyone's saviour. I'm just an ordinary guy who is in the wrong place at the wrong time."

Quinn handed the knife to Giovanni. He studied it a moment in his hand, finally satisfied with how things were shaping up.

"Okay, let's wrap things up," he said. He picked up the handgun that Hiram had dropped when he was shot. He then walked behind the altar to check on the ex-soldier's injury.

There was nobody there.

Giovanni's eyes widened as he saw the small pool of blood on the stone floor, but no sign of the man who had made it. Where had he gone? A sinking feeling hit him as he internally berated himself for being so careless.

Before he had time to react, Hiram appeared from the shadows, the big man slamming his body into Giovanni's. Both the handgun and the ceremonial knife went flying across the temple. Both men tussled on the ground. Hiram launched a barrage of punches to Giovanni's midriff with his un-injured hand. Having been caught off guard, Giovanni lifted his hands, palms out, to try and counter the blows. His opponent was strong, and with each punch, the man nearly knocked the wind out of him.

With the tables turning, Stefan sensed an opportunity. He picked himself up from the ground, and with fire in his eyes, he threw himself at Ted. Luckily for Ted, Quinn reacted faster than he did, and just before Stefan connected with him, she swung out a leg, tripping him. The man lost his balance and with it the element of surprise. Ted had a fraction of a second longer to react, but the man toppled into him all the same. Ted shoved him back, but then out of nowhere, a fist smashed into his jaw. He reeled as he felt something crack, his hand going to his mouth to nurse the injury.

Magda shook off her hand as she winced in pain, the force of her punch having had consequences for her too.

"You will make this sacrifice, Ted!" the woman yelled. "We've come too far to waste this opportunity."

"Grab the knife!" Stefan shouted. "Kill him, or kill her," he pointed at Quinn. "I don't care which. The ritual is almost complete. This must be done."

Magda raced across the temple towards the ceremonial knife. Hiram and Giovanni continued struggling with each other a few feet away, neither man able to take control of the fight. Giovanni knew that at full strength Hiram would have been too much for him, but the gunshot wound in his wrist was hampering him significantly. Hiram grabbed Giovanni by the throat, kneeling on top of him to pin him down. Giovanni spluttered as the air left him. His legs kicked out as he desperately tried to fend off his attacker. Hiram's fingers squeezed, and Giovanni felt the cavern close in on him. He flailed with his hands on the stone floor, feeling for anything to help his cause. Eventually, he felt the tip of a loose rock. He tried to grip it, but it was just out of reach. He tried again, this time the tip of his middle finger getting purchase on the edge of the rock. It slid towards him just enough for him to take hold of it. Clutching it, he swung his hand around and caught Hiram in the temple with the rock. Stunned by the blunt force, Hiram released his throat and Giovanni sucked in a deep breath.

Magda was almost at the dagger when Quinn intercepted her, knocking her to the ground. She let out a frustrated cry as Quinn smacked a tight fist into her cheek.

"Nobody punches my boyfriend!" she yelled, delivering another blow to Magda's side.

Ted watched on as he saw a side to Quinn he didn't know existed. She was ferocious. He couldn't help smiling as he heard her refer to him as her boyfriend. The moment was short-lived, however, as out of nowhere Stefan entered the fight, grabbing Quinn by the hair and pulling her off his colleague.

Quinn struggled against him, but Stefan didn't let go. He stamped on her foot, then dragged her a few feet across the stone floor. Magda got back to her feet, just as Stefan forced Quinn onto her knees. Magda took up position behind her to restrain her. Kneeling behind her, she held her arms tightly behind her back, while Stefan marched over to the ceremonial knife. He picked it up and watched the moonlight glint off its surface.

He turned to Quinn with malice in his eyes, then mumbled a few last words of the ritual. "Great Poseidon, commander of the sea, to you I make this sacrifice." He approached Quinn with the dagger raised, ready to bring it down on her. His figure loomed menacingly over her, a strange ethereal atmosphere filling the temple as he prepared to complete the ritual. She breathed hard, experiencing the strange sensation that each inhale she took could be her last.

Suddenly, a gunshot echoed around the cavern. Stefan's eyes widened and he froze in position, the hand holding the dagger still raised. Then, his grip weakened, and the ancient weapon fell from his grasp, clattering on the floor. Stefan looked down to his torso, seeing his shirt stained with blood. The bullet had travelled through his sternum, and the patch of blood grew larger and larger, a deep red spreading through the fabric of his clothes. With a look of confusion, Stefan looked in the direction the shot had come from.

Ted stood with Hiram's handgun raised, the barrel still smoking. His hand trembled as he watched Stefan's horrified expression turn to one of despair. The man fell to the ground, blood seeping into the stone floor. His body went still as life left him.

A scream came from Magda, who released Quinn and raced to her colleague.

"Stefan! No, no, no, no!" she panicked, tending to the lifeless Stefan. She cradled him in her arms, sobbing.

Quinn was stunned as she watched the woman grieve. She then rushed over to Ted, who was still pointing the gun, his hand shaking as the realisation of what he had done set in.

"It's okay," she said calmly, putting a gentle hand on his arm, slowly lowering the gun in the process.

"I... I..." he trembled.

"You did the right thing."

Across the temple, Giovanni had finally gotten the upper hand over Hiram. The ex-soldier had fought hard but had lost too much blood to keep up. He had slumped to the floor after Giovanni had smacked him in the side of the head with the rock, seemingly unconscious.

Giovanni got to his feet, using the altar to keep him steady as he coughed and wheezed.

"What a mess," he said at last, assessing the scene. He reached for his revolver and took stock of the dead frame of Stefan lying on the ground, his head in Magda's lap as she cradled him and wept.

"It's over," he said. "I'll take that gun, and that knife."

Something caused Giovanni's ears to prick up suddenly. It was an oddly familiar sound that evoked a very specific fear response inside him. The sound was subtle but unmistakable. A metallic pinging had come from behind him, and a small metal ring bounced off the altar next to where he was resting his hand. He turned to see Hiram sitting up against a pillar. He looked utterly spent. Blood continued to seep from the gunshot wound, and the ensuing fight with Giovanni which ended with a large gash to the side of his head had taken its toll on his strength. The whole side of his head was covered in dark red blood.

In his hand was a grenade, the pin having been pulled. Giovanni wondered where the hell had that come from. Had he been carrying it with him this whole time?

Hiram's eyes were heavy, and Giovanni could tell he was in his last moments. Giovanni knew that look. Hiram knew the end was coming for him; he was not leaving this place alive. Even if an emergency response team reached him now, there would be only a slim chance he would make it. Hiram knew the truth: he was dying. That knowledge made him dangerous. With no regard for his own life, and nothing but anger and thoughts of revenge on his mind, Giovanni could see he was about to make a stupid decision.

Hiram looked at the shocked expression on Giovanni's face, taking great joy in seeing him get the upper hand on him in a final twist of fate. He smirked as he spoke his final words.

"Go to hell, you bastard." The ex-soldier flung the live grenade towards the altar.

TWENTY-NINE

The grenade flew through the air, almost in slow motion. Giovanni watched as the metal casing clunked on the ground, then bounced up and ricocheted off the underside of the altar, before disappearing as it came to rest underneath the ancient stone structure.

"Move!" he yelled, diving for cover. He hit the floor just as the grenade went off. The explosion was deafening. The ancient altar was decimated, fragments of stone sent flying. The blast kicked up a cloud of dust that filled the air, obscuring everyone's vision.

One of the colossal pillars at the entrance of the temple cracked across the middle and began to crumble. There was a deep rumbling all around as the explosion had started a chain reaction of events. The old cavern that had diligently preserved this small piece of history for so long had been ruptured. The top of the stone pillar broke away, taking with it part of the ceiling of the cavern. A large fragment of earth fell, leaving a gaping hole from which moonlight now streamed in. The ground beneath their feet continued rumbling as the whole place shifted from the force of the blast.

Having heard the shouts of Giovanni, Ted had reacted by leaping to the steps leading up to the entrance of the temple. Having survived the initial blast, he, like those around him, was in the path of the falling debris. Seeing the chunk of earth breaking away from the ceiling, he rolled to his side, narrowly avoiding it as it crashed down onto the ground.

There was something strange about the way the earth moved at that moment. The vibrations from the ground felt akin to an earth tremor. His mind flashed to the story of the destruction of Atlantis, and how Poseidon had caused earthquakes that ravaged the city, destroying it to make way for something new.

The pillar that had started to crumble split in the middle, the top half toppling like a felled tree. The ancient stonework crashed down away from the temple, slamming into a dark corner of the cavern.

Dust filled the air and Ted's field of vision was short. He coughed as he got to his feet and tried to get his bearings.

"Quinn!" he called, worried that he couldn't see her. He hadn't heard another voice since Giovanni shouted for them to take cover.

He heard more coughing coming from somewhere nearby. Something brushed past him, but whatever it was had disappeared into the cloud of dust before he had a chance to turn around.

"Ted!" Quinn's voice came suddenly, and then she was beside him. "This place is coming down."

The dust settled and the group could see more clearly. Magda was still sitting next to Stefan's body, holding him close. Giovanni, who had been closest to the blast when the grenade went off, was tentatively getting to his feet. A thick streak of blood ran down the side of his face. He leaned onto a nearby pillar for support, his lack of balance accompanied by a loud ringing in his ears. Ted and Quinn then looked past him to where Hiram had sat propped up against the pillar he had thrown the explosive from. A pile of rubble concealed all but the sole of his boot. There was no way he had survived that.

A scraping noise came suddenly from across the cavern. Ted and Quinn spun around to see the platform that had taken the group down from the proving chamber kick into life. Turning slowly the opposite way it had come, the platform began to ascend, following the corkscrew tracks back up the shaft. On the platform was Natalia, the ceremonial knife in her hands. She gave a last look at the others before the platform rotated her away and she disappeared.

Quinn swore loudly. "She's leaving us for dead! How are we going to get back up?"

Ted's heart raced. Debris continued to fall all around them. He saw the grooves carved into the wall on one side of the shaft, remembering seeing them on the way down.

"The ladder," he said. "Isn't that how you came down?"

Quinn shook her head. "It was, but Natalia just took the lift back up. I think the ladder is only viable when the platform is at the bottom. It will block us from getting through the top."

It was Ted's turn to swear aloud. He looked around desperately for options. The cavern ceiling continued to crumble, and a large chunk of earth plummeted into one of the other pillars of the temple. There was a thud as the two materials came together, before the pillar splintered, sending large fragments in their direction. The heavy stone rained all around them. Ted and Quinn took cover, shielding their faces with their arms. Had one of the chunks of stone hit them, they would have been knocked unconscious at the very least. The way things were developing around them, that would mean certain death; the whole cavern was collapsing in on itself. Luckily, the debris missed them both.

"We need to find another way out," Quinn took Ted by the hand and pulled him down the steps to the temple entrance. As they approached the spot the platform had been moments earlier a tremendous crash sounded, and the cavern wall to the side of it caved in. Quinn stopped in her tracks as a huge pile of rubble blocked their path. Even if the ladder had been an option, there was no way of even getting to it now.

They both looked around helplessly. They were trapped. As stone and earth rained all around, Quinn took Ted by the hand and stared deep into his eyes. Dust and dirt covering their faces, a single tear escaped from the corner of her eye. Ted wiped it away with a gentle hand.

"I love you," he said. "I've wanted to tell you that for so long."

Quinn's lip trembled as she battled a complex mix of fear and warmth in her heart.

"I love you too," she replied, wrapping her arms around the back of his head, and pulling him close for a kiss.

Time seemed to stand still for a moment, before at last a voice cut through from across the cavern.

"Over here!" Giovanni called. He was standing by the shallow pool of water that flooded in on one side of the subterranean space.

The pair hurried over to where he was standing. As they ran, Quinn spotted another large rock flying in their direction, grabbing Ted by the arm to pull him out of the way. The rock missed them by inches.

When they finally reached Giovanni, he was standing in the pool, the water up to his waist. Water dripped from his head, as though he had dived or fallen in.

"I think there's a tunnel through here that leads to the sea," he said. "It's our only way out." He turned to Ted. "Can you swim?"

"Yes," Ted replied, wondering why the man was asking him specifically, and not them both.

"Good. Go now." Without warning, he dipped down into the water and was gone. A few bubbles remained on the surface where he had been, but Giovanni was nowhere to be seen. Either unconcerned about their safety or trusting them to look after themselves as they escaped, the private investigator had wasted no time in securing his own exit from the crumbling cavern.

Ted watched the surface of the water for a few moments longer, as though expecting the man to appear again. The fact he didn't return convinced Ted that his hunch that it was a viable escape route had been correct.

"Okay, you want to go first, or—" Ted turned to Quinn but found that she had disappeared. He saw her at the steps of the temple, pleading with Magda to follow them.

"I'm not leaving him," Magda said stubbornly.

"But you'll die here!" shouted Quinn. "He's gone, Magda."

Magda stayed with Stefan, unmoved by Quinn's protestations.

"Quinn, come on!" Ted called. The cavern looked like it was going to collapse completely at any moment.

"I can't stay here any longer, and neither can you," Quinn said. "Stefan wouldn't want you to die too."

Magda was unmoved. Quinn had done all she could. It was Magda's life, her choice. She raced back to Ted and dove straight into the cold pool of water, disappearing beneath the surface. Ted gave her a second to give her space to swim ahead of him, then gave a final glance back at the crumbling ruins of the temple. This ancient monument had been preserved here in secret for centuries. With one foolish act, the whole place was being destroyed, sentencing it to a sudden and unceremonious end.

He plunged into the cold water. The rumbling and crashing of the collapsing cavern dulled the instant he plunged underwater. The water was just clear enough to see the faint outline of Quinn kicking her legs as she swam down and underneath the rock wall of the cavern. An opening in the wall revealed how the water had poured in from the sea, and Ted watched as Quinn disappeared into the flooded tunnel. He spread his arms out long in front of him as he prepared to begin swimming. He kicked his legs as he pushed his arms out in a breaststroke pattern.

Debris fell into the water, the dust and dirt making it murkier, obscuring Ted's vision. The tunnel was starting to give way, and Ted's heart pounded in his chest, adrenaline coursing through his veins as he raced against time to escape. The tunnel was narrow and claustrophobic, the rocky walls pressing in on all sides as he propelled himself forward with powerful strokes of his arms and legs. His lungs burned as he held his breath and swam on into the darkness.

With each passing moment, the pressure mounted, driving him onward with a desperate urgency. He could feel the tunnel narrowing ahead, the ceiling pressing down on his back as he struggled to maintain his course.

Just when he feared that he could go no further, a faint glimmer of light appeared in the distance, beckoning him onward. With renewed determination, Ted pushed himself forward, until finally he burst through the surface of the water and into the open sea.

Gasping for breath, he began to tread water for a moment, blinking as his eyes adjusted to his new surroundings. The full moon glowed in the sky and the stars were out in force. He found himself in a sheltered cove, enveloped by towering cliffs and crashing waves. There was a small light attached to the side of the cliff which provided ample visibility of his surroundings. The light bounced beautifully off the sea, giving it an aura that made it shimmer.

"Ted!" Quinn was there, just a few feet ahead of him. "Are you okay?"

He began to swim towards her, still panting hard as he regained his breath. "Yes," he spluttered. "Keep going."

With a final effort, the pair swam around the edge of the cliff and towards the safety of the shore, the adrenaline still coursing through their veins.

As the shore came into sight, Ted could see the small boat they had taken to the small island, the vessel bobbing up and down in the gentle waves that lapped against the beach. For the first time on this journey, Ted felt free, their ordeal finally at an end as he made his way back to solid ground.

When they were finally out of the water they collapsed onto the beach, shattered.

Lying on their backs, staring up at the starry sky, listening to the gentle lapping of the waves, the moment was almost peaceful. They found it difficult to enjoy it, however. If only the moment hadn't immediately followed a near-death experience to conclude a nightmarish few days.

"I can't believe it's over," said Ted.

"I can't believe we actually made it out," Quinn replied. "If he hadn't told us about the underwater tunnel…" she trailed off, contemplating the alternative.

"But he did, and we're here," said Ted.

Quinn let out a long exhale, feeling relief begin to outweigh the other emotions. "I was so worried about you. After I learned about the Order of Poseidon, and what Stefan and Magda were planning with us. With you." She reached for Ted's hand. "I thought I'd lost you."

Ted felt her fingers touch his and held her hand tightly, interlocking his fingers with hers. "Thank you for coming after me."

"Guess it makes us even," she said with a smile.

Ted laughed, which quickly turned into a coughing fit as his lungs still burned from the intense period of underwater swimming. "I'm glad you brought backup," he managed at last. "Who was your friend, anyway? I heard him say detective something or other."

"Yeah, weird one. From Interpol, or under orders from Interpol, or something," said Quinn. "He came to talk to me about Sigma at the police station and asked me to help him track them down."

"Shit," Ted whistled. "Wonder if he caught up to Natalia."

"Hmm."

A minute went by as they listened to the sound of the sea and regained their energy.

"I killed Stefan," said Ted solemnly. "I killed him. I mean, I had to. I think I had to. It was him or you."

"I know," said Quinn softly.

Another long silence followed.

"Hey," a thought arrived in Ted's head. "Why did you go back for Magda? She was part of that cult too."

Quinn looked up into the stars. "At that point, it felt like everything before didn't matter anymore. We were just people trying to survive. I didn't want her to die."

"You're a good person, Quinn Miyata."

It was then they heard footsteps coming down the path towards them.

THIRTY

Getting to their feet, Quinn and Ted watched as a figure emerged from the dark of the path that led up the cliff towards the old church. The silhouette drew closer and then seemed to stop on seeing the pair. They made an involuntary noise that relayed their surprise at seeing them there.

"How on earth—" Natalia's voice came before she stepped into view. She appraised the pair, surprise etched across her face, clearly shocked to learn that they hadn't perished in the cavern after she had taken the lift back up to the church, leaving them all for dead. The ceremonial knife was in her hand, and the pair suddenly had an uneasy feeling of vulnerability. Perhaps it was the way Natalia was looking at them both. She seemed disappointed to see them alive and well.

"It seems I continue to underestimate you both," she said, seemingly regaining her composure. "How on earth did you get out?"

The two looked at her with stern expressions, saying nothing. Natalia waved a hand dismissively and made her way to the boat.

"It doesn't matter. It is unfortunate, though." She waded through the knee-high water and placed the ancient dagger on board before pulling herself up into the vessel. "I was hoping you would be dead already. I do hate loose threads." She knelt on the boat and rummaged around in a backpack that had been left there.

"You're a monster," said Quinn. "All of this, the death and destruction; it was all for your petty ego, wasn't it?"

Natalia's brow furrowed. She finally found what she was looking for and stood up, revealing a small pistol.

"Hiram was a resourceful one," she said with a wry smile. "He mentioned he would keep one here, just in case. Well…" she paused as she spared a moment of reflection for the mercenary that had so diligently protected her. She sighed. "Finding protection that you can trust is harder than you think." She levelled the gun in the direction of Quinn. "It is not about ego, my dear. It is a matter of justice. You have somehow robbed me of that justice. Like a couple of cockroaches, you just simply don't seem to die. If I didn't know better, I might say that those delusional Poseidon worshippers were onto something. Maybe there is some divine entity lingering in that place, and it took their lives to save yours. Unfortunately, that does not have agency over me."

"You can't do this," Ted pleaded. "Murdering us is not justice; it's not even close to the same thing we did. Your mother is alive. She's in prison for crimes *she* committed."

Natalia paused, a thought coming to her. She lowered the gun a fraction, rethinking her decision. "Mr Mendez, you are absolutely right. There is no justice in killing you."

Ted felt himself relax a little. There was a real unpredictability to the way Natalia stood on the boat, brandishing a firearm. She had proven herself to be emotional in her actions, often betraying the calm and controlled exterior she tried to maintain. Which way this exchange was going to go, Ted had no idea.

"I won't kill you," she said at last, the words spoken flippantly as though her decision had been a snap one. "There would be no sense in that. No, that would be too easy for you both. You should be made to feel the same way I feel. You should understand what it is to have someone you each care about be taken away from you." Natalia looked at them both with a stern expression, contemplating her next move. "I'll find a way to make that happen." She placed the gun down and began preparing the boat to go.

Quinn and Ted watched in silence. It looked like they were safe, for now, and they didn't wish to say anything further that might change that. However, Natalia's last words lingered like a bad taste in the mouth, and the pair couldn't help but wonder how the woman was planning to enact her vengeance.

Natalia bent down by the motor at the back of the small boat and began pulling on the cord to jump-start the 2-stroke outboard engine. It took a couple of attempts, but then the motor roared to life.

Over the rumbling of the motor, Natalia gave one last look at the pair.

"Don't get too comfortable when you get back home," she said. "I'm not finished with—"

Just then, a gunshot cracked, and Natalia stumbled, letting out a shout of pain. The sudden unexpected sound made Ted jump out of his skin. Compared to the cavern, the sound of the gunshot ringing out didn't have the same intensive impact on the shore. The acoustics were very different to that of the cavern, and here there was the added noise from the small boat engine. However, as Ted looked behind him, he realised why it had startled him so much. The revolver in Giovanni's hands had been shot only a few feet from him. They must have been over thirty feet from the boat at this point, but as Giovanni had said before, he didn't miss.

The PI marched over towards the boat, the water sloshing as he waded through the gentle waves that rose to his knees. Natalia's cries could be heard just above the rumbling of the motor, the woman having doubled over to nurse the wound in her side where the high-calibre bullet had torn through her flesh.

Giovanni heaved himself into the boat. He stood over the injured Natalia, revolver in hand. He flexed his off hand, before reaching down and picking up the ceremonial knife. Natalia cursed loudly, the searing pain spreading out from her side into the rest of her body.

"Who the hell are you?" she strained to get the words out. "I know a cop when I see one. That's not you."

"I'm like you," Giovanni said bluntly. "I take an opportunity when I see one."

Natalia looked up at the man with a pained expression. At that moment she knew it was over. But something inside her willed her to try. "How much?" she asked. "Name your bloody price!"

Giovanni shook his head. "I told you; I don't want your money. My client is already paying me very handsomely for my services. And believe me, these are not the kind of people you can walk away from. It is just business. You understand."

Natalia's face went ghostly white as the man levelled his revolver at her head and pulled the trigger. Quinn and Ted

The Atlantis Idol

saw the quick flash of light from the gun and heard the shot against the backdrop of the boat's motor.

A moment went by as the pair on the shore stood still, watching with their hands over their mouths. This detective had just gunned down a suspect with no attempt to arrest her or bring her in. Ted was suddenly aware of something the man had said in the cavern when trying to halt Stefan's ritual. He had said that backup was on the way, and that his colleagues would shortly be there to arrest them all. Well, so far, he hadn't seen any signs of police activity. If they were close by, there would be no way for Natalia to have sauntered down from the church back to the boat without being spotted and intercepted.

Giovanni holstered his gun and carefully placed the ceremonial knife inside his bomber jacket pocket. He then turned off the boat's engine and set about investigating the bags that had been left on the boat, as if looking for something else—further evidence of Sigma's activities, perhaps. The motor died down; the sound being replaced with the calming waves of the sea once more.

"Something isn't right," Quinn whispered. Ted could feel it too. There was something very off about it all.

"Are we safe with him?" Ted whispered back. Quinn hesitated before replying. She remembered the looks she had gotten when Giovanni had escorted her from the precinct in Rome and the way he had explained that the case he was working on was classified and not common knowledge to her arresting officers. Then her mind went back to Giovanni's apartment when he told her that his gun was not standard issue. Something was not adding up.

Quinn took Ted by the arm and began to back up towards the path that led up the cliff in the direction of the church. Giovanni snapped around, as though he had a sixth sense for fleeing witnesses.

"Stop," he said calmly. "I need to keep you close when my buddies arrive. They'll want to ask you a few questions."

"You killed her," Quinn said, her voice shaky. "You were supposed to arrest her."

Giovanni said nothing but kept his gaze on the pair. Quinn backed away, pulling Ted with her, her hand still firmly on his arm. She turned away as she eyed the path that led up the cliffside.

Giovanni reached for his holster and drew the revolver. "Stop," he said, more firmly this time.

Quinn closed her eyes and stopped dead in her tracks, hearing the hammer of the gun clicking. Her instincts had been right; something had felt off about him. He may have been good at hiding it until now, or perhaps Quinn was so wrapped up in the imminent danger with Sigma that she had been blind to it. Either way, this man was not who he said he was. No officer of the law would have gunned down Natalia like that, executing her even after she had been disarmed.

"Who are you?" Quinn asked.

Giovanni stepped down from the boat and waded through the shallow water to reach the shore. His revolver was trained on the pair the whole time. "Former detective Giovanni Rossi," he said candidly. I worked with Polizia di Stato for some years in Roma, but I work for myself now. I am a private investigator."

"So, you don't work with the police anymore?"

Giovanni gave a sly shrug of the shoulders. "Technically, yes. They hired me back temporarily to investigate Sigma. I would have committed to that task too, but I had a better offer."

Quinn shifted uncomfortably, trying to listen to what he was saying while staring down the barrel of his gun. "What do you mean?"

"It's ironic," Giovanni smiled. "All this time, that organisation tracing clues through the Catholic Church. It is ignorant to think that they would win against the sheer power of the Vatican."

Ted piped up. "The Vatican hired you?"

Giovanni nodded. "Even as a man of justice, when that conversation happens, you cannot say no. The orders were simple: follow Sigma, find Atlantis, and bring back anything of value for the Vatican's archive." He flashed the hilt of the dagger sticking out of his bomber jacket pocket. "I would say I have earned my pay." He appraised the surprised looks on their faces. "I would have tracked them down eventually, even if it meant taking this from them after they were long gone from here. But, after I heard an associate of Sigma was arrested, I spotted an opportunity to expedite the process. A good detective knows how to use the tools around them."

"You told me Interpol were after Sigma. They're not going to be happy when they find out you murdered their key target," said Quinn.

"And who will tell them this?" Giovanni cocked an eyebrow. "After I tracked Sigma to this place, they turned on their associate..." He gestured towards Quinn. "She was killed instantly, and I was attacked. I acted in self-defence, and unfortunately, the suspect was killed on scene."

"You won't get away with this," said Ted.

"I will," replied Giovanni plainly. "With no survivors, they will have only my account."

"The account of a reputable man of the law," Quinn scoffed. "You're a piece of work."

"I am good at my job," he replied assuredly. He aimed at Ted first. "I take no pleasure in violence, but unfortunately this is what must be done."

"Hang on a second," said Ted, stalling as much as he could. "Why tell us about the underwater passage if you were just going to kill us anyway?"

"Hindsight is a beautiful thing," Giovanni replied. "Perhaps I should have left you there. Or perhaps I hoped you wouldn't have crossed paths with her again, and you wouldn't have implicated yourselves in what followed."

"You don't have to do this," said Ted, shaking. "We won't tell anyone what happened."

"That's not a risk I can take." He closed one eye as he prepared to squeeze the trigger.

Just before he fired, a strange sensation hit him. A sudden cold feeling on the back of his head made him pause. It took him less than a second to register what it was. The small circle of cold steel buried into the back of his skull was the perfect shape of the barrel of a gun. His eyes widened, his brain shouting out alarm signals, but his body reacted too slowly. Before he had time to move, the gun went off. Giovanni fell forward, lifeless, onto the ground.

Stood in his place, with a solemn expression and water dripping from her hair and clothes, was Magda. Having escaped the cavern, she had witnessed the murder of Natalia and moved unseen to the boat to pick up the gun Natalia had retrieved from Hiram's pack. With Giovanni preoccupied with Ted and Quinn, she had been able to advance on him undetected.

Quinn and Ted's nerves were shot. They had whiplash from the coming and going between safety and staring down the barrel of a gun. First Natalia, then Giovanni, and now finally Magda.

A moment went by as they waited for a reaction. It felt like people had been queuing up to kill them these last few minutes. Would Magda be the last, and ultimately successful one in that line? Ted could see the conflict on her face, standing in front of the person who had killed Stefan, the person who had meant most to her in the world.

Magda held the gun lazily by her side as her fingers twitched on the trigger. Her eyes were puffy and red, her gaze held firmly on the pair, but her mind seemingly somewhere else. She looked exhausted. The lapping of the water filled the silence as Quinn and Ted waited anxiously for Magda's next move, their fate teetering precariously in her hands.

THIRTY-ONE

Months had passed since that fateful night on the shores of the small island of Irakleia. Before leaving Quinn and Ted alone on the beach, Magda had explained the change she felt after watching them escape through the underwater tunnel that led away from the Temple of Poseidon and to safety. Bereft of her colleague and best friend and watching everything they had worked towards come crashing down, Magda had been ready to give up and let the cavern take her life with Stefan's. But there was something in her—call it her body's primal need for survival, or something greater—that compelled her to go after the others and escape with her life. Seeing Giovanni murder Natalia and then confront Quinn and Ted, Magda felt a final sense of responsibility towards the two only innocent parties in this whole thing. Unexpectedly remorseful for her part in their ordeal, she saved them in hopes of expunging herself of some of the guilt that had lingered below the surface throughout the journey. She had been a dedicated member of the Order of Poseidon, and truly believed in the promise of a better world as much as Stefan had. But once the temple began to crumble, so too did her belief in the cause that had brought them there. She left on the boat, taking the ceremonial knife with her and issuing a final warning for Quinn and Ted to stay away.

What became of Magda and the dagger was a mystery. Quinn wondered if Magda would sell the artefact on the black market and use the money to retire somewhere away from the world. Perhaps she would eventually come back around to the Order of Poseidon and use the knife to attempt another ritual one day. However, the way she had spoken on that beach in Irakleia, it had felt like she was done with that life.

The following days and weeks had been strange for both Quinn and Ted. Navigating the trauma of the events as they tried to return to their normal lives, the world was not making things easy for them. Ted had lost his job, having been absent for so long without warning. He protested his case and explained what had happened, but it was no use. He was not sure if his boss believed a word of his story, or if they simply didn't care. The decision was made, and after accepting there was nothing he could do to help his cause, Ted left his workplace feeling like the universe was out to get him. He stormed out of that place, but not before telling his boss exactly what he thought of them and flipping them the bird. He met with Carl and Eliza for a drink to drown his sorrows. Ted couldn't tell if their beaming smiles that lasted all night were a valiant attempt at keeping his spirits up, or the lingering relief they shared at seeing their friend safe and well.

A trip to the police station had followed soon after he and Quinn had returned to London. They filed a report on Sigma and the Pembroke family and were told that the matter would be investigated. Weeks later, nothing had been done. With Natalia dead and her mother still in a Mexican prison, there was not much to be done. As far as they were concerned, Sigma as an operation had ceased to exist.

"That's it, Ted, you're doing great!" Quinn cupped her hands around her mouth to call back up the slope. Fifty yards up the gentle gradient, Ted had just exited the magic carpet and had begun sliding slowly down on a snowboard. The board perpendicular to the nursery slope, he tried to remember everything Quinn had taught him. He put pressure on his toes, keeping his hands up for balance as he started to pick up speed. He drifted off to the side, feeling the board steer out of control, and in a rush of panic he swivelled around until he was facing the other way. A clump of snow bumped underneath the board, and he lost his balance, falling forward into the snow with a thud. He bent his knees to take the brunt of the fall but couldn't prevent tasting a mouthful of the cold snow. He heard a chuckle from Quinn.

"You're getting better, I think," she said. "You're falling much better, anyway."

After getting back to normality, the two resumed their long-distance relationship. Things were going well. But, eventually, the time difference and mixture of late-night and early-morning video calls had taken their toll, and they couldn't go any longer without seeing each other in person. Quinn had managed to convince Ted to join her on the slopes of Aspen, to finish the vacation that had been interrupted when this whole debacle had started. It felt like a strange full-circle moment for her. This had been the place she had reconnected with Ted, right before Sigma had blackmailed her into joining them on their mission. Now, here they were together.

The snow season was ending now, but there was just enough of the powder to enjoy. Quinn was able to get up early, beating the crowds to the slopes to carve a path into the mountain in peace. She was completely in her element there.

Truth be told, Ted was not enjoying the snow all that much. Maybe it was just the learning curve, but he felt that snowboarding might not be for him. He got back up onto the board and let gravity do its thing, his arms flailing as the board went this way and that, carrying him down the final few feet of the nursery slope to the bottom of the magic carpet.

"We'll get you on the big runs next time," Quinn smiled as Ted started to free his feet from the bindings. He couldn't see from her goggles, but he was pretty sure she winked playfully as she said it. They both knew that was a long shot.

"I'm not giving up," Ted replied. "This slope will be very well acquainted with my arse by the end of this trip, but I won't let it beat me."

"Yes!" Quinn exclaimed jovially, throwing up a hand for a high five. Ted slapped it, their mittened hands creating a small cloud of powdered snow as they connected.

"Coffee?" Quinn suggested.

"Always."

Ted was ready for a break, and the prospect of a hot drink inside the café positioned nicely at the bottom of the slopes was too good to pass up. After propping up their snowboards outside they relaxed into the booth they had made theirs since arriving. The resort was quiet enough at the back end of the snow season that they could almost always get the spot they wanted, depending on the time of day. The smiling waitress brought over their hot drinks, and they warmed their hands around the mugs while they chatted.

"You know, I got Paige on the slopes last time," said Quinn.

Ted had just put the mug of coffee to his lips and choked on the hot liquid as he failed to stifle a laugh. Coffee sprayed out in front of him, hitting the table.

"I'm serious!" Quinn wiped her cheek, cleaning away a little bit of spatter that had made its way across the table.

"Paige?" Ted questioned. "I thought she came for the saunas and après ski."

"She did," Quinn conceded. "But I coaxed her into it."

"Blimey. That must have taken some doing."

"I can be very persuasive," she said with a suggestive look. Ted felt his heart skip a beat. Quinn took a sip of coffee while Ted took a mental note to pinch himself later.

"And?" He asked, eager to hear more.

"And what?"

"How did she get on?"

"Better than you," Quinn stuck out her tongue.

Ted feigned a dagger piercing his heart in mock hurt at her comment. The two laughed together, but the moment seemed to sour quickly as they both shared the same thought, their minds cast back to that dreadful night.

"Hey," Quinn leaned across the table, taking her hands on Ted's. "I love you."

Ted's eyes glistened at the words. They had made a pact in the months following their second ordeal with Sigma that whenever they would think about it and the trauma of the memory ate them up, they would say 'I love you'. It was usually Quinn who had the good ideas, but this one was Ted's. He said it was a way of taking control of the feeling and redirecting it to the one positive that came from their brush with Sigma: their relationship.

"I know," Ted replied coolly.

"Damn it," Quinn shook her head. "Can't believe you just Solo'd me."

The Atlantis Idol

On hearing her reference his favourite film franchise, Ted felt a strange warm sensation build inside him. He couldn't explain it, but it felt like the gentle squeezing of a hug, without anyone touching him. He looked at Quinn with doe eyes, wondering how he got so lucky.

To the side of their interlinked hands, lying flat on the table, Quinn's phone lit up. It began to buzz, the screen displaying an incoming phone call from an unknown number. The two looked at the phone, then at each other. Quinn shrugged her shoulders, withdrew her hands from Ted and picked it up. Tapping the green answer button on the screen, she put the phone to her ear.

"Hello?"

A clicking sound came through the receiver, and then a second of faint static.

"Um, hello?" Quinn furrowed her brow. She waited a moment, then decided it must have been an automated sales call that was taking a while to kick in. She was just about to take the phone away from her ear and hang up when a voice suddenly crackled through.

"Ms Miyata?" The voice sounded muffled. Quinn stood up and stepped out of the booth, as though trying to help improve the signal. The café did have dead spots where the internet got spotty; she figured it must be a similar story with the phone reception.

"Hello?" she tried again.

"Ms Miyata," the voice came through much clearer suddenly. Quinn stopped dead in her tracks, partly because she had found a good spot of reception, and partly because the voice on the other end of the phone was oddly familiar. It took her a second to place it, but she put the pieces together a split second before they spoke again. "This is Lillian Pembroke."

Quinn locked eyes with Ted, her expression alarming him. Just when they were moving on, the leader of Sigma had brought everything crashing back.

Ted narrowed his eyes as he saw the look on Quinn's face. He mouthed to her, asking if everything was okay.

Quinn took a deep breath, taking a moment to regain her composure. She reminded herself that she was in control, not this woman. "I'm hanging up," she said. "Don't call this number again."

"Wait, Quinn, please don't," the woman's voice sounded urgent, desperate, even. The tone defied the authority she commanded. Quinn thought about the woman's position and everything she had gone through in the months since that fateful night. Locked up in prison, away from her home, forced to grieve the loss of her daughter alone. Quinn actually felt sorry for her. Despite everything, she felt empathy for this person.

Sitting down at the nearest chair, Quinn ushered Ted over. He joined her as she put the phone on speaker.

"What do you want?" Quinn asked firmly.

"Is Ted with you?" Lillian asked.

Quinn hesitated a moment, as though contemplating whether it was a trick question. "Yes," she said at last.

"Good. I need to speak with both of you."

The pair exchanged a curious look as the woman continued.

"First of all, I wish to apologise to you both. Your involvement in my affairs was completely accidental and should never have happened. I'm grateful that you are both safe and well." She paused. "It should have ended the moment I was arrested. What happened after, while I've been in here…" She exhaled deeply. "That was most unfortunate. My daughter, Natalia. She was—" Lillian's voice cracked as she referred to her late daughter. "She was always very emotional. Petulant. She got that from her father. When I was sentenced, I told her in no uncertain terms that it was over. She shouldn't have continued in the way that she did, with any of the business I carried out." She went on. "I have amassed significant wealth and considerable power and influence with my organisation over the years, but at the heart of it, I am a collector. And what use is a collection when I can't even see it?"

Ted folded his arms, wondering where she was going with this. Was this phone call an apology, or was it leading to something? He was sceptical it was simply the former.

Lillian went on. "I had no idea of the agreements she made. That business with that damned cult, and her mindless obsession with the two of you." They heard another long exhale through the receiver. "It was unforgivable. I am sorry for the pain she caused you. I'm sure it is of no comfort to you, but I would like you to know that I had nothing to do with it."

"Is that what you called for? To absolve yourself of blame?" Ted questioned.

"You're angry, I understand," she said. "I will get to the point. You see, I've had a lot of time to think in my time here." She paused while she coughed violently. "Excuse me. I've been thinking a lot about the future, of the legacy I will leave behind."

Ted cocked an eyebrow at Quinn.

"I'm dying," said Lillian. "Cancer, you see. The doctor told me it's terminal."

"I'm sorry," Quinn found herself saying on impulse.

"Like I said, what is the use of collecting with no means to enjoy the collection? Now comes the crux of what I wanted to say to you both. When I'm gone, my legacy, Natalia's legacy, the legacy of Sigma, it will be marred with the unfortunate events of recent times, and the, shall we say, less than moral deals I brokered before."

Ted remembered the news report he had read after her arrest that talked about her business with notorious drug cartels in Mexico.

"I wish for something more. As I said, I've been doing a lot of thinking; thinking about the life I've led, and how my obsession for the artefacts I collected, the wealth and power, moulded the daughter I raised. I failed her, and I blame myself for the path she took. My only wish now, my last wish, is to take all that I have accumulated, and put it into something good."

"Like giving it all to charity," suggested Ted. A chuckle came down the line, followed by another bout of coughing.

"Like I said, I want my legacy to mean something. Something that will give a better purpose to Sigma, and what it stands for."

"What do you mean?"

"Let's start with this," Lillian said. "I would like you to arrange for the release of my full collection of artefacts to their rightful place. I don't want them to be dumped into some vault or driven to the nearest museum. I would like each piece to be handed back to their country of origin, for the appropriate authorities to handle. Don't worry, I have contacts I can trust that will help you with this."

Quinn nodded. "I like this."

"I knew you would, dear," she replied. "Now comes the legacy I've been speaking of. I want Sigma to become a force of good. I would like it to work towards the preservation of history, actively working to understand more about the cultures of the ancient world and ensuring that any tangible part of that is kept in its rightful place."

The Atlantis Idol

"That sounds nice," said Ted. "Good luck with that. What does this have to do with us?"

"My dear," Lillian sighed. "I would like the two of you to take over Sigma. I'm handing everything to you. My wealth, my contacts, all of it. I think the two of you have an odd knack for this sort of thing, and I truly believe you are good people."

A long silence followed. The pair said nothing, in shock at Lillian's proposition. Quinn considered what the woman was asking of them, and the vision she had shared.

"You want us to become professional treasure hunters?"

"I want you to become the guardians of history," Lillian retorted. "There are plenty of others out there who care little for the preservation of human history. There is a whole world of treasure hunters and black-market traders who care for nothing but the monetary value of what they take. I'm speaking from experience."

Quinn and Ted were quiet, both thinking about her proposition and what it meant for them. They would be given more money than they could ever dream of to work on a project that, in theory at least, would help contribute to the discovery and knowledge of the ancient world, while protecting that history from being ripped from its origins and sold for profit. They had tried to hide from the pain that Sigma had caused them, but perhaps this was a way to take control of it and turn it into something better; something that actually benefitted the world.

A smile crept across Quinn's face. Ted could see her train of thought; he was thinking something similar. What surprised him was how much the proposition excited him. Perhaps he was getting a taste for adventure after all.

"So, what do you think?" asked Lillian.

Quinn looked at Ted. The two didn't need to confer, sharing a smile that told them everything they needed to know about their decision.

"Okay," said Quinn. "Let's do it."

Acknowledgements

Thank you for reading this novel! If you enjoyed the experience and would like to share it with others, please leave a review on Amazon, Goodreads, or your book forum of choice. Your feedback means a lot to me.

I'd like to say a huge thank you for the encouragement I continue to receive from my loving wife, Hollie, my wonderful son, Oscar, family, and friends. Finishing that first draft can be a long slog and your kind words motivate me to push on to reach the end.

Printed in Great Britain
by Amazon